Scavengers

Also by Steven F. Havill

The Sheriff Bill Gastner Series

Scavengers

Steven F. Havill

THOMAS DUNNE BOOKS
ST. MARTIN'S MINOTAUR ❧ NEW YORK

THOMAS DUNNE BOOKS.
An imprint of St. Martin's Press.

SCAVENGERS. Copyright © 2002 by Steven F. Havill. All rights reserved. Printed in the United States of America. No part of this book may be used or reproduced in any manner whatsoever without written permission except in the case of brief quotations embodied in critical articles or reviews. For information, address St. Martin's Press, 175 Fifth Avenue, New York, N.Y. 10010.

www.minotaurbooks.com

Havill, Steven.
    Scavengers : a Posadas County mystery / Steven F. Havill.—1st ed.
    p. cm
    ISBN 0-312-28833-6
    1. Gastner, Bill (Fictitious character)—Fiction. 2. New Mexico—Fiction. 3. Sheriffs—Fiction. I. Title.

PS3558.A785 S28 2002
813'.54—dc21

                                                                2002071273

First Edition: September 2002

10 9 8 7 6 5 4 3 2 1

For Kathleen

Acknowledgments

◆◆◆◆◆

Special thanks to Ralph Altizer, Virgil Hall, David Martinez, H. L. McArthur, and Larry Youngblood.

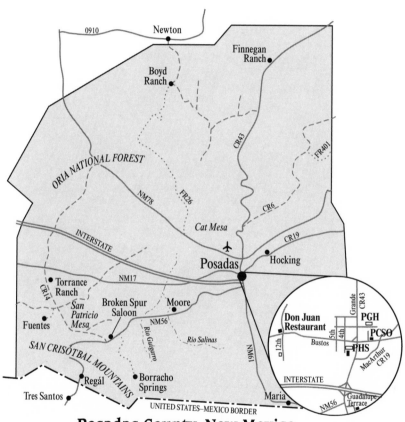

0910
Newton
Finnegan Ranch
Boyd Ranch
CR43
FR401
ORIA NATIONAL FOREST
NM78
FR26
CR6
Cat Mesa
CR19
INTERSTATE
Posadas
Hocking
Torrance Ranch
NM17
CR14
San Patricio Mesa
Broken Spur Saloon
Moore
Fuentes
NM56
Rio Guiguro
Rio Salinas
NM61
SAN CRISOTBAL MOUNTAINS
Regál
Borracho Springs
Tres Santos
Maria
UNITED STATES–MEXICO BORDER

Don Juan Restaurant
Grande
CR43
PGH
5th
4th
PCSO
PHS
12th
Bustos
MacArthur
CR19
INTERSTATE
NM56
Guadalupe Terrace

Posadas County, New Mexico

Scavengers

Posadas County Undersheriff Estelle Reyes-Guzman parked her Expedition between the deputy's unit and the chain-link fence surrounding the gravel pit. She sat for a few minutes with the engine switched off and the driver's-side window open. Five hundred yards east, Deputy Jackie Taber stood on a slight rise in the prairie, waiting.

With the radio on the short-range frequency, Estelle pushed the transmit bar. "Do you need anything from your vehicle, Jackie?" Given the choice whether to jolt and jar over the prairie in the stiffly sprung department unit or walk, it was predictable which route the deputy had taken. It wouldn't have surprised Estelle to see Jackie sitting on a rock, sketch pad in hand.

"That's negative, ma'am."

"I'll be over in a few minutes." The radio barked static twice by way of confirmation. In the distance, a raven vented a single raucous croak of his own, irritated at being driven away from his lunch. The sound floated clear and clean with no wind to play tricks. Beside the Expedition, a few sparse wands of prairie grass stood delicately motionless, their seed hulls long since blown.

The rest of the prairie was bare limestone gravel, a rough table of rocks running the gamut from irregular pinhead grains to great sharp-edged slabs the size of Volkswagens. Wedged in here and there were scrawny creosote bushes with February-bare limbs, cholla cacti spotted with the peculiar mange that reduced them to gray skeletons,

1

and little gray stick-sprays that in a few months would bloom tiny flowers the color of the blistering summer sun.

Dispatcher Gayle Torrez had hit it right when she'd described this particular patch of southeastern Posadas County as "bleak." Estelle Reyes-Guzman had worked for the Posadas County Sheriff's Department for twelve years, not counting the nine months that she, her physician husband Francis, and the two boys had spent in Minnesota. Not once in more than a decade had she occasion to visit this spot. Not once had the need for human law intruded on this stretch of nothing.

An enterprising goat would have to work hard to keep his belly off his backbone here. Rattlesnakes could find a lizard, horned toad, or packrat to sink fangs into every couple of weeks. An ambitious coyote might find something lean to kill on his way through to greener pastures. The ravens would clean up slim pickings afterward. That was it. Even the easy-to-please vultures were still wintering down south where there'd be lots of dead things stinking in the sun. And now someone had found a pile of bones that hadn't once been a jackrabbit, steer, or lonely, wandering burro.

Estelle didn't bother to ask dispatch for details. If Jackie Taber said a body was lying out on the prairie, then there was a body. With a fatality, no matter the cause of misadventure, the call from dispatch to the sheriff or undersheriff was automatic. Estelle regarded the expanse of barren prairie in front of her. Whoever had died had done so without much of an audience.

To the south, the nearest set of prying eyes lived at the Bordwell ranch, but it was unlikely that old Milton Bordwell had ridden this far afield to find a place to drop dead, even though this land had once been his. And if Milton had witnessed the incident, he would have called Sheriff Robert Torrez. The two were hunting buddies from decades back, until Milton became too crippled to hike the rugged San Cristóbals.

With no oil lurking in underground puddles, no uranium ticking away in the rocks, and no copper spreading its filaments through the matrix, Milton Bordwell had grown tired of paying property taxes on prairie too useless to graze a steer. He sold five hundred acres to Dale and Perry MacInerny for two hundred and fifty dollars an acre and figured he'd made the best of the deal.

Dale and Perry knew exactly where the wealth was. Had this day not been a Sunday, the cacophony of their stone crusher, front-end loaders, and the ponderous trucks with their belly-dump trailers would have made the Posadas County undersheriff's quiet contemplation impossible. MacInerny Sand and Gravel supplied builders and highway contractors across southern New Mexico and northern Mexico. Dale hadn't told his brother yet, but when the hole behind the chain-link fence sank deep enough, he planned to offer it as a landfill to some rich, garbage-fouled city.

Estelle looked at the massive padlock that secured the gate through the MacInerny's fence and let her gaze travel along the silver expanse of fencing toward the east, beyond the final corner post that marked MacInernys' gravel pit, out five hundred yards to where the deputy waited patiently.

Jackie Taber had found a spot where she could watch both her vehicle and the bones. She stood on the rock-strewn rise, silhouetted against the morning sun. From any other direction, the buff tan of her uniform blended with the roll of prairie to make her all but invisible. A large woman with square shoulders and thick waist, her military experience still showed in the calm, easy way she carried herself.

Estelle grinned. *"Perfecto,"* she said aloud, and rummaged through the bulky camera bag until she found the lens that would let her frame the picture as she saw it in her mind's eye. She twisted the lens onto the camera and got out of the Expedition, bag slung over her shoulder.

The deputy didn't stroll to meet her, didn't wave or shout. She stood quietly in her chosen spot and waited, a study in patience. Estelle hiked half the distance, stopped, and unslung the bag. She knelt and braced the camera, composing the scene so that Deputy Taber's figure stood on the left, backlit by the hard morning sun, sharply contrasted with the tawny reach of prairie in front of her. No other man-made object intruded to spoil the view—no road, no power line, no stock tanks. The natural rise of the terrain hid the corpse. That was just as well. The victim was not Estelle's idea of calendar art, regardless of his condition.

After shooting four different exposures, the undersheriff bagged the camera and continued on. Other than turning her head to watch Estelle's progress over the rocks, Deputy Taber hadn't moved an inch.

"This is a peaceful place," Estelle said as she approached.

"It is now, anyway," Jackie Taber replied. Her soft, gentle voice contrasted with her burly appearance. Stetson riding a military two fingers above the bridge of her nose, Jackie stood with her hands at her sides, perfectly at ease. She didn't ask why Estelle had taken the long-range photographs, but had watched the undersheriff choosing her route, taking time to examine everything—as if the five-hundred-yard hike was a Sunday outing with no particular agenda.

Reaching the deputy, Estelle halted and turned, looking back toward the gravel pit for reference. "Wow," she said. She lowered her heavy camera bag to the ground as she looked for the first time at the body.

The corpse lay fifty feet away on an east-facing grade, spread-eagled on its back. From a distance, the body looked complete and fresh.

"Anyone we know?"

"I'm not sure that there's enough there to recognize," the deputy said.

Without drawing any closer, Estelle regarded the corpse for a moment, and then looked east. Power line towers marched north–south, visible now from the rise as black Ts against the brown prairie more than a mile away. To the south, she could see the foothills of the San Cristóbal Mountains. The interstate five miles to the north was out of sight and hearing, an asphalt slash across the prairie.

Jackie Taber watched as Estelle turned in place, taking in the panorama. Completing the circuit, her inspection returned to the corpse. "You didn't see any tracks anywhere? No vehicle tracks?" Estelle asked.

"No, ma'am."

"What a hike. Who called it in?"

The deputy looked up at the blank sky and then grinned at Estelle. "A student pilot was flying over here this morning on a flight from Las Cruces to Lordsburg. She saw it."

"You're kidding."

"No, ma'am. She reported it to Jim Bergin at the airport."

"She just looked down and saw him?"

"Yes, ma'am. That's what she said."

"It'll be interesting to hear just how she did that," Estelle said.

"She's still at the airport. After Jim called us, they flew back over here in Jim's plane. I drove out and she was able to pinpoint the spot for me from the air. Saved us lots and lots of time. I could have been walkin' around out here for a long time. I asked if she'd stick around for a little bit . . . that you'd want to talk with her."

"We'll see," Estelle said. "How did you approach?"

"Right from here, ma'am. Straight in. Straight back. I didn't touch the body or the clothing. I haven't checked for ID or anything like that." They heard the growl of vehicles and turned to see a red Jeep join the impromptu parking lot, followed by a small station wagon and one of the Posadas Emergency units.

"We have a few minutes before they make it over here. Let's take a look."

Before she'd finished the sentence, the radio on Deputy Taber's belt squelched. "Three ten, can we drive over there?"

Estelle shook her head.

"That's negative," Taber said into the radio. "The ambulance may want to work its way over, but that's all the tracks we want at the moment. Take your time."

Estelle set off at a tangent, turning to walk a circle with a fifty-foot radius around the body. When they completed the circle, Estelle stopped, once more standing beside her camera bag. She frowned and turned to face west, toward Posadas and the two figures making their way across the prairie in front of the rocking and bouncing ambulance.

"The county road in to the MacInernys' is the only access from State Sixty-one. Am I remembering right?" Estelle asked.

"Yes, ma'am. There's an old two-track south of here. I would guess a good two miles. It goes over to an abandoned windmill and stock-tank."

"So this guy walked in here," Estelle said. "I didn't see a single track from any kind of vehicle. Not even a mountain bike."

"It's pretty rocky."

5

Estelle nodded. "Not enough to hide vehicle tracks, though." She nudged a football-size rock with the toe of her shoe to show its light-colored underside. "Not a single rock out of place."

With one camera slung over her shoulder and another in hand, she stepped toward the body, scanning the ground. "Let's see what he can tell us," she said.

At first glance, the corpse looked like a Halloween prank, a suit of clothes stuffed with rags or crumpled newspaper for exaggerated form. The black nylon windbreaker was unzipped, falling away on the sides to reveal what had once been a white T-shirt. The jeans were worn and faded with the cuffs beginning to show signs of fraying, pulled up just far enough to reveal white athletic socks.

"Fancy shoes," Deputy Taber said. The man's multicolored running shoes were the sort of off-brand imitations that discount stores sold for nine bucks during special sales.

"We'll want Linda to take close-ups of the soles," Estelle said. "Cactus spines, pebbles, that sort of thing." She said it more as a reminder to herself, and the deputy turned at the sound of voices and the idling engine of the ambulance.

"I'll keep 'em back until you're ready," she said.

"Right where you were standing when I walked up," Estelle replied. "But have Linda come over." She knelt by the corpse's head. Much of the soft tissues of the exposed face and neck were gone, leaving just the jagged, vague suggestion of features. Prairie scavengers might have accounted for much of the facial damage, but not the condition of the skull. From the prominence of the left mastoid, that bony protuberance just behind the ear, to the upper temporal ridge of the parietal bone, the upper left portion of the skullcap was missing.

Estelle settled back on her haunches and frowned. The frown deepened at the sound of a siren in the distance. A marked county unit arrived by the gravel pit in a cloud of dust, and she could hear the bark of Deputy Taber's radio as the new arrival announced his presence. Deputy Dennis Collins liked to talk on the radio, the telephone, over E-mail, or a cup of coffee. Jackie was quick to cut him off, and in a moment, Estelle saw him jogging across the prairie, leaving the county car behind. Fortune had smiled when airport manager Jim Bergin first called the Sheriff's Office and Deputy Collins hadn't been in the building to respond first to this call.

Estelle beckoned to Linda Real, and when the photographer joined her, said, "Sorry to tear you away on a Sunday morning."

"Is okay, is okay," Linda said, eyes flicking over the corpse and the surrounding prairie. "This is gross."

"Yep. And really interesting." Estelle knelt and pointed at the skull damage with the tip of her pen. "We can blame the ravens for a lot of the soft tissue loss, but not for the open fractures."

"That's more than I need to know already," Linda said, but her hand was opening the cover of one of her camera bags. "Do we know who this is?" Linda wrinkled her nose and avoided kneeling down for a closer look.

"Not yet."

"Gunshot?"

"I don't know. It doesn't look right, somehow. With a gunshot, there's usually some wound of entrance that's more or less obvious. I don't see that. Of course, with most of the face missing . . ." She shrugged. "It's just hard to tell. Gunshot is the most likely thing, I suppose." She straightened up and looked at Linda. "I took a few general quick shots. What I'm most interested in are closeups of the victim's shoe soles, this head damage . . . before he's moved."

"You got it."

"And anything else that you can think of," Estelle said. "Film's cheap." She lowered her voice another notch. "And by the way, I think I've got a good photo of Jackie for February."

Linda flashed a lopsided smile. "Neat," she said. "And I got an unbelievable shot yesterday of Tommy. He was in his grubbies, up to here"—she tapped her left elbow with her right hand—"working on his motorcycle." She glanced around to make sure none of the others were within earshot. "Just the sheriff, Collins, and Abeyta to go, and we'll have the whole gang." She flashed a wider smile. "So neat."

She gently placed her voluminous camera bag several paces from the corpse. While she rummaged for her equipment, Estelle motioned for the others to approach. Dr. Alan Perrone, the Posadas County Coroner and assistant state medical examiner, walked with his hands in his pockets, one click faster than a shuffle. His eyes were glued to the rough prairie under his feet. Dennis Collins hustled.

"What, did some wetback get lost?" Deputy Collins said as he started to step past Estelle. She reached out a hand and caught him by the sleeve of his uniform jacket, gently bringing him to a halt. He shot a puzzled glance at her, but she waited until Perrone, Deputy Taber, and the two EMTs had joined them.

"Nothing's been disturbed, sir," she said to the physician.

"Just my Sunday morning," he replied. "Who's this?"

"I have no idea."

Perrone nodded and surveyed the landscape. "Huh," he said at length. "How's little Carlos, by the way?"

"A miserable little kid," Estelle said. "And now mother is down with the same crud, I think."

"She wouldn't get a flu shot. That's what your husband said."

"Nope. She wouldn't. Last fall when we were still up in Minnesota, Francis even threatened to stick her with the shot while she was asleep. That didn't work, either. Stubborn to the end."

Perrone chuckled. "Let's see what trouble this one got into," he said, and ambled toward the corpse. He stood with his hands still in his pockets, looking down at the body. "He sure as hell is dead," he said. Deputy Collins circled around to the other side and bent down, reaching toward the pocket of the victim's jacket. Perrone held up a hand. "Not yet, Dennis. Nothing gets moved yet."

Collins took a deep breath of exasperation, and Perrone added, "Once the body is disturbed, that's it. You never get a second chance."

"I know," Collins said, the reply an automatic reflex rather than the truth. "I was just going to check for some identification." Estelle watched him closely to make sure that his hands didn't stray, glad that it had been the formidable Perrone who'd spoken up. Collins was scheduled to attend the next session of the law enforcement academy in Santa Fe. Until then, he was an uncertified gopher—spending his time delivering unglamorous civil paperwork and champing at the bit.

"That can wait," Perrone replied. For the next twenty minutes, they worked the area without touching the body. It was Perrone who froze in his tracks, looking down.

"And what's this," he said, beckoning Estelle. He knelt and pointed with his chrome pen. "Good-sized chunk of skullcap, is what I'd guess," he said. He turned and regarded the corpse, fifteen feet to the east. "So we know one thing," he added as Estelle silently examined the fragment of bone. "He wasn't killed somewhere else and dragged here. My first guess is that he was shot, and dropped in his tracks. Either this flew over here, or some critter toyed with it for a while, cleaning off all the good stuff."

"Gross," Linda Real said again. Collins looked expectantly at Estelle, as if waiting for her to pronounce some profundity that would lead directly to someone's arrest. The undersheriff remained silent, after a minute handing the bagged skull fragment to Collins for labeling.

"What do you want me to put on here?" he asked.

"Just fill in the blanks, Dennis," Estelle said. "Date, time, location. Use 'skull fragment' for description."

Linda continued with an array of cameras, photographing in color, black-and-white, and finally with video—close-up and panorama. Jackie Taber methodically collected samples of the stained gravel under the man's head and shoulders and passed them to Collins, whose printing on the evidence bag labels turned out to be so neat and precise that at first glance the lettering looked as if it came from a word processor.

Perrone's interest focused on the head wound, but he was noncommittal. "Interesting," he allowed. "Maybe gunshot, maybe more than that. Really interesting."

He reached out and lifted the corners of the black jacket. The V-necked white T-shirt was bloodstained near the collar but otherwise showed no evidence of intrusion. "Huh," the physician said. "I don't see evidence of any other wounds other than what I'd expect from the ravens. Let's roll him over."

Estelle nodded. Linda crouched off to one side, the video camera watching the process.

Deputy Collins put a hand on the man's shoulder while Perrone lifted at the hip. With the body rolled just far enough that it rested on its side, Perrone stopped, frowning. The small of the victim's back had been resting on a football-size rock, the sharp corners of the limestone digging into the skin where the T-shirt was hiked up.

"Huh," Perrone murmured.

Clare Parker, one of the EMTs who had been standing patiently to one side, stepped forward and added his leverage so that Perrone could free his hands.

"Linda," Perrone said, "Get me a picture of this, will you? A still, not video." He crouched, head close to the earth. When Linda joined him, he pointed with the eraser end of a pencil. "I want this area right here. It looks like the rock caught him on the back when he fell." Collins's face was pale, but he and Parker held the body in place as Linda Real fussed with her light meter.

"When was the last moisture out here?" Perrone asked.

"Three weeks, at least."

He pushed his glasses back up his long, slender nose and turned his attention again to the wrecked face. "The ravens and a coyote or two could account for most of the soft tissue damage to the face and neck in just a day or two. But that's after the body is ripe enough to attract their attention. With the condition of the rest of the body, my guess is that he hasn't been here too long. I'm not talking months. Two weeks, three maybe. If a vehicle left tracks, they'd still be here." He drew a pair of surgical gloves from his pocket and snapped them on. Collins looked eastward, his face paling a shade or two, as the physician gently probed around what was left of the victim's lower face.

"His jaw's been pulverized," Perrone said. "I'm guessing somebody really pounded on him. Several really hard, sharp blows." He held up a splinter of white. "This is part of a healthy tooth, Estelle. He's been hit so hard that his teeth and jaw bones are just splinters. Nothing much on the ground, though, except blood. So he was lying pretty still when they worked him over."

He gestured with his right hand. "Let him go on over." Collins let out a sigh of relief as he released his hold on the corpse and stood up. "Now you need to check his pockets," Perrone added.

The search didn't take long.

"No wallet, no money, no nothing," the deputy said. "Not even an inspection label." He looked up, shaking his head. "Black hair, though. Small stature. I'll bet he's Mexican. He got himself cross-wise with somebody."

Alan Perrone looked up at Collins and grinned. "Black hair and small stature sure narrows it down, doesn't it?"

"Well, it's just most likely, is all," the deputy said. "Out here, I mean. The border's just a few miles south of here." He stood up, hands on his hips, and turned his attention ninety degrees to the west. "The MacInernys' is closest, though," he said. When he noticed that the undersheriff was looking at him with interest, he added, "I mean, that's a place to start, wouldn't it be? The closest, most obvious place?"

"Yes, it is," Estelle agreed. "While Jackie finishes up here, I'd like you to go have a chat with them. They should be home on a Sunday morning. See if they remember anything unusual in the past few weeks. Get back with Jackie as soon as you find out." Almost as an afterthought, she added, "And Dennis, they don't need to know the specifics of any of this."

"You think we ought to tip our hand with them?" Collins asked. "I mean, if they're involved somehow . . ."

"That's unlikely," Estelle said.

"I mean, it could be someone who works for the MacInernys."

"Think about that when you're talking to them," Estelle said. "Use a light touch, as an old friend of mine likes to say."

Perrone stood up and stripped off the rubber gloves. "There's enough blood soaked into the ground or dried on the rocks to be consistent with this kind of injury, but that's always kind of a puzzle. It's just hard to tell. Although with this kind of head wound . . ." He frowned and glanced at Estelle. "Could have happened any number of ways, I suppose."

"That brings us back to the problem of vehicle tracks," Deputy Taber said. "Something has to show." She turned at the waist, scanning the prairie.

"That's right," Collins said, a light suddenly dawning. "There aren't any tracks out here from the gravel pit, are there?"

Estelle Reyes-Guzman glanced at her watch, ignoring Collins's

11

revelation. "Jackie, I'm going to run home for a few minutes, and then go down to the airport. I'd like to talk to the pilot before she flies off into the sunset."

"Huh," Alan Perrone said suddenly, and he reached out toward Estelle as if to hold her in place. "No, forget it," he said with a shake of his head. "Let me talk to you later, all right? We'll do a preliminary and see what it turns up." He nodded at the two EMTs. "You can go ahead and pack him up," he said. "I've seen all I'm going to be able to until we take him apart."

"I keep thinking that we're missing something," Jackie said.

"You are," Perrone agreed. "A whole lot of somethings. Find the weapon that bashed in his face. That's a good place to start." The physician grinned without much humor. "And the one that blew his skull to pieces. And while you're at it, a current driver's license would be nice."

Estelle shouldered her camera bag. "You'll give me a call?" she said to Jackie, and the deputy nodded.

"I wanted to look around a bit more," Taber said. "Then I'll be in."

"Look for a fist-sized chunk of rock with blood and tooth fragments," Perrone said holding his hand as if cradling the weapon. "It takes more than one blow to cause that kind of skull damage. You're talking about repeated blows to the face. Half a dozen or more." He nodded at Estelle. "I'll walk back with you."

"You think there's a chance he was killed somewhere else and dumped?" Collins asked. "What about the tracks, then?"

Perrone shrugged. "I'm glad all I have to do is tell you what killed him." He reached out and patted Deputy Collins on the arm. "Have at it."

IRMA Sedillos, known simply as Nana to little Carlos and his five-year-old brother Francisco, had arrived at the Guzmans' at seven that Sunday morning, ready to cope. It was the third day of the siege. Under normal conditions, the usual frenetic schedule imposed on the household would have been sufficient challenge, with a surgeon father, an undersheriff mother, and an elderly grandmother whose English was fluent on those rare occasions when she chose to stray from her native tongue.

With illness settling like a gloomy blanket on the Guzman clan, Irma set out to brighten the house on Twelfth Street in Posadas, beginning in the kitchen, where she excelled. Irma was not the least concerned that she might catch one of the rampant flu bugs herself. If she thought of the possibility at all, it would be dismissed with a sunny shrug. She saw herself simply as a sixth member of the Guzman clan.

When the family had moved to Minnesota the previous spring, Irma had been encouraged to go along—but hadn't. For months after the family left Posadas, she had felt that some portion of her insides had been torn away. In early December, just in time for the Christmas holidays, the Guzmans had moved back to New Mexico. Francis and Alan Perrone began plans for a new clinic, and newly-elected Sheriff Robert Torrez named Estelle as undersheriff of the Posadas County

Sheriff's Department. Irma glowed. Things were as they should be. A little illness went with the turf.

"Carlos is messy," Francisco announced loudly when Estelle returned home shortly before ten that morning. *"Corriendo de las dos puntas."*

"But he's asleep now, so be quiet, *niño*," Irma called from the kitchen.

After being awake most of the night "running from both ends," as his older brother had been pleased to announce, three-year-old Carlos Guzman had finally fallen into a fitful sleep, sprawled across his bed like a little, fragrant beanbag—a sorry little *sacito,* as Irma Sedillos was fond of saying. Estelle touched his forehead lightly and then rearranged the feather-light blanket to cover the back of the little boy's neck.

In her own bedroom down the hall, the boy's favorite companion in conversation, Estelle's frail, tiny eighty-two-year-old mother, had also spent a long night, racked by aching joints and a dry, painful cough. She too now slept, curled on her side.

Dr. Francis Guzman appeared in the kitchen door, a cup of coffee in hand. He had decided years before that blue hospital scrubs were the ideal Sunday morning lounge-around-the-house garments. He regarded Estelle over the top of the cup as she gently closed her mother's bedroom door.

"How did it go?" he said.

"Bizarre," Estelle replied. "Adult male, no ID, no *nada*. Misadventure out in the middle of nowhere." She shrugged. "*Mamá* seems a little more at ease."

Francis nodded. "She finally let me give her something to calm things down so she could get some sleep. I told her it was either that or the hospital where none of the nurses would listen to her." He extended the cup toward her. "Something hot?"

Estelle sighed. "When I come back, maybe. I need to stop out at the airport for a little bit."

"Someone else can't do that?"

Estelle reached up and traced two fingers down her husband's cheek, across the silky hair of his beard. The dark circles under his own eyes were pronounced, the reward for working with the designing architects for the new clinic, his own practice, and the demands of being on the lowest rung of the hospital's primitive on-call system. "It'll just be for a few minutes. If *Mamá* is resting, I don't want to disturb her. I really need to talk to the young lady who first spotted the body. Then I'll let Jackie take it from there. I'll be back in half an hour."

Her eldest son bolted into the kitchen and latched onto his father's hand.

"I'm going for a hike," Francisco announced. His father refused to budge away from his comfortable leaning spot against the kitchen doorjamb.

"You're going to eat some breakfast before you do anything," Irma said over her shoulder. "Come help me."

"Big help," his father said, and thumped Francisco gently on top of the head with a closed fist. "And by the way," he said, turning back to Estelle, "Bob Torrez called a little while ago from Virginia. I told him that as far as I knew, things were going fine, and that you were out in the boonies, collecting bones. He'd like you to call him later this evening when you get the chance. The number's by the phone."

Estelle knew that Sheriff Robert Torrez had been loath to spend two weeks in Virginia at the FBI's seminar for newly elected county sheriffs. Torrez considered anything east of the Pecos River to be one big housing development full of people with strange accents. His sojourn in Virginia hadn't coincided with any of that state's big game seasons, either—a screwup that he contended the Federal Bureau of Investigation could have avoided if they'd used half a brain when putting their seminar calendar together.

Estelle glanced at her watch. "I'll be back by lunch," she said. "Irma, do you need anything?"

"No, ma'am," Irma said. "Did you remember to tell *Padrino* not to come for lunch today?"

Estelle groaned. "No. I didn't. And that's all he needs, to be exposed to this crew." She smiled ruefully at her husband. "Would you give him a call, when you get a minute?"

"Sure." Dr. Guzman scooped up Francisco, holding him upside down. "We'll walk you out to the car." He carried the boy outside, draped over one arm like a sack of potatoes. The wind had stopped, and the high February sun had pushed the temperature above sixty. Despite Irma's ministrations inside, Estelle welcomed the clean, fresh winter air with a comfortable sigh. She settled behind the wheel and pulled the door of the Expedition closed.

"I could go," Francisco said. "You could take me to *Padrino*'s."

"Not today, *hijo*," she said and kissed him in the middle of the forehead as her husband held him up against the door. She glanced at Francis and held up her hands in surrender. "I know the look," she said, and grinned at her husband's scrutiny. "I'm fine. Really. And this will only take a minute."

"Okay," he said, sounding skeptical.

"And Alan said he'd probably want to talk to you this afternoon when he's ready to do the prelim on the body."

"How come *Padrino* isn't coming today?" Francisco asked, and Estelle looked down at him.

"When we're all better, Francisco. He doesn't want to see a bunch of stinkies."

"Carlos is a stinky," he said. "I'm not."

Dr. Guzman laughed and stepped back with his hands locked under the little boy's armpits as Estelle pulled the Expedition into reverse. "Hurry back," he said.

Estelle drove north on County Road 43, then west on the state highway that ran past the airport at the base of Cat Mesa. As she turned into the airport parking lot, she saw the small white-and-blue Cessna parked on the painted doughnut around the fuel pumps. Jim Bergin, the airport manager, was standing on a short aluminum ladder, topping off the left wing fuel tank.

He glanced around when he heard the crunch of tires on gravel. By the time Estelle had left the truck and walked across the tarmac to the pumps, Bergin had tapped the last drops of gasoline from the nozzle, screwed on the cap, and stepped down.

"Hey there," he said. With a deft pull, he activated the recoil, and fed the hose back onto the spool. His motions were economical, almost graceful. With his leathery, wrinkled face, perpetual careless facial stubble, and ice-blue eyes, Estelle could picture him in a movie about World War I aces, wrapped in leathers and flying a Spad. "Did you find it all right?" He didn't elaborate what the *it* was.

"Yes," Estelle replied. "Jackie said that you flew the young lady out there to spot for her."

"Yep."

"Thanks for taking the time to do that."

"You're entirely welcome. One of my great pleasures in life is watching the county commissioners blanch when they get my bill for flying county charters." He grinned at Estelle, showing a mouthful of colorful teeth that had seen better days. They both knew that the "blanching commissioners" was wishful thinking. Jim Bergin rarely billed the Sheriff's Department for anything.

"Have at it," she said. "Is this is her plane?"

Bergin rubbed a smudge from the Cessna's white propeller spinner. "Yep. She's inside, talking with Flight Service." At that moment, the door of the mobile home that served as Bergin's FBO office and the airport terminal opened. The young woman who stepped out looked as if she'd be more at home on the ski slopes—long blond hair in a single Heidi braid down her back, bulky white Scandinavian sweater with blue reindeer cavorting across the shapely chest, tight black nylon stretch pants, and flashy multicolored jogging shoes—the expensive kind.

With her logbook in one hand and dark glasses in the other, she strode across the apron toward them.

"Terri Keenan," Bergin said, "This is Undersheriff Estelle Guzman."

"Hi," the girl said. Her smile was a tribute to either the right genes or an orthodontist's skill. She extended her hand, and her grip was brisk. "You're not exactly what I expected when they said that the undersheriff wanted to talk to me." Her smile widened and her green eyes flicked over Estelle's tan pantsuit. "I met Deputy Taber earlier. Are all the officers in your department women?"

"You just happened to hit us on a good day," Estelle replied.

"Sixty-seven fifty-five," Bergin said. He took the credit card that Keenan extended to him. "And by the way, you two are welcome to use my office if you need it."

Estelle shook her head. "The sun feels good."

"Suit yourself." He waved the card. "I'll go write this up."

Estelle watched him stride toward the office. Terri Keenan opened the passenger-side door of the Cessna and put her logbook on the seat, snugging it down behind a leather camera bag.

"I left Las Cruces this morning at six o'clock," she said, and slammed the door. She ducked out from under the wing. "I was supposed to fly nonstop to Lordsburg. That was the plan, anyway." She grimaced.

"How did you happen to catch sight of the body?"

"I . . . uh . . ." She glanced toward the FBO's office, then smiled conspiratorially, moving a step closer to Estelle and dropping her voice. "I probably wasn't doing what I was supposed to be doing."

"And what was that?"

The woman rested a well-manicured hand on the engine cowling. "There was this eagle? I saw him soaring just about the same altitude I was flying at? And I thought how neat it would be to take a picture of him. In flight, you know?" She shrugged. "I mean, the air was like silk. How dangerous can it be?"

"That would be spectacular."

"Well, it didn't work out. I tried circling around him, you know? Trying to match my speed in a bigger orbit, outside of his and stuff? I closed to about fifty yards once, and zoom! He just turned a feather and shot straight up, way out of range."

"Wonderful."

"And basically, that's what happened. I was turning to head toward Posadas, and I saw the ravens down below. I still had the camera out, and the thought crossed my mind that a flock of them might make a picture too. Then something spooked them, and they all kind of took off and started milling. That's when I saw the body."

"How high above the ground were you?"

"About fifteen hundred feet. Maybe a little more or less. When I saw what I thought might be a body, I spiraled down some. Probably lower than I should have been."

Estelle's gaze turned to the airplane, a small two-seater that looked like the aircraft version of a tiny economy car. "You're a student pilot?"

Terri Keenan nodded. "I'm getting ready to take my flight test next week." She watched as the undersheriff stepped close to the window on the pilot's side and peered inside.

"It must be something of a challenge to fly and take pictures at the same time."

"I think it's easy," Keenan replied. "My instructor would have a cow, naturally. I don't see why, really. I mean, it's easy to *feel* what the airplane is doing and stuff. And my camera only requires one hand."

Estelle smiled and stepped away from the airplane. "Did you happen to take any photos of the body?"

The young woman hesitated. "Yeah, I guess I did. It was too far away to see any detail, though. It must have been at least a thousand feet. Even with the telephoto, that's too far. Just a dot, maybe. Basically, it was a waste of film." She held up her hands, rethinking the framing of the photo. "Some nice shadows, though. Early morning is really neat, you know? The sun's all at an angle on the grass and stuff."

"I'd like to see them, Terri. Sometimes, a photo shows something that the eye doesn't catch."

"Sure. The only other thing on that roll are a few pictures I took at the Las Cruces airport this morning. The sun wasn't really up yet, even. There was an old C-Forty-seven there. I think it lives over at Mesilla." She opened the passenger-side door and lifted the camera out of the bag. "It had been to some big air show out in California. I forget where. One of the engines was blowing smoke when they flew in a few days ago, and they had it all torn apart. Beautiful old thing."

She started to rewind the film but stopped, fingers poised on the crank. "Do you want me to have them developed and send them to you, or . . ."

"If we could just have the roll, that would be fine," Estelle said. "I'll make sure you get the negatives of anything we don't use. We really appreciate it." Terri nodded and rewound the film. She popped the canister out of the camera and handed it to Estelle.

"I hope it helps," she said.

"We'll take all the help we can get," Estelle said. "When you flew over that spot, did you happen to notice anything else?"

"Like what?"

"Any sign of human activity. Tracks, vehicles—anything at all?"

The young woman shook her head. "Nothing like that. Just a lot of open desert. But then again, I wasn't really looking, you know? The eagle got me all excited, and that's where my mind was." She grinned. "He was quite a sight."

"And nothing had changed out there when you went out again with Jim Bergin? Other than that the eagle had left the scene."

"Not that I saw. The body was still there. I was going to try for a picture when he buzzed the spot, but it went by too fast. Sorry. Do you know how long it had been out there? The body, I mean? Is it something that just happened, or what?"

"There are still lots of questions to answer, Miss Keenan. Nobody is sure of anything yet. It may just be someone who got caught unprepared, out in the cold, after dark. It'll take a while to sort things out."

Terri Keenan looked skeptical as she opened a fresh package of film and reloaded the camera. "That's a long way from anywhere just to be out hiking around in February, isn't it?"

"Yes, it is," Estelle said.

When Estelle didn't elaborate, Terri shot her a wry smile. She handed the undersheriff a business card, unadorned embossed gold lettering on ivory stock that announced the practice of Terri W. Keenan, DDS. "In case you need to reach me," she said. "First thing in the morning is always easiest, before I'm up to my elbows in someone's mouth."

"I'm sure that won't be necessary, Dr. Keenan," Estelle said. "We'll want to get the film back to you, and if you should think of anything else that might be important to us, I'd appreciate a call." She extended one of her own cards to the pilot. Terri Keenan frowned as she read it, then looked up at Estelle with a bright smile.

"When your deputy said that the undersheriff wanted to talk to me, I pictured some big guy with a potbelly and bad teeth. I don't know why. I mean, I've been told about a thousand times that I don't look like your average dentist, either."

"And I'm sure you're not," Estelle said, and extended her hand. "Thanks for your help this morning. We'll be in touch."

She left Terri Keenan to her preflight chores, and ducked her head inside Bergin's office on the way out. "Thanks, Jim."

"Don't mention it. Interesting gal, isn't she?"

"Yes."

"Looks too young to be a dentist, though. She talks more like a high school kid . . . and stuff." He grinned. "Makes me want to go to Las Cruces for a checkup."

"Win the lottery first, sir."

Bergin nodded slowly, pencil poised over his weather station log. "That's the impression I got, too," he said.

BY the time Estelle Reyes-Guzman reached the Public Safety Building on Bustos Avenue, she was sure that someone had rapped both knees with a ball-peen hammer after first clamping her elbow joints in a steel-jawed vise. She forced herself to concentrate as she filled out the evidence tag and tracking slip for Dr. Terri Keenan's roll of film, and then double-checked to make sure that she had put the film and paperwork in Linda Real's drawer.

She closed the cabinet and turned to find Gayle Torrez, the sheriff's wife and chief dispatcher, watching her with sympathetic eyes.

"You need to go home," Gayle said.

"Yes, I do." She shook her head in frustration. "Go home and join the rest of *los miserables*. If you see Linda before she finds my note, would you ask her to process that roll of film as soon as she can?"

"Sure. You'll be home, then?"

Estelle nodded. "A nap and I'll be fine."

"How's your mom?"

"Yuck," Estelle said. "She and Carlos are a pair. But I think they're over the hump now."

"And now you?"

"Don't say that. I'm just tired."

"Well, take your tired self home, and stop breathing on the rest of us." Gayle smiled. "Jackie said that she's going to spend some more time out at the scene. Widen the search circle a little."

Estelle nodded and then rocked her head from side to side to remove the kinks. "Bobby called the house this morning and talked to Francis. No emergency or anything. I guess he just wanted an update."

"And he called here. I don't think he cares much for Virginia. He said he hasn't seen the sun since he got there. He's homesick, Estelle."

"Me, too." She opened Linda's workstation again to make sure the bagged roll of film was where she remembered putting it, slid the steel drawer shut, and locked it. "If anyone needs me, tell 'em I went . . . somewhere."

"Did you see the note from Bill, by the way?" Gayle pointed toward Estelle's mailbox.

"Nope." She pulled the *While You Were Out* message from the slot, penciled not in Gayle's neat script but in the heavy, blocky printing of the state livestock inspector, Bill Gastner.

"When was he in?"

"Half an hour ago or thereabouts."

"He was supposed to come over for Sunday dinner today, but not with the stinkies, as Francisco calls them."

"That's what he said. He just missed you when you went to the airport, so he stopped here to leave a note."

" 'I need to borrow Linda,' " Estelle read.

"He's working some complaint about a bunch of mules or something," Gayle said. "He wanted Linda to take some pictures. Apparently the light's not very good, and he needs her expertise."

"He's got it," Estelle said. "When Linda comes in from . . ." She waved a hand eastward. The spot where the corpse had been found was so bleak no one had thought of an appropriate locator name for it. ". . . from out there, would you tell her to get in touch with him?"

"Sure. But he said there was no hurry on it."

"And that means *inmediamente*," Estelle grinned. "We know how he is." She slid the note into Linda Real's mailbox and puffed out her cheeks at the effort of moving the single sheet of paper. "I'll be home."

When she entered the house on Twelfth Street, the light tangy fragrance of simmering chicken greeted her, along with a silent house. Irma appeared from one of the back rooms.

"It smells wonderful," Estelle said. "How's everybody doing?"

"Chicken soup," Irma Sedillos said, affecting a heavy New York accent tinged with her own Mexican border lilt. "That's just what you need. Chicken soup." She took Estelle's jacket before it landed on the foyer floor and hung it up. "We had an early lunch, and then everybody crashed."

"Francisco, too?"

"His dad stretched out for a bit, and *el niño* couldn't resist. He's a smart kid. You need something to eat, and then you do the same thing." Irma waggled an index finger. With a gray wig and a touch of stage makeup, she could pass for sixty, rather than the twenty-six that she was.

"The nap sounds good."

"You want some soup first," Irma insisted, adding over her shoulder, *"No estás pegando en cuatro, Estelle,"* and headed for the kitchen. "You can't start skipping meals, now."

With too many knots in her joints to argue and in absolute agreement that she wasn't firing on all cylinders, Estelle did as she was told. The soup was so good that she lingered at the kitchen table, letting the vapors drift up from the bowl.

Irma chatted about this and that, but most of what she said drifted past Estelle unheard, comfortable kitchen chatter that didn't require an answer.

Estelle surprised herself by finishing two bowls of soup before putting down her spoon and straightened her spine against the back of the chair. "Okay," she said. "Now I can make it down the hall." She glanced at the kitchen clock. "Give me an hour and I'll be good as new."

In their bedroom, Dr. Francis Guzman was sleeping flat on his back, one arm thrown over his eyes. Francisco was curled beside him. Estelle left the door open and went to the boys' bedroom, where little Carlos was curled into a ball about the size of a cocker spaniel. She stretched out on Francisco's bed and, soothed by the smell of fresh linens and the regular, relaxed breathing of her youngest son across the room, fell asleep.

She awoke to the sound of her husband's quiet voice drifting into the darkened bedroom from somewhere in the front of the house. By turning her head a fraction, she could see the outline of Carlos, still sleeping peacefully. He had adopted a favorite position, scrunched on all fours with his legs drawn up under him and his rump in the air as if he'd fallen sleep while crawling.

Estelle sat up and swung her legs over the side of the bed. With a start, she saw that it was almost five in the afternoon.

Francis appeared in the doorway. "How are you doing?"

"Okay . . . I think."

"You slept like a stone," he said. He stepped into the room and peered at his youngest son. "This guy wanted to wake you up a while ago, but I told him that wasn't such a good idea."

"Y mamá?"

"Sleeping. This sleep is good stuff," Francis said. "Irma took Francisco with her to do a little grocery shopping. I'm surprised you didn't hear him."

Estelle pushed herself to her feet. "I didn't hear anything. Did Jackie Taber call, by any chance?"

"Nope." Francis followed her out of the bedroom. "Alan did, though. I just got off the phone with him. He said to tell you that John Doe was shot once in the head, probably either with a rifle or a large-caliber handgun."

Estelle stopped in the kitchen doorway and leaned her weight back into her husband's hands as he kneaded the muscles at the nape of her neck.

"Someone worked his lower face over, too," Francis added. "Alan wanted to talk to you about that. At first, he thought it was a case where the victim was beaten severely, and then shot. But apparently that's not the situation here."

Eyes closed, Estelle tried to picture the scenario days earlier out on the prairie east of the MacInernys' gravel pit. "What does he think happened?"

"Shot first, then a systematic effort made to destroy the dentition," Francis said.

Estelle turned and looked at him, frowning. "That's what he said out at the scene. That it looked like someone picked up a good-sized rock and did a number on his face."

"That's what Alan thinks. Ragged sort of injuries. Not the sort of thing you'd see if he'd been bashed with the butt of a rifle or hit with a baseball bat."

"Whoa," Estelle said, and rubbed her eyes.

"This, by the way, is chicken soup," Francis said, pointing at the crocked pot on the counter by the sink. "Enough for a fair-sized army. And the pot on the stove is *posole*."

"I had some of the soup," Estelle said. "What time did Irma go?"

"Not more than twenty minutes ago. She had one errand to run at home, and then she'd be back. She was planning to spend the night again, by the way."

"She doesn't need to do that. I think the worst is over."

"She thinks she does. I'm on call. And she was worried about you."

"I'm fine. I might have some more soup." She made no move toward the Crock-Pot. Francis sat down at the kitchen table and watched his wife think. Her thick black eyebrows knit together so tightly they nearly collided over the bridge of her nose. After a minute, she stepped close to the stove and lifted the lid off the simmering *posole*. Whether she actually saw it was another matter. Francis knew that her mind was somewhere east of Posadas, out on the rolling, rock-strewn prairie.

"I really question whether there was enough blood on the ground or on the rocks for him to have been shot there," she said finally.

"He could have been lying out there for a long time, Estelle. Several weeks, anyway. Between weather and critters, who can say?"

Estelle frowned and shook her head. "There hasn't been any precipitation since January fourth, and that was less than an eighth of an inch of snow, barely a frosting. Alan thinks the man was killed about three weeks ago, and that puts it at the end of January or early February, when the ground was dry. If this guy was standing when he was shot in the face, he would have pitched right over backward. There'd be blood and tissue and bits of bone all over the place."

"Scattered, though." Francis grimaced. "Or sprayed, might be a better way to describe it."

She looked at her husband. "We found a single skull fragment. Jackie found some small chips that may test out. Not much else. There was some dried blood under his head. But not much. Not a whole lot."

26

Francis shrugged. "The skull fragment says that he was shot there. It's hard to argue with that. Coyotes cleaned up, maybe."

"With his face bashed in for good measure," Estelle said. "And somehow whoever killed him managed to do it without leaving any tracks."

"From out of the clear blue," Francis said.

"No," Estelle said, taking him literally. "If he'd been dropped from a plane, every bone in his body would have been broken, not just his face. Did Alan say anything about any other injuries?"

"Nothing except the damage to the head. No bruises, no fractures, no defense wounds, no nothing."

"It's possible the film that our dentist shot will show something," Estelle said to herself. She glanced at Francis and read correctly the expression of combined curiosity and patience. He wouldn't ask where she'd been, any more than she would pester him to replay the mental tapes of his treatment of patients. "That's who I talked to at the airport, *querido*. A young dentist from Las Cruces saw the body and called it in." She stepped toward the phone. "You said you were on call tonight?"

Francis nodded. "Why don't you just let things mellow for a few hours?" he said. "Stew about it until morning. Maybe something will come to you. The guy's as dead as he's ever going to get."

"Just two things," she said as she dialed. "I need to know what's on the film, and I need to know if Jackie found anything else when she was out there. That's it."

"Uh-huh," her husband said. "And if either Linda or Jackie had new information that was of any importance, what would they have done?"

"Called me," she said, listening to the phone ringing at the other end.

"Posadas County Sheriff's Office, Wheeler." Francis could hear the dispatcher's voice across the kitchen.

"Ernie, is Linda still downstairs?" Estelle asked.

"She was. She and Jackie went back out to the MacInernys' about an hour ago. Make that an hour and a half."

"Did either one of them say why?"

"No, ma'am. I asked Jackie if she was going to work three shifts

27

in a row, and she just looked at me." Estelle smiled and glanced at her husband across the kitchen.

"Who's working swing tonight? I didn't look at the schedule when I was in there earlier."

"Tom Pasquale. He's headed out that way too, by the way. Maybe he thinks the girls are going to get lost in the wilderness or something."

"That's likely," Estelle chuckled. "If they need to reach me, I'll be home, Ernie."

She hung up and grinned at the pleased look on her husband's face. "The trouble is, this stuff smells too good," she said, lifting the lid on the *posole*. "It makes me want to forget everything else."

"That's likely," Francis said.

4

ESTELLE awoke with a start, nearly dumping her youngest son on the floor. She didn't remember hearing the soft ring of the telephone, but became aware of Irma's voice out in the kitchen in one-sided conversation.

"*Hijo,* we almost had a crash," Estelle laughed, and Carlos smiled up at her. They were sitting in the tall-backed rocker in the living room, a rocker that was all hard spindles and unforgiving maple armrests—and inexplicably, the little boy's favorite piece of furniture. She pulled him back up on her lap and wrapped the knitted shawl over his head so that he looked like a miniature Bedouin.

"You stopped reading," the three year-old said from underneath the shawl. It was just a droll reminder, a bookmark of a comment. Estelle leaned over to retrieve the little boy's literary passion that particular month. *Los Tres Pequeños Jabalíes* lay on the floor behind the rocker, just out of reach. She remembered reading the page that included the DO NOT DISTURB sign over the two sleeping Javelinas, comfortable in their house constructed of saguaro cactus ribs. Apparently the suggestion of the pigs' comfortable snoozing had been effective. She had no recollection of turning the page after that.

She looked at her watch and saw that it was eight-thirty. A half an hour had disappeared somehow.

"That's because it's time for bed, *querido,*" she said.

"Abuela can read."

Estelle leaned forward and let Carlos slide to the floor, shawl dragging between his feet. "Abuela's asleep, *hijo.*" She collected the book, straightened a bent page, and held it out to the boy. "Take it to bed with you."

Irma giggled and then she appeared in the doorway, the phone mouthpiece covered with her hand.

"It's Jackie Taber. Are you home?"

Estelle nodded. "You bet." She ushered Carlos and his book toward the hallway, taking the phone from Irma at the same time. "I think he's feeling better," she said as Irma turned to follow the small moving shawl toward his bedroom. "Jackie, what's up?"

"But are *you* feeling better?" Deputy Jackie Taber's voice was soft. "Gayle said you went home lookin' kind of punk."

"Sure. A passing moment," Estelle replied. "It's been an interesting week around this place." In the background, she could hear the distorted, metallic conversations of the police radio.

"Hold on just a sec," the deputy said. "They're yackin' at me." Estelle made her way back to the rocker and sat down. "Three oh six, go to the phone," Jackie said, and then to Estelle she added, "Pasquale is trying to reach me. Can I buzz you back in about five minutes?"

"Sure. I'll be here," Estelle said, and switched off. She rested her head back against the warm wood of the chair and closed her eyes. Nothing ached, nothing twinged, nothing pounded, but there wasn't much motivation to move, either. Sitting still felt just fine. In a moment, she could hear the muffled voice of Irma Sedillos in the boys' bedroom, continuing the harrowing tale of the three *jabalíes* and their continuing struggle with southwestern building codes and threats from the mangy coyote. Because there were no pleas to start the story all over again, she knew that Francisco was sound asleep. Were her oldest son awake, there would be argument and discussion about every move the *jabalíes* made.

In less than five minutes, the phone chirped again. Estelle put it to her ear without opening her eyes.

"Guzman."

"Estelle," Jackie said, "did Linda find you yet? She had some photos that she wanted to show you."

"She hasn't been by. The last I heard was this afternoon, when you two were going back out to see what you could find. Did Dennis talk to the MacInerny brothers, by the way?"

"That's part of what I wanted to tell you. Dale was home, and we drew a blank there. He doesn't remember anything out of the ordinary during the past weeks. But Collins caught up with Perry MacInerny at their parents' home in Lordsburg. Perry remembers hearing shots, but he says that someone is always shooting out that way, someplace. But what stuck in his memory is that a week or two ago, he heard shots in the evening. After dark. That's unusual enough that he took notice."

"Was he able to come closer with a date?"

"He told Collins that he *thinks* that it was a Friday night, two weeks ago. He says he couldn't swear to it, but he thinks that's when it was."

"Did he say why?"

"He said that he stayed late at the pit, working on some piece of cranky equipment. It was getting dark, and he says for a change the wind wasn't blowing. It was real still. Whatever job he had to do involved lots of oil, and I guess he was eager to take the opportunity to work without blowing sand. He remembers hearing the shots, and he told Dennis that his first thought was that it was probably jacklighters over east somewhere."

"Did he count the shots, by any chance?"

"We should be so lucky," Jackie said. "More than one, he said. He thought it was hunters. That's about as descriptive as he was willing to get."

"That's interesting," Estelle said. "If it was dark, how could Perry see what he was working on?"

"He told Collins that he's got a light that he strings from his pickup truck. Plugs into the cigarette lighter."

"I'm impressed," Estelle said.

"What . . . that he's got a light?"

"No," she chuckled. "That Collins thought to ask in the first place. There's hope, maybe."

"Maybe."

"Dennis had to drive to Lordsburg to talk with him, though?"

"Apparently so. He said he didn't want to do it over the phone, and didn't want to wait until Perry came back late tonight. Deputy Collins brought back a signed deposition, on top of that."

"I'm doubly impressed," Estelle said, amused when her remark brought no comment from the other end of the line. That Jackie Taber didn't hold Dennis Collins in particularly high regard was no secret, but they rarely crossed paths. Jackie preferred the dark times and solitude. Dennis liked the political visibility of daylight.

Jackie's voice dropped another decibel, barely more than a whisper. Estelle shifted the phone so that she could hear. "But here's the deal," and she hadn't finished the sentence when the police radio blared in the background. "Just a sec," Jackie said, and her voice drifted away as mike replaced phone. "Three oh one is ten-seven, just coming up on Pershing Park." The park was in the middle of the village, two good stone throws from the Public Safety Building and dispatch.

"Ten-four, three oh one."

"Let me turn this radio down so I can hear," Jackie said. "There's two points of good news, actually. Perry MacInerny said that the day after he worked on the rock crusher, or whatever it was, he had to buy a couple parts for it. He says he's got the invoice in the office at the gravel pit, and it would have the date on it. Collins was going to check with him and get a copy. If his memory is accurate, that date will give us something."

"That's good. What else?"

"The photos that the woman took from the airplane show a double set of tracks, Estelle. They're pretty clear. They come in from the east, and one photo shows them clearly enough that we were able to establish the point of origin from a roadway."

Estelle frowned, eyes still closed, picturing the empty sweep of eastern Posadas County. "What roadway, though?"

"There's a power company service road that follows the main transmission lines north–south. That's about, what, two miles east of the gravel pit, give or take? That's where the tracks lead. Linda and I went down to Maria to catch the service road where it leaves the state highway. We followed it north to see if we could find where the tracks join up, if they do. And sure enough the sand is soft along there, and they're pretty clear. Linda took shots using a flash, but she's almost certain that won't show much of anything. We need the strong morning light." Jackie took a deep breath, as if she'd caught herself being uncharacteristically blabby and needed to decide whether to confide more information. "And in one or two spots," she added, "the tracks in the sand are clear enough that we might make a casting work."

"You're sure it's the same tracks that extend all the way west to the body?" Estelle asked.

"We can overlay the photo on a map, and extend the tracks to see if they intersect with the road. I'm pretty sure that they will. That's what Linda's working on now, I think. She was going to print the photo so that its scale matches a map she ran off the computer's topo program. A more or less match, anyway. Then she'll burn a transparency on the copier."

"When you say a double set of tracks, what are you talking about? Two vehicles, or one coming and going?"

"Well, the photograph just shows traces, you know. Unless we find something at the west end—maybe evidence of a turnaround—we might not be able to tell. Two cars? One car? I just don't know. Another thing that's interesting is that one set goes in a pretty straight line. The other wanders a bit more. Maybe dodging terrain, or maybe one of the drivers was a little stoned. But they both sure enough go from somewhere over by the power lines to about fifty yards from where we found the body. They end just over a slight rise from that spot. If we had walked a bit farther east, I think we would have seen them."

"You said that Linda was able to take pictures of the tracks, though?"

"She thinks that she got something, but we were running out of light. She wants to be out here first thing in the morning, when the angle of the sun is real low. She thinks that she can pick up some contrast that way."

"Okay. She's not still out there, is she?"

"No, no. She wanted to work on the photo blowups. I go back on for graveyard, and wanted to catch some sleep before the shift starts. I wanted to ask if we could have Tom Pasquale sit the spot for a while between now and then, just to make sure nothing is disturbed."

"Of course. Mears is on tonight to cover, isn't he?"

"Yes, ma'am. And it's been quiet."

"Who's on graveyard with you? Sutherland?"

"Yes, ma'am."

"That'll be fine, then. Make sure that he knows when you go out there, Jackie."

"And there's always the possibility that the tracks don't have anything to do with John Doe, either," Jackie said. "We haven't hiked along the tracks from the power line road to where we found Mr. Doe. They might not even connect."

"There's always that," Estelle replied, knowing that it was a distant possibility at best. "You guys be careful."

She switched off the phone and sat quietly for a moment, her mind out on the empty prairie. The various scenarios were intriguing, including something as simple as Perry MacInerny lying to Deputy Collins. But if John Doe had run afoul of one or both of the MacInerny brothers, why would they bother to lug the corpse—or march the still living John Doe at gunpoint—a thousand yards from the yawning gravel pit, when the pit itself offered ample and permanent burial space? One dip of the MacInernys' enormous power shovel would scoop out a grave big and deep enough for a dozen John Does, and no one would be the wiser.

Estelle closed her eyes. The very spot chosen for the victim's disposal was interesting. If the tracks that the deputies had discovered were in fact related to John Doe's death and final resting place on the open prairie, the likelihood was great that the killer was no stranger to Posadas County. A killer didn't stumble onto a spot like that just by passing through.

The transmission line ran into the county from the east, passing just north of the tiny village of Maria. Maria itself was basically on the road to nowhere, snuggled up against the U.S.–Mexico border fence without a crossing station. From Maria, the line swept northward until, after twenty miles, it crossed the interstate and shed a few watts in the direction of the village of Posadas before angling out through the northwest corner of the county. Anyone living in Maria would know how to access the service road that followed the power line—a road in name only. And anyone who had bumped along that path would know that the transmission line passed through the most desolate acreage in the county.

Estelle could visualize the massive two-legged giants lugging their copper cables across the prairie, wind singing through the latticework of steel braces, just the hint of a road brushing their legs where once or twice a year a power company truck would jounce past.

She opened her eyes and smiled. On the short list of people who might know that country, two names came to mind. One was Sheriff Robert Torrez, who hunted every square inch of the county on a regular basis. The open reaches of eastern Posadas would be home to a few wandering antelope, certainly, and maybe even *los jabalies*. It wouldn't have surprised Estelle if, at some time or other, Bob Torrez had walked across the very piece of prairie that had become John Doe's final resting place. But the Sheriff wasn't going to be of any help. Sworn into office less than a month before, he was stewing in Virginia.

She turned the phone over, switched it on, and dialed. It rang six times before the *former* sheriff of Posadas County picked it up.

"Gastner . . . goddamn it . . ." A clatter followed, along with another curse. Estelle waited until the ruckus died down. "Gastner," he said again.

"Good evening, sir."

"Well, it was. Now I've got pieces of coffee cup and spilled coffee all over my kitchen floor."

"Sorry about that."

"It's not your fault, sweetheart. Normal folks can manage a god-damn telephone and a cup of coffee at the same time. That's why we have two hands. But something about that skill escapes me." William Gastner chuckled. "Ah, well. I was about to go out to eat. I got stiffed today on a dinner invitation, and I'm starving. What are you doing?"

"I'm sitting in a rocking chair, thinking."

"That sounds productive. How's your mother?"

"Better, I think. And Carlos is having a bedtime story finished up for him by Irma, so he's feeling better, too."

"He still into the three javelinas?"

"Same story."

"Christ, he ought to know it by heart by now. I read it to the two of them last week, myself. And I know they've heard it fifty times before that."

Estelle grinned at the memory of the howls of laughter as the boys' *padrino* tried to wrap his hopelessly Anglo tongue around the Spanish words, simple as they were. Francisco had laughed himself into a bout of hiccups that lasted the rest of the evening.

"At least fifty times. By the way, when I stopped by the office, I saw your note about needing to speak with Linda," Estelle said. "Did she call you yet?"

"Nope. But I could use a good hand with a camera—either Linda or you. I got me a nasty little deal going on with Eleanor Pope. You remember her?"

"Vaguely. As I recall, she lives over south of you a bit."

"Not far *enough* south. I can hear her damn dogs most of the time."

"So you're going to take pictures of Eleanor and her dogs?" Estelle stirred up a vague memory of a waddling, fat woman given to wearing long, flowing dresses and dirty white tennis shoes. "If I remember correctly, a year or two ago Howard Bishop tried to negotiate a fence dispute settlement between Mrs. Pope and one of her neighbors."

"Good memory," Gastner said. "But that wasn't just a neighbor. That was Eleanor Pope's son."

"That's right . . . it was. I don't remember how that turned out, either. Except Howard went out there about a dozen times."

"What happened is that the son moved to Deming for a while, until the fence either rotted away, or Eleanor forgot just what it was for. The son's name is Denton, by the way. Denton Pope. Goes by 'Woody.' And we're all happy to know that Denton is back, although he's not living next door to his mother this time. He's living *with* her. And none of that gossip, for what it's worth, is why I need a photographer. I can use one of those point and shoot things, but this is a little more tricky. What do you have on the agenda tomorrow? Gayle tells me that you have a little problem out east of the MacInernys' gravel pit."

"A John Doe."

"Ah, one of them."

"Found dead with a gunshot wound to the head and facial damage where someone pounded his teeth to pieces with a rock."

"Huh. Anybody we know?"

"Not yet."

Gastner chuckled. "You're a wealth of information, sweetheart."

"We just don't know much yet, *Padrino*. Jackie Taber is working through a lead or two. We'll see what she turns up."

"Jackie's coming along pretty well, isn't she? I was always impressed with her. A good, solid cop."

"Yes, she is."

"So can you fit in a few minutes tomorrow? It's got to be in the morning, though. Fairly early."

"That's not possible for Linda, then. She and Jackie are planning to be out at the MacInernys'. They need the early sun. I'll swing by, though. Just what is it that we're taking pictures of?"

Gastner hesitated. "It'd be easier just to show you."

"Is eight too early?"

"Eight would be just right. Why don't I pick you up. We'll do breakfast. It's a great way to start the week."

Estelle grinned. For Bill Gastner, *padrino,* or godfather, of her two children, retirement from the Sheriff's Department hadn't brought a change of habits. For him, the day was half over by eight o'clock, and he'd no doubt be on his second breakfast . . . maybe third, depending on how much of the night before he'd been up and prowling the county. For him, insomnia was more of an old friend than an affliction.

"That sounds good, sir," she said. "Take care of yourself." She switched off the phone, trying to conjure up a clear picture of Eleanor Pope's place at the end of Escondido Lane, almost on the southern outskirts of the village. She knew the property ran right up to the tall board fence that marked the back of Florek's Auto Wrecking yard. Beyond that, she drew a blank—particularly about what Eleanor and Denton "Woody" Pope might be doing that would attract the attention of the New Mexico livestock inspector.

THE village of Posadas, seat of a New Mexican county with fewer residents than an average suburban shopping mall on a busy Saturday, nestled against the southern skirts of Cat Mesa. Twenty miles south, the San Cristóbal mountains formed an east–west buttress between Posadas County and northern Mexico.

The rise of Cat Mesa and the spread of the border mountains molded a giant funnel for the prevailing west winds that bent the range grass into permanent tawny arcs with all the seed heads flagging eastward.

When she stepped outside that Monday morning, Estelle Reyes-Guzman felt the chill of the wind even as it bucked and swirled around the protective mass of her Twelfth Street home. Although the temperature hovered in the low forties, and before noon would break sixty that late February day, the open, windswept prairie east of the village where Linda Real and Jackie Taber were working would live up to its bleak reputation.

A battered white Ford four-wheel-drive pickup truck with state government plates was parked at the curb in front of the Guzmans' home. The faded spot on the passenger door's paint marked where the magnetic New Mexico Livestock Inspector's shield usually was affixed. Bill Gastner watched Estelle approach, then leaned across the seat, yanked the door handle, and shoved the passenger door open.

"Hey, there," he said.

"Good morning," Estelle replied, not altogether sure that it was. She slid the heavy camera bag on the floor in front of the seat and clambered up into the high-slung truck. Something as simple as getting into a vehicle had become a major effort, and Estelle puffed out her cheeks and shook her head. "Sorry about yesterday."

As she settled onto the seat, Gastner hunched forward with both hands on the steering wheel, regarding her critically. "Nothing to be sorry about. You're moving kind of slow this morning, too," he said.

She leaned back and let her hands relax in her lap. "Twice as fast as yesterday, though."

He pulled the truck into gear. *"Y Mamá?"*

Estelle nodded. "She asked this morning if we could drive down to Tres Santos sometime soon. That means she must be feeling better."

"That might be kinda good for her," Gastner said. "To get out and about like that. Is someone staying in her old place down there?" Compared to the tiny Mexican village where Teresa Reyes had spent her entire life and where Estelle had spent her childhood, Posadas was a metropolis. In Tres Santos, Teresa Reyes's four-room adobe house nestled under a grove of unkempt cottonwoods. One stump, close to the riverbed, bore so many carved initials and signatures on the smooth, iron-gray wood that it had become something of a historic directory.

Estelle remembered long, patient sessions as a child, rubbing the faint older markings with paper and pencil, trying to decipher them. Her favorite had been an ornate *PV* polished by the years of wind and weather until the serifs that ended the strokes were just a hint in the wood. Below the initials was the ghost of a date, and Estelle had stroked the paper with the smooth graphite until she was sure that it read *1911.* Her active imagination conjured up a burly Pancho Villa standing in front of the cottonwood, six-gun strapped to his waist, sun hot on his shoulders, penknife in hand, its sharp tip delicately nipping at the gray wood. At that time, her young mind hadn't seen the sense of admitting that the initials could just as easily have been carved by Pablo Vallejos, who had lived across the river behind the school, or Porfirio Villanueva, who for more than three decades had managed one of the copper mines.

"You remember the Diaz family?" she asked. "They live next door to *Mamá*'s?"

"Sure."

"Roberto, the oldest son, was renting *Mamá*'s for a while. He and his wife. But they moved to Juarez."

"Your mother lived in that little place for a long, long time."

"Her whole life," Estelle said wistfully. "That makes an even eighty years. And then one morning she trips doing something as simple as emptying a pan of water out the back door, and there goes the hip."

"God," Gastner grunted. "The thirty-five years that I've been in this town seem like an eternity. I can't begin to imagine *eighty* years looking up at the same bedroom ceiling."

"Maybe it's a comfort in some ways," Estelle said. "I think that's why she wants to see the village again. It brings back memories for her."

"I suppose it would." He glanced across at her. "How about you?" She looked quizzical. "Do you miss it ever?"

"Mexico, you mean?"

"Sure."

"Tres Santos will always be a special place for me." She looked off through the passenger window as they approached Bustos Avenue, the truck grumbling along as if they had the whole day to waste. A jogger could have lapped them, but Estelle had long ago become accustomed to Gastner's sense of pace. On rare occasions, she had ridden with him when the patrol vehicle screamed at over a hundred miles an hour. But far more often, she had seen the value of his *idling,* as she called it—drifting along with the windows down, listening to his county.

She turned and looked at him. "There are times when I miss it, of course. When things get hectic around here, sometimes the yearning to head south of the border is pretty strong." She smiled, but didn't elaborate. Bill Gastner was well aware of her past—orphaned at age two and taken in by Teresa Reyes, then forty-six years old, a childless widow.

The little black-haired, black-eyed child, her native blood echoed in the angular planes of her face, could as easily have become a ward of the church, destined for one of their orphanages. But something about the sober, quiet child had touched Teresa Reyes's heart.

She sighed. "I'd like the boys to have more time down there. With *Mamá,* if possible. They love talking with her. Especially Carlos. There's something between the two of them that's very private. A world all their own that's a mystery to the rest of us."

Gastner laughed. "He's a chip off his mother's block. And I've known your mother for what . . . twenty years? She sure as hell is a mystery to me, too." They moseyed out into the intersection of Twelfth and Bustos, with Gastner hesitant to turn east on the main drag. Directly across the intersection, a large, flat-roofed restaurant dominated the corner. Estelle knew exactly what was on her old friend's mind. "Have you eaten something?" he asked.

"Sure. Irma held me hostage until I did. She's worse than a mother hen. But if you need to stop, go ahead."

"You need to listen to Irma once in a while. And no, I'm all set. I ate a couple of hours ago." He waited for an eastbound vehicle to pass and lifted a hand in salute as the other driver waved at him.

As he turned the truck onto Bustos, Estelle saw the quick, perhaps wistful glance that he shot toward the Don Juan de Oñate restaurant. The place was his favorite haunt. She knew that to pass up a second smothered burrito grande before tending to business was something of a feat for him. After another ten blocks, they turned south on Grande Boulevard, heading toward the interstate exchange at a pace that, had there been a rush hour in Posadas, would have earned impatient gestures and glares. "Anything new on Mr. Doe, by the way?"

"Not a thing. At least not that I've heard," Estelle said. "Linda and Jackie were going out there first thing this morning."

"Theories?"

Estelle grinned. "It's probably a shorter list to assume what didn't happen."

"That's generally the way it is, more often than not."

"And by the way, what is it that we're doing this morning?" she asked.

Gastner frowned and shook his head. "We're going to stop by

Cameron Florek's first. He's got a problem with Eleanor Pope's goats, among other things."

Estelle laughed. "With her goats?"

"This is serious stuff, sweetheart," Gastner said with mock severity. "The goats are just the tip of the iceberg, though. Have you ever actually been in Florek's?"

"Ah . . . no."

"Cameron Florek has eight acres of automotive history behind that fence of his. And that fence is part of the problem. He has the misfortune of sharing a property line with Eleanor Pope." He glanced at Estelle. "But you know that already. Cameron's complaint started when he found several of Eleanor's goats inside his wrecking yard."

"I remember a tall board fence that circles the place. The goats are getting through that somehow?"

"Apparently it's more complicated than that. Mrs. Pope is aiding and abetting."

Estelle's left eyebrow drifted up and Gastner laughed. "Florek maintains that he drove the goats out a couple of times, and blocked all the likely places where he figured the critters were getting in. But despite his best efforts, they continued to trespass, and so he went back and looked more carefully. Someone—he says Eleanor or her son—had pried the nails out of one of the fence boards so that it worked like a kitty door." He swung his hand back and forth. "The goats were free to come and go as they pleased."

"And they were eating all his valuable license plates and fenders?"

Gastner shot a quick glance across at Estelle. "I can see you're not taking this case with the seriousness it deserves," he chuckled. "These are weighty matters."

"Sorry, sir." Estelle replied. "So you want a photograph of a goat chewing on a wrecked 1955 Oldsmobile? Is that it?"

"There you go again," he said, and held up an admonishing finger. "What's sort of interesting in all of this is that the goats are not why you and I are visiting Florek's Wrecking Yard."

"I was beginning to think that maybe you had too much free time, *Padrino.*"

"I wish. No, see, Cameron Florek doesn't really care about trespassing goats . . . they probably help to keep the weeds down, anyway. If that were the extent of it, he never would have called me in the first place."

They drove under the interstate, and in another quarter mile Estelle saw the tall board fence around the acres of wrecking yard. What passed for zoning in the village required the fence to shield the public's tender eyes from the eight-acre sea of decaying metal, plastic, and rubber . . . a fence that for most of its vast length was uglier than the scenery it obscured.

Near the entrance, an array of several thousand hubcaps had been tacked to the fence in wonderful patterns—so many hubcaps that village teens had long since given up trying to steal them all. It would have been a life's work to pry the entire collection loose.

On the opposite side of the entrance gate was Cameron's collection of license plates—rows and rows, decades and decades, every state and several foreign countries represented.

Parked in front of the fence was a vehicle welded together out of a vast conglomeration of mismatched parts. Looking like something out of a sci-fi film about Earth after the great atomic war, it sported a cow-catcher on the front, what appeared to be a large caliber howitzer on the roof, and rear fins made from what could have been parts from a retired corn harvester. Giant chrome exhaust stacks sprouted aggressively from the hood, in counterpoint to the four tires that had been flat for so long that the rims dug into the sand. The road warrior was evidence that even the busy Cameron Florek had spare time to devote to the pursuit of fine art.

Gastner pulled the truck through the front gate. Cameron Florek emerged from the battered Airstream trailer that served as his office. His coveralls had once been a natty, uniform Carhart brown. Over the seasons, they'd faded and been stained and patched to a perfect camouflage pattern for a wrecking yard. His giant beard splayed outward from a round face, combed meticulously into a great bib that hung off the bottom of his chin. Estelle grinned. Cameron Florek would look good motoring down the highway on a chopper, the wind lifting and caressing his beard.

He lifted a hand in salute when he recognized Bill Gastner, and the livestock inspector pointed toward the back of the yard. Florek nodded and went back inside the Airstream, apparently seeing no point in offering an escort service.

The lane that Gastner chose through the meandering rows of automotive carcasses was narrow, and Estelle watched the flow of vehicular history with fascination until they pulled to a stop in front of a Nash Ambassador.

Estelle looked at the forlorn heap, the teeth in its grill shed of all their chrome like an old man who'd spent his long life eating, drinking, and smoking all the wrong things. "It's hard to imagine that car sitting on a showroom floor," she said.

Gastner grunted, "My father owned one, can you believe it?" He nodded at the camera bag. "Do you need a hand with the camera gear?"

"No. I can manage."

"It's not too far, but there's so much shit in the way that we have to hoof it."

"I can't wait. Beware of the goats," she said as she slid out of the truck. Bill Gastner hadn't revealed the actual reason for their visit to Florek's, but Estelle could see that he was enjoying himself. And she knew that if their expedition hadn't been important, even for the most obscure of reasons, he wouldn't have bothered her.

"Goats are the least of our problem," Gastner said. "They're just the admission ticket." She followed him through the maze of dead cars and trucks until they reached an area where the vehicles were stacked three high. He stopped and stood still, hands thrust into his pockets. "There's no easy way through this goddamn mess, so you be careful. If there's an earthquake tremor or a sonic boom, run for your goddamn life."

"I'll just follow you, *Padrino*," she said. Bill Gastner had recently celebrated his seventy-first birthday, and *spry* wouldn't have been the first word Estelle would have chosen to describe his movements. At that particular moment, she was glad of it. Thirty pounds overweight, with bifocals that he'd worn for ten years but never gotten used to, Gastner stepped with methodical care, often punctuating a lapse of balance with colorful expletives reminiscent of his early years in the Marine Corps. More than once, he reached out to pat a thrusting

45

fender, and whether it was to restore balance or just a moment of private reminiscence, Estelle couldn't guess.

After working their way back through another decade of cars, they reached the tall, weathered board fence that marked the rear boundary of Florek's Wrecking Yard. Set tightly edge-to-edge when they'd been first nailed into place thirty years before, the six-foot tall boards had shrunken over the years, leaving a half inch gap between.

"The spot I want is right beside that old dump truck," Gastner said, pointing to his right. The Diamond Reo truck was doing a fair job of sinking into the sand, its stripped remains bleached by the New Mexico sun and rusted to an even reddish-brown patina.

He picked his way along the truck's hulk to a spot where the rear of the frame was snugged up against the fence. "Box seats," he said. With one hand on the fence boards, he stepped up onto the frame with a grunt. He extended a hand to Estelle. She rested the camera bag on the truck's brown skeleton and stepped up beside Bill Gastner.

Feeling like a little kid outside the fence at a baseball game, Estelle leaned against the warm wood. A dozen yards from the fence, five goats looked up at her, their eyes noncommittal and jaws idly oscillating. Eleanor Pope's dwelling was one of those interesting affairs that had grown over the years into a hodgepodge of angles and alcoves. What had started out as a single twelve-by-sixty mobile home was now two trailers, joined in a T, with a framed addition budding out of the middle, its roof somehow tarred onto the metal of the trailers. If it didn't rain, it didn't leak.

A vast collection of outbuildings filled the acre behind the house, together with half a dozen fifty-five-gallon drums lying on their sides. Two of the ones closest to the fence had wire mesh over the open ends. Estelle frowned. "What's in the drums?"

"Rabbits," Gastner muttered. He nodded off to the right. Meeting Florek's fence at a right angle was a row of metal-roofed sheds, each with a fair imitation of a two-by-six framed half door. "Here. Take a close look at the sheds." He held out a small pair of binoculars. Estelle took them and adjusted the focus and spread until the images jumped into sharp detail.

"What are those? Burros?"

"Miniature donkeys," Gastner said.

"It's hard to see with the shadows." She scanned the four stalls.

"How many do you count?"

"It's almost impossible to tell," she said. Bracing the binoculars against the wooden fence, she concentrated on the first stall. "They're packed in there like sardines. I think I see six in that first stall, maybe—but I can't see into the back. It's too dark."

"I counted eight yesterday," Gastner said. "And I estimate that stall is twelve by twelve. No bigger than that. Eight animals in one stall."

"And the others are the same?"

"I expect so. Maybe thirty of the damn little things in four stalls. It's a wonder that they don't kick themselves silly. Might as well jam 'em all in a livestock trailer."

Estelle lowered the binoculars and turned to look at Gastner. "What's going on, sir? What's she doing with them?"

"If I had to guess, I'd say that she's acting as a motel."

"I don't follow."

"A bit of a tip came my way. These little guys came up out of Mexico. Cameron Florek happened to see the truck that brought 'em. It's hard to imagine, but there's a good market for 'em. The folks who own all those half-acre ranchettes, and want to be real cowboys? Drop a burro or donkey in your front yard, and you've got a piece of 'living sculpture,' as a friend of mine calls 'em. Sidestep the permits and health inspections and all that government trivia, and there's a fair amount of money to be made." He leaned on the fence. "My guess is that these animals haven't been here for more than a couple of days. And I'd guess that they won't stay here long, either."

"You want to go in there with a warrant for a surprise visit. That's what this is for?"

"You betcha. I'm not going to chat with Mrs. Pope first, that's for goddamn sure. A good picture or two will help me convince Judge Hobart to cut a warrant loose, but I think I want to wait a bit."

"I can't imagine that the judge would hesitate," Estelle said.

Gastner shrugged. "Not with the animal health problems we've got now. Everybody's worried, you know, and not just in England or Europe. That hoof-and-mouth disease thing is a real nightmare." He nodded at the sheds. "Bring in animals like these, without proper health inspection, and we're just asking for some real trouble."

He paused. "Transporting these little guys around the state without a permit is just a misdemeanor. Hobart's not going to get excited about that. Me neither. But if these animals are headed out of state, that's a different story altogether. That's felony time." He thumped the fence with the palm of his hand. "She's got 'em packed in those stalls like cordwood. Maybe that's what bothers me most."

"Bizarre," Estelle said, and handed the binoculars back to Gastner. "It'd be interesting to know where they're going."

"That's the deal. If I just bust in there and confiscate 'em, I might never find out what her connections are."

"Let me see what it looks like," Estelle said. She bent down and unzipped the camera bag, selected the largest lens and screwed it onto the camera body. She rested the lens in the V formed by the top of two boards. "Are the Popes home now?"

"Eleanor works three days a week at Price's HairPort, today included. So far I haven't been able to establish what her son does. I'm assuming he's home."

Estelle adjusted the exposure and frowned. "What I can get is a sea of brown, fuzzy backs and a bunch of ears," she said. "Even with the sun shining into the stalls, there's just too much shadow and obstruction for much else."

"That's good, though. Two ears per beastie." Gastner chuckled softly. "That gives us a good count."

"It'd be easy with a flash if we were closer."

Gastner shook his head. "I don't want to be closer. I don't want them to know I'm interested. I just want to find out what the hell they're up to."

"The donkey source," Estelle said.

"That's it."

"They're cute little beasts. At least their ears are."

"Yes, they are. That's why the market for 'em is so strong. They're cute and small. You can keep one in the backyard. Use him to kick and bite the crap out of the neighbor's poodle."

Estelle snapped several more photos of each stall. "That's the best

I can do, without going into the yard. I think you can get an ear count, though."

"That'll do nicely."

"I'll have Linda develop the film today."

"Wonderful. Cliff Larson's giving me a hand watching the place. There's only the one driveway out onto Escondido Lane, so they're not going to slip away on us."

"How's he doing, by the way?"

"Cliff? Not well." Gastner grimaced. "He's dying, and he knows it. Something like this gives him something to do with his time, I guess."

Larson had become an institution as the district livestock inspector, and had asked Bill Gastner to fill in for him "on a temporary basis" after the November elections and Gastner's retirement from the Sheriff's Department. The filling in had become permanent as Larson's illness blossomed.

"You ready for some breakfast now?" Gastner asked as Estelle stepped down from the truck's frame.

She grinned at him. "Sure."

Walking back toward Gastner's truck, Estelle could smell the metal, grease, and oil as the sun gradually warmed the sea of car hulks around them. The inside of the state truck was warm, and she could cheerfully have settled back into a nap. With no place to turn around, Gastner backed the truck half a football field before a nook presented itself and he could swing into a space between a rusted Plymouth Valiant and a crushed Jeep Wagoneer.

Cameron Florek was standing by his Airstream as they approached. He crossed the driveway and Gastner opened his window and pulled the truck to a stop.

"You find the parts you was after?" Florek's beard bobbed as he talked, and the deep crow's-feet at the corner of his eyes crinkled. "That kinda worries me, I'd have to say."

"Sure did. Thanks for letting us look," Gastner said.

"Anytime, Sheriff." He glanced across at Estelle, letting that suffice as acknowledgment of her presence.

Gastner laughed. "God, don't say that," he said. "I'm not sheriff anymore."

Florek flashed a smile and jerked his beard toward the inside of Gastner's truck. "You got your scanner turned on?"

Gastner glanced at the radio slung under the dash. "Nope."

"Didn't think so. You wasn't in any hurry." He rested both hands on the door of the truck and rocked it gently. "You might want to give your office a jingle, ma'am," he said to Estelle.

"What's going on?" Gastner asked.

Before Florek could answer, and even while Estelle was pulling her small cell phone out of its belt holster, the gadget chirped urgently. "There ya go," Florek said. He patted the door of the truck and stepped back as Gastner pulled it into gear.

THE second corpse lay in the shallow grave with his feet pointing south. Estelle stood with her hands in her pockets, gazing down at what no doubt had once been a young man who had entertained all manner of exciting ideas about his future. Those ideas had been cut short when a heavy caliber bullet had smashed through the xiphoid process on the lower end of his sternum and then minced the internal organs that bone was supposed to protect.

"Juan Doe," as Deputy Thomas Pasquale had dubbed him, was no more than twenty-five years old, slight of stature with a lean, swarthy hawklike face, and long, black hair pulled tight behind his head in a short ponytail. He was dressed in blue jeans and a heavy denim shirt. A brown windbreaker had been tossed into the grave, perhaps as an afterthought, and lay across the man's knees. Other than laboriously removing the dirt using first the small short-handled spades that the deputies routinely carried in their units and then by hand, the body hadn't been touched or moved.

The grave was no more than eighteen inches deep, just enough to frustrate all but the most diligent coyotes. Estelle stood with her hands on her hips, surveying the distant horizon. Whoever had chosen the spot had worked at it. They had bounced along the rough service road that paralleled the power lines north from Maria for eleven miles. Five miles north of where she stood, the transmission lines crossed the interstate—and it was conceivable that the killers had gained access to the service road and driven south to this point. From whichever direction they'd come, this spot had served their purpose. They'd gouged out the young man's final resting place under the hum of commerce overhead.

Estelle turned and looked west to where a shovel lay a couple dozen yards out on the prairie, partially concealed by a runty creosote bush—marked now by a bit of red flagging tied to one of the bush's brittle limbs.

At a glance, it appeared to be a standard issue contractor's shovel, long of handle with an elliptical blade and good, sturdy blade shoulders that would take a beating from heavy-soled work boots. The shovel was new enough that portions of the label still clung to the hickory handle.

Following Estelle's gaze, Deputy Tom Pasquale said, "World class dumb. Somebody goes to all the trouble to dig a grave and then leaves the shovel behind."

"Let's hope so," Estelle said. "If the shovel and grave are related in the first place." She backed up half a dozen steps until she could lean against the eastern most upright of the huge transmission line support. It had taken nearly two hours to meticulously uncover the corpse, one careful scoop of desert soil at a time. She slid down the warm steel until she was resting on her haunches, arms comfortable across her knees.

"The crossroads," she murmured, and pointed west. "I can make out the tracks that head out from here." The sparse grass, bent and broken by the vehicle's tires, would remain so for months, until summer rains hastened the decay of the vegetation, and new sprouts took their place. "And Perry MacInerny told Collins that he heard shots on the evening of Friday, February second. He's got a parts receipt from the next day to lock in the date. All the way from here, you think?"

"Easily," Tom Pasquale said. "Unless the wind was howling from the west."

"MacInerny said it was calm."

"Then he could have heard gunshots from miles away . . . especially heavy caliber artillery."

Estelle nodded. "If the two killings are related, then Perry would have heard this shot first," and she nodded toward the grave, "followed by the ones that killed number one, way over there to the west." She turned, scanning the prairie. "I wonder how long."

"How long?"

"MacInerny doesn't remember an interval between the shots. If this one was first, and then"—she pointed to the west and stopped, brow furrowed—"that could be five minutes, ten minutes . . . almost anything." She shook her head in frustration. "We're going to have to work on Perry's memory a little bit." Turning to Jackie Taber, she said, "Tell me again what you saw."

The stocky deputy pushed her Stetson back on her head and squinted up into the sun, now harsh and winking on the power lines overhead. The wind was strong enough to touch the expanse of power lines between each tower, flexing them slightly, making them moan.

"I was sitting in the unit, right there," she said, indicating where the department Bronco was still parked. "I was waiting for Linda to come out. We were going to walk the tracks that showed up in the aerial photo. I saw where they took off to the west, right here, so this is where I parked. I was watching the changes in light, and I was getting ready to do some sketching. And that's when I saw the pattern."

Estelle regarded the grave expressionlessly. Scant as the vegetation was, there were an infinite number of places where a dedicated gravedigger could find a patch of earth two feet wide and five feet long without disturbing any plant life. Of all the places in Posadas County likely to remain undisturbed, and thus be suitable for an unmarked grave, the eastern Posadas prairie should have topped the list.

The transmission line service road, nothing more than a rude two-track in the best of places, paralleled the power lines just to the east of the tower's legs at this particular point. The grave was across the two-track, its northwest corner forty-five feet, nine inches from the tower's eastern support leg.

Estelle clasped her hands together and rested her chin on her intertwined fingers. "The pattern," she repeated.

Jackie Taber's were the eyes of an artist, Estelle knew. Why the young woman chose to spend her time as a graveyard shift deputy sheriff instead of using her GI bill money to attend a university and pursue her art was a question only Jackie could answer—and so far she had kept her reasons to herself. But the large eleven-by-fourteen sketch pad that was the deputy's habitual companion included detailed pencil or pastel drawings that often revealed more than the impersonal wink of a camera's lens.

"When the sun's low, just when it starts up over the horizon," Jackie said, holding her hand flat, palm down, "the way the light trips over things is really interesting."

"Deputy Picasso," Pasquale said.

Linda Real was standing within striking distance with her elbow, and did so. "She's right, bozo."

"I know she's right," Pasquale said easily and with a touch of admiration. "I tried one of those matchbook art contests once. It was so bad that when I tried to mail it in, the Post Office refused to deliver it."

"What's interesting is that this prairie is covered with rocks, all sizes and shapes, but uniformly covered, you know?" Jackie said. "If you want to sit down, you're going to have to nudge a couple of rocks out of the way, no matter what. You look at Linda's panoramic photos when she develops them, and you'll see the grave, too. Whoever did it didn't bother to take the time to kick the dirt smooth, so there wouldn't be a hump. And they sure didn't go back and duplicate the pattern of rocks."

"Did you do a sketch?" Estelle asked.

"Yes, ma'am."

"I'd like to see it." She pushed herself upright and waited, one shoulder leaning against the steel support while Jackie walked to the Bronco. She returned with the pad, opening it carefully so that the wind wouldn't grab the pages. She extended it to Estelle, who shook her head. "My hands are dirty," she said. Jackie held the pad while the undersheriff scrutinized the drawing.

"There's even a sort of windrow of rocks that got left after the construction crews went through, isn't there," she said. "Whoever dug the grave disturbed some of them." She looked up at Jackie and smiled.

"Yes, ma'am. And it looks like whoever dug this grave didn't take much time with it. They didn't go a millimeter deeper than they had to."

"So you saw this first? The grave?"

"I saw the disturbance of the ground, and that kind of tickled my imagination. I mean, this is a big prairie. To have an out-of-place feature of any kind . . . I mean, we're interested in the tracks that lead over this way from the MacInerny site, and so that's what I was looking for. Any kind of mark on the ground, any kind of disturbance. But I didn't make the connection at first. I mean that it might be a grave." She shrugged. "I mean, it could have just been a spot where one of the line crews parked a Bobcat or something. They let the blade down and made a mark."

"A neat two by five," Pasquale said.

"Well . . ." Jackie shrugged again. "And then I saw the shovel. The sun caught the blade. At first I thought it was just a tin can or something, then I saw the handle." She grinned and flipped the sketch pad closed. "The handle makes a nice, hard straight line that's really out of place. My first thought was, 'Ah-ha, I've got me a nice new garden shovel, free of charge.' And as I was getting out of the unit, it felt like somebody came up behind me and whacked me upside the head with a billy club." She tapped her forehead with the palm of her hand. "I'm thinking, whoa! Over here's what *looks* like a grave, and over there's a shovel. And a mile or so due west, if we maybe follow a vague set of vehicular tracks, is a corpse that didn't get buried at all . . ." She stopped and looked at Estelle. "It all hit me at once."

"He'd still be comfortable under the dirt if they'd picked up their tools when they were finished," Pasquale observed.

"Likely so," Jackie said. "When Linda got here, she took a bunch of pictures, and then I dug down as carefully as I could, at one corner. You know, maybe somebody just buried a bunch of garbage or something. Or maybe it was nothing at all. I took about five little bites with the shovel, and uncovered the tip of one of his shoes. With my fingers, I dug down just far enough to determine that there was a foot inside the shoe, and stopped."

The phone in Estelle's pocket chirped, and she fished it out. The conversation was brief and one-sided. She snapped the phone closed. "They just turned on the service road down in Maria," she said. "That's what . . . almost eleven miles? So we've got about twenty minutes if they're really hustling." She turned in place, head down.

With the toe of her boot, she loosened a small mound of sand and watched the wind rearrange it. "Any tracks have been obliterated long since," she said. "And that's too bad, because we've got some questions here." Without moving, she turned and looked at the grave. "Forty-five feet, nine inches from here to the grave," she said, tapping the vertical steel of the tower. "And how far in the opposite direction to the shovel?"

"It's sixty-one feet from the tower's northwest leg."

"And so we've got more than a hundred feet between the grave and the shovel that dug it . . . if we want to make the logical assumption that the two are related."

"That's a far toss," Linda Real said. "But it doesn't make sense that they'd throw the thing in the first place."

"No, it doesn't. Did you check it for blood or anything like that?" Estelle asked Jackie.

"Not yet. I haven't touched it. Linda took pictures of it in place, and I flagged the bush. I didn't touch the shovel. There were no tracks in the immediate area, nothing but the shovel. And the way it's caught in the bush, it sure *looks* like it was thrown."

"But from where?" Estelle said. "No one's going to dig a grave way over here, and then when they're finished, wind up and hurl the shovel about a hundred feet west, assuming that they'd miss the framework of the towers. And assuming that they could throw it that far in the first place." She thrust her hands in her pockets. "Why throw it at all?"

"I wonder how many more of these little surprises we've got out here," Tom Pasquale said. He grinned at Jackie Taber. "You see any more patterns, Picasso?"

"No," Jackie replied without a trace of humor. "Except I'll be willing to bet that when we move Juan here, we won't find any ID. That's a pattern. And whatever weapon took off the back of John Doe's head over by the MacInerneys' could sure enough have punched that big hole through this young man's chest. That's a pattern."

"The answer's with the shovel," Estelle said more to herself than anyone else. She ducked her head against the wind, hunched her shoulders, and walked across the rough prairie toward the creosote bush in whose angular, spiky limbs the tool had lodged.

She walked around the bush, turned her back to the wind, and knelt, hands on her thighs. "TemperRite," she said, reading the remains of the label on the handle. The tiny rectangular price tag was worn smooth, the printing nothing but a faint trace.

Jackie Taber knelt beside her. "The finish on the handle is smooth enough that we're going to get some prints if we're lucky," Estelle said. "And we've got a price tag that might give us a point of purchase." She rested her hands on the ground and leaned close. The shovel was turned slightly, and she could see the back of the blade, where the steel formed a deep grove to the handle socket.

"And there we have it," she whispered. Against the earth-polished steel, the dark russet of dried blood might as well have been glow-in-the-dark paint. Caught in the folded steel, near the junction of metal blade and wooden handle, were several hairs. She leaned back and looked at Jackie Taber. "An interesting question."

"A shovel makes a mean weapon," the deputy said softly.

"Sure enough. But if it connected with somebody's head *before* the grave was dug, then we wouldn't expect to find blood and hair still on the blade."

Jackie stood up with her hands on her hips, frowning down on the shovel. "It's way up high, though. And on the back." She grimaced. "Hard to tell." She turned full circle, seeing Tom and Linda standing near the front fender of Jackie's Bronco, their own and Estelle's units nose to tail in a row behind it. In the distance, she could see a column of dust rising and then being whipped away in a spreading plume as the medical examiner and the EMT ambulance made their way up the rough, bouncing trail from Maria.

"This place gives me the creeps," she said.

ESTELLE was surprised to see her husband riding with Dr. Alan Perrone. Although the friendship of the two physicians reached back more than a decade, and had been strengthened by their recently organized joint venture to build a new clinic in Posadas, Francis Guzman had expressed only a passing interest in the forensic side of medical practice.

Still, he assisted Perrone that morning as if the two had teamed at a hundred crime scenes. The two men worked, a study in opposites, quietly talking back and forth, never raising their voices so that anyone else was privy to their conversations.

Perrone would have looked at home behind the wheel of an elegant Dusenberg in a 1930s movie. Hatless even in the chill of the February wind, his long blond hair was parted in the middle and combed straight back, held in place as if molded out of yellow fiberglass. His lean, clean-shaven face was benchmarked by an aquiline nose, intense blue eyes, and full, sensuous mouth—his appearance drawing quick second looks from strangers who knew that he must *be* somebody.

Alan Perrone was of average size, but Francis Guzman made him look delicate in comparison. Well over six feet tall and powerfully built, Estelle's husband had inherited an exotic combination of his family's Andalusian and Moorish genes, from the dark polish of his mahogany complexion to the proud, ruler-straight bridge of his nose and his wide, expressive mouth. A year before his thirtieth birthday and his marriage to Estelle Reyes, Francis had grown a full beard—and was astonished when it sprouted fully salted and peppered. Nevertheless, he'd kept it and at the same time earned the nickname *oso viejo,* or old bear, from Estelle.

Perrone stood at the foot of the grave with his hands in his pockets and regarded the corpse with an expression of sad resignation. Francis Guzman's frown of concentration was dark and formidable as he paced a slow circle around the shallow pit.

"This appears to be a dangerous spot of nowhere," Perrone said without looking at any of the officers. "Until yesterday, I'd never been to this miserable little patch of the county. Now we're having reunions out here." He glanced up at Estelle. "Do any of you know this gentleman?"

"No, sir."

"Interesting," Perrone said, and knelt at the side of the grave. Francis Guzman did the same on the opposite side. Estelle stood a pace or two back, wishing that she had one of those nifty polyester folding chairs. She knew that the examination of misfortune's target by the two physicians would be methodical and thorough . . . and she also knew that neither physician wanted to narrate every step of the process for an audience. At that moment, the persistent wind became an ally—without it, Estelle knew the warm sun would make the drowsies unbeatable.

Estelle watched Linda Real reload her thirty-five millimeter camera three times before Alan Perrone finally straightened up and brushed off the knees of his trousers. He turned and beckoned to Estelle.

"This isn't going to give you much," he said. "One gunshot, through and through. He wasn't lying in the grave when it happened, so the odds of you finding the slug are slim and none." He flashed a tight smile and shrugged. "If the bullet fragmented, we may find some pieces when we autopsy, but don't hold your breath. That exit hole is only moderately larger than the entrance, so whatever tore through him did its damage and then just kept going." His gaze wandered out toward the open prairie, and he shrugged again.

"What about the angle?" Estelle asked.

"My first guess—and it's just a guess, remember—is that the trajectory was dead on, or nearly so," Perrone said. "The slug exited through the seventh thoracic vertebra, so you *maybe* have a slight upward slant. Maybe. It's impossible to say how the shooter was standing, or how your victim here was standing. And even as powerful as that weapon obviously was, it's impossible to predict how the bullet is going to wander around when it starts smashing through things. My best off-the-cuff preliminary maybe guess is a dead-on shot." He made a face of indecision. "No powder burns on the jacket or shirt, so there's a little distance there."

"A maybe guess." Estelle grinned at Perrone.

"That's it," Perrone said cheerfully. "There's a lot of blood in the grave, though, under the corpse. My guess is that he was shot while standing fairly close by. Hell, I don't know. Maybe he dug it himself. And that was that. Bang. One shot, and in he goes."

"You're thinking that someone made him dig his own grave?" Tom Pasquale asked.

Perrone shrugged again. "It's a good guess, isn't it? If I'm holding a gun on you, why should *I* bother to dig the grave? My hands are full, for one thing. I'm busy holding the weapon."

"He could have been shot first, and then the grave got dug."

"I don't think so," Perrone said.

"It would take ten minutes at the least to dig that pit," Francis Guzman said. "Maybe longer, depending how frantic the worker was. If your Mr. Doe had already been shot while all that was going on, he would have bled out with a wound that size. By the time he was placed in the hole, you'd be lucky to have a teacup drain into the soil. That's not the case here."

"Huh," Pasquale said, and frowned.

"Huh, is right," Perrone added. "My hunch is that the victim dug his own grave. Or at least took part in the ceremony. But that's just a hunch. It'd be nice if he had great big shovel blisters on his hands, but he doesn't." He knelt down and turned one of the victim's hands palm up. "This young man was used to work." He traced along the plastic bag that covered the man's palm. "No dude here. I'll take a closer look and see if anything interesting shows up." He stood up. "And by the way, the same thing is true of Mr. Doe from over west of here. You've got two hard-working men who ran afoul of somebody with a quick trigger finger. John and Juan Doe."

He turned to Jackie Taber who had meticulously retrieved, bagged, and tagged the shovel. "The state lab is going to want to go over that, too. We might get lucky."

"I think we did, sir," Jackie Taber said. "There's what looks like blood and human hair on the backside."

"Better and better," Perrone replied. As he talked, Estelle had been watching the progress of a yellow truck as it approached from the south. "The landlords," she said. In another moment, the truck pulled to a stop behind the ambulance, and they could see the round Posadas Electric Cooperative shield on the door.

Marvin Hudson got out and hesitated, one hand anchored to the truck. As Estelle approached, he remained in place, forehead in a worried frown. Another man whom Estelle didn't recognize remained in the vehicle.

"Good morning, sir," she said.

"They told us over the radio that there was all kinds of traffic up this way," Hudson said. "The supervisor said it might be a good idea to drive on up and see what was going on. See if there was anything we could do."

Hudson's eyes darted this way and that, taking in all the vehicles and the small group standing by the pile of dirt not far from one of the power poles. He was a chubby man, his brown utility shirt stretched tight across a gut that draped over his belt. He turned and looked at Estelle, eyes inventorying her slender figure and then retreating back to her face.

"I guess we've met, ain't we?" Hudson said, and extended his hand.

"I believe so, sir. I'm Undersheriff Reyes-Guzman."

"Okay," Hudson said, as if all the memory cells had been jogged on-line. "I got used to always workin' with old Bill Gastner. He's as much of a fixture as I am."

"Yes, sir."

"How's he doing, by the way?"

"Fine, sir."

Hudson released his hold on the truck and took a step forward. "So what's the deal here?"

"One of the deputies discovered some human remains, sir," Estelle said.

"No shit?" Hudson said. "Who is it, do you know?"

"No, sir, we don't."

"Know how it happened?"

Estelle shook her head. "We don't know that either, sir."

"Well, I'll be damned," Hudson added. His eyes narrowed. "Is this related to that thing yesterday? I'm hearing that they found some guy dead over in the MacInerys' gravel pit."

"We don't know, sir." She said it pleasantly enough, but it wasn't the informative answer Hudson was looking for. Estelle saw a brief flash of irritation cross his face, then a shift of the eyes at the same time as gravel crunched behind her. Tom Pasquale ambled up and leaned an arm on the hood of the company truck. Hudson put his hands in his hip pockets.

"What are you guys up to?" Pasquale asked. He turned slightly and aimed an index finger at the young man in the truck cab and flicked a couple of shots off with his thumb. The target lifted a hand in tentative greeting.

"Just drove on up to see who the hell was messin' with our electric lines," Hudson replied. "Looks like you guys got quite a deal goin' on."

Tom nodded and cocked his head at Hudson. "When did Eurelio start workin' for you folks?"

Hudson shot a glance at his partner. "Hell, it's been a couple of months now. You two know each other?"

"Oh, sure," Tom said. He patted the hood of the truck and ambled around to the passenger side.

Hudson took a deep breath. "So," he said to Estelle. "Is there anything you need from us?"

"Not at the moment, sir," Estelle replied. "If either of you happen to remember seeing or hearing anything out in this area in the past couple of weeks—any unusual traffic, anything at all—I'd appreciate you giving us a call."

Hudson grunted in dismissal. "This ain't the sort of place I hang out much, young lady. You might talk with Eurelio, there. He's one of the locals. You want me to give Matt Tierney a buzz?" Estelle knew that Tierney, as area manager of the Electric Coop, would be interested to know that the transmission line right of way was being used for the disposal of more than beer cans.

"I'll be talking to him later today, most likely," she said. "There's nothing else we need at the moment. Right now, we're waiting for the coroner to finish up. That always takes a while." She smiled at Hudson. "How often do you get up this way?"

"Blue moons," Hudson said. "This line here is just a straight shot, you know. No pots or anything. Not much is going to happen. Once in a while some damn kid from Maria wanders up this way to shoot snakes or something and ends up doing a little target practice on things he shouldn't. But most of the time, we don't have much cause to come up this way. Hell, I haven't been up here since before Thanksgiving. There's a routine inspection schedule, but I don't know what it is offhand. Tierney would know." His lips pursed. "Technically speaking, this transmission line doesn't even belong to us. Sort of a reciprocity thing with the big guys, you know."

She saw Hudson's neck stretch and turned to see the two paramedics maneuvering the corpse into a black plastic body bag. "Geez," Hudson said. "Tried to bury him and all, eh? This ain't the easiest diggin' in the world, out here."

"No, it's not," Estelle agreed.

"What, was he shot, or what?" Hudson sounded as if he were fishing for a tour invitation, and of course an opportunity to gape at the corpse would be a nice bonus.

"That's what the coroner will tell us, sir."

Even Marvin Hudson was bright enough to know that Dr. Alan Perrone wasn't about to sit down for a nice chat. "Well," he said, reaching for the truck's door handle, "if there's anything we can do for you, you let me know."

"I'll be in touch, sir." She heard Tom Pasquale chuckle at something that Eurelio said, and then Hudson climbed aboard and started the truck.

"There's a good clear spot right behind you there," Pasquale said helpfully, and they watched the power company truck kick rocks as Hudson backed up over a small berm and cranked the wheel. He lifted a hand in salute as he drove off.

"I think that old Marvin doesn't like me much," Tom Pasquale said.

"I noticed that."

"I gave him a ticket last week. He didn't say anything about it, did he?"

"No, but he was pretty quick to put his hands in his pockets so he didn't have to shake hands with you."

Pasquale laughed. "Oh, yeah. You noticed that, too."

"Who's Eurelio?"

"Oh, him? That's Eurelio Saenz. You know the intersection in Maria? He lives in that house with the turquoise trim on the south side of the road. His mother owns the bar right next door. La Taberna Azul, I think it's called."

"Paulita Saenz is his mother?"

"That's the one. Most of the family lives across the border. I think Eurelio's got about a hundred cousins down there."

"Paulita was originally from up north, though. Chama, I think," Estelle said. She smiled at the quizzical look on Pasquale's face. "Once upon a time, she and my Uncle Reuben had a little thing going."

Pasquale wagged his eyebrows. "You and Eurelio might be cousins then," he said. "You might be one of the hundred."

"That would be interesting," Estelle said, amused at the young deputy's good-natured insolence. She watched the dust from the electric company's truck fan out across the empty prairie as it headed south. "Eurelio didn't happen to say that he was missing a couple of those relatives, did he?"

"No. But he's spooked."

She looked at Pasquale sharply. "How do you mean?"

"He wasn't all that eager to get out of the truck, for one thing. But just in the little while that I stood there and talked with him, he kept tuggin' at his shoulder harness, like he needed something to hang on to." He saw Estelle's left eyebrow drift upward. "Well, it's just a little thing, I know. But it's the impression I got."

"Some people get nervous when they know there's a corpse in the neighborhood, *Tomás*."

"Nah," Tom said, waving a hand in dismissal. "He and the rest of the bunch hunt all the time."

"He didn't hear or see anything unusual in the last week or so?"

"He *says* not—but then again, he didn't say a whole lot about anything. He did volunteer that working with Marvin Hudson was something of an experience."

"Imagine that," Estelle said. "If that pair had to dig a hole, guess who'd get to run the shovel?"

STATE 61 plunged south from Posadas and passed through Maria as the highway wound along the state's southern border toward El Paso and Juarez to the east. The State Highway Department had recognized the tiny community's existence by hammering in a sign at each end of the village pleading for forty-five miles an hour. Wary of radar and the threat of languishing in a redneck jail cell, only tourists bothered to lift their foot.

Locals took potshots at the signs, most often when they wandered out of la Taberna Azul, the small saloon owned by Paulita Saenz. Bullet holes punctured the reflective surface of the sign and paint from bumpers and fenders scarred and bent the supports below.

Most of the paint had long since worn off the sign swinging from the two-by-four support nailed to the porch of la Taberna Azul. When locals mentioned the place, years of comfortable usage had worn down the name, too. Estelle could remember her Uncle Reuben referring to the Blue Tavern in Maria simply as *la Barra*.

Paulita Saenz walked to work each day from her square adobe house just east of the saloon. Her thirty-five- or forty-step journey crossed a stretch of worn bricks. The idea at one time had been to construct a neat patio between home and saloon, creating a sheltered spot for outdoor tables. Over the years, the bricked yard had become a convenient spot to stash those items not urgently needed in either building. Paulita's walkway had been forced to meander as the space filled with worn-out plumbing fixtures, great mounds of cans and bottles that were always going to the recycler next week, and a jumbled collection of various bargains in roofing materials.

Diagonally across the street from *la Barra,* Wally Madrid's dingy gas station and convenience store dominated the north side of the intersection of State 61 and J Street, J being the only cross-street in the village. No one in Maria recalled how the dirt lane had come by its cryptic name.

Wally was Paulita's first cousin. He resented that fate had allowed Paulita possession of a liquor license, and hadn't spoken directly to her in more than a decade.

Wally's store carried so few items that *convenience* was pure euphemism. By pricing his gasoline well over the sensible limit and keeping his store inventory down, Wally had found that he could avoid most things that reminded him of work. The west-facing window that would have looked out on J Street was covered with various posters and advertisements, bleached nearly printless by the sun. That was also a comfort to Wally. Had the window been clear of trash, he would have been able to glance out and see la Comida de Lucy, his wife's diner, and the third and final commercial establishment in Maria.

Lucy Madrid and Paulita Saenz were also first cousins, and enjoyed a common contempt for Wally. The Madrids were no longer on speaking terms either—a relationship that took considerable evasive skill in such a tiny community.

Should a famished tourist stop at the gas station to inquire about a place to buy lunch, Wally would point at the rack holding the slender choice of Doritos, but he would never recommend Comida de Lucy. And, on the rare occasions that Lucy filled the gas tank of her 'eighty-one Chrysler New Yorker, it wasn't at Wally's pump. Each Madrid found peace by pretending that the other didn't exist.

Lucy's diner was a plump, tidy adobe house with what passed for a commercial kitchen in one room, a single bathroom with all kinds of interesting messages on the walls that spanned generations, and enough space left over for a small counter that seated three, the customers' backs to the four tables that filled the dining room.

Lucy Madrid had long since given up worrying about whether her *comida* was good . . . or even edible. The same few people who lived in the environs of Maria bought the same items off the breakfast and lunch menu according to their own predictable schedules. Occasionally tourists chanced Lucy's. Had the tiny diner actually fronted on the state highway, Lucy's business might have overflowed the four tables. But being half a block off the main flow, traffic tended to pass the place by.

Tourists occasionally drove up J Street beyond the café, and saw that Maria boasted four or five more dwellings, clumped haphazardly around the little wart of a mission, la Iglesia de Santa Lucia.

Estelle Reyes-Guzman opened Lucy's front door and paused. A single fluorescent light unit hung by tenuous grip from the ceiling, the Sheetrock sagging from repeated roof leaks. An old man sat by himself at one of the tables, hands folded, a cigarette lodged between two gnarled fingers. He appeared to be meditating—or counting the tiny bubbles that might have been detergent dancing on the surface of his coffee.

"How about by the window?" Estelle said, and Francis nodded.

"A view of the surf," he sighed. They sat down and Estelle bent forward as if she were going to rest her forehead on the table, stopping with eyes closed just short of contact. "Too long a day for you, *querida,*" Francis said.

"*Sí.*"

He pulled the menu out from behind the empty napkin holder. "You actually want something to eat here?"

"No thanks." Estelle ignored the menu. "If she has tea, that would be nice." She lifted her head and smiled at her husband. "Tea's safe, no?"

Francis shrugged as he surveyed the laminated menu card. "That depends on where the water comes from, *querida.*"

Lucy Madrid appeared from the kitchen, a square, generously padded woman. "I thought I heard somebody," she said, doing her best imitation of a good-humored bustle to their table. She stopped short, eyebrows knit together in concentration, staring at Estelle. "You're on that show," she blurted.

"That show?"

"I've seen you on the TV." She cradled one hand in the other and looked up at the ceiling. "Now what's the name of that . . ."

"I don't think so, Mrs. Madrid," Estelle said. "Thanks for the compliment, though."

"I know you from somewhere, then. I know I do."

"My Uncle Reuben used to come down here a lot," Estelle said. "Reuben Fuentes?"

Lucy Madrid beamed, her teeth twinkling. "Thaaaaat's it. You're that girl."

"That one," Estelle said.

"Old Reuben, he was a one, that's for sure. He died, no?"

"Yes, he did. About five years ago."

"Too bad. I liked him." Comprehension turned up her smile another watt. "I read about you in the paper, that's where."

"You might have."

"You're sheriff now."

Estelle nodded, impressed. "Undersheriff, Mrs. Madrid. Bob Torrez is sheriff."

Lucy looked toward the door. "So where's Bobby?"

"He's in Virginia, ma'am." No doubt, Robert Torrez and Lucy Madrid shared family ties, however distant. Estelle saw a flicker of puzzlement flit across Lucy's broad face. Virginia was too much of a leap, and she changed course. "You're this one's husband, then," she said to Francis.

"For sure," Francis said. "And my wife would like a cup of tea, if you have it?"

"Hot or cold?"

"Hot, please."

"I got that. And that's it?"

"I'd like a Dr Pepper," Francis said. He slid the menu card back behind the salt and pepper shakers.

"I don't got that stuff. I don't like it. You want a Coke?"

Francis grinned. "That'll be fine."

She nodded and turned away from the table. "I close at two, you know." Without waiting for a response, she added, "That Bobby . . . he ought to come down this way more often. All we get are those federal *mierdas* . . ." She waved a hand in dismissal.

Estelle watched the woman waddle off. "I think she's talking about the Border Patrol," she said to Francis. "I would imagine that they find this little place pretty interesting."

"I bet they do." He looked out the window at the dusty street. "How far is it to the border fence from here?"

"A hundred yards behind the saloon . . . at the most," Estelle said. She rested her chin in one hand, elbow on the varnished table. "I was surprised to see you riding with Alan."

"We were right in the middle of a planning session when the call came in," Francis said, and shrugged. "So I came along." He reached across the narrow table and took hold of Estelle's wrist just below where her hand supported her chin. He shook her arm gently, just enough to joggle her head. "I was a little bit worried about you."

"I'm okay. Just tired."

"So . . . can you go home now? I mean, after your gourmet tea?"

"Sure. Jackie is doing just fine. There's just one or two things . . ."

Francis leaned back, his mouth opening in a wide, silent laugh.

"What?"

He bent forward and lowered his voice to a whisper. "Always one or two more little things . . . that's what they're going to carve on your tombstone, *cariño*."

"Well," Estelle said, "when I'm staring something interesting right in the face, I can't just ignore it." She closed one eye. "You can't either, you know."

"So . . . what's staring at you now?"

She frowned as Lucy Madrid approached, a heavy porcelain mug in one hand, a can of Coke in the other.

"Let me get you a glass," she said. "You want ice?"

"That would be nice, thanks," Francis said.

Estelle reached over and moved the napkin dispenser slightly. A small poster sat on the windowsill, facing J Street where both pedestrians would see it. She reached out and lifted it off the sill, turning it just enough to see what it advertised. La Iglesia de Santa Lucia was hosting a yard sale. No doubt Lucy Madrid felt a kinship with her matron saint. She arrived and slid the glass with two small ice cubes in front of Francis.

70

"Thank you," he said. "And?" Francis prompted Estelle after Lucy had moved on.

"Digging a grave takes time."

"Sure. Even a shallow one, when the soil is so full of rocks."

"Here's what makes sense to me," Estelle said, and encircled the mug with both hands. "John Doe was being chased. He was running west."

"John's the first victim that you found, right? The one that the dentist saw?"

She nodded.

"So what makes you think that he was running?"

"Suppose," Estelle said slowly, "that John and Juan Doe were together somehow. Maybe they're even related."

"Odds are," Francis agreed.

"It's too bizarre a place for them to be separate incidents. The tracks are circumstantial right now, but they make sense. But imagine this,"—she straightened up and held out her hands—"suppose John Doe had the shovel in his hand. He's either digging the grave, or helping, or something like that. The killer shoots Juan, and he either falls into the grave, or is dumped into it. John sees his chance, and hits the killer." She swung her arms in a short, choppy baseball bat stroke.

"That would explain the blood on the shovel," Francis said. "But we don't know about a match to either victim yet."

"No, but we will," Estelle murmured.

"So you think John Doe takes a swat with the shovel, and gives himself a few minutes head start. He turns to run, and after a few steps, realizes he's still holding the shovel, and tosses it into the bushes. And he runs away from the road, in a panic, knowing that he's next on the hit list."

"That would make sense."

"And after he recovers a little, the killer staggers to his truck, or his car, or whatever, and chases John Doe across the open prairie."

"He could have done that," Estelle said. "That would account for the tire tracks. And he caught up with him after a thousand yards or so."

"And because John tossed the shovel, he doesn't have anything to defend himself with. There's nowhere out there for anyone to hide. He's winded from running."

Estelle shrugged. "I think it's possible."

"Anything's possible. Why didn't John just take the vehicle after hitting the killer?"

"I don't know. Maybe the keys were in the killer's pocket."

"Why didn't he make sure the killer was out cold? Hit him again. Take the gun. Take the keys."

"Panic," Estelle said. "A basic instinct is to run. Fight or flight. If he's not a fighter, if he's scared to death, he's going to run. For one thing, if Perry MacInerny heard the shots, we know it was dark when this all happened."

"So the poor guy thinks he can get away in the dark."

Estelle nodded. "But that makes it hard to run."

"Hard to shoot, too."

"If the killer drove after him, he had his headlights. Enough for a quick shot or two."

Francis poured the remains of his soda into the glass, watching the two ice cubes drift in the current. "I suppose. The killer gets close enough for a head shot. John Doe is tired of running, staggering, out of breath. He turns to face him. Boom."

"I can understand the facial trauma, then," Estelle said. "The killer is in a rage. The head shot isn't enough, and he makes sure with a rock. When he's finished, he's probably in such a lather that he doesn't even realize that he doesn't have the shovel—even if he had the inclination to bury the second victim. He's confident that identification is going to be next to impossible, on the off chance that someone discovers the body."

"Interesting scenario," Francis said. "John Doe would have been the one with the shovel, too."

Estelle nodded. "Even if Juan dug his own grave, someone had to cover him up. The killer has the gun, John gets the shovel. And somewhere along the line, he sees his chance."

Francis looked over the top of his glass at his wife. "And if we're wrong?"

Estelle smiled. "Then we're no further away from an answer than we are right now."

"If you're right, you're looking for a man with head trauma. That shovel would have made a nasty cut." Draining the last of the soda into the glass, Francis squeezed the empty can neatly in half, set it on the table, and nudged it to rocking. "And now?" He watched his wife's face. Two sips of tea and a few quiet moments hadn't erased the dark circles under her eyes.

Estelle cradled her head again, gently shaking it back and forth. "I don't know." She lowered her voice even more. "I wonder about Eurelio."

"Who's that?"

"The young guy who was riding with Marvin Hudson today, from the electric company. He's Paulita Saenz's son."

"From the bar across the street, you mean?"

Estelle nodded.

"I saw you talking to the one who was driving. The fat one? That was Marvin? What did his partner do to attract your attention?"

"He didn't do anything." Estelle pushed the tea to one side, rested her chin on her hand again and gazed out the dirty window. "He didn't even get out of the truck."

"Why should he?"

"Tom Pasquale walked around the truck and talked to Eurelio. He said that the boy was nervous."

Francis chuckled. "Tom Pasquale has never impressed me as the most keenly observant type, *querida*."

"Exactly. If the boy's behavior caught Tom's attention . . ." She shrugged. "Loose ends, is all," she added.

"Things to keep you awake at night."

She nodded, almost imperceptibly.

"Did you run all this by Jackie? To see what she thinks?"

"No. Not yet."

"Well, you should," he said. "*Padrino*'s right when he calls you inscrutable, you know. The deputies can't read your mind. And Jackie's pretty savvy."

"Yes, she is. But she has other things to think about just now,"

Estelle said. She pushed her chair back and sighed. "Sometimes, until I know the direction I want to go, it's easier if I don't muddy the water. I'd hate to send somebody off on a wild-goose chase." She smiled at Francis. "Anyway, I did tell someone. I told *you, mi corazón*." She pushed herself to her feet. "You ready?"

"Sure."

Lucy Madrid hovered near the aging cash register, and Francis handed her a five dollar bill and waved away the change. "What do you do?" she asked.

"I'm a physician," Francis replied.

"Well, that's good," Lucy said. She nodded at the old man who still sat quietly, smoking and stroking his coffee cup. "He's deaf, you know."

"I didn't know," Francis said. Lucy looked at him expectantly, as if he was supposed to produce a pocket cure for deafness on the spot. "You have a nice day," he said.

Lucy snorted. "Ain't they all?"

Outside, Francis waited while Estelle unlocked the car, and then he slid into the passenger seat. "So . . . Eurelio's nervous, and on top of that, he lives right over there?" He pointed at the tavern, its adobe bulk visible beyond the corner of the service station. "He's sure in the neighborhood, isn't he?"

"The thought had crossed my mind."

"Well, now you can lie awake all night long, tossing and turning."

Estelle smiled as she pulled the car into gear. "You catch me, okay?"

ESTELLE looked at the vast mess in the middle of the kitchen linoleum with satisfaction. The original four colors of the modeling clay bricks were fused into one amorphous brown hue through long sessions of mangling, and were now sculpted, carved, and twisted into shapes that would have made Dalí's head spin.

Five-year-old Francisco built upward, squishing the clay into columns that supported odd creatures who lurked atop their pedestals. Carlos let his creations fan outward, preferring the horizontal line. The clay smashed into roadways along which strange vehicles gouged their way toward destinations unknown. The two youngsters chattered constantly to their father as they built. Francis presided over the vast conglomeration, lying on his side on the floor, his pager mercifully silent.

In her favorite spot in the north corner of the living room, engulfed by the wings of the overstuffed chair, Estelle's mother dozed, her hands folded in her lap. To the right of her chair within easy reach, her incongruously high-tech aluminum walker waited. On the end table to her left was a small brown thing Francisco had fashioned from the clay. Looking like a prairie dog who had tried to stand up on his hind legs to whistle and then had begun to melt in the sun, the creature's two eyes guarded the old woman while she slept.

Irma Sedillos, convinced that each member of the family was finally on the mend, had gone home after dinner, first to tend to her cats and then to spend time with her patient boyfriend, Manny Garcia. Manny, a math teacher and three-sport middle and high school coach, could count the number of his free evenings each week on one finger—and Monday was it.

Estelle sat at the kitchen table with a yellow legal pad in front of her. Over her right shoulder on the wall behind her were the three ancient *retablos* of *los Tres Santos* from whom the tiny village had taken its name, and that Estelle's mother had refused to leave unattended in Mexico. *Los Santos* Mateo, Ignacio, and Patricio, each carved in cottonwood that had cracked and polished over the decades, watched in silence as Estelle sketched on the pad.

As if the two sips of awful tea at Lucy's had destroyed the last vestiges of pathogens in her system, she felt a deep sense of contentment and well-being. Part of that contentment was being able to glance up and see every member of her inner universe at once—the boys and her husband playing on the kitchen floor, her mother napping peacefully across the living room. Her contentment, she knew, also was familiar to people addicted to jigsaw puzzles when they first broke the cellophane wrapping from around a new challenge and dumped the pieces out on the table.

The first five pieces of the undersheriff's puzzle lay in front of her. In neat black ink, she had drawn the transmission line support tower, the service two-track, Juan Doe's grave, the shovel, and far to the left edge of the paper, the site where the first victim, John Doe, had been found. In a tiny bracket, she had written the measured distance between the two victims—1,740 yards, give or take a detour or two around bushes and cacti. John Doe had managed to race just shy of a mile across the dark prairie before his pursuer had caught him.

Jackie Taber, Tom Pasquale, and Linda Real had walked along the faint trail across the prairie that afternoon. Jackie had taken the walking wheel, clicking off an accurate measurement. Other than the yardage, their hike had revealed nothing. But it was more than assumption that linked the two victims, and Estelle frowned, staring at the schematic diagram. One set of smudged prints from the shovel handle had presented three points of positive comparison with those taken from John Doe, enough to establish reasonable suspicion. A defense attorney would laugh five points out of court, but it was a start.

Perrone had said that it was likely that the two men had died at roughly the same time. *Likely. Roughly.* How long did it take to run a mile across the prairie, driven by panic?

The two men were dressed in casual clothing, equally innocuous in style. They were more or less the same age, although each lacked any form of identification.

Despite a lack of firm ballistic evidence, it was a logical assumption that somehow the two men had also shared a similar fate. It was easy to assume that they had, for a brief terrifying moment, both stared down the same gun barrel.

Estelle drew a neat compass rose in the upper right-hand corner of the diagram, and Francis happened to glance up at her in time to see the faint trace of a smile touch her lips.

"You making progress?" he asked.

"No."

"Too much distraction?"

"No, that's not it," she said, and sighed. "I just have movement problems, that's all." She rested the pen on the pad. "Jackie walked up the service road along the transmission line to the north, well beyond the grave site. There's no indication whether the vehicle—the vehicle we *think* had to be there—came in from the south or the north."

"I didn't think you had hard evidence of a vehicle in the first place," Francis said. "Other than the tracks on the prairie, and there's no way to tell about those."

"These are tracks," Carlos said, and used his fingernail to trace two lines in a section of clay that swerved around a smooth depression reminiscent of a dry cattle tank.

Estelle laughed. *"What do your children do?"* she said, mimicking an invisible audience. "Oh, they mold crime scenes out of clay." She pushed her chair back and reached for the telephone that had rested all evening, uncharacteristically silent. As her hand touched the instrument, it rang—and Estelle jerked back as if stung.

"A little stressed, are we?" Francis chuckled. He handed her the pen that had launched from the table at the same time as she lifted the receiver. "And I'm not home."

"Guzman residence," she said.

"Estelle, this is Jackie. I'm sorry to bother you, but I thought you'd want to know."

"It's no bother," Estelle replied. "What do I want to know?"

"Dr. Perrone did some preliminary tests for us on the shovel before we packed it up. The blood is human, and doesn't match either victim." Estelle's eyes widened as she stared at the diagram in front of her. "Estelle?" Jackie said after a moment.

"I'm here."

"John Doe was AB negative. The victim in the grave was O positive."

"And the blood on the shovel?"

"AB positive."

"Perrone is sure?" Estelle knew the question was unnecessary.

"I think so. He's going to let the lab double-check his results. But he's willing to bet."

"And the hair?"

"Human. No match with either victim, although he's less sure about that. Eyeballed through a microscope, it's easy to make a mistake. He did a DNA quickie with markers, and didn't get a match. It's dark brown, almost black. And curly. No record of any treatment for a head injury at any of the area hospitals, though."

"We should be so lucky. Any other injuries on either victim other than the obvious? Did Perrone say?"

"Nothing at all. Not a bruise, not a cut."

"Are you at the office now?"

"Yes, ma'am."

"Did Linda take a facial of Juan?"

"She's printing it now. I'll run copies soon as I can."

"Good. We might get lucky. I'll be down in a couple of minutes," Estelle said. "Good work."

She hung up, letting the phone settle gently, eyes already back in the diagram, her mind out on the prairie.

"What did they find?" Francis asked. His wife didn't answer, and he pushed himself to a sitting position, careful not to kick any of the creations spreading around him. He rose and leaned on the table. "Something unexpected?"

Estelle looked up quickly, as if surprised to see him. With a little sigh of apology, her hand strayed to cover his. "Sorry. I was off in orbit somewhere."

"What did they find?"

"The blood and hair on the shovel are both human. And don't match either victim." She stood up. "Some interesting possibilities with that."

"That supports what you were thinking earlier, then. You have a third party walking around somewhere, holding a bandage to his head."

"Maybe."

"And now you have a set of tentative prints that link—which one is it? John Doe to the shovel? Maybe it's just like you said. He dug, he swung, he ran."

"And he died," Estelle murmured.

"So was it just the three of them, or was there somebody else who just stood around with his thumb in his ear, watching all this go down?"

"That's an interesting image, *querido,*" Estelle said. She drew a small, neat question mark on the diagram halfway between the shovel and the grave. "We don't know." She looked up at her husband. "At least not yet."

A series of muffled thumps came from the living room, and Estelle's mother appeared, maneuvering the walker. She stopped, blinked at them, and then poked Carlos in the rump with one of the aluminum walker legs.

"Hace rato que deberías estar durmiendo, chinches," she said. Her voice was small and raspy, but still carried the melody of her native tongue. *"Y yo también."*

"Abuela is right, bedbugs," Francis said in English. "Past bedtime, past time to get this mess cleaned up." He watched with the assessing eye of an attending physician as the tiny woman started down the hall, gnarled knuckles wrapped around the cushions of the walker.

"Good night, *Mamá*," Estelle called.

"Debes cuidarte más, mija," she added without looking back.

79

"Mañana, voy a ir a casa. Puedes ser que vaga." She didn't wait for an answer, didn't offer any explanation of how she was going to go to her home in Mexico the next day if Estelle didn't accept the invitation to go along as chauffeur.

Taking a day to relax and stroll the property in Tres Santos, a day to spend with her mother without interruptions or nagging puzzles, was appealing . . . and impossible.

"I don't think tomorrow's the day to go back to Mexico, *Mamá*," Estelle said more to herself than anyone. She stood, staring at the sheet of paper. Her finger traced an invisible line southward. No other direction made sense.

10

◆◆◆

THE darkroom's red safety light illuminated the prints that had been spread out on the counter. Estelle Reyes-Guzman felt a twinge of sympathy for the man whose face stared up at her through the yellowish haze of darkroom chemicals.

"Hang on a second," Linda Real said. She transferred the print to the rinse tray, and then shuffled boxes, securing the black foil wrapping over the unused print paper. "Okay," she said, and snapped on the overheads. Estelle flinched against the burst of light and then tapped the tray in which floated the head and shoulders portrait of Juan Doe, his swarthy complexion and black hair sharply contrasting with the polished stainless steel of the morgue table.

"We need to make copies and fax them out," she said, and Linda Real nodded. "Every county agency first, including Texas and Arizona. And the *Judiciales* in Juarez, Agua Prieta, and Nogales. I'll be talking with Captain Naranjo tomorrow, and I want him to have a look, too. Copies to the Feds, the Border Patrol, the whole nine yards. Somebody has to have seen this guy. Somebody, somewhere, knows him. And maybe we'll get lucky with the fingerprints."

"You're thinking they were from Mexico, then?"

"Maybe. Right now, one place is as much a possibility as another."

"I've never worked with the *Judiciales* before," Linda said. "I was impressed when Captain Naranjo came up for Bill Gastner's retirement dinner last November. That was the first time I'd ever met him."

"He's a good man, Linda. If he can help us, he will. He's a master at cutting through that famous Mexican red tape."

"Dr. Perrone said John Doe doesn't have a single tattoo, birthmark, or scar to help us out," Linda said. She leaned against one of the long counters in the darkroom while Estelle examined the photos.

"But they both have fingerprints," Estelle said, and then looked skeptical. "Of course, if they're not on file somewhere, all the prints in the world won't do us a bit of good. If that's the case, the killer accomplished exactly what he needed to do, regardless of his motivations," Estelle mused. "Smashing in the dentition with a rock was either cold calculation, or done in a fit of rage. Payback time."

Estelle frowned, pausing by the drier to scrutinize one of the eight by tens of John Doe's shattered face. "Mexican dental records are often a whole lot less formal than ours," she said. "Somebody from a rural community, or without the means for top-notch care, might not have any records at all—so these injuries are a puzzle. Why batter a man's face to pieces after you've already blown the back of his head off with a high-powered rifle?"

Linda Real remained silent, watching Estelle sift through the photos. "Either way . . ." the undersheriff started to say, then shrugged. "If Jackie hadn't found her 'pattern,' John Doe would be all we'd have, and we'd be stumped."

Linda laughed. "I'm glad to hear we're not stumped," she said.

Estelle straightened up. "Just temporarily confused."

"They finished sifting the grave site, by the way," Linda said. She shook her head. "Nothing except blood-soaked prairie soil. No fragments, no nothing."

"As expected," Estelle said. "The bullets that killed both of them are still out on the prairie somewhere. Even if we knew to the inch where all the participants were standing when the shots were fired, it'd take a million dollars worth of man-hours to hunt for the bullets. And even then, no guarantees."

She sighed and dropped the photo back on the counter. "And speaking of hours," she added, glancing at her watch. Her mother and the two little boys had trundled off to bed, but Estelle's system had refused to shut down on demand. "You're working more tonight?" she asked.

"Tom's on until midnight," Linda replied. "I wanted to finish up here, so I thought I might as well come in, too."

"And be sure that you put in for every minute that you work," Estelle said, and when she saw the doubtful expression on Linda's face added, "Let the county share a little of the load, even if it's just scraping to find the money to pay you guys."

"Mostly, I was just cleaning up my mess," Linda said.

"Regardless," Estelle said, and handed Linda the remaining photos to be slipped with the others into an envelope. "I need to find Tom and talk with him for a minute," Estelle said. "Jackie is off tonight, isn't she . . . or at least is *supposed* to be."

Linda flashed a lopsided grin, as familiar as anyone with the odd hours that members of the small department chose to work. Estelle saw that the harsh light of the darkroom overheads accentuated the scar traces on the left side of Linda's face, the last physical memories of a long night six years before when, as a newspaper reporter riding along with one of the Posadas deputies, she had caught a shotgun blast in the face, neck, and left shoulder. The deputy had been killed, and Linda Real had suffered through nearly two years of therapy and rehabilitation, face scarred and blind in her left eye. Her remarkably resilient spirit had refused to be crippled.

Instead of resuming her career as a reporter, Linda had chosen to seek employment with the Posadas County Sheriff's Department, bringing along her considerable photographic talents.

Long before the shooting incident, Linda Real's crush on the young, brash deputy Thomas Pasquale had been a source of department amusement. Finally, in what then Undersheriff Bill Gastner had described as "a tribute to what little common sense Pasquale possesses," the friendship between Linda Real and Thomas Pasquale had blossomed into something more. Now, they split the rent on a small house on Tenth Street.

"By the way," Estelle said, turning toward the strips of negatives hanging in the dust-free drying bag, "did you happen to run that roll I shot for Bill?"

"That was next on my list," Linda said.

"A strange case he's working on. It looks like Eleanor Pope is running a donkey motel over at her place on Escondido."

"I know her."

"She works at the HairPort," Estelle said.

"No, I don't mean from there. She and I shared a little time a couple of weeks ago waiting at the insurance company, and we got to talking." Linda ducked her head. "She lugs around one of those oxygen tanks that emphysema patients sometimes have to have? She seemed like a nice lady."

"Maybe she is," Estelle stepped out of the darkroom and ducked around one of the furnace ducts. "I'm not sure about the pictures, though. A bizarre setup she's got going there. The light was really hard, so I'll be interested to see if anything came out. If they didn't, we're going to have to reshoot. Bill wants them to twist a warrant out of Judge Hobart."

She climbed the stairs slowly, feeling the stuffy basement air lighten as she reached the well-lighted first floor. Ernie Wheeler looked up as she emerged from the Hole.

"Sheriff Torrez called a few minutes ago," he said. "He didn't want me to interrupt you, but he asked that you call him back when you have a chance." He held up a Post-it note with the Virginia telephone number.

"He's homesick," Estelle laughed.

"He sounded like it," Ernie agreed. "And Bill Gastner was just here." He nodded toward the back door. "He walked out that door about ten seconds ago, so you can probably catch him."

Estelle stepped quickly toward the door, saying over her shoulder, "Would you find Tom Pasquale for me? I need to talk with him if he's not in the middle of something."

Without waiting for a response, she stepped outside and saw her old friend's stout figure moseying toward the white pickup truck parked in the spot reserved for Judge Hobart.

"Sir?"

Bill Gastner turned around at the sound of her voice and stopped, hands thrust in his pockets. "Hey, there," he said.

"We were in the darkroom. You should have come on down."

"The less time I spend in the Hole, the better," he said. "Too many stairs, for one thing. I need to save my knees for the Boston Marathon, or something equally important."

"Linda is going to process your roll of film tonight."

He nodded. "Good. You heard that Bobby called?"

"Yes. Did you happen to talk with him?"

Gastner scratched his scalp and then resettled his cap. "As a matter of fact, I did," he said. "He was wondering if he should take an early exit from his school and fly home."

"I hope you told him to stick it out, sir."

He chuckled. "He thinks he's missing all the fun stuff. But I told him we'd save some for him. He didn't believe me. He wanted you to give him a call."

"So Ernie said. Are you in the middle of anything right now?"

"Do I look like I'm rushing off somewhere?" Gastner grinned. "I would have stayed for coffee, but there wasn't any. The goddamn *tea* generation has hit this place."

"You'll learn to like it, sir. It's good for you."

"No, I won't. And no, it's not. And you're looking better, by the way. You homeward bound now, or is something on the wind?"

She nodded. "I was about to track down Pasquale. I think he's got one of the pieces to the puzzle. And I'm not sure he knows it."

Gastner smiled broadly at that. "Sometimes Tom Pasquale can be a surprise," he said.

"That's for sure. Would you like to ride along?"

"Let me check my social calendar," Gastner replied. He glanced quickly at his wristwatch. "Sure. Why not?"

Estelle turned toward the door in time to nearly catch it in the face as Ernie Wheeler thrust it open.

"Pasquale is down near Maria," he said quickly. "He's got a vehicle stopped on Sixty-one, and wants a female officer."

"Tell him we're on our way."

Gastner remained silent as they settled into the unmarked Crown Victoria that Estelle favored. They were just pulling out of the parking lot when the radio crackled.

"Three ten, three oh six."

Estelle gestured at the mike, and Gastner picked it up. "Three ten is just leaving the parking lot," he said. "ETA about eleven minutes."

"Ten-four." Pasquale's perfunctory reply. "We're at the junction of the power line service road and Sixty-one. PCS, I need wants and warrants on New Mexico one three three Echo Baker Nora."

By the time Ernie Wheeler repeated the number, the underpass of the interstate loomed ahead of them, with the sharp left-hand curve to State 61 just beyond.

"No telling what HotRod Pasquale is up to," Gastner commented. "Although he's never let the gender barrier slow him down before."

"No telling," Estelle said. She nudged the accelerator and they shot under the interstate.

"Maria has gotten to be a popular place all of a sudden," Gastner said. "It lies comatose since the day Coronado walked through, and now all of a sudden it's the center of the universe."

ITS top rack dancing a kaleidoscope of red and blue, Deputy Thomas Pasquale's patrol unit was parked well off the highway, nosed in behind a primer-gray 'fifty-eight Chevy pickup. Beyond, Estelle could see the scattering of lights that marked Maria . . . few enough to count and have fingers left over.

The glare of headlights picked up the power line support tower nearest the highway, and the dusty tire marks pulling out onto the black asphalt of State 61 were clear. The old pickup had bumped out of the two-track that followed the transmission line, to be stopped immediately by the deputy.

Estelle snapped on the grill lights and slowed. Pasquale was sitting in his unit, door ajar. Another individual sat in the backseat behind the security screen, features no more distinct than a shadow. Bracketed by the headlights, a young woman stood near the front of the pickup. She turned her back to the road as the unmarked car passed, then looked into the night sky. She shook her head in frustration, as if her night was rapidly going from bad to worse. Estelle swung the car wide in a U-turn, and parked on the opposite side of the highway so that Pasquale's big, boxy unit wasn't blocking her view of the pickup.

She heard Gastner mutter, "They're local kids."

"I can't see who Pasquale's got sitting in the back," Estelle said. "And I don't know the girl."

"That's Tori Benevidez," Gastner said. "Her dad is the restaurant manager at the Posadas Inn, home of the worst food this side of the Country Club. Last time I knew, she was working as a teacher's aide over in the elementary school."

Estelle glanced at Gastner with amusement. After thirty years with the Posadas County Sheriff's Department, his mind was a gazetteer of county trivia. She had decided long ago that William G. Gastner was simply one of those human beings who enjoyed *knowing*—whether it was the intricacies of the Battle of Chickamauga or the background of the new couple opening a craft shop on Sixth Street in Posadas.

He saw the expression on her face and grinned. "That's okay," he nodded. "Don't worry, I can't remember anything important."

Deputy Pasquale got out of the Expedition, glanced over his shoulder at the empty highway, and walked across toward them. His brow was furrowed in concentration, and he appeared to be reading something on his clipboard. Estelle lowered the window of the car and waited.

"Hey," Pasquale said by way of greeting. He shot a glance back at the young couple, then bent down, nodding toward Gastner. "Evening, sir."

"Thomas," Gastner said. Pasquale shifted position so that Estelle had an unobstructed view across the highway.

"This is kind of interesting," the deputy said. "I saw this vehicle coming down the two-track back there," and he nodded toward north. "I didn't recognize the truck. Turns out it's an old heap that belongs to Eurelio Saenz's dad."

"I thought Monroy Saenz was dead," Gastner said.

"Well, *belonged* to Mr. Saenz," Pasquale corrected. "It hasn't been registered since 'ninety-six. Eurelio says that he uses it to go out in the boonies. Doesn't drive it on the highway." He grinned. "He says." He extended the wrinkled, out-of-date registration stub toward Estelle. She waved it away, waiting for the deputy to make his point. Tom Pasquale's comfortable face was eager and Estelle knew that the deputy was hunting more than expired registrations.

"It's a good truck for rough country," Gastner said. "Nice big roomy cab. He and Miss Benevidez can go out and study nature in peace and quiet. Watch the moon."

Pasquale grinned. "Uh-huh. Maybe that's what they were doing on a nice quiet Monday night. I don't know." He rested his arm on the top of the car. "They were driving out that road without lights. They popped 'em on when they got to that real rocky section about a quarter mile from the pavement, and that's when I saw 'em. Funny, 'cause Eurelio was exactly the person I was cruisin' to find."

"Your lucky night," Gastner said.

Pasquale bent down, his face serious. "They've been drinkin' some, but not a whole lot. I asked 'em to step out of the unit, and Eurelio didn't have any trouble with the field sobriety test. He said he'd just had a beer or two. I think that part's probably true."

Estelle tapped her fingers on the steering wheel. Tom Pasquale didn't need help with a routine traffic stop even if the truck was unregistered, even if it was overflowing with beer cans, open or sealed. And under normal circumstances, Eurelio Saenz would be standing on the shoulder of the road, looking miserable or maybe arguing with his girlfriend about whose fault it all was. Instead, he was sitting in the secured portion of Pasquale's unit, for all practical purposes under arrest whether the announcement had been formally made or not.

"What were they doing up there?" Estelle asked. "I mean, beyond the obvious."

"That's what I was curious about." He opened the clipboard's spring with one hand and released a small plastic evidence bag. "When I asked Eurelio to step out of the truck, I saw this on the floor, kind of caught by the rubber mat. Right in front of the seat brace."

Estelle took the bag and twisted to turn on one of the overhead reading lights, focusing its narrow beam carefully. The brass cartridge case, fresh and polished, winked in the light. Her pulse picked up a beat. She turned the bag so that she could see the head-stamp on the casing.

"Forty-four Remington Magnum," she said. "RP."

Gastner leaned on the center console, looking at the casing through his bifocals. "Still fragrant?"

Estelle had already opened the small bag and held it to her nose. "Hard to tell." She handed it to Gastner, who inhaled deeply, shrugged, and handed it back. She zipped the bag closed again. "What's Eurelio say?"

"He doesn't know anything about it," Pasquale said.

"Of course not." She handed the bag back to the deputy and gazed across the road. At that moment, Tori Benevidez put her foot up on the front bumper of the pickup as if she wanted to kick the aging truck back up the road. Her shoulders were hunched and her arms crossed over her chest. Estelle watched her for a moment.

"How does he explain it?" she asked, knowing that there were a dozen ways, in the middle of country known for hunting and sport shooting, that an errant cartridge casing could go astray. Whether the Department of Game and Fish liked it or not, a few quick shots from the vehicle were often the most expeditious way to nail an unsuspecting antelope, deer, or javelina that strayed too close to the road. Unsuspecting cattle weren't any safer. A rifle could as easily pitch an empty casing into the truck as not, even if the marksman was standing outside, beside the vehicle.

"He claims that they drove up that road about four miles, then turned around. He said that they were heading back to town when I stopped 'em. He says that he was going to show his girlfriend the spot where the body was found, but they changed their minds when they got to where we strung the yellow tape restricting the area. He said that after a little bit of that road in the dark, another five miles or so didn't seem like such a good idea. He said that Tori wanted to go back." He turned and looked across at the girl. "She was afraid that they were going to get into trouble."

"Smart girl."

"That's what he says."

Estelle looked down at the casing in the bag. "He has no explanation for this, then?"

"Nope."

"He doesn't own the rifle, or whatever it was?"

"He says not. And an empty casing by itself doesn't tell us much, either."

"It's consistent with the wounds on both Does, though," Estelle said.

"That's a tough cartridge to work with, Estelle," Gastner said, and she looked over at him. He held up a hand. "A whole slew of companies manufacture handguns in that caliber. And on top of that, a couple of 'em manufacture semiautomatic carbines that take the same round. And then there's all the lever-action rifles and carbines chambered for it. Just about as bad as finding a casing for a damn twenty-two. Without some hint about what the gun was, it's about impossible to tell what you're dealing with."

Estelle nodded. "But it's a piece."

Gastner grinned. "Maybe. One thing's for sure," he added as Estelle held the bag up, closer to the light. "Bright and shiny as this is, it hasn't been lying on the floor of that old truck since the old man used to drive it."

"What's Tori say?" Estelle asked Pasquale.

"I haven't talked with her yet." He turned and regarded the old truck. "First thing I did was separate them, though. They haven't had a chance to discuss anything. That's why I called in for you. If we decide to transport 'em, I don't want 'em sitting together."

"Let's see what she knows," Estelle said. She reached back and slipped her cap out of its niche behind the passenger headrest. As she zipped up her down jacket, she glanced at Bill Gastner. "You don't have to stand out there and freeze, sir," she said.

"No, I don't," Gastner laughed. "You enjoy."

Estelle hefted her heavy flashlight and slid out of the car. The wind was a gentle hand, sliding down the highway from the northwest. Promising warmth earlier in the day, the air was now sharp. With no cloud cover to blanket the prairie, what progress had been made toward spring radiated away the moment the sun set.

"You want to talk with Eurelio?" Pasquale asked.

"Not yet, Tom. Let him stew," she replied quietly. The highway was empty, and she crossed the pavement, eyes on the girl. Tori Benevidez's body language spoke irritation and pout, not nervous guilt.

The young woman favored black. Her black jeans were poured on tight, the cuffs just so over the arches of her black, pointed-toe boots. Her quilted jacket was black, and Estelle could read the gold lettering that arced across the back, proclaiming the *Wausau Winter Nationals*.

"Ms. Benevidez?" Estelle said as she approached, and the young woman turned at the sound of her name. A strikingly attractive girl, Tori Benevidez apparently saw no need to leave anything to chance, but in the uneven reflected light, her heavy makeup, from the long, assisted eyelashes to the improbably wide, scarlet lips, thickened and coarsened her features. A small gold cross nestled at her throat.

"Ms. Benevidez, I'm Undersheriff Reyes-Guzman."

"And this is important because . . ." Tori said, drifting off into the affected pause that said "and I'm so bored." Estelle wondered if the elementary school kids with whom Tori worked talked to her in the same tone.

Estelle stepped close enough that she could smell the cloying perfume of beer on the girl's breath. Tori's eyes swept down Estelle's trim figure and then shifted immediately to Tom Pasquale, who had ambled across the highway and stood at the door of the pickup, playing his flashlight methodically around the interior.

"Ms. Benevidez, do you know why the deputy stopped Eurelio?"

"I have *no* idea."

The corner of Estelle's mouth twitched with the beginnings of a smile that just as quickly vanished. Tori caught the expression and rolled her eyes. "Well," she said, "this dumb old truck, I suppose."

"It would help if it were licensed," Estelle said pleasantly. A pair of headlights appeared from the north, and Estelle stepped around the front of the truck, clear of the pavement. Approaching rapidly, the black-and-white patrol car abruptly slowed as it passed, then turned off the highway onto the shoulder, coming to a stop fifty yards away. Light reflected off the New Mexico State Police shield and diagonal door stripe.

"That's Jack Adams," Tom Pasquale said. "I'll go talk to 'em." He snapped off his flashlight and trudged up the shoulder of the highway just as the trooper pulled himself out of the car.

"Tell him that he'll be getting a fax within the hour for identification," Estelle said. "Any help they can give us . . ."

"Will do."

She turned back to Tori Benevidez. "Tori, that applies to you, too. Any help at all."

"With *what*?" the girl said, making it sound pathetically plaintive.

"Eurelio didn't tell you why he wanted to drive up along the power line road?"

"Just that he had something he wanted to show me."

"He didn't say what?"

"No."

"And did he show you something?"

"No. We just drove up to where there's a yellow ribbon strung across the road. That's where he turned around."

"Did he tell you why there's a yellow ribbon there?"

The word *no* was about to escape and Tori bit it off, thought for a few seconds, and then nodded.

"What did he tell you?"

Tori lifted her foot and toed the truck bumper, hugging herself even tighter. "Just that they'd found a dead body up there somewhere. And they were talking about that in school, today, too. Some of the teachers. They said you'd found a second victim, or something like that."

"He thought that might frighten you? Why did he want to show you?"

"Who knows? It's gross."

"What did you guys do then? When you came to the yellow tape?"

"I told you. We turned around. I told Eurelio that I wanted to get out of there before we got into trouble."

"So you know why the deputy stopped you, then."

"Yes."

Estelle nodded. Even a begrudging *yes* was progress. She reached out a hand to touch the hood of the old truck. "Nice smooth ride," she said, but Tori didn't respond. "Do you guys use this for hunting?"

"I guess he does. I don't know."

"You don't hunt?"

Tori made a little noise affirming that hunting was far outside her universe. "So are we getting a ticket, or what?" she asked instead.

"That would be up to the deputy who stopped you," Estelle said easily. She extracted a business card from her blouse pocket and handed it to Tori. "If you should happen to remember anything that you think we should know, my number's on there. Anytime."

"About what?"

"Anything at all," Estelle said pleasantly.

"Can we go now?"

"Not yet, Tori." Estelle's answer evidently surprised the girl, who had been in midturn, heading for the passenger door of the truck. She stopped. "A few more minutes," Estelle added. She pointed away from the truck toward the highway right-of-way fence. "If you'd step away from the truck." Up the road, Pasquale and the state trooper were still in animated discussion. A laugh punctuated the conversation and Adams turned back to his car.

Estelle walked around to the passenger door of the old truck. When it opened, the hinge squawked loudly, and she felt the resistance of a sprung hinge. The interior was surprisingly clean, without the usual eclectic clutter of junk that graced the broad, convenient dashboards of working trucks. What looked like a saddle blanket was folded neatly on the seat, protecting rumps from spring ends that had begun to project through the original fabric.

Behind the seat, a rifle rack spanned the back window. Empty now, the rack had been used enough over the years that the vinyl coating on the bottom set of hooks had worn through.

Estelle stepped forward and bent down to look under the passenger seat. A beer can sat on the transmission hump, just behind the tall, angular shift lever. She touched it with the eraser of her pencil and felt the weight of at least half a can.

The beam of her flashlight swept under the seat, where the collection of the ages hadn't been disturbed. Popcorn was the leading contender, the pale kernels tied together with a rich layer of dust and cobwebs. Crumpled Styrofoam cups, an empty box of Wildcat .22 ammo, and assorted nails, paper clips, and ballpoint pens added to the wealth.

"You want to spring the seat forward?" Tom Pasquale asked. He had appeared at the driver's side.

"Yes. Pay attention to the highway, though," Estelle replied.

"You bet. Watch your head." She straightened up as he yanked the seat lever and pushed forward at the same time. The bench seat slid forward, hung, then slid the rest of the way. He folded the seat back up against the steering wheel.

The generous space was filled with a large handyman jack, lug wrench, and a portion of what looked like a shop vacuum hose. Crushed against the right rear bulkhead was an empty cereal box, surrounded by wadded tissues.

"Yuck," Pasquale said.

"What's that?" Estelle pointed toward Pasquale's side. The yellow paper was caught in the seat's release mechanism.

Pasquale gently tugged it free and opened it. "A receipt from Posadas Auto Supply for a case of oil," he said. "Don't I wish that's what it cost nowadays."

"Dated?"

"August two, nineteen eighty."

"Not exactly the stone ages," she said. She pulled the cereal box free from its nest. The ad on the back promised a free Frisbee with return of the coupon inside, plus postage and handling. With her pencil, she moved the tissues, finding a small crescent wrench, a ballpoint pen cap, a six-inch length of electrical wire, and dust.

Estelle bent forward, surveying the trash. "Not much," she said. "What's that thing?" She focused her flashlight on Tom's side of the transmission hump, near the heavy jack's ratchet mechanism.

Pasquale wedged his large frame farther into the truck. "Whoa," he said.

"Whoa what?"

He reached in and nudged the object with his pen. "Huh," he said. "It's a little cylinder of some sort."

"It looks new," Estelle said.

"I think it is. It's blued, like a gun part of some kind." He looked up at Estelle, then up at the rifle rack in the truck's back window. "This is where we need the sheriff," he said. "He's the gun man."

"And the gun man is in Virginia," Estelle said. "Maybe Bill knows."

"Bill knows what?" a quiet voice behind Tom Pasquale said. "Bill is out here directing traffic." He appeared in the doorway and rested a hand on Tom's shoulder. "What have you got?"

"Sir, before we move it . . . would you take a look?"

Pasquale pulled himself out of the truck, and Gastner struggled to push his bulk past the seat. "This thing?" he said, pointing the beam of his flashlight.

"That."

"I don't know."

"It looks pretty new," Estelle said. "Tom says it's blued, like something off a gun."

"I agree with both." He shook his head. "I still don't know." He looked across at Estelle. "It shouldn't be hard to find out." He pushed himself free of the truck.

"Tom, you might call the county yard and have a wrecker come out. I think we're going to hang onto this truck for a little bit."

12
◆◆◆

As a child, Estelle Reyes had joined forces with the ragtag urchins who stalked the various eight-, six-, four-, two-, and no-legged beasts of the Chihuahan desert that encircled Tres Santos, Mexico. The sly, cautious jackrabbits had been her favorites.

She soon learned that when a jackrabbit knew that he was being hunted, he'd often crouch low, sometimes sneaking along on his belly behind the brush, hoping to avoid detection, hoping to avoid the risky, rocketing dash through the open spaces. The jackrabbits had played hide-and-seek with her, ducking behind the twisted acacia, greasewood, or cholla. Her skinny arms had hurled the sharp rocks that were her only weapons. When the rocks snapped too close, the hares had raced away in a blur, ears up, eyes wide.

Eurelio Saenz, sitting in the secured backseat of Tom Pasquale's vehicle, reminded Estelle of a jackrabbit. He hunkered down low as she approached, head hanging but eyes wide and watchful.

She opened the front passenger door and climbed into the Expedition. Reaching across the broad seat, she snapped on the overhead lights and then settled, regarding Eurelio. He was a good-looking kid, with slicked back raven hair and the wink of a gold ear stud. If he let it happen, he'd age into one of those old men with the craggy face, lined walnut skin, and twinkling eyes.

As Estelle remained silent, he ducked his head and swallowed hard. She looked at the small evidence bag that contained the metal cylinder, turning it this way and that, letting the silence grow heavy.

Estelle had never met Eurelio Saenz, unless it had been when he was a grubby little kid playing around the Taberna Azul. She had no recollection of her uncle taking her inside that establishment, but Paulita Saenz, the young man's mother, was enough of a memory that their paths might have crossed a time or two.

Tom Pasquale had judged it right, Estelle thought. There was something there. Eurelio Saenz should have greeted a routine traffic stop with bravado and attitude, especially with Tori Benevidez riding shotgun, ready to be impressed. Instead, he was playing jackrabbit.

"Do you know why the deputy stopped you, Eurelio?"

He nodded. He was trying for stoic and not doing very well—pretty much the same expression she would have expected from her son Francisco when he was hoping that her anger about modeling clay smeared on the carpet would deflect her attention away from a larger crime elsewhere in the house.

"Why do you think he stopped you?"

"The truck."

She turned and looked out the windshield. Tom Pasquale was standing with Tori Benevidez beside the right-of-way fence. Tori's posture had relaxed. With her hands in her hip pockets, she dug the ground with the toe of her boot, nodding in response to what the deputy was telling her. Bill Gastner had ambled back across the road. He stood near the front of the unmarked car with his hip leaning against the fender. He appeared to be counting the stars overhead.

Exaggerated calm, Estelle thought. Everyone's calm. She shifted position and rested her left arm across the back of the seat, her face close to the wire mesh.

"Tell me what you know about the dead man, Eurelio."

His eyes jerked up from their study of the seat back stitching, met Estelle's for only a heartbeat, and then shifted away. For a moment, it looked as if he was going to say, "What dead man?" He settled for silence instead.

"Did you know him?"

"No." His answer was immediate.

"How do you know that?" Estelle's voice was almost a whisper.

Eurelio's eyebrows knit together as he considered where the traps might be.

"I don't know what you're talking about." It sounded lame, and the expression on his face agreed.

"You didn't get out of the electric company truck this morning," she said. "When you and Wayne Hudson came out to check up on us. You didn't walk up to where the body was."

"So? Why should I? And the cops wouldn't have let me anyway."

"And you didn't have any questions about what was going on? About who the victim might have been?"

He shrugged. "Hudson was talkin' to you. If there was something that the cops wanted me to know, I figure they would have told me." Estelle smiled at that. Start a scuffle in school, and students mobbed the action, vying for a look. Blood was neat, a torn blouse was neater. Eurelio was only four, maybe five years removed from that mindset. But if there was something to see, he'd gawk with everyone else—unless there was a good reason not to.

"You weren't curious, Eurelio?"

"No." A little starch crept into his voice.

"I think you already knew, didn't you?"

Eurelio looked out the side window. Estelle held the evidence bag up and shook the blue-black cylinder into the opposite corner. She held it against the security screen. "Tell me what this is." He turned, leaned forward and looked at the bag briefly when Estelle held it against the screen.

"How should I know that?"

"It was in your truck."

"Is that right? That's my dad's truck, anyways," Eurelio said quickly.

"Ah, your *dad's* truck. And the shell casing that the deputy found—that was in your *dad's* truck, too."

"I don't know about any bullets."

"Did you used to go hunting with your dad, Eurelio? Back when you were a kid?"

"Sometimes."

"Where was his favorite spot?"

Eurelio shrugged. "All over."

"No one spot that he liked more than the others?"

"He'd go over to Silver Springs Canyon a lot of times."

"That's west of here, isn't it? Right at the foot of the San Cristóbals?"

He nodded.

"What did he hunt?"

"Javelina, mostly."

"And you went along too."

"Sure. Sometimes."

"So you know this country pretty well."

Eurelio nodded absently and turned his attention back to the side window of his small automotive cell.

"Do you ever let anyone else use your father's truck now? Does anyone ever drive it besides you?" The young man took a long time mulling the question. "*Su madre* . . . maybe your mom loans it out?"

Estelle watched him with interest as a dark frown of irritation touching his face. He shook his head quickly as if to say "Don't drag my mother into this." Turned sideways in her seat, the undersheriff rested her chin on her left arm. Her silence, her settling into patient comfort, goaded Eurelio as surely as if she'd prodded him through the security mesh with a stick.

"You going to arrest me, or what?" he said.

She didn't answer immediately, but then said, *"Cuéntame cómo su madre, Eurelio."*

The light was poor, but Estelle thought that she could see the deep flush of embarrassment creep up Eurelio's neck from the collar of his T-shirt. Paulita Saenz would be tending bar that very moment at the Taberna Azul, a thousand yards down the highway. But Eurelio's twenty-first birthday was two years history. As far as the law was concerned, it didn't matter what *Mamá* thought.

"My mom don't have nothing to do with any of this stuff," Eurelio snapped. His brows furrowed with anger and he glared out the side window.

"Any of what *stuff*, Eurelio?"

Eurelio Saenz started to say something and thought better of it. His eyes blinked rapidly. "Me usin' this truck or anything."

"Do you think we care whether or not you use your dad's truck, Eurelio?"

"Well, it ain't licensed."

"No, it's not. And it's not insured. And right now it smells like a brewery." She sighed and lowered her voice to a soft whisper. "And it turns up in the wrong places, Eurelio."

He turned and looked at her, forcing himself to hold her gaze for a few seconds. "Me and Tori were just out, that's all. We drove up that road a little ways, turned around at the yellow tape, and drove back. That's all we did. It's no big deal."

"Okay."

He seemed to relax back against the seat. "So can we go now?"

Estelle pushed herself away from the comfortable support, turning her back to the young man as she opened the door and slid out of the vehicle. "I don't think so, Eurelio." He had started to say something when she closed the door, cutting him off. In frustration he slammed the security mesh with the palm of his hand.

Tom Pasquale's left hand drifted out and touched Tori Benevidez's right elbow as Estelle approached. She nodded at the girl. "Miss Benevidez, where do you live?"

"North Fourth Street." As if finally realizing that being helpful might be to her advantage, she hastily added, "Seven oh one North Fourth."

"Is that where your folks live?"

"No. I share an apartment with a friend of mine."

"We'll drop you off there, then. Is that all right?" Estelle said, and indicated the unmarked car parked across the highway. Without waiting for a response, she said to Pasquale, "Is a tow truck on the way?"

"Yes, ma'am."

"Good." She turned and studied the old pickup one last time. "And make sure that it gets parked in the secured bay," she said. "We're going to want to take it apart tomorrow."

"I really don't understand any of this," Tori Benevidez snapped. "Eurelio hasn't done anything. I mean, so there's no license on this old heap. Big deal. That's no reason to arrest him, to treat him like some criminal or something."

Estelle nodded. "You're right, Tori. Driving an unlicensed vehicle is no reason to arrest him." She started across the highway, but the girl held back. "You want a ride home, or are you going to walk?"

Tori Benevidez shook her head in exasperation and followed across to the unmarked car. "Can't I ride with Eurelio? Aren't you letting him go?"

"No," Estelle said, opening the back door of the sedan for her. "You can't ride with Eurelio."

"I don't understand this," the girl said. She slid into the back of the unmarked car, muttering to herself. Bill Gastner had been standing beside the passenger side of the car, watching. He grinned at Estelle. She shook her head and looked heavenward.

Halfway back to town, they passed the tow truck headed toward Maria. "Interesting, interesting," Gastner said. Estelle didn't respond, and they completed the rest of the trip into Posadas in silence. Tori Benevidez's address on North Fourth was a tiny place, a four or five room fake adobe, its cinderblock skeleton showing here and there where the plaster had chipped away.

Estelle got out and opened the back door. Tori slid by without looking at her. "If there's anything else that you think of, I'd appreciate hearing from you," Estelle said. The girl mumbled something that might have been agreement and hurried inside.

"And now?" Gastner said when she had settled back in the car. "You look beat."

"I am," Estelle said. She glanced at her watch and saw that it was just moments before ten. "I've got energy for one little errand. Then I'm going home to collapse."

"The little errand can't wait until tomorrow? That's my old trap, you know. Just keep going until . . ." He made a fall-on-your-face motion with his hand.

"This really is little," she said. "It's time Bob Torrez did some work."

"Sweetheart, he's in Virginia, last I heard." He glanced at the clock on the dash. "And it's about midnight there, or after."

"Yep. Right in the middle of FBI country. We need to know what that little *cosa* is that we found in Eurelio's truck." She grinned as she pulled the patrol car away from the curb. "And that's the fastest way I know of to do it. And as Eurelio took pains to remind me, sir, that's Eurelio's *dad's* truck, not his. The dead dad."

"And you think Bob will know?"

"If it has to do with guns, he'll know. Yes, sir."

"You don't have much to hold Eurelio on."

Estelle nodded. "We don't. Not yet, anyway. But DUI, unregistered, uninsured, and open containers in a motor vehicle should get us through the night. We can stall that long. Let him call his *mamá,* if he's got the guts." She glanced across at Gastner. "That ought to be interesting. He didn't sound like he wants her involved in his mess."

"Smart kid."

Back at the Public Safety Building, Estelle nudged the steel cylinder out of the evidence bag, onto the glass surface of the photocopy machine. After a couple of experiments, she managed a reasonably clear image. Above the image, she wrote, "What is this?" and signed it.

She handed it to dispatcher Ernie Wheeler. "Bob didn't leave me a fax number, but there has to be one, Ernie. See if you can dig it up, and get this off to him just as soon as you can."

"You want me to give you a call when I hear back?" Ernie asked.

Estelle found herself nodding, and pulled up short with a sudden shake of her head. She held out a hand. "No. Not unless Bob comes up with an answer in the next five minutes, no. Just put it in my box. Or Jackie's. That'll give us a running start in the morning." She took a deep breath and looked up at the clock. The minute hand jolted forward to 10:34 P.M. "Uh," she groaned. "In fact, if the world comes to an end, let me find out about it tomorrow."

"Yes, ma'am." As usual, Ernie Wheeler took her seriously.

13

◆◆◆

WHEN the telephone rang at seventeen minutes after midnight, a nine-year-old Estelle Reyes-Guzman was twisting a small knife into a rotten spot in one of her mother's cottonwood stumps in Tres Santos. She had discovered a carefully folded letter. The document was locked in place by the folds of wood, the paper stained from the occasional rains that collected in the crotch of the stump. Using one of her mother's paring knives, she had coaxed the letter from its tomb. Hands shaking with excitement, she unfolded it far enough to see the bold signature of Pancho Villa.

The telephone interrupted her before she could unfold the document further and discover what *Generalísimo* Villa had written—and to whom he had written it.

The purr of the phone was soft, and if her husband heard it, he showed no reaction. Estelle jolted awake with a stab of regret, the letter now and forever a mystery. Even if she had been able to restart the dream on command, she knew that somehow, her mind would find a way to cheat her out of knowing the letter's contents.

"Guzman residence," she murmured, not sure that she had the correct end of the phone pressed to her ear. She squinted at the clock.

"You awake?" Bill Gastner's gruff voice flooded into her ear, and her pulse kicked up a beat. Gastner was a world-class insomniac, but he didn't expect the rest of the world to be. She rolled over on her back.

"I am now, sir."

"Sorry about that." Even as he spoke, she could hear sirens in the distance. "Someone's going to get around to bothering you anyway, and I figured it might as well be me."

"What's going on, sir?"

"For starters, we've got a hell of a fire on our hands. If the wind switches, I might end up being barbecued myself. Apparently a propane tank exploded at Eleanor Pope's place. Or a propane stove. Something propane, anyway. It took the house. Now it's spread through the yard and outbuildings and working on Florek's fence, burning into his wrecking yard."

Estelle groaned. "Mrs. Pope's all right?"

"She wasn't home at the time of the explosion. But it looks like she's lost everything, so needless to say . . ."

"Her son?"

"No one knows just where Woody is at the moment. His car was in the driveway. Right now, it's a black puddle."

"So he could be inside the house?"

"He could be. It's possible. No one's been able to get that close yet." She heard voices in the background, and Gastner spoke to someone else. "No, I don't know if he is or not." More voices were a jumble, and she lay quietly, waiting. Finally, Gastner said, "I need to get off the line, Estelle. Eduardo Martinez asked if you were on your way, and I told him I'd find out."

"I'm on my way," Estelle said. Martinez was chief of the Posadas Village PD, a force of two and a half, including himself. If people drove slowly through the school zones, Eduardo was happy. Anything more serious he gladly handed off to the county Sheriff's Department.

"The fire chief has his command post set up on State Sixty-one in that wide spot in the highway in front of the wrecking yard. There's another traffic jamb on Escondido, a ways past my place."

"Where are you, sir?"

"Right now, I'm with Cameron Florek. He's trying to clean out his office in case they can't get this thing under control."

"I'll be there in a few minutes." She switched off the phone and swung her legs out of bed. Francis hadn't moved, but his voice was calm in the dark.

"The world is coming to an end?"

"Just about, *querido. Una conflagración espectacular.* Down behind the wrecking yard, south of *Padrino*'s place."

"Down where you were taking pictures of *los burros*?"

"That's it."

"So now they got roasted *burritos*. No wonder Bill is down there."

She tossed her pillow at his dark form. "A propane tank exploded, *querido*. And now the fire's spreading into the wrecking yard. Lots of gasoline, oil, all those neat things."

His tone turned serious. "Injuries?" She turned on the light, and he flinched, sitting up in bed.

"Sin duda," she replied. "You might as well get dressed. Your phone rings next."

"I'm not on call tonight."

"Oh, sure," she said, and pulled on a pair of jeans and a sweatshirt, then slipped into running shoes. *"Everybody* is going to be on call by the time this mess is cleaned up." She hesitated, thinking about the roster of volunteer firefighters—and the names included most of the Posadas County sheriff's deputies. With both hands behind her back, she worked the stiff clip of her holster over her belt. "Will you give Irma a call?"

He grimaced as he rolled across the bed and picked up the phone. "She's going to love that. If she's in bed with Manny, what do you want me to say?"

Estelle flashed a smile. "Tell her to bring Manny with her." She leaned over the bed and Francis caught her around the small of the back.

"Monday nights are supposed to be her reprieve from *los locos,*" he said. "Somebody's not paying attention to our schedule." He looked hard at Estelle. "How are you doing?"

"I'm doing okay. I slept for a little while."

Their eyes met for a long moment, and he reached up and swept the fall of hair away from her face. "Remember that *Mamá* expects you to take her to Tres Santos today."

She kissed him and pushed herself up right. "She won't even remember that she wanted to go when she wakes up in the morning," she said.

"Oh, sure." Francis pressed the phone buttons with his thumb.

"Maybe it can be an outing for Irma and the boys."

Francis glanced up at her, skeptical. "She wants to go with *you, querida.*"

Estelle nodded impatiently. She padded down the hall, footsteps inaudible on the carpeting, and peered into the boys' room. Both were asleep. Irma had aired out the room during the day and changed the bedding again. If not smelling like a flower garden, at least the small room was fresh and welcome. For what seemed like a long time, she stood silently in the doorway, hand on the knob, listening to her husband's quiet voice down the hall. Of course Irma Sedillos had answered promptly. The thought of leaving her phone off the hook would never have occurred to her.

Her mother's door was closed, and for a moment Estelle hesitated. The knob turned noiselessly and she cracked open the door.

"Estelita?" Her mother cleared her throat and repeated her name.

"I have to go out for a while," Estelle said. She crossed to the single bed and knelt down.

"I heard the sirens," her mother said in Spanish. "And an explosion."

"It's a bad fire, *Mamá.* Over by *Padrino*'s house."

"Then you be careful."

"I will. *Oso* is on call, too. But I think Irma is coming over."

"That's not necessary, Estelita. I'm awake now."

Estelle reached out and took her mother's hand. "The boys are sound asleep. They'll be fine."

"They wear me out."

Estelle laughed. "I know. Me, too."

"You be careful."

"I will."

"Does Irma drive?"

"Of course she does, *Mamá.*"

"Then maybe she can take me to Tres Santos later today."

Estelle bent over, holding her mother's hand in both of hers. "I want to do that, *Mamá.* But maybe not today. We'll see."

"It's something I want to do."

"I know it is."

"Then maybe we won't wait too long, *hija*."

In the distance, the wail of another siren floated on the night air. "You better go. Be careful." The old woman's tiny, thin hand pressed Estelle's with surprising strength.

"I'll be back soon."

"That's good. Close the door, please."

Estelle left the room to find Francis standing in the hall, phone in hand.

"She heard the sirens," he said.

"Irma did?"

He nodded.

"I seem to be the only one who didn't," Estelle said.

"Sleep is a good thing," her husband said. "If only for an hour."

"You sound very doctorly," Estelle grinned. She took her coat off the back of one of the kitchen chairs and shrugged into it, then grabbed her husband in a fierce hug. "Thank you," she said.

"For what?"

She stretched up and kissed him. "Just on general principles." She turned toward the door just as the phone in Francis's hand rang, and she stopped in midstep. She could hear the loud, clear voice of dispatcher Ernie Wheeler from three paces away.

"She's on the way, Ernie. She's just walking out the door now."

He clicked off the phone. "They found Denton Pope."

14

Denton "Woody" Pope didn't look much like Denton Pope any longer.

The corpse lay against the back of what once might have been a freezer. Small patches of the appliance's white enamel showed between the tears, dents, smudges, and scorch marks. Originally, the freezer had been in a small utility room immediately beside the furnace closet. Blackened stumps of wall studs marked where the furnace closet had been. The freezer was skewed out into the middle of the utility room.

Heavy smoke and the heat of the mobile home's buckled steel chassis had kept firefighters at a respectful distance, but it was obvious that heroic resuscitation efforts for Denton weren't necessary.

"You shouldn't be here yet," Tom Mears said. He'd traded in his deputy's uniform for the bulky yellow and black firefighting apparatus, an airpack strapped to his back. He reached out a protective hand and touched Estelle's elbow as she stepped through the twisted rubble that surrounded the mobile home. A section of wall had crumpled to form a jagged barrier. Behind them, three firefighters kept a constant stream of water directed at the two hundred and fifty gallon propane tank, even though the fire had moved on to more productive pastures.

"I just need a quick look," she said.

"Be careful where you step. We'll be setting up a generator here after a bit. Then we'll have some light."

Estelle nodded. She held the flashlight over her head and directed the beam through the debris. Denton Pope's corpse was wedged between the bulk of the freezer and a pair of charred wall studs. One hand was visible, nothing more now than a stump, clawed upward as if he'd thrown up an arm to ward off the explosion even as the blast was sifting him through the wall. Estelle leaned forward, putting her weight against a section of the trailer's unburned skirting. Denton Pope was clearly holding something.

Perhaps mistaking her movement, Mears shouted in her ear, "You okay? There's an awful lot of smoke still." She glanced at him and saw the anxious expression of a fireman feeling sidelined. He knew that Denton Pope would keep, and there were other places he needed to be.

"What's that in his hand?" Estelle asked. She directed the beam of light, squinting against the sting of the smoke.

"A screwdriver or something," Mears said. "Nobody's going to touch it."

"That's good." She shifted the light. "Does anyone have any idea what he was doing with it?"

"Haven't a clue," Mears said. "Adjusting the furnace, is my guess."

Estelle shook her head in wonder. "He adjusted it, all right." She glanced back at Mears just as a dull, heavy *whump* jerked his head around. Behind them, the fire had found interesting feeding in the wrecking yard. A plume of flame and a great rolling ball of smoke billowed upward, followed by the raucous bawl of a fire engine as the driver leaned on the air horn.

"Go ahead," she shouted. "We'll make sure this stays cordoned off." Mears nodded and moved off, a walking mound of protective gear.

For a few moments, Estelle was by herself. She could feel the heat radiating out of the destroyed home. Picking her way carefully, she circled the structure, keeping away from the snarl of barbed wire fencing on the southeast side.

Denton Pope's car was a black puddle of melted plastic, metal, and rubber in the driveway, its yellow license plate incongruously unscathed.

Unsure of herself, Estelle stood very still. What was left of the dwelling's floor tilted at a crazy angle in front of her, the steel floor joists of the mobile home melted and twisted. There was no obvious place to step that wouldn't send her crashing through the sodden, smoking wreckage.

She tried to find an island of silence in her mind, a place where she could push away the assault of the senses. A cacophony of voices, all high-pitched and frantic, competed with the roar of vehicles, the incessant shriek of sirens, and the distant jet-engine bellow of the flames, contained now in the wrecking yard behind the Popes'. Her eyes stung from the acrid smoke. Out of reflex, she raised her arm and buried her nose deep in the folds and creases of her elbow.

"I'm establishing a line . . ."

She heard the shout and turned. One of the village part-timers, Perry Kenderman, waved his arm toward the knot of people who stood in the middle of Escondido Lane, front row seats for the show. "I'm establishing a line right there," he shouted again. Estelle saw the village patrol car turned sideways in the street, roof rack flashing.

"This whole area needs to be cordoned off," Estelle replied. She saw Mears making his way back toward her. "Has anyone called the Fire Marshall's office?"

"I don't think so, sheriff."

"But Perrone is on his way?"

He nodded. "I'll put a call in to the state."

Estelle caught him by the forearm. "Let me," she said. "You're needed here."

The Popes' home was a conglomeration of two trailers with a pitched roof added over the junction. Estelle caught up with the village cop. She swept her arm in an arc to include the whole thing. "Make sure that nobody gets anywhere near any of this, Perry," she shouted as he bent close to hear. "And if I don't see them first, make sure you contact me when either the coroner or the state investigators show up. All right?"

He nodded, knowing as well as she did that the first investigator from the state office could be expected by late morning, if they were lucky. Estelle was surprised that Alan Perrone, the coroner and assistant state medical examiner, wasn't on the scene already. But Denton Pope could wait.

"We'll get everyone here to help you that we can," she added, and grimaced as a wave of heat touched her face. She turned toward the backyard and saw that the fire had leaped from the house to a brush hedgerow that had provided a windbreak for the barns, and then had found the dry wood and straw of the *burro hotel*. Beyond those buildings, an empty lot had offered two acres of winter-dried brush and unkempt bunch grass, and the fire had darted there eagerly while the flank of the blaze ate into the board fence around the wrecking yard.

"Where's Mrs. Pope?" she shouted. "Her car's not here. Did somebody locate her?"

"She's at bingo," Kenderman shouted.

"Where?"

He stepped closer. "Bingo." He waved a hand in the general direction of Escondido Lane. "One of the neighbors said that she goes to Monday Night Bingo at the First Baptist Church."

Estelle glanced at her watch. "That's long over with."

Kenderman shrugged. "I don't know, ma'am. You want me to check on that?"

Estelle nodded. "And did anyone have a chance to move the animals?" she shouted, but Perry Kenderman had already hustled away.

She surveyed the backyard and its hard shadows cast by the flames and floodlights from the fire trucks. The fire had scorched a crescent, leaving the southwest corner, that area that included the goat pens, untouched. The goat pens were empty.

Picking her way carefully, using the heavy body of her flashlight for balance, she followed the black avenue left by the fire. Through the remains of the wrecking yard boundary fence, she could see that the firemen had managed to contain the blaze in an area triangulated by two of the lanes that meandered through Florek's property.

The spot where she and Bill Gastner had stood to take photographs of the burros earlier was now a gaping, smoking hole fifty yards long. She turned and looked at the sheds, wincing at the thought of the twenty-odd animals trapped and driven to panic as the flames burned their woolly hides.

She had no desire to peer into the pens, but found herself drawn there anyway. With a mixture of relief and puzzlement, she found the pens empty. The remains of the wooden half doors that secured two of the pens were open, standing ajar the width of a donkey. Short steel livestock panels had been used for the other two stalls. The chain that secured each panel would wrap around one of the stanchions and then be spring-clipped to itself. Both chains hung loose, the panels open.

Estelle allowed a small sigh of relief. Goats, dogs, donkeys— maybe even a few ducks and geese—who knew what else, except Eleanor Pope. Estelle stood in front of the barns, feeling the heat and smelling the sweet-sour odor of things burned. She tried to visualize a neighbor, perhaps glued to the late night television, hearing the *karrump* of the exploding stove. From any window in the neighborhood, the soaring flames would have been visible.

Within minutes, the joined, aging mobile homes would have been consumed, the sort of blaze that firemen hated. The blaze, with oxygen chimneys formed by the narrow hallways and fueled with the thin press-paper paneling and polyester carpeting, would have erupted throughout the dwelling long before the first firefighting units of the volunteer department arrived.

Had Denton Pope been snoozing on a living-room couch instead of dinking around the furnace when it blew to pieces, he still might not have escaped as the dense fumes from melting plastic and polyester overwhelmed him.

Estelle thrust her hands in her pockets, trying to replay the scene in her mind, trying to understand the awkward geometry of the property. Seeing the blaze, the neighbor would have had to run across the front yard, down beside the burning buildings, and then, ducking the sparks, embers, and roaring jets of propane-powered flame, dash to the barns and release the livestock . . . running in exactly the same direction that the wind drove the flames.

Maybe, when the first firemen arrived on the scene, during the initial moments of confusion and disorganization, they had had the heroic moment necessary to turn the livestock loose.

"You can't be here!" a voice shouted behind her, and Estelle startled and turned. One of the firefighters had scrambled along the charred fence line, with two others following close behind. He held a lethal-looking ax in his hand. "We're going to move one of the pumpers in along here," he shouted at Estelle, and stepped close, flipping up his visor. Under the burden of his equipment, with a grimy face and a sheen of sweat on his forehead, Dennis Collins looked as if he'd aged a decade.

"Sorry, I didn't recognize you at first," he bellowed. He turned to face the wrecking yard. "I think we've got it pretty much contained, sheriff. We're going to circle around and mop up some along the fence." He flashed a smile of confidence. "It ain't going anywhere now."

"Good!" Estelle shouted back. "Where are all the livestock? Do you know?"

"Scattered all over hell and gone, as far as I can tell," Collins replied. He waved a hand toward the south, through Florek's. "I saw a bunch headed through there, ahead of the fire. Maybe four or five little horselike things."

"Donkeys?" Estelle said, and Collins nodded and started to move away.

"You ought to have some gear on if you're going to be in here," he said. "There's still a lot that's unstable."

"I'm leaving," Estelle replied. "And by the way—I need to talk to you about what you found out from Perry MacInerny earlier." Collins stopped in his tracks, puzzled by the sudden switch from fire to law.

"Who . . ." he started, then nodded quickly. "Oh. Sure. I'm off on Tuesdays, but anytime, sheriff."

"Later this morning would be fine," Estelle said, and caught the flicker of resignation on Collins's face. "I'll catch up with you. Don't worry about it." Her radio squawked 310, and she pulled it out of its belt holster, holding it close to her ear.

"Guzman."

Static cracked dispatcher Ernie Wheeler's voice. "Three ten, be advised that the information you wanted from Sheriff Torrez is here in the office."

114

For a moment, Estelle's mind went blank, and then clicked into gear. "Ten-four." What a bizarre time to call, she thought, but her puzzlement didn't last long.

"And he's en route," the dispatcher added.

Estelle's finger had been about to press the transmit bar for the routine response, but she hesitated. "Ten-nine?"

"He's en route from Virginia. His flight reaches El Paso about five-thirty A.M. local today."

"Has he been advised about the fire?"

"That's affirmative. And Dr. Guzman called from Posadas General, ma'am. He'd like you to stop by there when you're clear."

"Ten-four," Estelle replied, and slid the radio back into its holster. "When I'm clear," she said aloud. She made her way back across the yard, skirting the burned out building. Perry Kenderman had strung the yellow tape across the head of the driveway, looping it around the newspaper delivery box and tying it off in a grove of elm saplings that served as a hedge.

As Estelle approached, Kenderman was in animated discussion with his chief, Eduardo Martinez. Martinez leaned against his huge brown Buick, arms crossed over his chest. He saw Estelle and straightened a bit, hands moving to his hips as if poised for action.

"What did you find out?" he asked by way of greeting.

"It's a mess, sir," Estelle said. "Dr. Perrone hasn't shown up yet?"

"No . . . well, I haven't seen him. Not yet. Maybe there's not much he can do until they get all this quieted down some."

Estelle surveyed the small crowd standing behind the yellow tape. "Who called this in, do we know?"

Before Eduardo could say that he didn't know, Perry Kenderman turned and pointed toward a small mobile home perilously close to the arroyo behind Escondido. "Dispatch says that Mary Salazar called it in. She and her husband are standing right there by the streetlight."

"Time?"

"She called just after eleven-thirty, sheriff." He pulled a small notebook out of his pocket and ruffled the pages; turning so he didn't shield the light. "Eleven thirty-three Monday night is what Ernie said."

115

"Did she hear the explosion?"

"Sure did. Then looked out and saw the flames. She said that the first thing she did was call nine-one-one, and then she and her husband came outside. She said that they were going to go over, but the flames were already above the tops of the trees, and they didn't see what they could do."

Estelle turned and looked down the driveway at the smoldering wreckage of the Popes' home. "They didn't approach at all?"

"She said that her husband started to, but that the car parked in the driveway had already started to burn, and they were afraid of the gasoline. And the propane tank, over there." The big silver missile rested on four concrete blocks on the opposite side of the driveway. Estelle hissed out a breath.

"Did they believe that anyone was home?"

"They thought that Denton was. They'd taken an evening stroll, and seen him earlier, working with the animals out back."

"What did you find out about his mom?"

"She was playing bingo," Kenderman said. "Won one hundred ten dollars, and took a couple lady friends of hers to the Don Juan for a treat. One of the neighbors called her. She didn't even make it out of the restaurant before she collapsed. She's at Posadas General now."

"I talked to her for just a minute in the emergency room," Eduardo Martinez said. He put two fingers at his nostrils. "She wears that air thing, you know what I mean?" He shook his head sadly. "A real shock, you know? This is just a real bad thing. Old Denton, he was okay."

"I'll go over in a few minutes to talk to her, sir. If we can. Did you want to go with me?"

The chief shook his head quickly, a wobble that was half positive, half negative as if to say, "No, you go ahead and do it." "She's taking this real hard," he said.

Hard was an understatement, Estelle thought. The woman, frail enough to be wearing an auxiliary oxygen tank, had lost her son, her home, everything but her aging car, the clothes on her back, and the remains of the $110.

"Did anybody see the animals loose after the explosion?" Estelle asked. "When you talked to the Salazars, what did they say? Did they see anything when they came outside?"

Kenderman glanced at Chief Martinez and then at Estelle. "Ah . . . I didn't ask."

"I didn't see any dead," Estelle said. "They're scattered halfway to Deming by now, I imagine. But they're the least of our problems at the moment."

Over Kenderman's shoulder, Estelle saw Linda Real's little red Honda ease into a spot on the opposite side of the road. "Excuse me, gentlemen," she said.

Linda had two camera cases slung over her shoulders and slammed the car's trunk closed as Estelle approached. "I hope you brought plenty of film," the undersheriff said, and Linda grinned, pulling her Oakland As baseball cap down firmly on her head.

"I'm about to buy stock in the company," she said. No look of worry or concern crossed her face. "This looks like a real messaroo." She stood for a minute, assessing the challenge. "And by the way—when I stopped by the county building, I saw Pauline Saenz, Eurelio's mom?"

"She wants her son out of jail, no doubt."

Linda nodded. "And she wants to talk to you."

"Queue up, Mrs. Saenz," Estelle said. "Let me show you what I need here. And Bill Gastner's around here somewhere. He's going to need some shots, I'm sure."

"This is the place with all the illicit donkeys?" Linda said, falling in step with Estelle.

"This is the place, except all the livestock beat a hasty retreat when the fire started. I have no idea where they went, but if you're lucky, you might get some action shots you can sell to *Rodeo News.*"

"Who turned them all loose?"

Estelle watched Linda duck under the yellow ribbon. "That's one of the interesting questions," she said.

Mary Salazar cowered next to her husband, her arms hugging her silver vinyl coat around her body as if caught in the middle of a raging blizzard. Nestor, in jeans, slippers, and a T-shirt, draped one beefy arm across his diminutive wife's shoulders as they stood on the edge of the stirring, chattering crowd of spectators. The couple stood quietly, not joining in on the conversations.

From fifty yards away, the woman's posture spoke eloquently—"If only we could have . . ." Estelle felt a pang of sympathy as she approached the couple.

Seeing the undersheriff, Mrs. Salazar drew her coat tighter, leaned harder against her husband, and seemed to shrink into herself. Standing there in the February night, unsure of what was going to happen next in her world, Mary Salazar didn't look like the woman she would have to force herself to be in a few hours, confidently herding her twenty-three second-graders through their day at Posadas elementary school.

As Estelle drew close, Mary Salazar stretched out her hand—not a handshake, but a gathering in, as if Estelle were one of the woman's small charges who might wander into danger. To the best of her knowledge, Estelle had never met Mary Salazar. Mary obviously knew who Estelle was, despite the undersheriff's casual dress. Even as Mary turned away from three other woman and an elderly man who were standing close by, Estelle found herself wondering what Mrs. Salazar's relationship would be with little Francisco in two years time. Mary didn't look like the steely-nerved type.

"This is so . . ." Mary said, and stopped, biting her lip.

"Mrs. Pope is safe," Estelle said. She nodded at Nestor Salazar. "She's at the hospital now." Voice husky from the smoke, Estelle wasn't sure that Mary had heard her.

"But Woody . . ." Mary said.

"I'm sorry," Estelle said.

"So awful."

"Could we find a place to talk?" Estelle glanced toward the Salazars' mobile home. A tiny white dog sat on the metal step by the front door. The dog's short leash was snapped to the handrail, and he shifted position every couple of seconds, as if unsure what vantage point might allow him to keep all the incomprehensible human activities in view.

"We can go to the trailer," Mary said, and Nestor nodded—the closest he had come to a comment. One of the other women, demonstrating either acute hearing or adept at reading lips, orbited back into the group, reached out and grasped Nestor by the upper arm.

"I've got coffee on," she said. "You're welcome to it."

"I'll just need a few minutes," Estelle said, and nodded toward the Salazars' trailer.

"Surely," Mary said, and for the first time, some of her occupational confidence crept back into her voice.

"Thank you," Estelle said to the other woman, who looked disappointed. "Maybe a little later. We appreciate your kindness." Following the couple toward their home, Estelle saw that the Salazar lot was as orderly as the Pope property was junk-struck. Mary's Camry was parked in the driveway, with the Nestor Salazar Plumbing and Heating truck snugged in behind it. Even the truck was neat—and probably more expensive than the older model mobile home beside which it was parked.

As they reached the trailer, the small dog became a white ball of constant motion, its tiny feet dancing on the metal step. Nestor unclipped the leash and the animal darted into the trailer ahead of them. Inside was uncomfortably warm as Nestor closed the door behind them. The dog danced around her feet, black nose twitching. "He won't bother you," Nestor said. "Scampi, come here."

The animated dustmop hurtled itself into Nestor's beckoning arms, pink tongue darting out as it panted.

Mary Salazar perched on the edge of the sofa, still wrapped in her silver coat. She made no move to offer the ubiquitous cup of coffee. "Mary and Nestor," Estelle said, and sat down in the wooden rocker across the rug. "One of the village officers told me that you had seen Denton Pope earlier in the evening. Is that correct?"

Mary nodded. "We walk every evening. Nestor and me. We had Scampi on the leash."

"And you saw Denton?"

"Yes. Woody, we all call him."

"Do you remember what time that might have been?"

"Right at nine o'clock," Nestor said. His voice was rich and authoritative. He sat down beside his wife on the sofa and brushed some of the fur away from Scampi's face. The dog had eyes, buried deep behind its coiffure, and the little black dots flicked this way and that.

"And did everything appear normal at that time?"

"Well, I suppose so," Mary said, and shrugged. "We saw Woody when he came out the side door of his place. It was dark, but when he opened the door, the light, you know?"

"Did you see where he went?"

"No. We didn't pay any attention. I think he turned toward the backyard."

"You didn't speak to him, though?"

"Oh, no," Mary said. "We just saw him. He was busy, and we wanted to walk."

"Eleanor was not home at that time?"

"I don't think so. Her car was gone. And she usually plays bingo on Monday nights."

"And Wednesday. And Friday. And Saturday," Nestor added. "She's a bingo addict."

"When was the last time you spoke with her?"

Mary frowned. "Oh, my. It's been a while, I think. I mean other than just to catch sight and maybe shout a 'good morning.' She's going to be all right, isn't she?"

"We don't know, Mary. She's being kept at Posadas General for observation. We'll know more by morning."

"Such a shock."

"Yes, it is. When was the last time you actually spoke with Denton? Do you remember?"

"Well, other than earlier . . . but we didn't speak to him then. I guess I chatted with him some on Saturday afternoon. I was thinking that it might be fun to have the second-graders out here to meet all the burros while they still had them. Denton suggested that maybe it would be better if he brought one or two over to the school sometime."

"Maybe easier on the donkeys," Estelle said. The image of Livestock Inspector Bill Gastner flashed through her mind. The second-graders would find him entertaining, too. "You said 'while they still had them.' Were they planning to thin the herd a little?"

"I don't know about that," Mary said. She looked at Nestor. He stroked the dustmop's head and shrugged. "This little one," and she nodded at Scampi. "He's enough of a handful. I can't imagine having animals all over the place the way they do."

"I never see them," Nestor said, as if that settled that. "The Popes, I mean. You know, I get busy. We all do. And I probably should have taken the time. Maybe Woody wouldn't have blown the place up."

Estelle nodded with sympathy. "Mr. Salazar, had he ever mentioned furnace problems to you before this?"

Nestor shot a glance at his wife. "He didn't. His mother did." Estelle remained silent, waiting. Nestor shrugged. "She said that they were both getting tired of having to get up and relight the pilot. She wondered if I'd come over and take a look at it some day when Woody wasn't home."

"Some day when he *wasn't* home?"

Nestor shrugged again. "Old Woody, he was kind of an odd duck. Figured there was nothing on the planet that he couldn't do. Mr. Fix-it-himself." A trace of a smile touched Nestor's pudgy face. "Eleanor was afraid he'd screw things up. She didn't like gas in the first place, and was always after him to put in a woodstove. He wasn't much for

121

that. It'd be my guess that gas furnace came with the place when it was new—sometime in the stone ages. I mean, we've replaced our heater, what, three, four times?"

"Did you actually ever look at it? At their heater, I mean?"

"Nope. Should have, obviously. She told me that it was starting to get noisy when it lit . . . you know the way those old ones do. Kind of goes *whump* after enough gas collects. The baffles were probably shot, is what I think."

He transferred his hand from Scampi's head to Mary's forearm and patted her. "We sure feel bad about all those animals. My gosh, what a mess now."

"I think all of the animals were able to escape," Estelle said.

"That so? Well, good, then. I know some of 'em were loose, but I wasn't sure about the rest." He nodded and patted his wife's hand. "Just about a zoo, is what it is over there. The wife don't mind all the animals, but it's kinda strange, if you ask me. Wind gets just right, you can smell that place." He waved a hand in front of his nose. "Too many critters in too small a space, if you ask me. 'Course, I don't suppose that has anything to do with the fire. I guess now they're going to be rounding up goats and donkeys and whatnot for the next month. Don't know what will become of them."

"Do you have an idea who might've turned all the animals loose when the fire started?"

"I have no idea," Nestor said. "They sure enough got out of there in a hurry, though. They was runnin' every which way when we went outside."

"You heard the explosion?"

"Sure did," Nestor said, and Mary winced, not sharing the eagerness of her husband's memory. "Just *whump,* like that. Real loud. Actually, it was sort of a double *whump,* just the way propane does sometimes."

"But a single explosion, then. There wasn't a long time lag between the two?"

"Just *whump WHUMP,* like that. And then kind of a roar that built up. I knew right away what had happened."

"You ran outside at that time?"

"Sure did. Me and the missus. We could see the fireball just about

122

taking out the whole west side of their trailer, there. It's actually two joined together, you know. I shouted for Mary to call in, and I started across the street to see what I could do."

He held out a leg with one of the furry slippers. "And then I realized I wasn't going to be able to do a damn thing. That fire," and he paused and drew himself forward on the couch. Scampi shifted nervously. "That fire, sheriff, was already above the trees, there. You know them two elms that grew right beside their propane tank? It was higher than that, and already workin' on his car, parked right there. And with the car burning, why, that propane tank was just a few feet away—just across the driveway. And that's enough to scare anybody." He reared back as if seeing the fire again. "I could see that there wasn't anything I could do." He drew a horizontal circle in the air with his finger. "So I come around the east side, to see if I could maybe reach the door there." He shook his head. "But they've got this snarled up old barbed wire and chicken wire conglomeration of a fence on that side."

Holding up his right arm, he displayed a short, reddened scratch on the underside of his arm. "I started to get all caught up in it, and saw right away that even if I did get through, there wouldn't be much that I could do. About that time, I heard the first siren."

"And the animals were loose then?"

"There was animals *everywhere*. And I mean *everywhere*. They're pretty smart, you know, if they got a choice. They was goin' this way and that, trying to figure out the best way, and the fire just kind of drove 'em off the back of the property, there, over in those woods. And some of 'em broke through into Florek's, and God knows what all. Like I said, they're going to be finding strays for a long, long time."

Estelle frowned and rested her elbows on her knees. "I'm trying to understand this, sir. When you ran around the house to the east side, to the fence that snagged you . . . at that time, did you see animals loose?"

"Sure enough did. All over the place."

"But you didn't see who turned them loose."

Nestor shook his head, puzzled. "Nope."

"You didn't see anyone else in the area, or on the Popes' property?"

He leaned back against the sofa and looked at Mary. "Didn't see a soul," he said.

"Maybe they just neglected to hook the chains, or whatever they have on the stalls and such," Mary said.

"Well, no," Nestor said. "I see what the sheriff's sayin'. They might forget to hook one gate, maybe two. But as far as I could tell, the whole damn menagerie was on the loose. Hell, she's even got a half dozen ducks over there, and I *know* they keep them penned up, 'cause of the coyotes and coons. But they was already squawkin' through the weeds there, headin' east for all they was worth." He reached out a hand and scooped up Scampi. "You got any ideas about all this, Sheriff?"

"No," Estelle said, and took a deep breath. She pushed herself out of the chair. "I'm sure there's a simple explanation. We're just glad no one else was hurt. We'll find out what caused the explosion, and I'll talk with Eleanor later today."

Nestor heaved himself to his feet, threatening to crush the small dog between the folds of his belly. "I *know* what caused the explosion, sheriff. There's no mystery there. They was using an old, worn out piece of junk to heat that place. Should have been red-tagged a long, long time ago."

"You think it just caught up with him, then."

"Yes, ma'am. That's what happened. I *know* that's what happened. You see, those baffles prevent the gas from collecting in one spot. They kind of guide the flow of propane across the burner, keeping it even and under control. That was the problem there."

"Interesting," Estelle said, and extended her hand to Mary, and then to Nestor. "Thank you both. We may need to talk with you again." She fished a business card out of her pocket and handed it to Nestor. "And should you think of anything else, feel free to call me."

"Let us know if there's anything we can do," Mary said. "I feel so awful about this."

"I certainly will," Estelle said.

The night was still full of people, the flicker of flames, and the roar of heavy equipment. Estelle stood on the shoulder of Escondido for a few minutes, watching. Dawn was four hours away. By then, the jets of water would have cooled the propane tank, the hot spots

124

would have been quenched, and the Popes' small patch of paradise would be quiet ashes.

Shouldering her own camera bag, Estelle walked along the shoulder of Escondido to the far west side of the Pope property, her slight figure unnoticed by the assembled curious. She slipped into her car and sat for a while, watching from the darkness.

It made sense that any number of things might cause an explosion in an old propane heater. The Guzmans had removed a unit from their own home when it started to *whump* uncomfortably each time it lit. Worn-out baffles, the dealer had said and Nestor Salazar obviously agreed. It made sense that, on a brisk February night, with his elderly mother soon to return from bingo, Denton Pope might have wanted the house warm and cozy.

Estelle could picture Denton, cussing the aging heater, cussing the faulty pilot light. She could picture him, screwdriver in hand, advancing to adjust the relic, perhaps even smelling the propane as he did so. But there was a catch in that scenario, a nagging catch. No one thought much of the risk when they did things like that. There was no reason for Denton to turn all the animals loose before working on the furnace, unless he was sure that the aging appliance was going to explode and take most of their little *ranchito* with it.

"Denton, what were you doing?" Estelle said aloud.

16

ESTELLE started when a knuckle rapped against the driver's-side window of her unmarked car. She wasn't sure where she'd been for the past several minutes, and she hadn't seen her visitor approach.

"So what have you decided?" Bill Gastner asked when she opened the window. "I saw you sitting over here in this dark corner, all by yourself. I could hear the brain waves."

"I wish I could hear them," Estelle said, and Gastner grinned. She motioned toward the passenger seat, and he settled into the car with a groan of relief. "How goes the rodeo, *Padrino?*" The smell of smoke and char was strong on his clothes.

"The rodeo." He laughed. "We've got thirteen mean little donkeys corralled up the arroyo a ways. One of the neighbors had some livestock panels we commandeered for a temporary pen. They ought to be fine until we can decide what happens next. Lots of good dog food there."

"Don't let Eleanor Pope hear you say that. It'll finish the job. And thirteen is a long way from all of them, isn't it?"

"Yep." Gastner twisted in the seat and leaned against the door, hooking his arm across the back of the seat. "This is a mess, that's for sure. And speaking of their owner, what's the word on Eleanor? One of the firemen said she was in the hospital. Is that true?"

"That's what I'm told."

Gastner grimaced. "I guess that doesn't surprise me. You ever seen the oxygen tank that woman lugs around with her?"

"Actually, I've never met Mrs. Pope, sir. But Chief Martinez visited with her for a bit just a little while ago. He filled me in."

"See," Gastner said, and reached out to thump the dashboard with his right hand, "if she'd been the one at home, I would have had it figured out in a heartbeat. She smokes, you know."

"While she's on supplemental oxygen?"

He nodded. "Yep. Every time I see her, it makes me feel in such good shape that for a few minutes I think I'm a teenaged track star. She's got congestive heart failure, she's got emphysema, she's got every goddamn thing that it's possible to have, and she still smokes like a chimney. How she's able to waddle around and feed all those critters is beyond me. I have visions of that oxygen tank of hers igniting one day and taking a tour of the neighborhood, with her hanging by her tubes, trailing behind."

"She was out playing bingo with the lady friends," Estelle said. "She was at the Don Juan, celebrating her winnings. A hundred and ten bucks. That's where she was when they broke the news. She collapsed right there."

"A hundred and ten won't even pay for an aspirin at the emergency room," Gastner said. "Have you talked to her yet?"

"No. Later, maybe. I was just sitting here, watching. Alan hasn't been here yet."

"What's the deal?"

Estelle glanced at him quizzically. "Sir?"

Gastner looked at her over the tops of his glasses. "I can hear the gears grinding, sweetheart. You haven't found out who turned the critters loose yet, have you?" He grinned at her.

"That's the major thing," Estelle said. "No one seems to know." She folded her hands in her lap. "It bothers me, is all."

"I would think so. It bothers me, too."

"I can understand the first fireman on the scene making a dash through the backyard, flipped doors open, shooing all the livestock to safety. That's a firemanly thing to do."

"Except he'd have to run between a burning house, burning car, and a threatening propane tank to do it, and I would argue that's more stupid than heroic. Plus, Salazar was over there *before* the fire department arrived. He would have seen something."

Estelle nodded. "And if a neighbor turned the animals loose, someone would say so. But no one did that, apparently. So that's a puzzle. The logical person would be Denton. But why would he turn them loose, down to the last two ducks, *before* he worked on the furnace? That just doesn't make sense, unless he was thinking suicide."

"Nobody commits suicide by exploding a propane heater, sweetheart."

"I've been sitting here stewing about that." She looked over at Gastner. "One of the assumptions we've been making is that Denton was working on the furnace. What if that's *not* what he was doing at all? What if he was in the pantry or something, in that little room with the freezer, just trying to pry open a can with a screwdriver?"

Gastner shrugged. "Maybe."

"Opening a can of paint or something. I agree that it looks like he was blown through the wall, but it might not have happened that way at all." Estelle took a deep breath and exhaled, as if trying to clear the greasy smoke from her lungs. "He has a screwdriver clutched in his hand. Like he was going to work on something when the furnace blew up."

"Only one small catch," Gastner said. "Here's an interesting little piece of information to add to your puzzle mix—it isn't a screwdriver that he's holding in his hand."

She turned and looked at him. "What is it?"

"I believe that it's an awl."

"An awl?" She raised her hand and made a twisting motion. "One of those things that you drill holes in leather with?"

He nodded. "Or in anything else, for that matter. Maybe Denton thought he had a clogged gas line, and was trying to break the obstruction loose. Who the hell knows."

Estelle gazed out the window for a minute. She could see Linda Real's stout figure working around the wreckage, the explosion of white light from her camera flash marking her path. "Take a walk with me," Estelle said, and opened the car door.

"I was just getting comfortable," Gastner replied as he heaved himself out of the car. He turned as more flashing lights swept the area, and stepped around the car as an ambulance pulled up, headed for the yellow tape. "Perrone is not far behind," he said to Estelle. "What did you want to look at?"

"Show me the awl, sir," she said, hefting her flashlight.

"Okay. Go slow," he replied, and she gestured for him to lead the way. She fell in step behind him, watching how carefully the older man placed his feet in the vague light. "The Gastner Shuffle," she had called his manner of moving about a crime scene—hands thrust in his pockets, head down, eyes covering every inch of ground. Occasionally he would stop and look up, scanning the charred remains of the trees, the blackened utility pole, and as they drew closer, the building itself.

Linda Real was standing at the northwest corner of the burned trailer, the nearest point to Denton Pope's corpse that she could reach without actually climbing up into the structure.

"The flooring's burned away a little further over," Gastner said as he approached Linda. She held up both hands, camera in one of them, as if she was unsure of what to do. "I think we can pull some of the skirting off, and then we can duck under," Gastner said. "I've got gloves. Let me in there." He yanked at a piece of thin sheet metal as Estelle held the light. With the skirting peeled back, the space underneath the trailers yawned black.

Gastner dropped to his hands and knees, playing his own flashlight through the wreckage. "This is nice," he muttered. "At least all the spiders are cooked." He shuffled a few inches and stopped. "We don't actually have to go under. It's all right here," and Estelle could see the beam from his light lance up through the burned floor joists, touching the dark lump that was Denton Pope's charcoaled head.

"I'm too fat for this," he said, and twisted around to wave at Estelle. "You're nimble. If you watch yourself, you can work your way right where you want to go. Just don't go under the main structure. Stay on the perimeter here."

"*Want* to go, sir?" she replied, and Linda knelt at her elbow. Wisps of acrid smoke still stung her nostrils, and Estelle could feel the residual heat above her, along with the odd popping and groaning of cooling metal. But the force of the flames had been upward. The bare earth under the trailer was almost cool to the touch.

"Right there," Gastner said, pointing with his flashlight.

Estelle could see Denton Pope's hand. The floor around the mangled propane heater had disintegrated, but portions of it still remained in the utility room where Pope lay. Negotiating carefully, Estelle and Linda were able to approach within a foot or two of Pope's body. Linda crouched as if ready to dive out from under the hulk at the least provocation.

On one knee, maintaining her balance with one hand in the soft dirt, Estelle could see that the man's right hand—at least it appeared to be his right—was a blackened stump, fused tightly to the tool's handle. Three inches of soot-covered metal projected, ending in a sharp point.

"Can you get a photo of that?" she asked Linda, and the photographer grunted something as she shifted position.

"Sure," she said. "Why not." She knelt for a moment, thinking. "We'll try a couple different ways." Estelle cringed away from the flash as Linda shot directly, then tried bouncing the light from various angles. "That'll work," she said.

Voices approached, and then another figure knelt beside Gastner. Estelle turned to see Alan Perrone rest a hand on the older man's shoulder. "Can't stay away, eh?" the physician said.

"I'm looking for strays," Gastner said, and motioned toward the two shadows ahead of him. "They're trying for a portrait."

"I see," Perrone said. "Just the one victim?"

"As far as we know."

"Denton Pope? That's what Chief Martinez said."

"We think so. There's not a whole lot left."

Estelle crab-scrambled out from under the trailer, followed by Linda Real. Perrone regarded the two skeptically. "You know, the firefighters can lay a couple of nice planks across that floor for us. That might be preferable to risking your necks under all this mess."

Estelle nodded and reached for her radio. "It's an interesting angle, though."

"I'm sure it is. But they're going to have to plank it anyway for the EMTs to remove the body."

Estelle favored Perrone with a warm smile, and reached out to tug at his sleeve. "And once they lay those planks in place, the scene is never the same, doctor. I needed to see it before they did that."

"Ah," Perrone said, and glanced at Gastner. "This is something other than a flash trailer fire? It's pretty common that folks don't get out of these old tin cans in time."

Gastner held up both hands. "I'm just looking for burros and such. You'll have to ask her."

"Uh-huh," Perrone said. Estelle had turned away, talking to dispatch, and he nodded at her as she turned back. She slipped the radio back in its holster.

"They're finally able to spring a couple of the firemen clear, Alan. I asked if Mears and Collins could bring a couple of walkways. They'll be here in a minute."

"And by the way," Perrone said, raising a hand as if he expected silence. "Francis said that if you hadn't left for the hospital yet, to put it on your list of things to do ASAP."

"That's my next stop. I need to see Eleanor Pope, for one thing."

"See Francis, too."

"He must be in his worry mode," Estelle said.

"I think it's your mother that he's worried about," Perrone said, leaning close.

Estelle looked at him quickly, but his expression didn't give anything away. She knew that Francis was reluctant to use *the Curse,* as he called the cellular phones, maintaining that most humans couldn't resist a ringing telephone no matter how inappropriate the timing.

She turned to Linda. "I need to go. Would you make doubly sure—maybe even triply—to cover this from every which way? I'm probably just running spooked after this weekend, but I want to be sure. And I'm going to ask Tom Mears to do a preliminary on this mess, too. He's the closest we've got to an arson investigator until somebody from the state shows up, Lord knows when. I don't know if there's enough left, but if he can get us started, that'll help."

Estelle took Gastner by the elbow and they walked several steps away. "I can't believe how shorthanded we are, sir. Is there any way you can . . ."

He grinned. "I'll stick around and be a gofer. Mears is good, Estelle. Not to worry."

"I know he's good. But we're being drawn fifteen different ways here. The best news I had all night was that Bobby was catching a plane back."

Gastner's eyebrows shot up. "From Virginia?"

"His flight arrives in El Paso at five-thirty."

"Well, good . . . although that just means he'll have to catch the class some other time. But we can use him. I mean, you can use him. Knowing him, he couldn't stand being cooped up in a classroom in Virginia, while you guys were having all the fun."

Estelle grinned ruefully. "I'm never going to complain about peace and quiet again, sir." She turned to survey the ruins of the Popes' home. "Ay."

By the time she pulled into the hospital's driveway, the clock on the dashboard had clicked 3:17 A.M. She parked in one of the reserved slots near the emergency room entrance, climbed out of the car and stood quietly for a moment, listening. Now out of the south, the wind had dropped to a gentle whisper, and she heard the faint, brief bleat of a siren.

She turned toward the hospital entrance, forcing her weary body to walk quickly. She had left the house shortly after eight Monday evening, planning a few quick errands. Now, an exhausting seven hours later, the priority list stretched in front of her, running off the bottom of the page. She still wanted to stop by the Public Safety Building to pick up the material that Bob Torrez had sent from Virginia. She wanted to be on hand as Deputy Mears started the laborious job of sifting through the charred remains of the furnace. And somewhere, perhaps, Paulita Saenz was waiting to talk to her.

Estelle pulled the door handle at the hospital entryway and her grip slipped when the door was halfway open. Jerking to catch it, she rammed her thumb against the polished stainless steel. The stab of pain lanced all the way up to her elbow. "There's a reason for just shuffling along," she said aloud, and shouldered the door open.

"Are you all right?" Debbie Peterson had watched Estelle's tussle with the door, and as it opened, had heard the undersheriff talking to herself. Estelle, in midgrimace as she massaged the bruised thumb, looked heavenward when she saw the ER nurse. Debbie's long, angular face softened in sympathy. "I hate that door," she added.

"Early morning clumsies," Estelle said. The nurse was balancing an impressive array of medical supplies on a clipboard, in the middle of something that didn't need an interruption. "I'm fine," Estelle added. "It's been quite a night."

"I'll say." Debbie's gaze inventoried Estelle from head to toe. She saw the grime of the fire scene embedded in the undersheriff's clothes, and could smell the acrid bouquet. But there were no projecting bones or blood . . . just the pale complexion of fatigue that the undersheriff's flawless olive skin couldn't hide. The nurse nodded down the hallway that skirted the two small emergency rooms and the radiology lab. "Your husband was here just a few minutes ago treating the officer. I think when he finished he planned to go back to the ICU."

Estelle's face went blank. "The officer? One of the firemen was hurt?"

"Collins, I think his name is. The one who ran the nail into his hand."

"Ouch. No, I didn't know about that. He's all right?"

"Sure. In fact, he headed back out to the fire." Debbie adjusted the placement of two of the small bottles on the clipboard.

"And Eleanor Pope—I understand that she was brought in earlier. Can you point me in the direction of her room?" Estelle asked.

"She's the one who's in ICU right now," Debbie said. "You might want to check at the nurse's station to be sure, but that's where they planned to take her." She smiled warmly as Estelle nodded her thanks and started down the hall.

Despite the ruckus at the opposite end of town, Posadas General Hospital was locked in the deep quiet of the predawn hours. The intensive care unit dominated the end of a long hallway out of the heaviest central traffic flow, the double glass doors opening to the ICU nurses' station.

Dr. Francis Guzman leaned both elbows on the polished wood of the counter with his face cradled by both hands. He appeared to either be asleep or reading the chart that lay on the counter in front of him. A gray-haired nurse whom Estelle didn't recognize stood behind the counter frowning at the floor, telephone receiver tight against her ear. The nurse saw Estelle hesitate at the door, and beckoned. Francis glanced up as the door glided open.

"Ah, good," he said. Estelle breathed in the aromas of him as he caught her up in a bear hug. Her aromas were a different matter. "You smell as if you've been inside somebody's chimney," he said. She managed to free her right hand enough to reach up and move the ballpoint pen in his pocket so that it didn't threaten her eye as he crushed her against him.

"You're going to need a fresh set of scrubs," she said.

"I got lots of those." He held her at arm's length and she grinned as he gave her his best critical physician's scrutiny. "How you holding up, *cariña?*"

"I'm okay. Is Eleanor still here?"

"No, no," Francis said quickly. "You're supposed to say, 'Can we go home now?'" He gave her another squeeze and then relaxed his hold. Estelle stood with eyes closed, using her husband as a leaning post. She thumped her head against his chest a couple of times and then looked up at him. "And yes, she's still here," Francis said. "And you're a smelly mess."

134

"I know, but I need to see her."

Francis nodded in resignation. "I don't think that's going to do any good, *querida*." He turned, one hand still on her shoulder. "We're trying to keep her as quiet as we can." Estelle started to move off toward the nearest sliding curtain that provided a modicum of privacy for the patient behind it, but stopped when she felt the trace of restraint from her husband's hand. She realized that the nurse was watching as well.

"What?"

"I brought *Mamá* in with me, Estelle."

Estelle's first reflex was to look across the hall toward the small ICU waiting room with its three vinyl-covered chairs and single sofa, but just as quickly she realized what Francis had meant.

"She's here? What happened?"

Francis rested a hand on his chest, fingers splayed like a spider's legs. "She was having a little trouble breathing. I wanted to be able to keep an eye on her."

"She's sleeping peacefully now," the nurse said. The woman rounded the end of the counter and held out a hand toward Estelle. A small spray of delicate paper flowers obscured a portion of the staff name tag, but Estelle could read *Sadie McC* and then *RN*. As if her soles had been welded to the floor tiles, Estelle stood motionless. Francis saw the darkness gathering on her face and sighed.

"*Querida,* I wanted her here so I could keep an eye on her. That's all. With both of us out on call, I didn't want to put Irma in that position. Your mother was having a little respiratory discomfort, and I had to be here. You were out at the fire, and I just thought it would be easier. It's as simple as that."

"There's nothing simple about ending up in ICU," Estelle snapped, and instantly regretted the outburst. She closed her eyes and shook her head in apology, leaning her weight against him as she felt Francis's arm.

"Come on," he said gently.

Even though she knew it would not be so, Estelle had recoiled from the vision of Teresa Reyes lying helpless—intubated, IVed, and sedated, completely at the mercy of this sterile place despite the woman's wishes to the contrary. Francis pushed the privacy curtain to one side, and she saw her mother sleeping like a child, tiny and curled on her side. The clear plastic oxygen tube curled from her nose up around her ears, lost in the halo of wiry gray hair.

The analytical side of Estelle's brain understood perfectly well that, at age eighty-two with a failing heart, congested lungs, and the soaring blood pressure of brittle arteries, Teresa Reyes's hold on life was precarious at best. Still, that portion of Estelle's brain that entertained dreams of Pancho Villa's tree and the recollection of her mother's voice on the peaceful Mexican air of her childhood refused to accept the inevitable.

"Hay una gran distancia la que va de ayer a hoy," she whispered, and then found herself wishing that she could remember the exact circumstances when her mother had said that to her for the first time. *A great distance between yesterday and today.* The analytical clock said that great distance happened in an infinitely small time, the click between midnight and a heartbeat afterward. What did the clock know?

"She accepted medication?" Estelle asked.

"After I explained exactly what I was giving her and why. If we can relieve her lungs a little, she'll be more comfortable." Estelle lowered the security railing on the side of the bed and sat on the edge, acutely aware of how perfectly white the linens were in contrast to her smudged clothing. Her left hand rested lightly on her mother's hip. "She's not interested in anything else," Francis added.

Estelle nodded. After a long moment, she said, "That's why she's been talking about Mexico lately."

"Sin duda."

With her right hand, she squeezed her husband's, feeling his warm, comfortable grip. "Can she go home?"

"Sure. When either you or I are there. Otherwise, we're going to have to find a nurse to be with her. We can't ask Irma . . ."

"No," Estelle agreed quickly. "That would be unfair."

"She'll probably sleep through morning. Until then, we've got the extra bed space here, and we might as well take advantage of some of the strings that I can pull. And by morning, maybe the world will calm down a bit."

"Unlikely," Estelle said.

"It's that bad?"

"Probably worse, *oso*," she said with a sigh, and stood up, careful not to jostle the bed. She bent over until her lips were brushing Teresa Reyes's ear. *"Mañana, Mamá. Vamos a ir a casa."* She straightened and touched a finger to her mother's cheek, then turned to Francis. "I need to see Eleanor Pope."

"I don't think she's going to tell you much," Francis said. He led Estelle deeper into the sanctum of the ICU to where the monitors kept track of Eleanor Pope's sagging functions. A great mound of a woman, Mrs. Pope lay wired and tubed, her round face slack-jawed, her ragged breath whistling in and out without the interference of her dentures.

"Ay," Estelle sighed.

"We were able to stabilize her a little," Francis said. "But we're at the hoping for a miracle stage now."

"She hasn't been the recipient of too many of those."

"Mrs. Guzman?"

Estelle turned at the sound of her name. Nurse Sadie McC leaned past the curtain, one hand raised as if asking permission to speak.

"We're done here," Estelle said.

"No, I don't mean to interrupt," Sadie said. "There's a woman waiting for you out in the hall. She wanted to make sure that you knew she was here."

"I'll be just a minute," Estelle said, and the nurse nodded and left. "There's a chance Mrs. Pope might be able to talk to us later in the morning?"

Francis held up both hands in a shrug. "We just don't know." He pulled the curtain closed. "When she was brought in, she was no longer lucid. Right now, her circulation system has basically collapsed. Her kidney function is nil. Things don't look good."

"I'm not sure what she could tell us even if she were alert," Estelle said. She ran both hands through her hair in frustration. "All we know is that it appears that her son was monkeying with the propane furnace when it exploded. We'd like to know why."

"Because it didn't work properly?"

She shot Francis a withering glance. "You're hired, *oso*," she said. They reached the nurse's station, and through the glass partitions that formed the ICU, Estelle could see the waiting room across the hall. Pauline Saenz sat on one end of the short sofa, an unlit cigarette in hand. She saw Estelle and jammed the cigarette back into her purse, then stood up and walked into the hall to meet her.

18

␣␣␣◆◆◆

WHEN Estelle walked out of the ICU, Paulita Saenz pulled the cigarette back out of her purse as if she intended to use it as a weapon.
She held it by the filter and jabbed it in Estelle's direction. "When
was the last time I saw you?" A large-boned, angular woman, she
stood a head taller than the undersheriff. She would make a formidable bartender.

Estelle remembered Paulita's husband, Monroy, as a short, stumpy
man who had driven a dump truck for the county. A combination of
alcohol and diabetes had killed him, leaving Paulita with a young
son to raise. The lean, darkly handsome Eurelio apparently enjoyed
the best genes from each parent.

Estelle extended her hand and waited while Paulita regarded it.
Finally the woman shifted her grip on the cigarette to accept the
greeting. "I think I was in the Taberna Azul with my Uncle Reuben
ten or fifteen years ago, Mrs. Saenz," Estelle said. Paulita's eyes narrowed as she ran through her own mental calculations.

"And not since then," Paulita said with just a hint of recrimination.

"No. Not since then."

"Reuben's been gone for five years now."

Surprised that the woman should have Reuben Fuentes's memory
on such fresh recall, Estelle wondered what the relationship between
the old man and the Saenz family might have been. She remembered
the tavern as a dark, musty, cool place, and could visualize little

more. Over the years, sheriff's deputies had responded to the inevitable bar fights at the *taberna,* but Estelle had never had occasion to go. In fact, it had been fully twenty-one years before when, as an eighteen-year-old, Estelle Reyes had stepped into the tavern and searched the dark corners until she had found Reuben. She had no recollection of the purpose of the errand, or what had happened after that.

Whatever Reuben's relationship to the Saenz family had been, beyond that of a casual customer at the bar, no doubt it was as evanescent as Estelle's own relationship with the ancient Reuben Fuentes, a man who was actually her mother's uncle . . . and thus her own adoptive *great*-uncle.

"Yes, ma'am. Reuben passed away in 1996," Estelle said.

"And your mother, she's living with you now, isn't she?" Paulita asked with just a light shade of triumph. The tendrils of information from her bartender's grapevine were impressive.

"Yes, she is."

"He's a good-looking man." The non sequitur caught Estelle by surprise until she turned and saw that Paulita was looking through the glass partitions of the ICU. Dr. Francis was shaking his head while Sadie McC appeared to be questioning something from the clipboard chart. Paulita didn't wait for confirmation. Instead she turned abruptly and walked to the waiting room, saying over her shoulder, "I heard that you're the sheriff now. That's what they were telling me."

Estelle followed her into the room and chose one of the corner chairs. "Bob Torrez is sheriff, Mrs. Saenz." She saw the furrow on the woman's forehead deepen, perhaps perplexed to learn that her source of information was faulty. To the general public, the distinction between sheriff and deputy was often fuzzy at best. "Do you feel comfortable talking here, or would you like to go somewhere else?"

"It doesn't matter where we talk," Mrs. Saenz said, and her tone took an edge. "I want to know why my son is in jail. And I want to know why he didn't call me." She rummaged in her purse, found a lighter, and despite the numerous signs throughout the hospital admonishing to the contrary, lit the cigarette.

"Have you been to the Sheriff's Office yet, Mrs. Saenz?"

"They told me you might be down here."

"They didn't allow you to see Eurelio?"

Paulita rolled the cigarette this way and that, watching the embers burn and shed. When she spoke, her voice sank to a whisper. "He didn't want to see me."

"There may have been a misunderstanding, Mrs. Saenz. With the fire at the Pope place, we're terribly shorthanded at the moment. If the dispatch deputy was by himself, he wouldn't have had the time to arrange a meeting with your son for you."

"My son didn't call me," Paulita said, in no mood to discuss fires or someone else's misfortune. "His girlfriend came and told me."

"That would be Ms. Benevidez?"

Paulita nodded. "And she didn't know why Eurelio had been taken off to jail. She said it didn't make any sense at all. They were drinking a few beers, that's all. Having a nice drive in that old truck . . ."

Estelle indicated one of the vinyl-covered chairs, and Paulita Saenz sat down. She reached out, folded down the corner of the cover of one of the news magazines on the coffee table in front of her, and ripped it off. With practiced skill, she folded the slip of paper into a small dish. She tapped the ash off her cigarette and placed the makeshift receptacle on the table. "So maybe you can tell me."

Estelle settled back against the hard plastic of the chair. Even at a perfectly temperate seventy degrees, the air of the hospital felt close and warm. It would have been welcome just to let her eyes close and rest her head back against the wall. "Paulita, I'm sure you're aware that we're investigating an incident involving the death of two men. Their bodies were found out on the prairie, north of Maria."

"Everybody's heard about that. Eurelio had nothing to do with that."

"I hope not."

Paulita frowned again, looking hard at the undersheriff. She prided herself on reading the faces of her customers at the Taberna Azul but this young woman sat quietly, hands folded in her lap, so calm, so serene, so controlled. Estelle Reyes-Guzman could have been sitting at the table in the back of the *taberna*, those same hands holding four aces with a mounded pot, and she would have given away nothing.

Paulita opened her mouth to say something but stopped at the sound of footsteps in the hallway. They weren't the almost inaudible padding of a nurse's soft shoes, or the shuffle of a custodian guiding a dust mop, but were heavy and rapid.

Deputy Tom Pasquale appeared in the doorway. "Hey," he said by way of greeting and rested his hand on the doorjamb. He'd shed his firefighting gear and slipped into jeans and a T-shirt, incongruous with the black Sheriff's Department coat. "Mrs. Saenz, how are you?" Paulita let a nod suffice. Estelle saw the deputy's eyes quickly inventory the woman, from the lit cigarette to the outlines of things in the pockets of her own bulky coat. "Did you need me for anything?" the deputy asked, and Estelle realized that she was so tired she didn't really know the answer. The clock across the hall had ticked to 4:01 A.M.

"I don't think so, Tom. We're going to have to regroup after everybody gets some rest. The sheriff will be back, and we can see where we stand."

Pasquale nodded, still regarding Paulita Saenz.

"I appreciate your checking," Estelle said. "I think Mrs. Saenz and I are going to go on over to the county building and see her son for a few minutes."

"You're the one who arrested him," Paulita said to Pasquale, not bothering to add the "and it's all your fault" that her tone so clearly implied.

"Yes, ma'am," Tom Pasquale said.

"He had nothing to do with those two men."

Pasquale nodded, but said nothing.

"Do you know why he doesn't want to talk to me?"

"Not a clue," the deputy said. "Maybe he's afraid you're going to whup on him some." He smiled engagingly, but Paulita was in no mood to share the humor. Her lips pressed into a thin line.

"Maybe that's what I ought to do," she said.

"Mrs. Saenz, let's go over to the office," Estelle said. "Maybe we can straighten out a few things with Eurelio."

"Jackie's on the road," Tom Pasquale said as Estelle pushed herself to her feet. Jackie Taber was one of the few deputies who didn't

142

have a volunteer firefighter's rig hanging at the fire house. "She said she'd stay sort of central until everything quiets down."

"That's fine." She turned to Paulita Saenz. "Let me poke my head in and check on *mi mamá* one more time before I leave. I'll meet you right at the office by the dispatcher's desk in just a few minutes. Then we'll talk to Eurelio."

Paulita crushed out the cigarette. She gathered the makeshift ashtray and crumpling it carefully into a tight ball. "Now you—" She started to say, and stopped. Her face softened and she extended her free hand toward Estelle. "Teresa . . . she's in here?" She motioned with her head toward the ICU beyond the wall of the waiting room. "You didn't tell me that."

"She'll be fine," Estelle said. That wasn't the informative answer that Paulita obviously expected. Estelle touched the woman's waiting hand. "I'll just be a few minutes."

Tom Pasquale stepped out of the doorway to let her pass, and she squeezed his arm quickly. "Thank you." Her lips formed the silent words, and Tom nodded. "Did you get a chance to look at the information that the sheriff sent?"

"Haven't had a chance," Tom said. "I was thinkin' of doing that right now. How's Mrs. Pope, by the way?"

Estelle shook her head. "One in a million, maybe." The deputy grimaced. He watched Paulita Saenz as the woman made her way down the polished tile of the hallway.

"You're all right with her?"

"She's fine," Estelle replied.

"Apparently she was rip-roaring when she came into the office. Brent made the mistake of telling her where you might be. I chewed his ass for that."

"That's all right. She's a mom, you know. Moms go off the deep end now and then."

Tom Pasquale waved a hand in salute as Francis Guzman opened the door to the ICU and held it, obviously waiting for Estelle. "She's going to be all right?" the deputy asked. "I didn't know your mother was here."

"She'll be fine," Estelle said. "I'll be at the office in a few minutes.

You might hold Paulita's hand for a while until I get there so she doesn't have the chance to work herself up again."

"She'll pass out from the smell," Pasquale said, looking down at himself. "I need a shower."

"Not just you," Estelle laughed.

Other than the soft tick and hiss of machinery that ministered to Eleanor Pope, the ICU was silent. Standing at the foot of the hospital bed where Teresa Reyes slept peacefully, Estelle slipped her arm around her husband's waist and leaned her head against the heavy muscle of his upper arm.

"I'm not ready for this," Estelle whispered.

"Don't get yourself all worked up. She's doing a lot better," Francis said. "She really is. I want to make a change or two in her meds, and that's going to make a difference. She'll be back to her old self in a day or two."

Estelle sighed. "She's going to just keep getting older, isn't she?"

Francis laughed, quick to bite off the sound. He squeezed the base of Estelle's neck affectionately. "Good thing we aren't, huh."

"I feel about a hundred and six," Estelle said.

"But you're not going straight home to bed, are you?"

She ducked her head in resignation. "Sort of straight."

"Circuitously straight," Francis said, and swept the privacy curtain closed as they stepped away from the bed.

"And you don't think there's a chance that we'll be able to talk to Mrs. Pope later today?"

Francis paused with his hand on the door to the hallway. "Unlikely, *querida*. Unlikely today. Or any day. That would be my bet. Her system just isn't tough enough to take that kind of insult." He shrugged. "Of course, she may surprise us all. There's always that."

"I'm too tired for surprises," Estelle said. "But I'll take that one."

19

***

PAULITA Saenz had been sitting on one of the hard chairs in the foyer, perhaps expecting the undersheriff to enter the Public Safety Building through the front door instead of the side entrance that led directly into the dispatcher's domain. Whether alerted by the slight change in air pressure, the distant thud of the door, or the muffled voice of dispatcher Brent Sutherland greeting the undersheriff, Paulita turned and caught a glimpse of Estelle through the heavy glass of the dividers. She rose quickly and stood in front of her chair, hands clasped at her waist.

The deference now in her body language wasn't lost on Estelle. The undersheriff crossed behind Brent Sutherland's chair and opened the glass door that separated the dispatch console from the foyer. "Can you give me just a minute?" she said, and Paulita nodded. She turned as if to settle back in the chair, changed her mind and remained standing, her handbag resting on the chair's arm. "Thanks," Estelle said. "I won't be long."

Waiting was the order of the day, apparently. It seemed like a week had passed since Estelle had faxed her request to Sheriff Robert Torrez for information on the small gadget found in Eurelio's truck. His reply had been prompt, as if he'd been sitting by the machine at the Virginia end, waiting for something to do. The document now rested in Estelle's mailbox, where it had remained for most of the night. Estelle fished the paper out and unfolded it.

"Ernie Wheeler said to make sure that you saw that," Brent Sutherland said needlessly. Estelle glanced at the young deputy, expecting him to add something to the announcement that she needed to know. "I guess it came in sometime before midnight," Sutherland said lamely. "By the way, I'm sorry that I let that slip." Estelle saw his gaze flick out toward where Paulita Saenz waited.

"That's okay," Estelle said, her attention already back on the message. Bob Torrez's blocky printing surrounded the photocopied image of the small metal cylinder. Estelle could picture him in a lecture hall somewhere in downtown Quantico, Virginia, sitting in an auditorium seat with one of those awkward fold-down writing arms, one of two hundred sheriffs and sheriffs-to-be from around the country. She imagined his large frame scrunched up in the cramped seat, his fist clenched around his habitual felt-tipped pen. Down in front of the hall, an FBI specialist would be droning on about something wonderfully high-tech in the world of forensics, his lecture augmented by neat, colorful PowerPoint graphics projected onto a wide screen behind him. Sheriff Torrez wasn't listening.

Regardless of where the sheriff actually was, or what he was supposed to be doing, Posadas County was first in his thoughts— enough so that the new chain of events had sent him back to his motel room to pack after firing off his return fax. Estelle read his message, a smile deepening the wrinkles at the corners of her eyes as she did so. Robert Torrez was never happier than when he was hunting—and it didn't matter whether the quarry was wild game or people.

This item is a hammer spur extender for a lever-action rifle, probably a Marlin. It's usually supplied as an accessory by the manufacturer. It's fastened to the hammer with a set screw so that when a scope is mounted on the rifle, the hammer can still be cocked easily. Without it, there's not very much room between the body of the scope and the hammer spur for the shooter's thumb.

A drawing of what could have been a rifle hammer, a human thumb, and the tube of a telescopic sight followed. Estelle turned the

146

drawing this way and that. At the bottom of the page, Torrez had added:

This looks like a new piece, so I would bet that it's from a Marlin. Winchester uses something similar, but theirs is a little screw doohickey that threads right into the hammer. It's a lot smaller than this. Ask Howard if you want to see how one works. He has a Marlin .444 that he uses to miss elk with.

Estelle grinned and folded the paper so that she could slip it into the back of her notebook. "Ernie said that the sheriff was coming back early," Brent said.

"In about an hour, as a matter of fact," Estelle said without looking up. "Pop the main lockup corridor door for me, would you?" Sutherland reached over to the compact panel to the right of his desk and turned a large red switch. Off in the bowels of the building, they could hear the clang and draw of metal against metal.

Paulita Saenz still waited patiently in the foyer, and Estelle saw the woman jerk as the sound of the doors reached her. There would be a pang as the dismal sound reminded Paulita of exactly where her son was.

Estelle took another moment to pull a single, slender manila folder from the active case file cabinet. Eurelio Saenz's name had been printed on the label in Deputy Tom Pasquale's sprawling hand. She pushed the drawer closed. "We're going to be with Eurelio for a few minutes," Estelle said to the dispatcher. "His mother and I will just be in the corridor. No contact."

Sutherland looked up at the corridor monitor over his station. "He's our only guest at the moment," he said. "You don't want to use the conference room?"

Estelle shook her head. "No. We won't be that long." And there was something about the cold, passionless restraint of the steel cell bars that added to the ambiance, she knew—especially with an inexperienced kid. Sit at a nice mahogany table in a comfortable leather chair with your mom at your elbow, and there's always the tantalizing notion that you're going to go home if you arrange your lies just right.

She tapped the folder against her thumb for a minute, deep in thought, then turned and left dispatch. Paulita Saenz looked expectant as Estelle approached. Her gaze drifted down to the manila folder. "Let's find a quiet spot," Estelle said, and led the way to her own office just down the hall. She held the door until Paulita was inside, then closed it behind them.

"Before we talk to Eurelio, let me clarify some things for you, Mrs. Saenz." She nodded toward one of the large chairs beside her desk. "First of all, your son is over twenty-one."

Before Estelle could continue, Paulita's face scrinched up in a grimace. "I know what you're going to say," she said. "He's got to fight his own battles. He got himself into whatever mess this is, now he can get himself out." She nodded at Estelle as if to add "Am I right?"

Estelle set the manila folder carefully on top of several others that lay scattered across her desk, then sank into her own chair. She clasped her hands in front of her and leaned forward slightly.

"He's my son," Paulita said as the silence lengthened. "I have every right to know what's happening with him."

"Of course you do, Paulita," Estelle said. She took a deep breath. "Your son was arrested for driving an unregistered and uninsured vehicle, and later for suspicion of driving under the influence of alcohol." She reached over and opened the slender folder, thumbing the two single sheets of paper apart. "The deputy has also specified that there were open containers of alcoholic beverages in the vehicle when it was stopped."

She stopped and let the folder fall shut. "In this case, I really don't care about any of that, Mrs. Saenz." She leaned back in the chair. "If that was all that concerned us, your son would have been arraigned and probably released on his own recognizance, with a follow-up visit with the judge scheduled for later in the day." She shrugged and spread her hands. "That would have been that. And you and I wouldn't be sitting here in the middle of the night, wondering about what's going to happen to him."

"But that's not it, is it?" Paulita said.

"No, it's not." Estelle paused again. "Paulita . . ." She stopped, letting the single word hang all by itself for a few seconds. "Paulita, I'm worried about your son."

"This is the first time he's done something like this," Paulita said. "That old truck—usually it just sits, you know? Until a tire or something goes flat. He maybe uses it once or twice a year. Sometimes not even that."

"I don't care about the truck," Estelle said flatly, and Paulita looked surprised. "Your son knows something about the two men who were killed north of Maria. That's what worries me."

"No, he . . ." But Paulita stopped in midthought.

"Back at the hospital, you said that Eurelio didn't want to speak with you—that it was Tori Benevidez who told you that Eurelio was in jail. Didn't she mention the circumstances? Why wouldn't your son want you to know that he was in trouble?"

Paulita looked hurt and puzzled. "I don't know."

"I can think of a couple reasons," Estelle said. Her voice softened. "Maybe he doesn't want you to become involved in whatever trouble he's in. Maybe he thinks that he's protecting you from something."

"No," Paulita said, but then could go no further. Forehead wrinkled, she examined the edge of the desk. She lifted her hand and ran a finger along the polished wood. Estelle waited, seeing the understanding on the woman's face.

"Let me tell you what we found," Estelle said. "And then you tell me if we should be worried." When Paulita looked up, Estelle added, "That old truck . . . it was your husband's?"

Paulita nodded.

"Your son is the only one who drives it? That's what he told me."

"As far as I know. Maybe once in a while somebody else, but not often."

"Who might the 'somebody else' be?"

Paulita frowned. "Well . . ." And she paused. "I guess one of the boys borrowed it sometime last month. When they redid the roof across the street. They were throwing the old roofing down into the back of it so they could take it to the dump."

"One of the boys, Paulita?" Estelle said. "Was that Eurelio, you mean?"

"No, no. It would have been either Isidro or Benny Madrid. They were up here to do the roof on the service station for their father.

149

They put on new metal." She tapped a finger on the desk. "You were going to tell me what you found."

"Yes. The deputy found a cartridge casing in that truck, Mrs. Saenz. A recently fired shell casing. Eurelio says he's never seen it before, doesn't have any idea how it might have gotten in the truck, or when, or by who." She rested her chin in her hand. "I have two little boys of my own, Paulita. And when they're fibbing to me, I can tell. I'm sure that when Eurelio was little, you could do the same thing."

"Why would he lie about something like that?" Paulita said, but the answer was so obvious that it brought a pained expression to her face.

"We found another firearm-related item in the truck," Estelle said. "Eurelio denies any knowledge of that, too."

"Now all this you're telling me . . . all this. You're telling me that maybe my son has something to do with that awful business—those two dead men they found up on the prairie?" Paulita said. "That's what this is all about, then? Do you even have any idea who these two men are?"

"No, I don't." Estelle lifted her head off her hand. "I'd like to ask that you look at a couple of photos, though. You see people passing through Maria all the time. You know a lot of people. There's a chance." Estelle slipped a heavier folder out from under Eurelio's. "Will you look at them?"

"I guess so." Paulita's reluctance was understandable. The photos weren't for the faint of heart. Estelle saw the woman's jaw muscles twitch as Paulita clenched her teeth, hands rigid on the two eight-by-ten glossies.

"Jesús, Maria y . . ." she murmured, and then her voice trailed off. The massive head wounds and an indeterminate time out on the prairie would have made it difficult for John Doe's own mother to recognize him—perhaps the pattern of the hair line, the angle and arch of the one remaining eyebrow, the color of the hair would be familiar. Paulita looked longer at the morgue portrait of Juan Doe. The dirt had been cleaned from his face and hair.

Estelle watched Paulita's face. "You know them," she said when Paulita shuffled the pictures for the tenth time, as if trying to will the images to fade—or at least change into a couple of nameless strangers.

She held out a photo of the victim from the shallow grave. Estelle stretched across the desk and took it. "His name was Rafael. I remember that. I don't remember his last name. He and this other one . . ." She handed the rest of the photos across the desk. "They were like brothers. Rafael and . . ." She stopped, eyes closed. With a shake of her head, she added, "Maybe they were. I just don't remember. That one . . . Rafael? He did most of the talking when they stopped by. *Un verdadero payaso.* A real what-you-call-it."

"A comedian?"

"That's what he was," Paulita said and nodded vehemently. "He and his brother, they stopped at the *taberna,* I remember that. Before you know it, Rafael has us all in stitches. He reminded me of that guy who was so famous . . . the one with the small mustache who always did the funny bullfight scenes. He was in the movies all the time years ago, that clown."

"Contínflas?" Estelle prompted.

"That's the one."

Estelle looked the photo that lay on the blotter. Rafael hadn't died with a smile on his face. "These brothers . . . if that's what they were . . . they were from Mexico, then?"

"Sure. They were going to Mule Creek, up north there."

"Did they say why?"

"Rafael said that they were going to cut firewood on some big ranch up that way. He said that they were going to make a lot of money doing that. That they had at least a month's work, with room and board."

"When was this? Do you remember?"

"I don't know. It was after Christmas some time. I think that's when it was."

"So Rafael and his brother spent what, an evening? An evening at the *taberna*?"

"Yes."

"Do you recall who was there that evening?"

Paulita frowned and shook her head. "*Por Dios,* no." She looked at the photos again and shook her head sadly. *"Ay,"* she murmured. "I remember him doing a trick with whiskey tumblers . . . hands so fast. I couldn't figure it out. He made a few bets with that. I remember Eurelio crouching down so he could look along the table at eye level, you know. To see how Rafael did it . . ."

"So Eurelio *was* there."

Paulita looked startled. "I guess he was, then. And so were the boys."

"The boys?"

"Isidro and Benny."

Estelle sat quietly and watched the woman's face.

"They were there. That's right. Isidro was angry because Rafael won from him, oh, three, four times straight, and nobody could figure out the trick." She waved a finger in the air. "That's what it was."

"When Rafael and his companion left the *taberna,* Paulita . . . do you remember where they went? Were they driving their own car?"

"*That* I remember, and I know exactly why," Paulita said. "They had an old pickup truck. One of those square, really boxy things. It sagged in the middle, and when they started it up, the blue clouds were so thick they came in the *taberna.* One of the boys was standing in the doorway, and I had to shout at him to close the door. I remember we all laughed about that, too."

"Rafael was driving?"

"Yes. When they drove off, he was leaning out the window, beating on the door with his hand, trying to make the truck go faster."

"And that was the last you saw of them?"

"The last."

"Can you try to remember a date for me?"

"It was after Christmas, I know that. And New Year's." A recollection dawned on her as she looked up at the ceiling. "It was during that warm spell we had in early January. We had a week or so when we were all walking around in our shirt sleeves, wondering if the fruit trees were going to bloom."

Estelle nodded and tapped the photos into order before slipping them into the folder. "Mrs. Saenz, you've been so helpful. We need to talk to Eurelio. You say that he met these two that night. . . ." She rested her hand on top of the folder. "Maybe he'll remember something."

"What makes you think that he—"

Estelle shook her head. "I'm not thinking anything at the moment, Paulita. But yesterday evening, your son was in the area where the bodies were found, when he shouldn't have been. And he knew it. And he says that he has no idea how that cartridge casing got in the truck. The simple truth is that your son knows more than he's telling me."

Paulita's voice was almost inaudible. "How did they die? These two men," Paulita said. "I've heard a hundred crazy stories already. And I heard that the police are still diggin' up there, looking for more."

"They were both shot, Paulita. That's all I can tell you."

"And this bullet or whatever it was that you found in the old truck? That matches what you think happened?"

Estelle hesitated, then nodded.

"Eurelio hunts all the time."

"I imagine that he does."

"So . . ."

Estelle leaned forward. "There's something he's not telling us, Paulita." Mrs. Saenz frowned. "There's something that he doesn't want us to know, and something that he doesn't want you to know. That's why he didn't call you. That's what I think."

The undersheriff watched Paulita Saenz work that over in her mind for a few seconds.

"He knows something about the two dead men, Paulita."

20

♦♦♦

THE corridor door yawned open, and Paulita Saenz walked through with the small, hesitant steps that most civilians used when they first entered the cell area. By correctional standards, the detainment facility in the Posadas County Public Safety Building was miniature, with three small cells downstairs and two units upstairs for juveniles.

During the county building's remodeling and upgrading five years before, the architect had chosen a spiffy, off-white gloss finish for the brightly lighted cells and the metalwork that enclosed them. An improvement over the previous deck-gray finish, the cellblock still managed to look exactly like what it was: a jail.

Eurelio Saenz reclined across his cot in the center cell on the right, feet flat on the floor, the back of his head, neck, and shoulders against the smooth wall. His hands were shoved up to the second knuckle in his jeans pockets. A copy of *Field and Stream* rested on the blanket beside him, a not-so-subtle reminder that, were circumstances different, he could be other places, doing other things.

For ten minutes, Estelle knew, the young man had been sitting there, waiting for something to happen. The clanging as the corridor door slid open ten minutes before would have echoed through his cell. Had he been looking that way, he would have seen the bars gliding open. He would have sat there, expecting to hear footsteps on the polished concrete, waiting for the electric bolts of *his* door to rack open.

Eventually, he did hear footsteps. He looked up, saw his mother, and turned his head away, disgusted. Still moving as if she were walking on small stepping stones laid across a deep scummy pond, Paulita advanced to a point directly in front of the cell door. Eurelio pushed himself away from the wall, shrugging himself to an upright sitting position on the edge of the bed, hands still scrunched in his pockets.

Paulita regarded him silently for a moment. "You remember Rafael and his friend," she said.

Eurelio's gaze flicked first to her, and then to Estelle. "What are you talking about?"

"They found them. Those men that were killed, out there on the prairie? That was Rafael, the one with all the jokes and tricks. He and his brother."

"So?"

"So? That's all you have to say, is *so*?"

"What do you want me to say, *Mamá?*" Eurelio snapped. "I don't know anything about that. Me and Tori were just out having a beer. That's all."

"I don't mean tonight," Paulita said. "And you know we don't mean tonight, *hijo*."

Estelle moved close to the bars. "Come here a minute, Eurelio," she said. The young man remained on the cot. "Come here," she repeated. "I want you to see something." He turned his head sideways as he rose off the cot, his expression plainly saying that this was going to be the extent of his cooperation. Estelle held up a plastic evidence bag so that he could see it. "This is the shell casing we found on the floor of the truck, Eurelio. It's a forty-four magnum. It's fresh."

"I don't know nothing about that."

"So you said earlier." She held a second bag up for him to see, smoothing the plastic so that the hammer extender was plainly visible. "This was behind the seat of your truck, Eurelio. You see what it is, don't you?"

"How am I supposed to know what that is?" His eyes said otherwise.

"With a lever action rifle like a Marlin forty-four it's hard to cock with a scope, isn't it?" He frowned. "So this little gadget attaches to the hammer, and makes it easy. But sometime not too long ago, this little gadget fell off that rifle. Maybe while it was resting in the rifle rack behind the seat of your truck. Maybe while you were using it."

Eurelio grunted a derisive little puff of breath.

"Or maybe someone else was using that rifle, Eurelio. Maybe that could be it. Maybe when they borrowed your truck."

"No one's borrowed that truck," he said.

"Is that right?"

"Yeah. That's right."

"Did Isidro or Benny Madrid borrow it, maybe?"

"Why would they?"

Estelle looked at him for a long minute. He couldn't meet her gaze, and he avoided looking at his mother as well. When the cell was so quiet they could hear the tick of water in the pipes, Estelle said, "I thought maybe they might have used it last month when they put the new roof on their father's place across the street."

"Maybe they did. I don't know." This time, Eurelio shot a quick glance at his mother.

Contemplating the brass shell casing, Estelle said, "It's a beautiful finish for fingerprints." She looked at Eurelio. "You know what's going to happen if we process the prints on this and find a match to you, don't you?"

"You process all you want," Eurelio said. "That ain't mine."

Estelle slipped the two small evidence bags back into the folder she'd been carrying. "When Rafael was in the *taberna* with his companion back in early January, did you have a chance to talk with him much?"

"Who's Rafael?"

"Eurelio!" Paulita Saenz snapped, and braced her hands on her hips, elbows forward, chin pugnacious. "What is wrong with you, *hijo?* You don't even know what kind of trouble you're really in, and you play like this wise guy . . ." She glared at her son. Estelle watched them, wondering if the expression on Eurelio's face would crack if the cell door opened. The polished, sanitary bars provided a convenient bulwark between the young man and his mother's temper.

Paulita reached out and rapped her knuckle against a crossbar on the door. "You tell the sheriff what she needs to know, before you get into trouble that's over your head."

"Rafael and his companion stopped at the *taberna* one night in January, Eurelio," Estelle prompted. "Apparently Rafael was something of an entertainer. He won a few bets, showed some sleight of hand feats, had everybody—including you—laughing."

"Yeah. So?"

"So you remember now?"

"Sure, I remember."

"Do you remember the other one's name? Rafael's companion?"

Eurelio's eyebrows twitched. "Juan," he said, and smirked. He returned Estelle's impassive gaze for a moment, then looked away. "It really was Juan."

"Rafael and Juan. Surname?"

"I don't know."

"Were they brothers?"

"I don't know that, either."

"Did they ever say where they were from?"

"Not that I remember."

"And you didn't ask . . ."

Eurelio shrugged and said nothing.

"Were the Madrid brothers there that night?"

"They might have been. I don't know. They're around often enough. They could have been."

"You don't remember for sure?"

He shook his head, avoiding his mother's glare.

"*I* remember they were there," Paulita said. "And if an old lady like me can remember, then you can, too."

Eurelio ignored his mother and said to Estelle, "I don't remember for sure whether they were there or not. They might have been."

"Do you remember Rafael and Juan mentioning where they were headed after they left Maria?"

"Somewheres up north to cut wood for a couple weeks. I don't know where."

"They were headed to Mule Creek," Paulita prompted.

"If you say so," Eurelio shrugged.

"Eurelio, when's the last time you saw the Madrid brothers?"

157

"What, you mean in Maria?"

"Anywhere."

"I guess I saw them last week. In Asunción. That's where they're workin'."

Estelle tried to picture the tiny Mexican village, but too many years had slipped by. "What do they do there?"

"They were rebuilding the fountain in the square," Eurelio said. "And now there's a whole bunch of new shops going in there. They got a job working on those."

"Were Rafael and Juan from Asunción, too?"

"I don't know. I already said that."

"What were you doing down in Asunción, *hijo?*" his mother asked. He studiously ignored her.

"I guess maybe we'll have a chat with Isidro and Benny. It'd be interesting to see what they remember," Estelle said. She held the folder with both hands and took a deep breath. "The deputy will be around before long to schedule your arraignment with Judge Hobart, Eurelio. The judge may want to see you right away this morning, or it may be a day or two. I'm going to recommend that you be released on your own recognizance until that time." She smiled faintly. "Of course, Judge Hobart may have different ideas." She started to turn away. "If you should remember anything else that you think I should know, don't hesitate."

Paulita stood rooted, even as her son returned to the cot. "Your father would have been so ashamed by all this," she said.

"What, that I had a beer while I was driving his old truck?"

Anxious that the final conversation didn't degenerate into a shouting match, Estelle touched Paulita's elbow, ushering her back up the corridor. Brent Sutherland had been paying attention. As soon as the two women had stepped through the passageway, the heavy door slid shut behind them. Estelle held the solid hallway door for Paulita.

"He'll be all right," she said. "He has to figure all this out for himself first." She glanced at the wall clock. "The deputy will process him in a few minutes. That will give him a little while to be alone with his thoughts."

"He's been such a good kid," Paulita said. "He's never been involved in anything before."

"He's still a good kid," Estelle said. "He just needs some time to realize that he is."

Paulita Saenz paused in the foyer. "What should I do?"

"You should go home and get some sleep, Mrs. Saenz. This will all sort itself out."

"And your mother?"

The question caught Estelle off guard, but there was something in Paulita Saenz's face—perhaps the understanding of a perfect bartender—that prompted her to reply as she did. "My mother wants to visit her home in Mexico one more time."

Paulita reached out and touched Estelle on the wrist. "And you're going to do that for her?"

"Yes."

Paulita nodded vehemently. "Good," she said with finality. "Don't you be putting that off."

"No, ma'am," Estelle said. "I'm not going to put it off."

21

THE hand on her shoulder was gentle but insistent. Estelle pressed her eyes tightly shut, blocking out the artificial daylight from the hallway. "Your mother would like to talk with you," the voice said. "Are you awake?" Estelle cracked one eye and saw the blurry form bending over her.

"What time is it?"

"Six-thirty," the voice said.

Estelle groaned and burrowed her face in the folded jacket that had served as a pillow. "I'll be there in a minute," she said. "Thanks." The hard vinyl couch in the hospital's ICU waiting room hadn't been the most comfortable bed in the world, but it had been efficient. Her cellular phone and radio rested on the small end table, on top of a pile of months-old *Family Circle* magazines. The radio was turned off, and the phone had been mercifully silent for the past two hours.

Estelle swung her feet down and sat upright, rocking her head to relieve the crick in her neck. Her husband had been right, of course. Her own bed in her own home would have been a marvelous luxury, a tonic. She might have been able to sleep the morning away as Irma Sedillos, the ever skillful *nana,* guided the ruckus of the two small boys away from their mother's bedroom.

She sighed and reached across for the phone and radio. A small yellow note was pasted to the radio's leather holster. She peeled it off and held it to the light from the hallway, immediately recognizing

160

Tom Pasquale's scrawl. "ES ROR'd 5:15," the note read. "Mears wants to talk to you whenever."

"Whenever," Estelle said, and shook her head to clear the cobwebs. One of the nurses must have whispered in to leave the note. Had Tom Pasquale delivered it in person, he would have braked to an embarrassed halt in the waiting room doorway and said, loudly enough to awaken her, "Oh . . . are you asleep?"

She stood up and shrugged her clothes straight. She'd apparently slept like a stone, since neither her jeans nor the sweatshirt were wrinkled beyond what one would expect after catnapping on the ICU couch. Earlier, she had slipped home for a wonderful fifteen minutes under the shower, trying to rinse the acrid fire residue out of her hair. It would have been so easy to doze off right there, among the clouds of steam. But she had returned to the hospital, stretched out on the couch for just a moment, and fallen asleep. She shook out her jacket, clipped both radio and phone to her belt, and then paused at the small mirror by the door.

"We've never met," she said to her image, and ran her fingers through thick, tangled black hair until the stuff sat on her head roughly the way it was supposed to. She turned away with a sigh.

The night shift ICU supervisor looked up and smiled brightly as Estelle entered the unit. "Sleep some?"

"Too much," Estelle said, recognizing the voice that awakened her. "Thanks for coming to get me, Julie."

"You probably could have used another twelve hours or so," Julie Castañon said. "Your mother's been awake since about five, raring to go."

"Is Francis still here?"

"Been, gone, returned. He's down in the ER right now. Something about a two-year old, a vacuum cleaner, and a broken toe."

"All in the middle of the night," Estelle said. "As an old friend of mine is fond of saying, 'humans are interesting critters.' " She ran the fingers of both hands through her collar-length hair again and started around the nurses' island.

"I think that Dr. Guzman planned to take your mother home just as soon as he was finished down in the ER," Julie said. "He was going to let you sleep until he was finished."

Estelle nodded her thanks. "And Mrs. Pope?"

The nurse's face crumpled with sympathy. "She's stable, but that's the best I can say."

The privacy curtains were drawn around Eleanor Pope's bed, and Estelle slipped her hand around the end, lifting the white fabric just enough to slip through. The woman lay as before, jaw slack, eyes half-lidded, each breath coming as a major victory. Moving close to the bedside, Estelle took the older woman's left hand in hers, letting it lie flat on top of her own.

Whatever other health problems had plagued the woman, Eleanor Pope had been blessed with a strong pair of hands. Her skin was rough from the demands of garden and livestock. Bright red polish decorated fingernails that were rough and broken.

Estelle gently rolled the woman's hand palm up, seeing the calluses on each stubby finger. It wasn't hard to imagine those hands wrenching a hay bale off the pile, clipping the wire, and prying off a flake for each waiting pet—or temporary tenant. The old, worn-out, oxygen-starved body behind the hands was the problem, and Estelle could imagine Eleanor Pope puffing for breath as she waddled from stall to stall. When simply opening a can of cat food was a chore, tending a single donkey would be a monumental task. Running a donkey motel would have been far beyond Eleanor Pope's endurance. Denton "Woody" Pope must have helped with the daily chores.

"I wish you could talk to me," Estelle whispered. She squeezed Eleanor's hand gently. "But you're somewhere else now, aren't you?" The hand remained unresponsive. She felt a presence at her elbow and turned to see Julie Castañon. The nurse stretched over the bed and straightened an imaginary kink in the oxygen tube.

"Just a good rest," she said softly. "That's what she needs." At the same time, she glanced first at Estelle and then at the cardiac monitor, shaking her head. She patted Eleanor's shoulder, standing for a moment at the bedside as her fingertips kneaded the woman's ashen flesh with affection.

Once well away from the woman's bedside, Julie lowered her voice so that Estelle almost had to read her lips. "Being alone must be the hardest part," Julie said. "Maybe they can hear what we say to them, maybe not." She smiled again. "It's a challenge to stay optimistic, isn't it?" She moved toward the other end of the ICU, toward Teresa Reyes's bed. "I don't know how you do it, sheriff," she said.

"How I do what?"

"Stay optimistic. With all the things that you see."

"Sometimes I don't," Estelle said, and let it go at that, feeling too disheveled and weary to wax philosophical.

When the curtain parted, the first thing she saw was her mother carefully coiling up the oxygen tube around knobby, arthritic fingers.

"Aquí," her mother said to Julie Castañon, and she handed the tube to her. *"Es una lata."* she added, and Julie looked at Estelle, not following the rapid Spanish.

"She says it's a nuisance," Estelle said, and then switched to Spanish. "You should wait to see what Francis says, *Mamá.*"

"He's a nuisance too, that *oso,*" Teresa replied. She pushed herself up on one elbow and swung tiny feet over the side of the bed, barely giving Julie enough time to release the side rail. With a grimace she sat up straight, the thin hospital gown hanging like a tent around her tiny body.

Julie started to say something, but Teresa waved her away. "I'm fine," she said in English. "Leave me with my daughter."

"Don't you do too much, now," Julie said, and then to Estelle, "Call if you need anything. I'll check with Dr. Guzman to see how long he's going to be."

Teresa Reyes's black eyes watched the nurse as she left, and Estelle saw the crows' feet at their corners deepen. "She's a good girl," Teresa said, once more in Spanish. "She worries too much all the time, though."

"She's concerned about you, *Mamá.*"

"Well I am, too," Teresa said. "You look like you've been up all night, *Estelita.*"

"I have. We've got a real mess on our hands."

"The lady next to me?"

Estelle nodded. "That's part of it."

"She's gone, you know."

"I know, *Mamá.*"

"How's Carlos?"

"He's fine." Teresa looked sideways at her as if to say, "How do you know?" "Irma is with the boys. She said she'd stay with them until we get you home."

"That's today," Teresa said with surprising force. "There are places to hate, and this place tops my list." The sentence was almost too long for her air supply, and she straightened up and tried to take a deep breath. "It doesn't smell good around this place."

"You want to lie back down?"

"I think so."

"Did Francis say that you should wear the oxygen tube?" Estelle asked as Teresa settled back against the pillow.

"Of course he did."

"Well, then . . ." She slipped the oxygen tube around her mother's head. "It's no big deal, *Mamá*. It helps you breath, is all."

"I don't like it in my nose."

"There aren't too many other choices, *querida*."

Teresa chuckled, a dry, thin little sound. "So, are you going to take me home, or is Irma?"

"I'm going with you."

Teresa closed one eye, the other holding her daughter's gaze with amusement. "You can't afford the time, can you?" Before Estelle could answer, Teresa added, "but I feel like being selfish just now."

"It's not being selfish, *Mamá*."

"Oh, yes," the old woman said, and closed her eyes. "There's always something, I know that." She lay quietly, eyes still closed, Estelle's hand gripped tightly in hers. "It will be interesting to see what becomes of the boys."

"I'm not sure the world's ready for them."

"Well, it better *get* ready," Teresa said. She opened her eyes. "Time goes by so quickly, eh? It always surprises me."

"All of us, *Mamá*."

"No, in your case, you've got so much to do, all the time, day and night. You and that husband of yours. But me, what do I do? Still, the time just slips away so fast." She smiled at Estelle. "And if I don't visit Tres Santos today or tomorrow, I never will. And that's the truth. And I know it to *be* the truth." She squeezed Estelle's hand. "So I want to be a little bit selfish, *Estelita*."

164

"I'll talk to Francis as soon as he's out of the emergency room, *Mamá*. And then we'll go. Maybe right after lunch."

"That would be fine." Teresa raised her right hand, thumb up. "But no *maybes*. I might be standing out by the road like this. What do you call it?"

"Hitchhiking. Let me get my camera before you do that."

Teresa Reyes frowned with mock seriousness. "And don't you think I won't."

"You won't have to, *Mamá*." With a head shake of irritation, Estelle realized that she had been calculating how long the drive would take round-trip, how long they could afford to stay there, maybe visiting with neighbors . . . In short, how she could squeeze into a frenetic day a single monumental favor to her mother. "I look forward to going there with you. Do you want the boys to go along?"

"Tres Santos means nothing to them, *querida*. No, this time I want to be selfish. Just the two of us." She lifted her head off the pillow and stroked her chin as if deep in thought. "And maybe we don't have to take the police car, eh?"

Estelle laughed. "I'll leave the radio at home, *Mamá*. No one will be able to reach us."

"You know that's not true," Teresa said ruefully, and Estelle nodded with resignation.

"Bob Torrez is on his way back from Virginia, so maybe things will quiet down a little," Estelle said.

Teresa sniffed. "What difference will that make, *Estelita?* But maybe no one will tell him where you went."

The cellular phone on Estelle's belt chirped, and as she reached for it, Teresa said, "There. You see? They always know." She listened to the cryptic conversation, and when Estelle folded the gadget to put it away, Teresa said, "Right after lunch, then?"

"Right after lunch, *Mamá*."

"So, you're leaving now?"

"I have to. Just for a little bit. Francis will be back up in a few minutes."

"What do they want?" Teresa nodded at the phone.

"Interesting developments," Estelle said.

"And aren't they always?"

165

A few minutes later, as Estelle passed by on her way out of the unit, Julie Castañon paused with one hand on Eleanor Pope's privacy curtain. "Nice to see you," she whispered to Estelle. "Your mom is doing better, isn't she?"

"Much," Estelle replied. "We'll take her off your hands as soon as Francis is finished up."

"I wish I spoke better Spanish," Julie said. "She's so interesting to talk to. I wish I had the time just to sit down with her for a morning and listen to her."

"Me, too," Estelle said.

22
◆◆◆

Sergeant Tom Mears knelt in the middle of the rubble, feet close together on a two-by-twelve plank that had been laid across the mobile home's ruined floor. He pointed with the dark end of his flashlight as Estelle approached one cautious step at a time along the plank, shading her eyes against the first blast of early morning sun.

"You can step right there," he said, pointing at a small section of floor that had been directly in front of the propane heater. The flames had blistered the vinyl, but the small section of floor was still intact.

"You want me to find another bridge?" Tom Pasquale said from below, where he'd been standing with Linda Real and Dennis Collins.

"This is fine," Estelle said. She reached Mears and knelt down beside him. He held up a plastic evidence bag.

"This is what Denton had in his right hand," he said. "I thought at first that it was a screwdriver, but it's not. It's an awl." He handed the bag to Estelle, and she took it, careful not to push the point of the tool through either the small piece of cardboard that had been taped over its tip, or through the plastic bag. The tool was short, no more than three inches in the shank. Despite his chronic complaints about his bifocals, Bill Gastner had called it right. She grinned.

"What?" Mears asked.

"Nothing." She looked up at him. "So what was he using it for?"

"This is kind of interesting," Mears said. "You're going to have to

167

scrunch over here to see, 'cause the light's still not very good with all this crap obstructing the view." He pointed at the remains of the flexible steel feed line that had was attached to the propane heater's control valve. "This comes . . . or used to come, I should say . . . from the solid galvanized pipe that leads in from outside," he said. "The solid pipe came through the wall, and then there's a shutoff valve, and then this flex pipe." He sat back on his haunches, tapping the butt of the flashlight absently on the remains of the floor.

"The initial point of explosion was right inside the stove. That's interesting, too, but look at this first." Holding the torn end of the flex pipe gingerly with one hand, he pulled it up toward them, holding his light in his other hand. "Look about three inches from the stove end," he said.

By crouching low on her hands and knees, Estelle could move close to the pipe. At 7 a.m. with the sun still low, the fire scene was a mass of black shadows, one overlaid over another. She brought the flashlight close to the metal. "I'm not sure what I'm seeing."

"It looks like what Denton did was try to wedge the awl between the ridges of the flex pipe."

"Here?"

"Right."

"Why would he want to do that?"

"For one thing, he probably thought that it might be the easiest place to make a leak."

Estelle straightened her elbows and sat back on her haunches. "A leak."

"That's what it looks like. Not a huge hole or anything, but it looks like he managed to worry a pretty good opening."

"So what's the theory? That he thought the place would fill with propane fumes, and then, when the stove thermostat kicked it on, boom?"

"Well, that's interesting," Mears said. He let the flex pipe rest back on the remains of the floor. "That's *maybe* what he had in mind. But I don't think he wanted to leave anything to chance. This is kind of neat." He started to shift position, then took the evidence bag from Estelle and held it out toward Tom Pasquale. "Take this, please?" he said, and tossed the bag the short distance over the side of the ruined wall of the trailer to the deputy.

He pointed at the heater. "See this area here? That's just an empty space under the unit, right under the burners. Propane flows through the burner pipe across the front of the stove, the pilot ignites it, and all the heat goes up and out the chimney. During the best of times." He grinned at Estelle. "There's normally a decorative skirt around the bottom of the stove. Keeps us from having to look at all the dust underneath." He reached across and picked up a bent and twisted piece of metal. "This is the skirt." He handed it to Estelle. "And this is what used to be one of those disposable turkey basting pans." He pulled the crumpled, roasted aluminum from its place under the stove. The pan was no more than a wisp of its original shape.

"Linda has pictures of all this?" Estelle said.

"Of course," Mears replied. "Color, black-and-white, and video. Which is good, because this is the payoff here." He held the thin, blackened shard of aluminum to his nose. "The gasoline that he happened to have was for his string trimmer or lawn mower," he said. "Something that uses an oil-gas mix. Lots of oil in that, and a real characteristic smell. The lab will tell us the whole story, right down to the brand . . . probably even the refinery that made it."

"You lost me. He put gasoline in the pan? In this turkey basting pan?"

"I will bet my next week's pay that's what he did."

"Whoa," Estelle said softly.

"Why would he use an awl to wedge a hole in the propane line? So the house would be full of fumes, and when the thermostat clicked on, boom. With a nice pan of gasoline underneath, add another couple quarts of fuel to the explosion."

Estelle frowned. "I don't understand."

"Neither did old Denton," Mears said.

"No. The pilot light is always lit, isn't it? It burns all the time?"

"Sure."

"Then how could he put a pan of gasoline underneath the burners? Wouldn't the open flame of the pilot ignite it the second he did that?"

"In fact, the odds are good that it wouldn't. I tried it a few minutes ago and couldn't get a flat pan of gas to ignite until I flipped the match right in the liquid. You can drop a cigarette in a pan of gas all day, and most of the time, it won't ignite. The butt just drowns. It's a real *don't try this at home, kids* kind of stunt. And in this case, the pilot light is nearly a foot above the floor, so it's almost that far above the pan of gasoline." Mears scrunched up his face in wry humor. "What old Denton maybe didn't know is that propane isn't like natural gas—it's heavier than air, so it sinks. Turn on the propane, and just cover that pan of gasoline in a nice blanket of propane vapors. He made a bigger bomb than he thought."

"I can't believe he'd do something so stupid," Estelle muttered.

"Well, actually, if you're a gambler, it was a pretty good plan, up to a point," Mears said. "The pan of gasoline makes a nice afterburner. The leaking propane gently fills the place for the main bang. He could turn the thermostat down so that the house was kind of cool. His mother comes home late from bingo, feels the chill, and toddles back to the thermostat to jar it up a notch. She's even carrying an oxygen bottle, I'm told. That would make a neat torch."

"You're saying he wanted to kill his mother," Estelle said.

"Well, he sure as hell wanted to burn the place down," Mears said. "Whether he wanted an added homicide or not is conjecture. Then, I'm thinking that he could have turned the thermostat down. If he wanted a delayed explosion, he's going to have to do that, otherwise the stove would light. That would have made sense if he wanted to kill his mother. He was looking for an opportunity. Maybe she called him after winning bingo and told him she'd be home late. So that was his chance. He could set the thing up, then go out to a bar someplace, and wait for the bad news. With a good explosion, maybe he figured the odds of finding his tampering were small. Old heater, history of complaints—we've even got a contractor neighbor across the street who worried about the thing." He shrugged.

"But . . ." Estelle said.

Mears pushed his fire helmet back on his head. "Yep, there's a but." He stood up carefully and turned. "The wall with the thermostat used to be here," he said, drawing an imaginary wall in the air over the charred wall studs. "This," and he bent and pointed the flashlight at a misshapen piece of plastic, "was a thermostat." He took out his ballpoint pen and pointed with it. "It's hard to see, but the dial indicator appears to be pointing at the ninety-degree mark."

"That doesn't make any sense," Estelle said. She peered closely at the melted thermostat. "Why would *he* turn it up? If the furnace came on while he was standing there, even if the propane didn't have very long to leak, wouldn't there be an explosion? At the very least, wouldn't the gasoline in the basting pan ignite?"

"Exactly."

"And so?"

"The only thing that makes sense to me is that Denton wheedled the hole in the flex pipe with his little awl there, made sure the propane was flowing, and then slid the pan of gas-oil mix into place. He turned one last time to check the thermostat to make sure it was low enough."

"Oh, no," Estelle said, knowing exactly what had happened. "He turned it the wrong way."

"And turned it the wrong way." Mears grinned at Estelle, his teeth impossibly white against his smudged face. "He might even have had a millisecond of horror when he realized his mistake and just couldn't stop his hand in time."

"This reminds me of a guy up in Minnesota. He built a fire out of old boards between his hot water heater and the outside wall to keep the water pipes from freezing during a cold snap," Estelle said.

Mears shrugged, still smiling. "Sometimes things *seem* like a pretty good idea at the time." He turned back toward the remains of the heater. "Todd Paul from the State Fire Marshal's office said he'd be here by eight this morning at the latest. That gives us an hour. I'll be interested to hear what he has to say."

"You're confident that the fire did start here, though."

"Oh, yes. A thousand percent."

"If that's the way it worked, then Denton took the time to open all the animals' stalls and cages *before* he came back inside to mess with the furnace."

"A soft touch with the beasts," Mears said. "Roasted mom is one thing, but he didn't want fried donkey on his conscious."

Estelle grimaced. She looked across the wreckage at Tom Pasquale. "We need to find out who Eleanor had home owner's insurance with, for one thing," she said.

171

"And life insurance while you're at it," Mears added. "If Denton just wanted to burn the place down, maybe he was after the fire insurance. If he wanted to kill his mother in the bargain, maybe there was some life insurance to be had. That's unless Denton Pope was a really creative kind of guy and had some grand scheme that we haven't even imagined."

"Oh, he was creative, all right," Estelle said, and shook her head in wonder. "Creative . . . and really, really stupid." She stepped away from the wrecked furnace. "We're going to have to be creative, too," she said. "Eleanor Pope's not going to tell us much . . . if she survives the day. We need to find who she confides in. A good place to start is the three ladies who were with her at the Don Juan earlier."

"I can do that," Collins said.

"All right. As soon as the sheriff hits town, I'll bring him up to speed on all this. And then I'll be out of service this afternoon for a few hours."

"Sleep, huh," Mears laughed.

"No. Mexico. My mom wants to take a quick run down to Tres Santos. I'm going to take her down there, and try to touch bases with Captain Naranjo at the same time." She started to make her way back along the plank, and then stopped. "And by the way, Tom, did Eurelio Saenz say anything more to you this morning when he was released?"

"Just looked smug," Pasquale said. "His girlfriend picked him up."

"Well, we'll try and un-smug him. You got my note about the hammer spur thingy?"

Pasquale nodded. "Tony Abeyta was going to see what he could find out about recent sales of similar type weapons. It's a long shot, but we might get lucky. How many Marlin forty-four magnums could there be jumping off the shelves in this part of New Mexico?"

"Luck is what we need at this point," Estelle said. She turned to Mears, nodding at the wreckage of the furnace. "Nicely done. I'll be really curious to hear about the insurance angle. I can't imagine what else would have been on Denton's mind."

"The furnace is what he ended up with," Mears said.

23

SERGEANT Howard Bishop handed the short rifle to Estelle. "Right there," he said, and pointed at the hammer with an enormous index finger. She rolled the rifle sideways, looking at the cylindrical cocking device attached to the hammer. She didn't need to look at the piece in the evidence bag to know they were identical.

"And how old is this rifle?" she asked.

"I bought it a couple years ago," Bishop said. His big frame was perched on the corner of Sheriff Robert Torrez's desk. He breathed with occasional grunts, as if his huge belly was pinching his lungs.

Torrez, who had been back in Posadas for less than 30 minutes after a night as sleepless as the rest of his staff, sat heavy-lidded in his swivel chair, watching his undersheriff examine the rifle. Estelle pulled the lever down and saw the rifle's bolt draw rearward from the empty chamber, cocking the hammer. Sure enough, the hammer spur cleared the bottom of the telescopic sight by a fraction of an inch— not enough for a thumb's clearance if the weapon was cocked and the shooter wished to lower the hammer and still leave a shell in the chamber. The small cocking extension projected sideways, away from the body of the scope, allowing convenient access to the hammer.

After glancing inside the action, Estelle closed the lever, then used the extension to gently lower the hammer as she pulled the trigger. She rocked the cylinder with her thumb, frowning.

"And that one's loose, I see," Bishop said. He turned and grinned at the silent Torrez.

"It wouldn't be unusual for one to fall off, then," Estelle said.

"Easiest thing in the world," Bishop replied.

She handed him the rifle. "And these are made in forty-four magnum as well as whatever this is?"

Bishop nodded. "Correcto."

"Who's doing the weapon trace?" Torrez asked. He leaned his head back against the chair, folding his hands over his belly.

"Abeyta."

He nodded slowly. "What if Eurelio really didn't know that the shell casing was in the truck? Or that cocker doohickey either."

"Then someone else used the truck."

"Uh-huh. There's a pretty simple scenario that would explain a lot of this," he said. "From all I've ever heard, Eurelio's a pretty law-abiding kid. If he's as nervous about all this as you guys say he is . . . how about this. What if Eurelio purchased the rifle, and then sold it to someone else who turned out to be the shooter. . . ."

"He's got to be thinking he's in deep, deep trouble," Estelle said.

"Which he is," Torrez added. "I don't think there were hundreds and hundreds of those rifles sold around these parts in the past year or so. Find a rifle, it'll be real easy to match the fired shell casing. The bolt face and firing pin will leave a real individual print in the primer face." He looked at Estelle quizzically. "What's bothering you?"

"I can imagine Eurelio going to Albuquerque or Cruces, or some place like that to buy a rifle, and I can imagine him selling it to a friend—even a friend from Mexico. I'm sure it happens all the time. But I agree with Pasquale. When Eurelio came up to the crime scene with Marvin Hudson, we think he already knew what had happened. Maybe not the details, but he knew there'd been a killing. At the very least, that's what he guessed."

"Easy guess, Estelle. Why else would there have been a gathering of cops out there? You either have a homicide or a plane crash."

"But Eurelio knew."

"That's just an impression," Torrez said.

"Yes."

"A Tom Pasquale impression at that," he added, and a ghost of a

174

smile touched his heavy face. "Taking his girlfriend up there last night might have been a pretty natural thing for Eurelio to do, anyway," Torrez said. "Everybody's talking about it, he'd already been up there and knew the layout. Take along the girl and impress the hell out of her." He pursed his lips. "Natural as can be. Or he could be taking the opportunity to look for something that got left behind. There's all kinds of possibilities."

He put his big hands on the arms of his chair and pushed himself to his feet. "Okay, so who's doing what?"

Estelle held up her left hand, hooking her little finger with her right index. "Abeyta is looking into recent firearms sales that might give us a match. Collins is going to find out if Eleanor Pope had home owner's insurance as well as life insurance."

"How's he doing, by the way?"

"Collins? He's doing okay. He's eager."

"Keep the directions simple," Bishop said dryly.

Estelle held up her hand again. "Mears is working the fire scene with Todd Paul, when Paul gets here from Santa Fe. I'm going to be talking with Tomás Naranjo this afternoon. He might be able to help us out with IDing the two victims. Paulita Saenz says they were from Mexico, going up north to cut wood."

"You're running out of fingers," Torrez said.

"I know it," Estelle said with a grin. "It's a great time for someone to rob Posadas National Bank, that's for sure. Anyway, Paulita remembers the two men mentioning that they were cutting wood up around Mule Creek, and there's no reason to suspect that she'd make that up. I was going to ask Jackie Taber if she'd work that angle."

"Let me do that," Torrez said. "I've hunted up in Grant County a few times, and know a few folks. It'll give me something to do. You said that the nearest thing we have to a name is *Rafael*?"

"Correct. Rafael and Juan."

"And while all this is happening, who's sitting on young Mr. Eurelio?"

"I was going back down to Maria this morning for a little while," Estelle said. "A couple of names came up in all this mess. The Madrid brothers?"

"Oh, *sí*," Torrez said with a resignation that surprised Estelle.

"You know them?"

"Oh, *sí,*" he repeated.

"Apparently, they were working earlier in the winter, putting a new roof on the gas station for their father."

"*Working* is the interesting word," Torrez said. "Their mother, Lucy, owns that little diner just around the corner from Wally's place. Wally and Lucy haven't spoken to each other in a lifetime."

"They're divorced?"

"Sort of. *Apart* might be more accurate. Benny and Isidro live in old Mexico. Last I heard, down in Asunción or someplace like that. They drift back and forth across the border when the opportunity presents itself. Or when they want to hit *Mamá* up for a few bucks."

"They were working in Asunción," Estelle said. "That's what Paulita told me. And they were in the *taberna* the night that the two nationals stopped there. Rafael and his partner."

Torrez reached down and flipped open the manila folder. He stood with his head down, looking hard at the faces of the two victims. "Huh," he said finally, and flipped the folder closed. "These two guys work for a month in Mule Creek, earn some pretty good money, and head for home. You suppose it's ever happened before? Somebody with a good wad of bills flashes his money in a bar and gets rolled for his efforts when he walks outside?"

"About as common as dirt," Bishop said. "What happened to their vehicle, by the way?"

"That's part of the puzzle," Estelle said. "The last time Rafael and Juan were seen was when they drove away from the *taberna* on their way north, supposedly to Mule Creek. We don't know what happened after that."

Bishop looked resigned. "Anything you want me to work on?" he said, glancing first at Estelle and then at the sheriff.

"Actually, it'd be good if we had one officer who was freed up to do a little law enforcement," Torrez said. Bishop shifted position, straightening his back just enough to relieve the weight on his belt for a few seconds. "But that's wishful thinking. It'd help if you'd touched bases with Bill Gastner to find out what the deal is with the Pope livestock." He turned to look at Estelle. "You took some pictures for him whenever it was . . . last night?"

"Yesterday morning."

"Did he say why he didn't just go talk to the Popes then? I don't understand this surveillance business."

"He wanted to see where the animals were going," Estelle said. "It wasn't that the animals were being mistreated or something like that. It's that they were apparently being shipped without a permit. He thought that the easiest way to find out what was really happening was just to watch and see, rather than listening to someone's tall story."

"Huh," Torrez said. "Bizarre. Bill's got too much free time on his hands. Did the Popes see you two while you were taking pictures? Were you on their property?"

"No. We were behind Florek's fence."

Torrez grinned at that. "Knothole pictures," he said.

"Well, not quite. But it was a good view."

"Could Denton have seen you, and that maybe precipitated his little brain into doing something stupid?"

"I suppose that's possible. Had he been looking out a window at the time, he would have seen us, no doubt. We weren't sneaking, exactly."

"It's hard to imagine Bill sneaking," Torrez said. "So Denton might have seen you?"

"It's possible."

Torrez took a deep breath and stood up straight, hooking his hands behind his head. Joints popped. "It'd be so much easier if we could just hit the *replay* button," he said.

"How was your seminar, by the way?" Estelle asked.

"What I paid attention to was fine," Torrez said, and looked a little sheepish. "I'm going back in June."

"Choose a quiet two weeks, please," Estelle said. She picked up the manila folders from Torrez's desk. "I'm going to make a couple of calls, check out a couple of things, and then take my mother to Mexico."

"If you work it just right, she won't know it's a business trip," Torrez said. "Although knowing Teresa Reyes, I wouldn't be surprised if she's figured that out for herself already."

"More than likely," Estelle said.

"And by the way," Torrez said, "you might ask her about Lucy and Wally Madrid, and that whole gang down in Maria. Tres Santos isn't that far away and her Uncle Reuben used to hang out down that way. He liked *la taberna,* as I recall. I would be surprised if Teresa didn't know all about that."

Estelle nodded, not bothering to remind Torrez that what Teresa Reyes knew, and what she would choose to talk about, were often two very different things.

"Gayle tells me that Teresa's not doing too well," Torrez said.

"No, she's not."

"Well, take your time this afternoon," he said. "The rest of the world will wait. You taking Carlos and Francisco with you?" Estelle shook her head, and Torrez looked surprised. "I thought grandparents lived and breathed for the company of *los nietos.*"

"The past is on her mind just now, I think," Estelle said. "They'd wear her out."

"They'd wear *me* out," Torrez said, and rapped his knuckle on the edge of his desk. It was a small gesture that said the meeting was over. "Let me know what else I can do to help," the sheriff said.

As Estelle left the sheriff's office, she reflected that she'd never heard Robert Torrez, legendary for his taciturn, monosyllabic communications, so downright efficient and administrative. Perhaps the sheriff had listened to the seminars more carefully than he had supposed.

24

An exuberantly cheerful officer—and Estelle couldn't tell if the voice was male or female—informed her that Capt. Tomás Naranjo was not in his office. Somehow the dispatcher managed to sound triumphant, as if the good *capitán* had been locked in the district office of the *Judiciales* for weeks or even months and finally had managed to break out into the light of day, the dust cloud from his escaping truck rolling across the Chihuahuan countryside.

On the off chance that Naranjo might check with his office or that his infuriatingly vague office might initiate contact with him, Estelle left word that she would be in Tres Santos that afternoon and if the *capitán*'s dust cloud could drift over that way sometime between one and three, it would be appreciated. The dispatcher said that he—or she—would see what could be done.

By the time Estelle had returned to the hospital shortly after eight that morning, her mother's status had been upgraded from patient to guest, and a few minutes later, she sat comfortably in one of the hospital's wheelchairs, ready for the short trip out the front door to the parking lot. A warm blanket had been draped over her lap, and another one wrapped around her tiny shoulders.

Francis hung the oxygen canister over one of the chair's push handles.

"Is it nasty outside?" Teresa asked as they rolled down the polished hallway floor toward the double doors. "Earlier, it was nice. I know that."

"It's like spring," Francis said.

"That means windy," Teresa said, and pulled at the blankets.

"No wind," Francis assured her. "For a change, no wind. And it's going to be warm, too. Just perfect."

The doors slid open and he maneuvered the chair across the rubber entry mat. The county car was parked directly in front of the sidewalk and as her son-in-law rolled her wheelchair toward the dark blue sedan, Teresa Reyes grimaced with displeasure.

"I don't want to ride in that thing," she said, just loud enough to be heard but not vocal enough to make it a serious refusal.

"I guess we could always walk home, Teresa," Francis said cheerfully.

"You can take me in your car," she said, and leaned back in the chair as the physician pulled it to a stop at the Ford's front door.

"Just ten blocks, *Mamá*," Estelle said as she came around the front fender of the car. "It won't hurt a bit."

"They'll think I've been arrested," Teresa grumbled.

"A desperado," Francis said as he maneuvered the chair close to the curb and locked the wheels. With surprising agility, Teresa stood up, her daughter assisting at her elbow. She stretched out a hand to the car's roof for support, and Francis and Estelle eased her down into the seat.

"You'd think I was made of glass," Teresa muttered, and hauled her other leg into the car. "There. Close the door."

Estelle did so, and grinned at Francis. He slid the oxygen bottle into the back seat, along with the aluminum walker.

"Still Mexico this afternoon?" he asked in English.

"If we're up to it," Estelle said.

"Oh, *she's* up to it," Francis replied. "Just take things real slow. And encourage her to stay close to the oxygen bottle."

"We'll only be gone a couple of hours. I think while I'm down there, I'm going to see if I can talk to Naranjo. He's usually pretty cooperative. Is there anything new from Alan?"

Francis shook his head. "Not that we didn't already know. Except maybe the alcohol blood level. That came back moderate on both men. They'd had a few. The rest of the tox tests are going to take a while."

"I'm not expecting anything there," Estelle said. She stretched up and kissed Francis and then stood with her left hand hooked around his neck. "You'll be home in a bit?"

"Yep."

As Estelle slipped behind the wheel, her mother watched with a scowl. Teresa reached out with her left hand and with the back of her fingers flicked at the barrel of the shotgun that rested in its vertical bracket beside the radio stack as if it were an annoying insect. "This is nice," she said.

"It goes with the car, *Mamá.*"

Teresa Reyes sniffed and turned to study the world out the side window as Estelle pulled away from the curb.

"Do you remember Paulita Saenz, *Mamá?*" For a moment she didn't think that Teresa had heard her, and she glanced across at the tiny woman. Her mother sat with her right elbow on the door's arm-rest, index finger lying pensively across her lips.

"Is that what this is all about?"

Taking that as a *yes,* Estelle added, "Her son's in trouble. Do you remember Eurelio?"

Teresa's eyebrows went up a little. "I don't think I ever met him, you know," she said. "The last time I saw that girl Paulita was . . ." She hesitated, lower lip projected in thought. "Maybe twenty years ago. Maybe that long." She leaned her head on her hand. "What's her boy done?"

"We're not sure. We think he's involved somehow in the death of a couple of Mexican nationals."

"Ah."

"Do you remember the Madrids? Lucy and Wally?"

"They live down in Maria."

"Yes."

"No, I don't recall them."

Estelle smiled at the contradiction, the standard tactic to steer away from disagreeable topics of conversation. "They have two sons we need to talk to as well."

"Los hijos . . ." Teresa murmured.

181

"I think Reuben knew them, didn't he? Lucy and Wally, I mean?"

"I wouldn't be surprised. Your great-uncle knew everybody."

With a pang of nostalgia, Estelle remembered her great-uncle as she had seen him last—eighty-nine years old, unable to attend to even the most basic bodily functions. One by one, those functions had switched off until he lay in the hospital bed an empty shell. "I wish I had known him better when I was younger," Estelle said.

"No, you don't," Teresa replied, and the starch in her reply surprised Estelle. She could remember the man's quick, white-toothed smile and his mane of hair that had turned gray before he was thirty. Of the man himself, Estelle could remember little beyond those final impressions. "He cut a swath on both sides of the border," Teresa said. "I always thought some jealous husband was going to shoot him."

"I guess they never caught up with him," Estelle laughed. They turned south from Bustos onto Twelfth Street. "I need to go down to Maria for a few minutes this morning, *Mamá*. Then after lunch you and I will go to Tres Santos."

Teresa nodded. "That's good." Her arthritic fingers were already fumbling for the door handle as the patrol car pulled into the driveway.

Estelle switched off the car and got out.

"Hi, gang!"

She turned and saw Irma Sedillos standing on the small porch, holding the storm door open. Irma stepped outside and let the door close behind her.

"Captain Naranjo is on the phone, Estelle. From Mexico."

Estelle stopped, her mother's door half open. "Right now, you mean?"

"I told him you had just driven up, and he said he'd wait."

"You go ahead," Teresa Reyes said. She had both feet out of the car and one hand on the door, preparing for the effort to stand upright.

"Would you tell him I'll call him right back? Just have him leave the number where he's at. I'll be about five minutes."

Irma nodded and retreated inside.

Estelle bent down, wrapped her left arm around her mother's shoulders and with her right hand on the older woman's elbow, lifted her out of the car and to her feet.

"You're pretty strong, *hija*," Teresa said. "You always surprise me."

Estelle got the walker out of the back seat and handed it to her mother. "Do you want the chair?"

"No, this is fine," Teresa said. She settled some of her weight tentatively on the aluminum walker as if afraid it might collapse. "It might take me a while."

"We have all day, *Mamá*."

Teresa flashed a smile, her strong teeth good for another eighty years. "Wouldn't that be nice," she said. "Wouldn't that be nice." She looked toward the front door, fixing that in her mind as the destination, and then navigated around the car door so that Estelle could close it.

Five-year-old Francisco appeared in the doorway. "Where did you go?" he said to his grandmother.

Teresa stopped and rested both hands on the walker handle. *"Andando a la caza de pinacates, hijo."*

Francisco's black eyebrows knit together as his forehead puckered in a frown. "No you weren't," he said cautiously and looked around at Irma for confirmation. Surely *Abuela* had not been out hunting the first stinkbugs of the season without telling him.

"Here's one right here," Teresa said, and moved the walker delicately. Sure enough, one of the comical black beetles had decided that the heat bouncing off the concrete of the sidewalk and the house's foundation had moved spring ahead of the actual calendar. He was posed by the sidewalk, tail up in the air. "He walked all this way, just like me."

Francisco ducked his head, giggled, and bolted back into the house. *"Abuela's* back!" they heard him shout to Carlos, but the younger boy was not so easily dislodged from whatever engrossed him at the moment.

"Hijos," Teresa Reyes said as if that proved the thesis of some earlier conversation.

With her mother inside and tucked in her favorite chair with the oxygen tubes looped around her head like a high-tech necklace, Estelle paused for a moment in the middle of the small living room to slow the whirlwind that was her elder son. She clamped him in a bearhug as she said to Irma, "Did Naranjo leave his number?"

"He's still holding," Irma replied, and then lowered her voice. "He sounds like a movie star or something."

Estelle laughed and aimed Francisco toward Irma. "He doesn't need to hear that," she said, and went to the phone in the kitchen. During her various dealings with the Mexican policeman over the years, it had always been abundantly clear that Naranjo remained a bachelor at heart, despite his long and apparently happy marriage. His prowl had extended for decades.

"Capitán, buenos días. Lo siento la tardanza," she said in Spanish.

"Ah," Naranjo said. "It's good to hear from you, *Señora* Guzman." His English was flawless and elegantly accented, as if he were trying to imitate Ricardo Montalban. "My office told me that you called, and I knew it must be important." He chuckled. "Or at least, I hoped it would be. How is your mother, by the way?"

"She's fine. Just tired. I just brought her home."

"A remarkable woman. I hope you will give her my very best wishes."

"I'll do that," Estelle said, at the same time wondering when her mother and Tomás Naranjo had crossed paths. In his early fifties and having served in the *Judiciales* for nearly thirty years, Naranjo had become something of an institution in his district. "I was hoping that I could ask your assistance with a case we're working at the moment."

"Nothing would please me more."

"We have two homicide victims whom I believe are Mexican nationals, captain. They were apparently working up here for a month, cutting firewood on a large ranch near the community of Mule Creek, up in Grant County."

"With all the appropriate papers, of course," Naranjo interjected.

"Oh, of course. Actually, we really don't know. When we found the bodies, there was no identification . . . no wallets, no cards, no nothing."

"And no money, I'm sure."

"Certainly not that."

"Shot?"

"Yes. Large caliber, no casings left behind, no bullets or bullet fragments. One victim was buried, the other apparently was able to break away. His body was discovered a thousand yards west. Out on the prairie."

"I see."

"At any rate, some witnesses have placed the two men here in Posadas County earlier this winter—when they were on the way to their job. They stopped at the saloon in Maria."

"La Taberna Azul."

"That's correct. And they were seen by several people."

"What is it that I can help you with?"

"First of all, did you have a chance to see the photos that we faxed to your office yesterday?"

"No, as a matter of fact. But then, I haven't been *in* my office for most of the week, so that is not surprising." He made a sound as if he were trying to hum a tune. "Did you address them directly to me?"

"Yes sir."

"Well," Naranjo said. "That's the problem then. I wasn't in the office, and no one else looked at them. I'm sure that they're lying on my desk at this very moment."

"I see."

"But the message I received was that you would be in Tres Santos this afternoon? Is that correct?"

"Yes, sir. My mother would like to visit her home for a little while, and we thought that today would be good."

"May I meet you there?"

"I was hoping that you could. I'll bring copies of the photos with me. If you could be of assistance in identifying the two men, that would be a great help."

"Most certainly. We will do everything that we can." He cleared his throat. "Did you have a particular time in mind?"

"Would two o'clock be convenient?"

"I will make it so," Naranjo said. "And perhaps afterward, there is a small place in Asunción we might visit for dinner. It is a short drive, after all. I would enjoy the opportunity to visit with your mother once again."

"We'll have to see," Estelle said. "My mother tires easily. Even the short drive from here to Tres Santos is going to be a major undertaking for her."

185

"I understand completely. I must confess, I had—what do you call them—ulterior motives. We are currently investigating a nasty little incident at Asunción. I was going to lay it out for you, so to speak . . . to see what you have to say."

"I'd be interested," Estelle said, her pulse quickening.

"Then I think it will be a profitable afternoon," Naranjo said. "I will plan to arrive at your mother's house at two. Is that settled?"

"Thank you, sir. You know where it is?"

"Indeed I do. Until then."

Estelle hung up the phone, turned, and took two steps toward the living room. She could hear the two boys in earnest conversation with their grandmother, and then the shrill ringing of the telephone stopped her in her tracks. Even as she lifted the receiver out of the cradle, she could hear the radio traffic in the background.

25

ACCORDING to the story that Paulita Saenz recounted, she never would have looked south that morning had the sink in the women's bathroom not clogged. Paulita had run enough water to soak a sponge, and then saw the ugly puddle of soap scum, hair, and who knows what else as the sink refused to drain.

Unscrewing the big plastic lock rings of the sink trap was a simple job requiring no special tools and no particular knowledge of sophisticated plumbing. Paulita knew the trap, long neglected, was choked. With a sigh, she slid a pan under the trap, grunted loose the lock rings above and below the trap, and grimaced at the smell of the trapped, stagnant water as it cascaded into the pan. Long tendrils of hair nearly held the plumbing together, but eventually, Paulita managed to pull out the offending plug, her face screwed up in a puckered *eeewww* of disgust. She dug at the curtains of residue that hung from the now-exposed sink drain stub and wiped the elbow joints clean.

Reassembly took seconds, and she had closed her eyes and grunted with a dry rag wrapped around the lock rings, snugging them so they wouldn't leak. With a sigh, she had pushed herself up off the floor, holding a pan containing a quart of bluish-brown water and a large, ugly, fragrant glob of *caca asquerosa*. The logical place to dispose of the cargo was out the side door that led to the courtyard between house and saloon.

From there, Paulita turned right, unlatching the garden gate. As the rough, weathered board gate swung open, Paulita was treated to a view south, the early morning sun lancing across the desert. She paused, bowl of watery gunk in hand, riveted by what she saw. Then she dropped the bowl, ran inside and called the Posadas County Sheriff's Department.

Deputy Jackie Taber, off-duty when dispatch went on the air to locate an officer, had been methodically scouring the prairie around the grave site north of Maria, hoping to find a deformed bullet or another shell casing that might have hidden under a chamisa or cholla— something that had been missed in earlier searches. Sgt. Howard Bishop had just turned into the airport parking lot northwest of Posadas. Taber took the call, her Bronco airborne as often as not as she hurtled down the power line access road. She beat the undersheriff to the *taberna* by eight minutes.

"Stay here," Estelle Reyes-Guzman said, and Paulita Saenz stepped onto the flagstones of her patio and stood with her arms crossed, hugging herself like a small child waiting for a bus. Estelle followed Jackie Taber's boot prints where the deputy had walked the hundred yards from the back of the Taberna Azul to the border fence, four strands of barbed wire that had seen better days. Stepping directly on the deputy's prints, Estelle approached until she stood immediately behind Taber.

"No sign of anything?"

"Nothing," Jackie said, and lowered the binoculars. She offered them to Estelle, who shook her head. "This is a good bet where they crossed," she added. "Lots of boot prints, and you can see the scuffing in the dirt where they climbed over . . . or through."

The border security separating New Mexico and Texas from old Mexico ran the gamut from nothing—where the Rio Grande provided a natural barrier of sorts—to impressive chain link with barbed wire topping in urban centers. Out in the country, however, where tourists didn't need to be reminded which part of the desert belonged to whom, an aging barbed wire fence frequently served the purpose. At one time, a narrow dirt lane had been bladed along the border fence from one side of New Mexico to the other, but the lane served little purpose: no one drove east–west. It was north–south that interested most folks.

At formal ports of entry, the fence was bolstered by imposing block houses that protected American and Mexican customs officials from sunstroke. At the smaller crossings, like Columbus to Palomas or Regál to Tres Santos, traffic inched through a single lane, lined up for inspection.

The tiny village of Maria had never been lucky enough to warrant a crossing of its own. For one thing, the state highway that passed through Maria headed out of the village east toward Las Cruces, roughly paralleling the border rather than crossing it. In the other direction, State 61 veered north to Posadas.

Columbus, New Mexico, was matched on the Mexican side by Palomas, and westward, at the other end of the rumpled San Cristóbals, folks in Regál could see the lights of Tres Santos if they stood on the hill behind the water tank. Maria had no such sister village across the border.

The nearest pocket of population, Asunción, was tucked in a wonderfully shady little canyon some sixteen miles south of the border. Roads from Asunción led still farther south to Janos, east to Juarez, and even west to Agua Prieta. But south of Maria in Posadas County and the stretch of barbed wire that marked the border, the Chihuahuan desert stretched rumpled and desolate, marked only occasionally by a rough lane or two-track.

"Did you contact Mexican authorities?" Estelle asked.

"I did, but there's a problem." Jackie turned and nodded toward the saloon, and Paulita Saenz. "She saw a car, but doesn't know what kind it is—not the year, not even the make. She thinks it was an older model station wagon. And at the distance, she didn't recognize the two men who were with Eurelio."

"Could it have been the Madrid brothers?"

"She just couldn't tell. Apparently she didn't have on her distance glasses," Jackie said. "She was busy with the plumbing." She shrugged. "I talked with a Mexican officer named Bernardo. Luis Bernardo? He's a corporal in Asunción. Anyway, I told him that we'd be interested in anything he could do for us. I gave him a description of Eurelio."

189

"It's a place to start," Estelle said. She turned and regarded the saloon.

Had there been a window in the back storage room of the Taberna Azul, Paulita Saenz could have peered out and seen the sun glinting off the barbed wire border fence. But a window would have been an attractive nuisance. The back, southern-facing wall of the saloon was solid, secure adobe from ground to vigas.

The west wall of the *taberna* once had sported a window with a beautiful, deep sill. The view of the San Cristóbal mountains had been breathtaking when the dawn washed them in rose and purple. Three break-ins through that window had prompted Monroy Saenz to block up the window and plaster it over to match the rest of the wall. On the inside of the patched wall, he'd painted a window with shutters thrown open to reveal a colorful garden beyond, complete with a vineyard and improbably huge purple grapes glistening in latex splendor. It was a cheerful, secure view that never changed, the grapes hanging forever ripe.

Estelle could remember, during a visit to the *taberna* with her great-uncle when she'd sat quietly, waiting for Reuben to finish his business. She had watched the grapes, trying to imagine the movement of the leaves in the breeze.

The single front window of the saloon, protected by a heavy wrought-iron grill, looked out on the front parking lot, State 61, and across the way, Wally Madrid's gas station.

The Taberna Azul was a comfortable fortress. It was a place to sit in quiet darkness while the New Mexico sun baked the world outside, or the wind scoured it, or ambitious people blew themselves up trying to make a profit from it.

"She said her son went willingly, though . . . at least at the beginning," Estelle said.

"Until the very last, apparently," Jackie replied. "Then it turned into a tussle."

Estelle nodded. "Let me talk to her again."

Paulita Saenz was weeping and trying to hide the fact by wiping at her eyes with the sleeve of her blouse. She turned back toward the patio as Estelle approached, and the undersheriff heard a loud, heartfelt sigh from Paulita.

"Paulita, it's one thing if Eurelio just jumped the fence and took off with friends—he probably does that all the time. That's not what happened this morning?"

The woman wiped her eyes again with her sleeve and shook her head. She turned and tried to meet Estelle's gaze, but couldn't. "I saw them go over the fence," she said. "Their car was parked just beyond, on the Mexican side, on that little cow path there."

"I understand that. But what did you see, exactly? I really need to know."

"Eurelio was walking ahead of them, and they were all talking. I could see their hands moving, you know? I guess they must have come across and walked to the back of the house to find my son. I was busy in the *taberna*. I didn't hear them. I didn't see them."

And maybe it's just as well that you didn't, Estelle thought. "And then what happened?"

"I saw them hop the fence. And then they went to the car, and then I could hear their voices. Eurelio opened the passenger door in front and just as he turned to get in, one of the men hit him in the back of the head. I saw him do that." Paulita's voice quavered.

"With his fist, or did he have something in his hand?"

"I couldn't tell for sure." Paulita held out her right hand, palm spread with her fingers pointing up. She patted the heel of her hand. "It looked like this." And she punched sharply forward with her hand. "That's what I think. Eurelio, he turned then, and they struggled. Then he went down inside the car."

"Did your son fall?"

"I couldn't tell if he fell, or what," Paulita said.

"But it looked to you that he'd changed his mind about getting in the car?"

She nodded. "And the one man slammed the door on him. Then one of them got in to drive and the other got in the back."

"And you never saw any weapons?"

Paulita shook her head.

"Did they ever look back and see you?"

"No. I don't think so."

"And show me again what direction they went." Paulita pointed toward the southwest. "Toward Asunción, then?"

"Maybe. Maybe anywhere."

"It was a four-door sedan?"

"It was one of those huge old station wagons," Paulita said. "The kind with the roof rack on top."

"Deputy Taber said that you didn't see what model it was."

"Well, I remembered some. That's what it was. Just about the same color as the dust."

"Sort of a yellowish tan?"

"That's right. And big."

"And a station wagon."

"That's right."

"Did you ever have a chance to see the front of the car?"

"Yes, I saw the front. It was parked sort of angled toward the fence, you know. Yes, I could see the front."

"Would you recognize the front of it if we showed you a picture?"

"I think I might," Paulita said. "I remember the hood, you know. It was really long. A big old boat. The front fenders were really sharp. Creased on the top. They looked like cheeks."

Estelle glanced at Paulita with amusement. The woman had progressed from knowing nothing to a pretty comprehensive description. Jackie Taber approached, and Estelle turned to her. "I'd like you to run Mrs. Saenz up to the office and have her look through the Motor Manuals to identify the car that she's talking about. It sounds like one of those 'seventies model Ford wagons—those beasts with the hood about a football field long. See if that's the one."

"Yes, ma'am."

"But what about my son?" Paulita Saenz said.

"We have the Mexican authorities looking for him," Estelle said. "We're limited on what we can do on this end, Paulita. Until we have some word from them." She saw the look of desolation on the woman's face. "They don't have much of a head start."

"In that country you don't *need* much of a head start," Paulita said.

"We'll add the vehicle description to what we've already told them. If they have an officer in the area, they might be able to do some good." The words were hollow, and Estelle knew it. With a state policeman for every thousand square miles, capture in Mexico was more often the result of betrayal and ambush rather than simple pursuit.

Paulita's gaze traveled out to the fence and beyond, into the bleak reaches of the Chihuahuan desert.

"What sort of trouble is he in?" Estelle asked.

"I wish I could tell you."

"It wasn't the Madrids? Benny and Isidro?"

"It could have been. And it could have been somebody else. They had heavy coats on, and with the hats and everything, it was hard to tell. It might have been, though. One of them . . . I thought he moved kind of like Benny when they were going over the fence."

"Was that the one who hit Eurelio, or was it the other one?"

"The other one."

Estelle turned and looked toward Mexico. Eurelio had been turned loose by Judge Hobart early that morning. He obviously hadn't gone home and cleaned up for another workday with Posadas Electric Cooperative.

"Somebody knew your son was home, Mrs. Saenz. Less than three hours after he was released from our custody, you saw him bailing over the fence. Did you talk with him this morning? After he got home?"

Paulita shook her head. "He just said that he didn't want to discuss anything about it. He gets mad, you know. And then I can't talk to him."

"Somebody's talkin' to him now," Jackie Taber said, and Estelle saw Paulita Saenz flinch.

26

♦♦♦

WHEN Eurelio Saenz jumped the border fence—whether he'd been forced to or not—he had managed to throw up a considerable roadblock. Had the young man lit out for Phoenix, Denver, or even Cleveland, the long arm of American law enforcement could have kept pace with him at the speed of a computer's neuron. By going to Mexico, the rules changed.

Estelle Reyes-Guzman knew that Capt. Tomás Naranjo would help all he could. There had been numerous incidents in the past when the Mexican officer had simply ignored international boundaries—without trumpeting the fact to his superiors, of course. A rarity among his colleagues, Naranjo sliced and diced paperwork and protocol with an efficiency that sometimes left his counterparts north of the border in the dust.

But with a vast, rural jurisdiction and few men to police it, Naranjo's *Judiciales* worked at a disadvantage under the best of circumstances. Estelle didn't hold much hope that the Mexican troopers would catch sight of the faded station wagon and its three passengers. The country was full of old cars that sagged down the dirt roads, battered and smoking. Had the trio stolen a *new* car, it would have stood out like a beacon.

The young Mexican officer with whom Jackie Taber had made initial contact had sounded eager, the deputy said. Maybe they would get lucky. Maybe Eurelio would get lucky. Maybe he'd finish his deal

194

in one piece, whatever it might be, and sneak back over the border after dark. Maybe his mother would see him again.

Estelle continued to mull her options as she returned to the Public Safety Building in Posadas. She drove into the parking lot as if on automatic pilot and pulled the unmarked unit into a space without conscious guidance. For several minutes, she sat behind the wheel after the engine died, fingers tapping a featureless beat on the steering wheel. At last she got out, collected her briefcase, and entered the building. Gayle Torrez was standing in the door of her husband's office when Estelle walked in, and the dispatcher raised a hand. "Here she is," Gayle said, and then hesitated.

"What?" Estelle asked.

"It's just that you were frowning so hard," Gayle said. "I didn't want to interrupt you if you had to go write something down before you forgot it."

"I wish I *had* something to write down," Estelle replied. "What's going on?"

Torrez appeared in the door of his office, his huge frame filling the opening. "Rafael Smith and Lolo Duarte," he said without preamble.

Estelle stopped in her tracks. "Smith?"

"Well, *Smeeeth,* then," Torrez said. "At least that's the name he went by up north."

"They weren't brothers, then."

"Apparently not."

"You talked to the rancher involved?"

"I did. *Smeeeth* and Duarte worked for a rancher named Travis Fox from January sixth through the first week in February. I faxed the photos up to the Grant County SO for them to look at, but Travis was sure that's who the men were. His description was right on target. Apparently they've worked for him on other occasions."

Bill Gastner appeared in the doorway behind Torrez, and Estelle smiled at the older man. "Good morning, sir." The livestock inspector looked relaxed and alert, as if he'd spent the night sleeping like a normal person.

"Hey, there," Gastner replied. "You've had a busy morning. Young Mr. Saenz gave you the slip?"

Estelle looked heavenward. "We're going around in circles," she

195

replied. "I'm not even sure if that's what Eurelio did. He ducked across the border with two other men—that much his mother is sure of. Whether or not there was some force or coercion involved is another question. Naranjo said that he'd do what he could."

"Which may or may not amount to diddly," Gastner said.

Estelle nodded agreement and then looked at Torrez. "So the two of them were on their way home to somewhere, pockets full of money after a month's hard work."

"That's what it looks like."

"You show your money, you get robbed," Gastner said. "About as simple as that. Damn near biblical." He held an aluminum clipboard in one hand and used it to usher Torrez to one side so that he could slip through the office door. "I need more fuel," he said. He held his cup up toward Estelle. "Want some? Gayle just made it. There's some cinnamon buns in there, too."

"No thanks," Estelle replied. Her left eyebrow drifted up as she contemplated the floor. "That leaves us with a lot of questions, then," she said.

"Travis Fox answered one of them for me," Torrez said. "Smith and Duarte arrived in an older model Chevy pickup truck. Fox thinks that its about a seventy-two. The transmission blew a few days after they started work. They didn't want to spend all their earnings to have it fixed, and they asked Fox if they could leave it there for a while until they could come and get it. It's still parked out on his place."

"So they hitchhiked back down this way?" Estelle said. "And if their route took them through Maria, should I make a bet about where they're from originally?"

"Asunción," Torrez said. "Fox said that he and his family enjoyed having the two boys around. A couple of jokers, is how he described them. Told them to come back any time. That he'd have work of some sort."

She nodded. "If they're from Asunción, it makes sense then that they would stop at the Taberna Azul in Maria. They knew people there, and maybe figured that they could find someone who would run them the rest of the way home. There's no direct road across the border at that point. It would be a stout walk going cross-country."

"That's possible," the sheriff said. "Somebody offered 'em a ride, all right."

"Did Fox happen to say when the two of them finished their work up there?"

"They left his place on February second, midmorning."

"And we found them February eighteenth. It makes sense that they stopped here late in the afternoon of the second. That's the night that MacInerny heard the shots."

Torrez nodded. "Or on the third. Or the fourth." He held up his hands. "We're guessing."

"That's something, then," Estelle said. "If they stopped in Maria, then they were right in the middle of roofing season."

"I beg your pardon?"

"That's when the two Madrid boys were in town, fixing their father's roof. Paulita wouldn't swear to it, but she thinks that the two men with Eurelio this morning might have been Isidro and Benny."

"She doesn't know them well enough to tell?" Torrez said skeptically.

"Distance," Estelle said. "And maybe squirrelly light. And maybe a little denial thrown in."

"I guess." He sighed and put his hands on his hips. "With the kid split to Mexico, there's not a whole lot we can do, other than asking Naranjo's boys to make some inquiries for us."

"And they're doing that," Estelle said.

"Good. Bill and I were just tackling the problem of the donkeys," Torrez said. "And some bad news, by the way."

"Bad news how?"

"Eleanor Pope didn't make it."

Estelle felt as if she'd been punched in the stomach. She reached out a hand to the cool, smooth surface of the wall and stood silently for a long minute. The sheriff waited until she looked up.

"Francis called me just after nine this morning."

"Ah," Estelle said. By nine, her mother had decided that the new day held at least a few more promises. Eleanor Pope had given up on any she might have had left. "She took a lot of answers with her, then."

"Yes, she did," Gastner said. He took a sip of the coffee and grimaced—whether from appreciation or revulsion, Estelle couldn't tell. "Somebody made a deal with Billy White up in Belen," Gastner said. "He was supposed to take a look at the wee beasties this morning, and if he liked what he saw, haul off the whole bunch." Seeing the blank look on Estelle's face, he added, "White's a dealer. White and Sons Livestock. Actually, his specialty is draft horses." He grinned. "One extreme to another, I suppose. The idea of horse-things about the size of cocker spaniels appealed to him."

"Who called him?"

"He said that he took a call from Denton Pope earlier in the week. Pope offered the critters for sale."

"But White didn't talk with Eleanor?"

"Apparently not."

"And this Billy White person . . . he just called you from out of the blue? Had he heard about the fire, or what?"

"No, nothing like that," Gastner said. "There was a message on my answering machine." He flashed a quick smile. "A day or two old, I might add. You know how diligent I am about checking that damn thing. Anyway, White had been trying to get in contact with me for a few days, but I've been in and out, and we've managed to miss each other." Gastner took another swallow of coffee, and his right hand patted his shirt pocket as if there might be a cigarette there.

"White's a legit dealer who plays by the rules," he said. "Denton told him that he had all the paperwork, and I guess White asked him a question or two and didn't get the answers that he thought he should. He called me to make sure the deal was on the level. To make sure the livestock were as advertised before he drove all the way down here from Belen."

"Ah."

"Ah, is right," Gastner said.

"That's interesting," Estelle said, more to herself than to anyone else.

"Yes, it is," Gastner agreed.

"Did Denton suggest when Billy White would come to inspect the animals?"

"Apparently he did. White said he was supposed to come to Posadas this afternoon."

"And knowing that, Denton set the place on fire. After turning the animals loose."

"A truly great mind at work," Gastner said. "Makes it easy, number one, to tell me that the paperwork for the animals was destroyed in the fire."

"But there are copies," Estelle said.

"True enough." Gastner smiled. "We can excuse a man who would poke holes in a propane line for missing a salient point like that. And number two, my guess would be that Eleanor had no intention of seeing her herd of pets auctioned off. *She* didn't call Billy White, after all."

"If Denton stood to collect on house insurance, his mother's life insurance, and the sale of the animals, it would have been a clean sweep," Estelle said.

"Yep. Then Denton could fly off to Tahiti or some such place. And probably never break open another bale of alfalfa in his life."

"We don't know about the insurance angle yet," Torrez said.

"Collins is working on that," Estelle said. "Just Eleanor's medical bills alone would have been staggering, even assuming Medicare took care of most of it." She turned to Gastner. "What *are* you going to do with the donkeys?"

"They're sampling a piece of pasture over on Herb Torrance's place," Gastner said. "He's got a paddock with the boards set close enough together that they won't just slip under and wander off."

"You have them all?"

Gastner grinned. "I doubt it. But we will. A couple of the neighborhood kids volunteered to play cowboy, helping Herb and his son with the roundup. They think it's great fun."

"Has anyone heard from the Fire Marshal's office?" Estelle asked.

"Todd Paul showed up with a couple assistants," Torrez said. He glanced at his watch. "I was going over there in a few minutes to see what they found out."

"Are there relatives, by the way?"

"To the Popes, you mean? No, I don't think so. At least no one close."

"There's a cousin," Gastner interjected. "Well, her niece, his cousin. Something like that. One of the neighbors thinks that she lives in Denver, but doesn't know her name. An older woman, they said."

"We'll find her," Torrez said.

"Maybe she'll want a few ducks for her backyard pool," Gastner said, and waved his cup at the two officers. "I need to hit the road. If you think of anything else you need from me, just hesitate to ask." He frowned at Estelle. "You still headed to Mexico this afternoon?"

"Yes. Naranjo agreed to meet with me in Tres Santos. We'll compare notes."

Gastner nodded, taking a long, slow breath. "You be careful."

"Oh sure."

"And give my best to your mother."

"I'll do that."

Gayle Torrez reappeared, and gave Bill Gastner an affectionate pinch on the arm as he walked by. "Pam Gardiner on two, Bobby," she said to the sheriff, and Torrez rolled his eyes. His method of dealing with the *Posadas Register* had so far not progressed beyond the stage of ignoring its presence.

"Why don't you talk to her?" he said to Estelle.

Estelle smiled. "I'd rather go to Mexico," she said. They both heard Gastner's chuckle as he pushed open the outside door.

27

THE telephone caught Estelle in midstride between refrigerator and cooler. For just a moment, she looked at the instrument as if she could make it vanish before it triggered the answering machine on the fifth ring. She set the bottles of chilled juice down on the counter and picked up the receiver.

"Guzman."

"Estelle, Tony Abeyta." The deputy sounded as if he were holding his breath when he talked.

"What's up, Tony?"

"On December twenty-seventh of last year, Mountain Trails Sporting Goods in Las Cruces sold a forty-four magnum Marlin Model eighteen ninety-four lever action rifle to Eurelio Saenz."

The silence on the line hung heavy for a few heartbeats. The deputy anticipated Estelle's question. "The salesman remembers mounting the scope and bore-sighting the rifle for Saenz at the time. He remembers that Eurelio had an old scope with him, but that it was much too big for the rifle. He ended up buying another one that he liked better . . . the whole package. Rifle, scope, rings, and mounts."

"Uh," Estelle groaned. "I was hoping that wouldn't be the case." She sighed. "Have you passed word to Jackie yet?"

"No, ma'am. I just got off the phone with Cruces. Jackie's out on the prairie somewhere, sifting sand."

"I'd appreciate it if you'd get in contact with her first thing. She needs to know what you've found out. You have a record of the serial number and such?"

"Mountain Trails faxed me a copy of the ATF form. It's interesting, though. The salesman I talked to this morning remembers Saenz. He was absolutely sure it wasn't a straw sale."

"How would he know?"

"He says that Saenz came in by himself, and looked at several rifles before he decided on the Marlin. In fact, he came close to buying another weapon entirely. The salesman said that Saenz spent more than two hours making up his mind and then selecting the right scope and all. It wasn't as if he was buying the stuff for someone else. He made some interesting choices."

Estelle leaned against the kitchen counter. "In what way?"

"The salesman remembers Saenz talking a lot about hunting javelina in rugged country. He didn't want a high-powered scope. What he was looking for was something with relatively low magnification, but a wide field of view."

"And he found it?"

"Apparently so." She heard Abeyta shuffling papers. "He bought a little two-and-a-half power jobbie with a reticule that shotgun shooters like. It's got kind of a circle thing in the middle with crosshairs that lets you swing on a moving target."

"A man running for his life across the open prairie certainly qualifies as that," Estelle said.

"I guess it would," the deputy said. "And by the way, the salesman didn't remember one way or the other if the hammer extender was attached or not. He did say that if the store mounts the scope for the customer, they put the extender on as a matter of course."

"But he doesn't remember for sure in this case?"

"No, ma'am. He wouldn't swear to it. He says 'probably' is as close as he can come."

"Did he happen to remember if Eurelio purchased ammunition at the same time?"

"He didn't buy any. The salesman threw in a twenty-round box as part of the deal. Winchester Western, two forty grain jacketed hollow points. Sarge says that's the most common round."

"That doesn't give us much," Estelle said. "He would have shot that up in the first five minutes when he went out to try the rifle."

"His prints weren't on the shell casing from the truck, by the way," Abeyta said.

"I'm not surprised. Those were a different brand, as well."

"Sergeant Mears got a start on the prints before he was called away to the fire, but he's pretty sure. He was going to get back on it later today."

"You're at the office now?"

"Yes, ma'am."

"Have Gayle put out a bulletin for Eurelio Saenz. You heard he skipped to Mexico?"

"With interesting circumstances is what I'm told."

"That's right. And you might as well add Isidro and Benny Madrid's names to that, too. They're in on this somehow. Their little heads just show up too often. Anyway, make sure she gets that out ASAP. And then get ahold of Jackie. She needs to know what you found out, and she needs to get a search warrant from Judge Hobart. I'll be back from Mexico later this afternoon, and we'll see what we can find. If there's anyone we can spring free to keep an eye on the *taberna* in the meantime, we need to do that. You might pull Collins for that. Tell him that he's just to keep surveillance . . . nothing else. No confrontations, no nothing. I don't want him walking into the middle of something."

"No problem. On the bulletin for Saenz, you want A and D?"

Estelle sighed. "My intuition tells me that Eurelio is neither armed nor dangerous, but I wouldn't bet on the folks he might be with. So yes . . . I guess he's earned it," she said.

"That's what the sheriff said. And by the way, he's already requested the warrant. He wants to watch the place in the meantime, so we can use Collins for something else."

"That'll work. I'll be back as soon as I can," Estelle said.

"No problem," Abeyta said again. Estelle disconnected and stood in the kitchen with the phone in her hand, the lighted buttons inviting use. After a minute, she took a deep breath and hung up. Irma Sedillos had taken the two boys on an expedition up the arroyo behind

Twelfth Street, and the house was quiet. Her mother had traded her rocker for the living room sofa, and she napped peacefully, curled under the old afghan, the oxygen tubes trailing down to the canister on the floor.

Estelle retreated gratefully to the bedroom. Despite the earlier shower, she could still smell the various aromas of the long night. For what seemed like an hour she stood in the shower, the hot spray pounding the aches out of her body and the steam clearing her sinuses.

She stepped out of the bathroom, wrapped in a large white towel, to find her husband stretched out on the bed, eyes closed.

"Your mother's got the right idea," he said. "Smartest one in the bunch."

"I didn't hear you come in, *querido*."

He opened one eye. "Any good news?"

"Depends on the definition of *good, oso,*" Estelle replied.

Francis lifted a hand toward her, and Estelle moved to the edge of the bed. "No new corpses would be a start," he said. He slipped his hand through the folds of the towel and rested his hand on the flat of her belly.

She turned slightly toward his hand and sat down on the edge of the bed as Francis made room. "We're pretty worried about Eurelio Saenz," she said. "He's skipped across the border with a couple of men, probably the Madrid brothers—and maybe not voluntarily, either."

"That could be the last you'll see of him."

Estelle didn't reply, but she knew that Francis was probably right. He reached up and ran a finger under a tangle of damp hair, frowning.

"I wish there was more we could have done for Eleanor Pope," he said. "But her system just decided that enough was enough. Not twenty minutes after you and your mother left."

Estelle stretched out beside her husband. She put both hands over her face, her palms muffling her words. "Do you happen to know what kind of insurance she had?"

Francis laughed. "Ah, no." He lifted up one of her hands and looked deeply into her right eye. "That's an official-type question, isn't it?"

"Sure."

"One of the hospital bookies can tell you," he said. "I didn't give it a thought."

"Um."

"But you don't need to do that right this minute," he added. "It can wait."

"And you need a shower," she said.

"You were in there about a week. Did you leave some hot water?"

"Probably not. You should have come in." She rolled over to snuggle against him. "We could warm some up, couldn't we?"

He grinned. "That would be nice."

28
♦♦♦

TERESA Reyes straightened in the seat, leaning forward slightly. She pointed at a scar on the steep hillside ahead.

"I remember when they blasted that," she said. "I think all the adobes settled this far . . ." She held her hands several inches apart. Fluorite had initiated outside interest in Tres Santos shortly after the First World War, adding a dimension to the economy and culture of the tiny village that was a mixed blessing. Many of the miners' shacks still stood, most little more than piles of weathered boards pimpling the hillside.

"They haven't mined for years, though, have they?" Estelle asked. She could remember taking considerable delight in exploring the forbidden shafts, cuts, and holes in the mesa sides, looking for crystals that people with no imagination had earlier deemed worthless.

"No. They're all gone now."

Before the gray-brown hills and mesa flanks began to show the effects of haphazard boring and blasting, Tres Santos had concentrated on its central blessing—the Río Plegado. *River* might have been an exaggeration. The Plegado's trickle of water followed a circuitous path down the flanks of the limestone hills, through the *bolson* of the valley before finally disappearing underground.

After the brief flurry of the mines, residents of Tres Santos had subsisted from the fields irrigated by the Plegado and by the artistry of two extended families of wood-carvers—Roman Diaz, his eight children and their families, and the nine progeny of his father-in-law, the late Domingo Eschevarria. Eschevarria had been the first to understand that the thick, contorted stumps of Chihuahuan desert shrubs were the well-spring for a world of whimsically carved creatures. Tourists bought them by the hundreds, as fast as the Eschevarria and Diaz chisels could turn the figurines loose from the tough, gnarled wood.

Situated six miles from the border and on the main hard-packed dirt and gravel road to Janos and the interior, Tres Santos was a tourist's delight. Remote enough to be Old Mexico, the village gave tourists the impression that they might be the very first to have discovered the place. The dirt road wound down into the small valley, itself just enough of a depression in the desert that the horizon was always within reach.

The galleria of cottonwood, elm, and stunted walnut followed the river, and the lane itself crossed the water in a half dozen places, the flow rarely wide enough to splash both front and rear tires simultaneously.

The invention of the automobile had had at least one marked impact on Tres Santos. Over the years, derelict autos had been dumped into the river, forced up against the eroding banks on the outside of strategic bends. The automotive riprap worked pretty well until a cloudburst upstream created a bulldozer of chocolate-colored water powerful enough to rearrange the whole mess.

Estelle eased the van out of the fourth river crossing and turned sharply right, bouncing up and out of the riverbed. A high adobe wall greeted them. "I don't want to talk to anybody," Teresa said as they neared the gate. Ceramic letters over the arch announced *Casa Diaz,* and Estelle saw three vehicles in the driveway close to the portico. The one nearest the road was a familiar tan Toyota 4-Runner with government plates. "Maybe later," Teresa added.

Estelle understood her mother's reluctance to lay on the horn, bringing her neighbors out in force. The Diaz family, from the sixty-five-year-old Roman and his wife Marta, down through all eight children to little Tinita, included twenty arms powered by an endless need to embrace and hug, with back-slapping and rib-nudging thrown in.

If Teresa was to enjoy a few quiet moments at her former home, it would have to be before the village knew of her presence. And once the Diaz family knew, the rest of the community was sure to follow.

They drove along beside the high wall, following the curve of it toward a grove of aging cottonwoods whose roots were just a bit too far from the current riverbed. The trees looked as if they were patiently waiting for a spring flood to change the course of the Plegado back to their benefit.

Teresa Reyes's home was basically four rooms with a screened porch across the back. The tree nearest the front door had grown until its roots crushed upward against the stone foundation, sending large cracks radiating up through the wall, around the narrow, deeply cased window, and up to the vigas. Estelle turned off the lane, drove across the close-cropped weeds of the yard and stopped as close to the front door as she could.

"This place," Teresa said enigmatically. Estelle glanced across at her mother. Teresa propped her chin on her fingers, elbow on the door rest. She regarded the little building. The crow's-feet at the corners of her eyes deepened.

"It's held up pretty well," Estelle said. Except for a brief time when it had been rented by one of the Diaz sons and his bride, the place had been standing empty for three years. When Teresa had fallen at the back porch step and broken her left hip, she had moved from Tres Santos to Posadas. And when her daughter's family had gone to Minnesota for a brief interlude, Teresa had traveled with them.

"What do you want to do with it?" Teresa asked.

The question took Estelle by surprise, but she knew that her mother didn't mean the cosmetic cracks in the plaster, the cobwebs, or the mouse turds.

"I haven't thought about it," she said. "And it's not my decision."

"I talked to Roman last week," Teresa said. She pointed to the north. "Those trees over there died. You can see the school from here now." Sure enough, the small cinderblock building that housed the current iteration of the district school stood bleak and gray at the end of a field of rusting derelict cars. "It was better before the river took it out," she said, referring to the small, neat adobe building where she had taught for close to forty years before the Plegado had gotten angry after a cloudburst and straightened out a bend or two.

"What did Roman say?" Estelle asked. The telephone was among the many modern luxuries, gadgets, and annoyances that Teresa eschewed. Its impersonal nature somehow offended her. No telephone lines ran to the tiny house standing before them, and Estelle could imagine how serious Teresa's concerns must have been to prompt her to make a telephone call to Roman—and an international call at that.

"About the house?"

"Yes."

"Well," Teresa said, and shrugged. "It's something that has to be decided sometime."

"What do *you* want to do with it, *Mamá?*" She could see by the expression on her mother's face that there was no easy answer, and she didn't pursue the question. She pulled the door handle. The aroma of weeds crushed under the tires of the van was pungent. Her mother sat quietly. Estelle took a deep breath, trying to place herself on this tiny patch of dried Mexico. As a child, the valley had seemed limitless, the stream in constant conversation with itself, the hills studded with secrets. The squat, square adobe house was snug and cool, the supply of companions constant and close at hand. That was a different lifetime.

Even though the van was now parked a scant thirty miles south of Posadas, Estelle had visited her mother's house in Tres Santos no more than a half dozen times in the past three years—and more out of courtesy to the Diaz family, who kept an eye on the place, than anything else.

"Do you want to go inside?"

"Oh, I don't know," Teresa said. "The dust will make me cough."

"Let me go see," Estelle said, and stepped out of the van. Three steps carried her to the shade of the small front porch, itself no more than four feet deep and eight feet long. Estelle looked at the cracks in the plaster finish that she and her husband had applied five years before. She rested her hand on the warm adobe and looked up at the web-tangled eaves. She could smell the soft musty aroma forced out of the adobe blocks by the high February sun. The front door was without lock or metal latch. A carved block of wood turned into a slot in the jamb, snugging the door against the frame. The gray wood had shed most of its paint. She ran her hand over the sunflower that her great-uncle had carved in the slab wood and saw that traces of yellow enamel still clung to the petal impressions.

The other door of the van opened and her mother waved a hand. "Just go ahead," she called. "I might get there, and I might not."

By the time Teresa had managed to get out of the vehicle, Estelle was at her elbow.

"I can do this," Teresa said.

"I know you can, *Mamá*. But the last time you were here, you broke your hip."

"If I do that again, just roll me in the river and let it go at that." She stopped with one hand on the van's front fender, the other on her walker. "You wouldn't think that ten feet is such a distance." She pointed a finger to the north without releasing her hold on the walker. "You remember all the time you spent in that little village you built down in the trees?"

"Sure." The fist-size adobe houses, with roads, fields, gardens, and various other fortifications, lasted until one of the infrequent rains melted them into amorphous lumps, ready for urban renewal . . . or until Frederico Diaz conducted a raid from *his* town farther upstream.

"Francisco and Carlos would be right at home there," Estelle said. "I'd like to go look at the Villa stump before we go."

"Oh, I'm sure it's still there." Teresa nodded at the front door. "Let's see if there are any surprises."

Estelle knew exactly what she meant, since the little house offered protection for all kinds of creatures, and even a brief term without human interference made the zoo's residency all the more likely. Estelle stayed at her mother's elbow until they reached the door. The wooden latch lifted effortlessly.

Teresa wrinkled her nose at the strong odor of skunk. "Probably nesting under the floor," Estelle said.

"Well, he can have it, then," Teresa said, waving a hand in dismissal. She turned away. "There's nothing there anyway." Estelle pushed the door fully open and stepped across the threshold.

"It would be good to air it out for a while," she said. "Let me get the back." She crossed the tiny living room and kitchen and pulled the brass bolt to open the back door. The rush of cool air brought the scent of cottonwood leaves.

"It's not so bad," Teresa observed. She stood in the front door, both hands on the walker, nodding. A simple white kitchen table remained, along with two straight chairs and a small braided rug in the living room. Various nails projected from the wall, some supporting shadows. An unadorned crucifix hung by the front door.

Estelle looked into the tiny bathroom and bedroom, both neat, tidy, and vacant.

Teresa shuffled to the nearest chair and sat down carefully. "I was born here, you know," she said.

"I know, *Mamá*. And I know you always loved it here."

"That a house should stand so long."

"That too," Estelle laughed.

"I'm as old as the hills now."

"Not quite."

"I feel like it, sometimes." Off in the distance they heard someone's voice raised, but couldn't distinguish the words.

Estelle sat in the other chair, elbows on her knees. "I brought some munchies along, *Mamá*. Are you hungry?"

Teresa shook her head. She was smiling, and pointed out the door. At the same time, Estelle heard the pounding of feet on the earth outside. In a moment, a teenager appeared in the doorway, a hand on each side of the jamb as if holding herself back from catapulting inside.

"Tinita," Estelle cried, and was out of her chair and to the door in three steps. She wrapped her arms around the young girl in a ferocious hug and swung her off her feet. "Look at you," she said, finally releasing the girl to arm's length. Tina Diaz blushed. *"Mamá,* look at this one."

Teresa Reyes stretched out both hands to Tina, who had been greeted into uncharacteristic silence.

"I didn't know you were coming down today," Tina said when she'd caught her breath. "You didn't tell us!"

"Secrets, secrets," Teresa said. She sat holding Tina's left hand in both of hers. "And you didn't tell me that you'd grown into such a beautiful woman."

Tina ducked her head. *"Papá* said he saw your van drive by. He's talking with *Capitán* Naranjo. The *capitán* stopped by for lunch." She beamed at first Teresa and then Estelle. "He asked if you would come to the house."

"Which 'he'," Estelle almost asked.

"Oh yes," Teresa said. "But just for a moment, Tinita. We're tired, and we need to return to Posadas. This police officer here,"—she winked toward Estelle—"she's more busy than any five people. I've taken too much of her time already today."

She pulled her coat more tightly around her frail body. "I need the sun," she said. "This house has winter in it." She pushed herself out of the chair. "Why don't you help me out to the car, *hija,*" she said. "My daughter has a couple of things she needs to look at, and then we'll be along. You can tell *el Capitán* that she won't be late for their meeting."

She turned and smiled at her daughter. "Sometimes young hearing in an old head is a nuisance, don't you think?"

29
◆◆◆

THE Diaz family welcomed Teresa Reyes and her daughter as if the Mexican family had been waiting a decade for that very day. In the dining room, a large, slab-topped table was covered with food and drink, but the ponderous, high-backed wooden dining chairs had been drawn back against the walls, well out of the way so that people could circulate around the table and then, with plates full, retire to the comfortable study in the adjoining room.

None of the rooms of the Diaz home was large. All were low-ceilinged and round-cornered with walls fortress thick. The house included no space wasted in hallways. Instead, a tour of the home would pass through each room on the way to the next, the entire affair encircling a simple inner courtyard.

In the study, a narrow, deeply set window looked out on the tiled courtyard, and with great solicitation, Teresa was guided to a comfortable love seat by the window. Her oxygen tank was placed reverently by her side.

With a weary, almost theatrical shake of her head, Teresa declined the first offers of food and drink, but within minutes Estelle saw with amusement that her mother was enjoying a substantial plate of food—along with a remarkably robust tumbler of dark red wine.

The Diaz home was a wonderfully cluttered museum of the woodcarver's trade, and the study had become the focal point for the exhibition. Carvings ranged from tiny, whimsical creatures of the desert to large, prancing horses standing nearly four feet high. Each creation became a member of the family until it was sold but Estelle could see that several pieces on a shelf behind Roman's desk were obviously cherished family members of long standing. Roman had first touched knife to wood half a century before, at age six. The first horse he had carved, a grotesque little creature with ponderous head and wire legs, still pranced on a brass base on his desk.

Folded in the comfortable, aromatic support of a leather chair in Roman's study, well-fed and with a glass of wine in hand, Estelle let her eyes roam around the study as the conversation drifted from topic to topic.

"Now, you must tell me . . ." was Don Roman's favorite introductory expression as he grilled Estelle about her family and life beyond Tres Santos. Rather than a mere two years, the last visit with the Diaz family seemed several lifetimes distant, and Posadas now very far away.

Of the eight Diaz children, all but Roberto were home, and at various times made their appearances. Through the blizzard of reminiscences, Estelle made a point to glance Tomás Naranjo's way for the first signs of impatience. But Naranjo was as relaxed as if he were spending a week with his good friends. Soft-spoken and self-effacing, the state policeman spent most of his time in conversation with Mateo Diaz, the second eldest of the children—a thin, arthritically bent young man of perhaps nineteen or twenty.

Naranjo sat in a heavily carved rocker, a monstrous chair that rested on its own rug to protect the Saltillo tile underneath. His left leg from toes to midcalf was encased in a black plastic orthopedic boot. "It is nothing," was the sum total of information he dispensed about his injury. He waved off any sympathy with an impatient shrug of dismissal, but when Marta Diaz moved a leather ottoman within range, he accepted it.

Mateo had shown him a collection of small wood carvings, and Naranjo looked at each carefully, handing some back to Mateo, setting others on the floor next to his chair. From time to time, as he sipped from his wine glass, his eyes met Estelle's and a ghost of a smile would touch his face.

"Now, you must tell me," Roman said for the umpteenth time that afternoon, "what of the clinic? Is it true that your husband is to open a medical clinic in Posadas?"

"That's true," Estelle said. "We hope that ground breaking is within the month."

"Ah," Roman said. "That is wonderful news. You have acquired the land and all, then."

"Yes. Almost five acres from *Padrino.*"

"He's well? We don't see as much of him as we used to."

Estelle nodded. "Busier than ever. He's working for the New Mexico Livestock Board now as one of their inspectors. He enjoys it."

Roman scrunched up his face in doubt. "I was a little bit worried about him when he retired, you know. So many years, and then . . ." He ended Bill Gastner's law enforcement career with a slight chop of the hand. "But I'm pleased to hear that he's staying busy. This one over here," and he nodded toward Tomás Naranjo, "he stays busy too, even with his misfortune."

Naranjo grinned and shrugged. Roman Diaz carefully set his empty plate on a small table whose top was a fine mosaic of ceramic tile. "I know that you two need to speak in private." He flashed a smile at Estelle.

With a grace that belied his injury, Naranjo eased himself out of the chair, at the same time placing the small wooden horse he had been holding with his earlier selections. "My wife's shop will be graced by these," he said to Mateo. "As always." He turned toward Estelle. "Suppose we take a stroll around the grounds?"

Roman began a protest, but Naranjo waved it aside. "It's a sprain. A simple sprain during an unguarded clumsy moment. This magic boot allows me to walk with no discomfort at all, and the physician tells me that the more I make use of it, the faster I'll heal. So"—he held out a hand toward Estelle—"may we speak for a few moments?"

"Business, business, business," Teresa Reyes said from across the room. "The affairs of the world."

"We'll be but a moment," Naranjo replied, and Teresa glowered at him with half-serious impatience.

"We have much to talk about as well," Teresa said, including the ebb and flow of Diaz family in a graceful sweep of her hand. "But remember, *Estelita.* We're expected home at five."

215

Somehow, Naranjo managed with only a slight limp as he and Estelle strolled outside to the parked vehicles. "Your mother is a remarkable woman," he said, switching to English. "I'm sorry to see the oxygen bottle."

"Getting her to use it is a challenge," Estelle replied.

"We can all hope to be so acute at that age," Naranjo said. He leaned against the tan Toyota, arms folded across his chest, regarding Estelle. "You're looking well," he said. "No harm done during the visit to the north country."

"An interesting experience," she said.

"The same could be said of camping on an iceberg floating in the North Atlantic."

Estelle laughed. "I suppose."

"It's good to have you back."

"Thank you."

Naranjo shifted his gaze to a point near one of the mines on the far hillside. "I confess that it took me by surprise when I heard that Sheriff Torrez had named you as undersheriff." He looked back at her. "A tribute to his good sense. But it's a post you've held before, is it not?"

"Yes, sir, I did. And for that go-around, it was for the grand total of one week."

Naranjo laughed and pushed away from the vehicle. He turned in place, scanning the countryside. "I'm sure you'll find happiness now. This is such a picturesque place," he said. "Your mother was an institution here." Estelle remained silent. Naranjo smiled. "And your great-uncle, of course. But that was another time." He sighed. "And now I understand you have something of a mess on your hands."

"I have some photos in the car that I'd like to show you," she said. "It'll take me just a moment."

"The stroll will do me good," Naranjo said. "But before I forget . . ." He turned, opened the door of the Toyota, and retrieved a brown envelope. As they walked toward the Guzman vehicle parked in front of Teresa Reyes's house, he extracted a photo, glanced at it, slid it back in, and pulled out another. He handed it to Estelle. The photograph was of professional quality, and bore a gold sticker on the back announcing *El Estudio de Gutierrez* in Asunción. It showed

216

a large wedding party gathered on the front steps of the church. In center front, the bride and groom were radiant, the train of her dress arranged so that it swept down the remaining steps in front of her.

"This man right here," and Naranjo reached over as Estelle stopped. He pointed at the figure standing immediately behind the bride, a large, robust man obviously delighted with his daughter's match. "Is Juan Carlos Osuna. He is a building contractor in Ganos, a man of some distinction. As a matter of fact, the beautiful facade of this church that you see behind him? That is a restoration job completed only last year by Mr. Osuna's company. The church stands at the head of the square in Asunción. Beautiful, no?"

"Surely."

Naranjo took the photograph in exchange for two others. "And that," he said, "is what Mr. Osuna looked like three weeks ago." In the first photo, a man's body was sprawled on barren desert, one boot in the shade of a runty acacia bush. The corpse lay on its face, both arms spread as if the man had been flung to the ground and skidded to a stop on his stomach. A blue cap lay several feet away. The second photo was a close-up, and Estelle winced.

"It appears that the first shot grazed the left side of his neck from the rear," Naranjo said. "Perhaps not even enough to knock him down. The second round struck him in the back of the head, as you can see, and exited out the front."

"And not from particularly close range, either," Estelle said.

"Indeed. Such a blast from close range would have left residue, would have parted the hair—all those kinds of things." He touched the photo with a careful finger as if the image might smudge. "The blood on the left hand is interesting. It's Mr. Osuna's own. It's almost as if, upon feeling the first grazing wound that he slapped his left hand to his neck, so." Naranjo brought his own hand up quickly to his own neck. "In other photos, you can quite clearly see that the blood ran profusely onto his hand, and down his wrist, as we would expect if he were standing so, with his left hand pressed to his injured neck."

"And then the second round hit him in the back of the skull."

"That's what I think happened, yes."

"Where did this happen?"

217

Naranjo accepted the two photos and slid them back into the envelope. "There is a small road that lies between Ganos and Asunción. The country is as you saw in the photograph—bleak and desolate. The body was discovered less than a hundred meters from the road, less than ten kilometers from Asunción."

Estelle resumed her walk to her car, head down, her hands clasped behind her back. "Motive?"

Naranjo pursed his lips and shrugged. "Robbery, I think. Osuna was traveling back to Asunción late in the afternoon on a Saturday, four weeks ago. Among other errands, he was returning with pay envelopes for his five workers."

"He had a crew still in Asunción, then?"

"Most assuredly. They have been working on the central fountain in the square. It's a most impressive project, more than such a modest village could ever afford. It is entirely donated by Mr. Osuna and his company." Naranjo raised an eyebrow in question when he saw the expression on Estelle's face.

"You talked to the workers?" she asked.

"Of course. The project on the fountain was nearly complete when this tragedy occurred. In fact, among other things that day, Mr. Osuna was bringing a small marble icon that was to be included as a finishing touch. A sculptor in Ganos had created it." Naranjo nodded his head sadly. "The workmen were so struck by the tragedy that they completed the fountain project over the next couple of days . . . even without pay."

"The icon wasn't taken?"

Naranjo leaned against the front fender of Estelle's car with a sigh, as if the short walk had been a bit too far. "It was still in his truck, along with various tools and whatnot. Only the money was taken, including whatever funds Mr. Osuna had in his personal wallet, in addition to the pay for his workers. That's how the body was discovered, you see. His truck was left by the side of the road, and noticed by a passerby. But with the wind and so on, there were no tracks that were of any use to us. A petty theft that ended most tragically."

He rapped the hood of the vehicle with the edge of the brown envelope. "Carlos Osuna is—was—a rare man, Estelle. He was wealthy, but shared it. He built grand buildings, but always found

218

time to return to his home to lend the strength of his company to worthwhile projects such as the church in Asunción. Revered would be the wrong word, but Mr. Osuna was certainly highly respected. To lose such a life for no reason is a tragedy that our country can ill afford. The pressures on us to bring resolution to the case are remarkable, but so far . . . we have nothing." He took a deep breath. "So you see, when you mentioned your case, the similarities came to mind immediately. We have precious little to go on, as you can imagine. When such a thing is not witnessed, and occurs in such desolate country"—he shrugged again—"who's to know? Sometimes, though, with patience, if you talk to enough people, sometimes something slips."

"Who's to know," Estelle repeated. "You have no evidence from the scene, then, other than the body? No signs of a struggle, no spent bullets, no shell casings? Things of that sort?"

"Nothing. Troopers combed the area on their hands and knees. We have spent hundreds of hours at the location where Mr. Osuna's body was discovered. Both sides of the road, in an area of ever increasing radius. But nothing. I think we have spoken to every living soul in Chihuahua." He smiled. "And prayed to a few others."

"Did your medical examiner have an opinion about the weapon, based on the wound?"

Naranjo made a face as if he'd bitten into a lemon. "So little there, you know. Because the wound was through and through—and in the first case, only a slight graze—there was nothing, or next to nothing."

Estelle ducked inside the vehicle and rummage through her briefcase. When she straightened up out of the car, she said, "Fragments, you mean?"

"I don't understand."

"You said 'next to nothing,' Captain."

"Ah, well. A tiny piece of lead that had peeled off the core of the bullet when it shattered the skull at entry. Nothing else. And certainly not enough to establish the nature of the rifling, or the caliber of the weapon."

Estelle nodded. "Maybe in time it will help." She extended the photos to Naranjo. "These are the photos that we faxed to your office."

The state policeman frowned as he examined the grim images of Rafael Smith and Lolo Duarte. Again and again he shuffled between the two, and then laid the two photos on the hood of the car, resting his chin on the heel of his hand as he studied them. "Who identified them for you?" he asked finally.

"The rancher who hired them to cut wood."

"This man in Grant County?"

"Yes. They worked there for the better part of a month before heading back toward their homes in Mexico."

"Then it shouldn't be so hard to discover where they lived," Naranjo said. He rested his index finger on the photo of Rafael Smith. "This man . . ." He tapped his finger. "I'm sure that I have seen him, you know." He held up the photo, scrutinizing it. "But he is not someone with whom I am familiar. Maybe he simply reminds me of someone." He sighed and laid the photo down. "I would think that after all these years, I would know every solitary soul in all of Chihuahua, no?" He shook his head.

"There are a lot of strangers left in the world," Estelle said, and Naranjo laughed.

"And at my age, with my memory . . . how does that old joke go? I meet new faces every day, even among my acquaintances." He picked up both photos. "We have the names and a face. I should think we can find out for you by this time tomorrow. Unless something unforeseen intrudes." He tapped the photos once more on the hood and handed them back to Estelle. "And now tell me what surprised you so." He grinned at Estelle's guarded expression. "When I first mentioned Mr. Osuna's work on the fountain, I could see the spark in those wonderful eyes of yours."

Estelle laughed good-naturedly and shook her head in resignation. Her mother hadn't missed a thing . . . and certainly not the occasional, interested glances from Tomás Naranjo. Teresa's *five o'clock meeting* had been the gentle reminder of the habitual chaperone.

"We have two other names that interest us, too," Estelle said. "And they were last reported living in Asunción as well." She gathered up the photos. "And what you'll find most interesting is that at least one account reported that they had jobs working on the plaza fountain project in Asunción."

The flirtatious look of pleasant attentiveness vanished from the state policeman's face. "Two names?"

"The Madrid brothers. Benny and Isidro Madrid. They're handymen of sorts. For a period in January, they were in Maria, doing a roofing job for their father."

"Wally Madrid."

"Yes."

"An unusual circumstance. You see, my men would have talked to them in the course of this investigation. There was nothing to prick their curiosity."

"Well, they've pricked ours, sir. What is most interesting is that when Smith and Duarte stopped in la Taberna Azul in Maria on the way north to cut firewood, several witnesses place the Madrid brothers at the saloon at the same time."

"But not when they stopped on the return trip?"

"That we don't know."

"And the connection that makes you so uneasy?"

"The son of the tavern owner purchased a heavy caliber carbine in December. We're certain that a weapon of similar caliber was used in the Smith-Duarte murders. We learned this morning that the son, Eurelio Saenz, lied about the purchase of the weapon. We have evidence that suggests that the rifle was probably fired, at least once, from a vehicle that was being used, or had been used at some time, by the Madrid brothers. There's a connection there that we don't understand fully."

Naranjo's eyebrows drifted up. "Ah. What does Mr. Saenz have to say?"

"I wish I knew. He denied any information of the rifle, but that was before we had evidence that he was lying. Unfortunately, we had nothing solid enough to hold him on. Early this morning, Eurelio Saenz fled to this country in the company of two men. His mother witnessed the incident, and said that some coercion was involved. She also thinks the two men could have been the Madrid brothers."

"*Could* have been?"

"That's correct. She wasn't sure."

"And Mr. Saenz hasn't been seen since, I'm willing to wager."

"That's also correct."

Naranjo studied Estelle for a long time, but there was none of the suave, gentle Don Juan in his expression this time. "It seems to me that another trip to Asunción is in order," Naranjo said. He looked at his watch. "You have a previous commitment at five, I understand." He almost smiled when he said that, and quickly added, "And your mother is tired and needs to go home, I'm sure. Let me look into this. Perhaps there are some simple answers after all." He reached out a courtly hand for Estelle's elbow. "I'll pay my respects to Don Roman, gather my purchases, and be on my way. Expect to hear from me this evening. Will that be satisfactory?"

Estelle nodded. She let herself be escorted back into the house. Fifteen minutes later, with the dust from Tomás Naranjo's Toyota long dispersed, Estelle walked her mother out to the car for their return to Posadas.

As they drove out the lane, around the high adobe wall that marked the Diaz hacienda's grounds, Teresa sighed. "This is a nice little village," she said. "But you know . . ." She waved a hand, leaving the sentence unfinished.

"I hope we didn't pull you away from visiting your place too soon," Estelle said.

"No, no. I saw what I needed to see." She turned slightly in her seat, arranging first the pleats of her skirt and then the coils of oxygen hose. "You gave information to the captain that was of interest to him. I could see it on his face when he left."

"He has a case that's related to one of ours, I think," Estelle said.

Teresa nodded. "He left in a hurry. You, too."

Estelle eased the car up out of the arroyo, and turned on the single lane dirt road that lead north to the border crossing at Regál. "We both have five o'clock meetings, *Mamá*."

"Oh, okay," Teresa said. She covered her mouth with two arthritic fingers to stifle the smile.

THE leisurely drive back to Posadas included a brief stop at the small mission in Regál. Estelle had been surprised at the request, since her mother had shown no interest in visiting the church in Tres Santos. The original mission in Tres Santos had burned in 1960, and had been replaced with a conservative frame building, its sharply peaked, metal roof somehow incongruous in a village of flat-roofed adobes. Perhaps it was that design that offended Teresa.

In Regál, it took Teresa Reyes more time to get out of the van and walk up the three steps to the mission's cool interior than she spent inside. Once inside, what brief conversation she had with the various saints was a concise and private one.

La Iglesia de Nuestra Señora was without electricity or plumbing. The thick, immaculately white walls rose uncluttered to the heavy beamed ceiling, and the twelve stations of the cross were represented in small *nichos* around the perimeter. Other than the soft, distant knocks and pings of the roof as it cooled in late afternoon, the hush of *la Iglesia* was powerful.

Estelle stood just behind the last pew, watching her mother commune with the spirits. When after three or four minutes Teresa began the process of lifting herself from her knees, Estelle stepped forward to offer assistance.

"This is a good church," Teresa said. She didn't clarify whether it was the building that was stout and true, or whether she meant that the saints harbored in its cool silence were especially receptive.

"Yes, it is," Estelle said, and her mother nodded with approval that her daughter understood.

Back in the car, Teresa sighed with contentment and readjusted the oxygen tube without reminder. As they pulled back onto the asphalt of the state highway, she turned to her daughter to relate the decision after her consultation with the higher powers.

"What you're doing is a good thing."

Estelle glanced across at her mother. "Which thing that I'm doing is good, *Mamá?*"

"You know, I'm eighty-two years old. In all that time, you're the only policewoman I've ever known."

"You've lived a sheltered life, *Mamá*. That's why the word *policía* is feminine."

"That's true. That's true. But I've decided it's a good thing—what you do."

"Sometimes I'm not so sure," Estelle replied.

"The farmer says that, too, when it doesn't rain as often as he likes."

"I suppose."

"The devil knows more because he's old than because he's the devil, you know. And I've been around for a long, long time now." She gazed out the side window as the van wound its way up through Regál pass. "I'm glad we didn't wait until summer to visit the house. Do you remember how hot it would get in July and August?"

"For sure. We spent most of our time in the water holes," Estelle replied.

"Maybe you should take the boys down. This summer, I mean. Roman and Marta would like to see them—if you have the time."

"We'll make time, *Mamá*. Francis would enjoy that too. By then, he's going to need a break."

"Sometimes it seems like it's a hundred miles away, doesn't it?"

"Or more." As if it had been waiting patiently for them to clear the rise of Regál Pass, the cellular phone interrupted. Estelle thumbed it open.

"Guzman."

"Ma'am, this is Collins," the deputy said. "Are you back in the country?"

Estelle smiled and glanced at her mother. "We're just coming down off the pass, Dennis. We'll be back in town in about twenty minutes."

"Oh, good. Look, I talked with George Enriquez of National Mutual Insurance. His agency is the one who held Eleanor Pope's auto insurance. I got the insurance card from the glove box of her car? And her son's, too, what's left of it. I figured that maybe she'd have all her insurance with the same place. But Enriquez says that Mrs. Pope didn't have home owner's, at least not with NMI."

"Maybe with another company, then."

"He doesn't think so. He said that he'd tried to talk her into home owner's before, but that she didn't want it. He said that he tried pretty hard to convince her that she should have it."

"She didn't have a mortgage on the place, then."

"Why is that?"

"A lender would require insurance, Dennis. They've lived on that property forever, though. I suppose it was paid off long ago. Did you happen to ask about a life insurance policy?"

"No dice," Collins said. "She didn't have that either."

"At least not with NMI."

"Right. But Enriquez said he'd talked to her about that, too, on more than one occasion. She never mentioned that she had coverage with someone else. She just told him that she wasn't interested in more insurance."

"So, no life insurance, and no home owner's insurance," Estelle said, more to herself than Collins. "Unless she had it with another company. That's interesting."

"Kind of makes you wonder what old Denton had in mind when he decided to blow things up," Collins said. "Maybe it was just his way of winning the award for the most complicated suicide of the decade."

"Stranger things have happened. Did you happen to locate Mrs. Pope's checkbook, by the way? That's sometimes a good record of payments."

"I think Taber was going to go that route. And the Popes also had a safety deposit box at Posadas National Bank. Taber was going to see about getting a court order from Judge Hobart to have a look-see. Maybe there'll be something of interest hidden away, but I don't know if she did that yet or not. She might still be out in no-man's land, for all I know."

"That very well could be." She didn't bother to add for the high-octane Collins's benefit that persistent, dogged diligence sometimes uncovered things missed in the first, quick pass. "Who else did you talk to?"

"Ah, nobody, yet. I was kinda going on what Enriquez said."

"That's okay, but you need to make a quick run down the list of agents in Posadas, Lordsburg, and Deming," Estelle said. "Find out if Eleanor Pope was a customer. She might have been doing business with somebody else, and just didn't want to have to explain to Enriquez. And when you find out what bank she used, have a chat with them, too."

"All right."

"And then get together with Jackie to see about payments. Not very many people pay things like their monthly bills with cash. She would have been writing checks if she had insurance."

Collins grunted something Estelle didn't catch, then added, "I don't know about that . . . Tom Pasquale sure does. Cash or money orders."

Estelle laughed. "But that's Tom," she said. "If the whole world operated the way he does, the global financial system would be in chaos. You need to check with the other agencies."

"Will do. Everybody's closed now, though, so I'll get on it first thing in the morning."

"There's always . . ." Estelle stopped herself, the memory of a casual comment flooding back into her mind. "Have you talked to Linda Real about this?"

"Why her?" Collins asked.

"She mentioned that she'd talked to Eleanor Pope while they were sitting in the insurance office. Maybe she said something in that conversation that would be useful to us."

"I think she went home for a while."

She had been about to remind Collins that even after hours, there were home phones to contact, but she thought better of it. She knew that several of the deputies—herself included—didn't bother documenting overtime. Others—Dennis Collins included—turned in every minute over the standard forty hours, perhaps on the not uncommon assumption that they had a life, and the county's intrusion into that life was going to be a commensurate cost to taxpayers. She made a mental note to talk with Linda herself as soon as she had the chance.

"We'll see what develops," she said instead. "Keep me posted."

"Will do," Collins replied.

She switched off the phone and glanced at her mother.

"You know, my mother remembered Pancho Villa," Teresa said. "She met him once, less than a week before he was killed."

"I would have liked to have been there."

"Just another *bandito,* my mother said. Nothing more."

"History has given him some stature, then," Estelle said.

Teresa nodded. "These men you chase," she said. "The ones who left the two boys out on the desert to die. No such stature in them, is there."

Estelle looked back at her mother with surprise. It was easy to assume that an elderly woman, dozing in a rocking chair, wouldn't hear the conversations around her, or if she did, might not understand them or ruminate on them. "What do you think about it all, *Mamá?* Why would they do such a thing?"

"Because they have nothing else," Teresa said. "Tomorrow holds nothing for them. It is only what they can gain *today* that counts. Nothing else. And they are young, and that makes them dangerous. No wisdom." She grimaced and shook her head. "They are *young* devils, *Estelita.* They don't know anything about tomorrow. And that makes them dangerous." She took a deep breath through her nose, drawing in the oxygen. "As long as they don't know that you're coming up behind them, you'll be okay," she said.

227

31

THE new telephone line ran through the tree limbs along the river, then looped over one of the Villa stump's broken stubs before stretching across the open space to the house. The Diaz family waited outside in a neat queue along with a dozen strangers, all eager to go in the house and try Teresa Reyes's new telephone. Despite the hot sun, everyone waited patiently for the district telephone people to find the correct adapter to mate Mexican wiring to the telephone Teresa had brought with her from Posadas.

"Who was it?"

Estelle heard her husband's quiet voice, and Tres Santos sunshine gave way to the confusion of darkness. She didn't reply for a moment, letting the faint trickle of illumination from the hallway nightlight outline first the doorway and then, as her eyes adjusted and consciousness took over from sleep, the other familiar objects in the room.

"Who was what?" she said, and only as she started to turn toward Francis did she notice that the small telephone was lying beside her pillow.

"On the phone," Francis prompted.

Estelle levered herself up onto her elbows and stretched across to turn on the bedside light. "The phone rang, and you answered it," Francis said. He lay on his back, arm thrown across his eyes.

Estelle turned and looked at him, brows furrowed, phone in hand. "And what did I say?"

"'Uh-huh. Okay. Uh-uh. Right.'" He lifted his arm and squinted at her. "Those were your exact words. A deep, meaningful conversation if there ever was one. What time is it, anyway?" He lifted his head, looked at the clock, and expelled a loud sigh as the digits clicked over to 4:12 A.M.

"Tell me that didn't really happen."

"All right. It didn't happen." He reached and gently disengaged the phone from her hand. "If we're going to start having conversations in our sleep, we need one of those phones with caller ID and all that fancy stuff."

She shifted her weight to one elbow and reached for the phone again. "Let me call the SO. It was probably them."

"Or—" Francis was interrupted as the telephone once more came to life, its ring startlingly loud. "Whoever it was didn't believe you," he added.

"Guzman," Estelle said into the phone.

"Uh-huh, okay, uh-huh, right," Francis mimicked softly, and Estelle kneed him.

"This is Sutherland, ma'am," the voice on the telephone said. "I'm sorry to disturb you, but did you copy that message a minute ago?"

"No, I didn't," Estelle replied. She sat up on the side of the bed. "Thanks for calling back."

"No problem," Brent Sutherland said. "I didn't think you sounded awake."

"What's up?"

"We received a report of an unidentified male subject with unspecified injuries down on State 61, about three miles east of Maria. A trucker called in after stopping to render assistance. Deputy Taber is headed down that way and she wanted me to give you a call."

"Do you have an ambulance en route?"

"One is on standby. They haven't rolled yet. I was waiting until we had something a little more concrete to go on."

"No, no, don't do that. Go ahead and have them respond. Truckers aren't wrong very often. This isn't an MVA?"

"Apparently not. Unless it's a pedestrian involved with a hit-and-run."

"The trucker is still on the scene?"

"He said that he'd stand by until someone got there."

"The victim is alive?"

"The trucker *thinks* so, but he's kinda shook. He didn't sound like he was too sure about anything . . . kind of panicky."

"Where's Jackie now?"

Sutherland hesitated, and Estelle could picture him turning to look at the patrol log. "Ah, she was just taking a swing through Regál when I got ahold of her."

"How long ago did the trucker call in?"

"It's been about three minutes now."

"Okay. I'm en route. Are you still in contact with the trucker?"

"Yes, ma'am. I've got him on line three."

"Good. Tell him we're on the way. And you might give State Police dispatch a buzz and see if they have a man closer. Or the Border Patrol. Either one."

"I've done that. The closest trooper is in Lordsburg at the moment. The Border Patrol has a unit headed out east from Deming, but that's going to take a while."

"Okay, I'm on my way. And be sure that ambulance is rolling."

Estelle swung up and out of bed, tossing the phone to Francis.

"Alive or dead?" he asked.

"Don't know. But it's down by Maria, and we haven't been having much luck down that way recently."

Francis grimaced. "How many?"

"One."

"So far," he added, but he was already talking to Estelle's back.

In less than five minutes, Estelle was out of the house and swinging the unmarked patrol car eastbound on Bustos Avenue. She turned the radio up and dropped the mike in her lap as she powered through the intersection with Grande and headed south. Jackie Taber was driving one of the older Broncos, and even flailing the old thing for all it was worth, she would still be the better part of ten miles out on State 56. Because of the bulwark of the San Cristóbal mountains, the deputy would essentially have to drive all the way back to Posadas to reach the intersection with State 61 toward Maria.

Estelle keyed the mike. "PCS, this is three ten."

"Go ahead, three ten."

"What's the trucker's twenty?"

"He says that he can see mile marker one-oh-six just to the east of where he's parked. And the ambulance is en route."

"Ten-four. I see it." Ahead, the winking lights of the ambulance grew out of the darkness, and she snapped on her own grill lights as she overtook the slower unit. Ahead lay sixteen miles of empty road. As she accelerated, Estelle turned on the spotlight, letting the pencil beam lance out along the side of the road, giving her a small edge over the desert creatures that might be ambling out onto the tarmac.

Finally, she could see the sodium vapor light in the distance that hung in front of Wally Madrid's gas station, a single beacon in the otherwise blank, black canvas. As she slowed for the village of Maria, she heard Jackie Taber announce that the deputy was turning southbound on 61, sixteen miles behind her.

The unmarked car flashed through Maria in the span of two heartbeats. Estelle leaned forward, eyes straining to see beyond the walls of the light tunnel through which her car flashed. The highway swept up through a series of graceful chicanes, cutting through the first limestone hint of the San Cristóbals and then, after crossing a rumpled section of prairie cut by a dozen small arroyos, shot straight east. As her car crested a rise, she could see the running lights of the big rig's trailer along the south side of the highway.

Estelle slowed, planting the car dead-center on the dotted line. As she approached, she saw a single figure silhouetted by the rig's headlights. He stepped out and walked the length of the truck to meet her as she pulled in behind it.

"He's right over there by the fence," he said. The trucker looked too small for his rig—almost frail in build with the light breeze plastering his T-shirt against washboard ribs as he shrugged into a down jacket. The bulk of the truck's trailer blocked Estelle's view, and she pulled the car in reverse until the spotlight beam blanketed the shapeless lump by the highway right-of-way fence off to the right. "I seen him, and hit the brakes," the man said. "Then I backed up here on the shoulder so I could keep him in my lights."

"Okay," Estelle said, and picked up the mike. "PCS, three ten is ten-ninety-seven."

"Ten-four, three ten."

"Three ten," Deputy Taber's voice announced, "three oh nine copies. ETA about ten minutes."

Estelle clicked the mike twice, collected her flashlight, and swung out of the car. The trucker turned slightly sideways as she approached, stepping back toward his rig.

"I'm Undersheriff Guzman," Estelle said. "What's your name, sir?"

He fell in step beside her as she walked the length of the truck. "Noel Jones," he said. "I'm out of Emmetsburg, Texas."

They rounded the cab of the big truck. Its engine idled gently, a deep, guttural pulse.

"Would you shut down your truck, sir? It's difficult to hear over it."

"I guess I can do that."

"Thank you. And then I'd appreciate it if you'd remain here."

"Yes, ma'am." Estelle waited a moment as the man climbed back inside the unit. In a moment, the engine died. "Ya'all want me to leave the lights on for a minute?"

"Yes."

The man added something about his batteries, but Estelle was no longer listening to him. She walked along the shoulder of the road, flashlight illuminating the ground. The light from her patrol car's spotlight forced harsh shadows behind each clump of grass. At a spot directly opposite the lump of rags, she turned toward the fence. The four strands of barbed wire were tight, rigidly braced every eight feet with vertical stays. The fence was strung tightly enough that a man could clamber over it while the wires supported his weight.

As Estelle drew near, she saw a hand lift ever so slightly, the arm thrust under the fence but caught on the bottom wire. The man, barefoot but wearing a denim work shirt and blue jeans, was lying on his back. His eyes were closed, mere slits in a face puffed and swollen nearly round.

"We're here," Estelle said as she knelt down beside Eurelio Saenz. "Don't move anymore." She could see that the wire had torn the young man's arm in a dozen places, and then, moving the flashlight quickly to assess his injuries, saw that he was a mass of blood, flecked from head to toe. The front of his shirt was torn and blood-soaked. A groan of agony escaped his lips and his head jerked to the right. She saw that the gold ear stud in his left ear had ripped free. His hair, no longer shiny and well-oiled, was encrusted with the desert across which he'd crawled.

Taking his hand, she pulled the wire barbs out of his forearm to release him from the fence, and each touch brought another moan. He tried to flex one leg at the knee, but even that motion was impossible. The light caught the back of his hand, and Estelle saw the long cactus barbs embedded in his skin. She moved the beam and felt a swell of nausea as she saw that the young man's entire body appeared to be an enormous welter of cactus spines, as if he'd rolled through a patch, unable to stop until every inch of his skin had been stabbed and pinned.

"Oh my God," he managed through swollen lips, and one leg kicked feebly.

"Just lie still," Estelle said. "We'll get you out of here." She pulled the handheld radio off her belt. "PCS, three ten. We have one subject down, unknown multiple injuries. Expedite that ambulance."

"Ten-four, three ten."

Estelle turned and looked back toward the rig. "Sir! I need you over here."

He approached none too eagerly, stopping a dozen feet away.

"I need to get fencing pliers to cut these wires. Stay with him for a minute." The man hesitated. "Just for a minute. Talk to him. Tell him who you are." Before the man had a chance to protest, Estelle sprinted past him. At the county car, she scrabbled for the electric trunk release. In the trunk's cavernous interior, she found the canvas roll, flipped it open and pulled out the heavy fencing pliers.

With that and the large first-aid kit, she raced back. The trucker was bent over, hands on his knees. He straightened back up immediately and stepped away. "Here," Estelle said, forcing the fencing pliers at him. "You can do this ten times faster than I can. I need all four wires cut. Right at the post here. Then roll the strands way back out of the way."

"Highway department ain't going to like that," Jones said. He bent down, and Estelle put her arms over the injured man's face and turned her own head away, grimacing with closed eyes in anticipation as Jones clamped the pliers around the wire. The strand parted with a musical twang, curling back to the first vertical stay. One by one, Jones worked his way up the post until all four wires snaked back in a snarled jumble.

With the wires gone, she could crouch directly beside the victim.

"You're going to be all right, Eurelio," she said. The flashlight beam caught the stubble on his face. The cactus spines looked like large, coarse chin whiskers.

She bent down until she was just inches from his ear. "Who did this to you, Eurelio?" But all she got was a whimper in response.

32

◆◆◆

EURELIO Saenz breathed as if each tiny motion drove a pitchfork through his body. The continuous, feeble flexing of his limbs just made matters worse. He could not squirm away from the assault. After a moment, it seemed as if he was responding to Estelle's voice even though he didn't open his eyes. His hands stopped their aimless spasms and he lay still.

"Somebody hit him with a car, or what?" Noel Jones asked. He kept his distance, hands balled into tight fists.

Estelle didn't reply. Keeping the light out of Eurelio's face, she played the flashlight down the length of his body. His clothing was studded with cactus spines, but even the thousand barbs didn't explain the mass of blood that soaked his shirt front around a long, ragged hole. The barbs pegged the shirt to his skin as if he'd been transformed into living Velcro. When Estelle touched the fabric of the shirt, she felt his body tense.

"No, no," he whispered, and she could hear the panic in his voice. One eyelid flickered.

She turned to the first-aid kit and found surgical scissors. "Mr. Jones!" she called. "Come here." She heard his tentative advance behind her. "Hold the flashlight so I can see." He gingerly took the big aluminum light. "Closer, please." He took a step forward and aimed the light as if it were a fire hose, holding it with both hands at arm's length. Estelle could see that the jagged rip across the left breast of Eurelio's shirt was more than just a gash from a barbed wire prong. Blood welled up, and she took her hands away. "It's going to be all right, Eurelio," she murmured, knowing that it obviously wasn't going to be all right. She wanted to at least pad the gaping wound until the EMTs arrived, but there was no way to press a gauze pad over the field of heavy cactus spines without driving them farther into his flesh. There was no spurting of arterial blood, no deadly sucking sound of a hole punched through into the lung, and she hesitated to inflict any more damage. She sat back on her haunches.

"Christ," Jones said. "He took himself a header somewheres."

In the distance, they heard the wail of a siren. "Just hang in there," she said. She spread the pad out like a handkerchief and let it drift over the wound with just its own weight.

"Keep the light out of his face," she said, and Jones twitched the light back, grunting an apology. Crouched by the young man's side, Estelle waited with her back to the spotlight. Jackie Taber's unit arrived in the lead, with the ambulance less than a hundred yards behind.

Taber parked ahead of the truck, swinging wide to the left and then turning tightly so that she could catch the area in both headlights and spot. The ambulance stopped on the highway shoulder, and the first EMT out of the ambulance was a young girl who looked to be not much more than a teenager. Estelle stood up to meet them.

Reaching out a hand to take the young woman by the upper arm, Estelle bent close, her voice no more than a whisper. "Somebody's beaten him with cactus," she said. "There's another injury there, too, but I can't tell what it is yet."

"Oh my," the EMT said, and hesitated, turning to her partner.

"Let's see what we've got," he said. They knelt by the victim's side for a few minutes. Estelle bent forward until she could read Sam Ortiz's name tag.

"I don't think this is a sucking wound," Estelle said. She removed the light covering and the EMT, a heavyset man with a cleanly shaven bullet head, moved in close.

"Nah," he said as if he saw people rolled in cactus spines on an hourly basis. "No sign of anything broken?"

"I don't know. I didn't want to touch him. But I don't think so. Everything is straight and points where it's supposed to point."

"Let's find an open spot and get an IV started." He examined Eurelio's left arm, fingers poised. "Well, shit," he said. "Young fella, you sure got into it, didn't you." He bent back and fast-drew scissors out of his belt holster. With deft motions he cut through the shirt sleeve. "No, no, you can't pull it off," he said as his partner started to pull the severed sleeve away. A little high-pitched yelp emerged from Eurelio. "Just leave it."

He glanced up at Jackie Taber. "You might get the gurney," he said, and Taber nodded. "He ain't going to want to be rolled over," Ortiz added, and Eurelio moaned again, stabbed a hundred times just by the thought. "That's all right, now," the EMT soothed. He motioned to Jackie as she approached. "We're enough hands here that we can just levitate him on board," he said, holding his hands out flat. "Sheriff, you at his head. Jackie, you and me at his shoulders. Emma," and he stopped, looking around. "There's another one around, ain't there?"

Noel Jones had faded back toward his truck, hand at his mouth.

"Sir, we're going to need your assistance," the EMT shouted at the trucker.

"His name's Jones," Estelle said.

"Mr. Jones, you and Emma are going to be at his hips. One hand on his hip, one hand right at his knees. She'll show you how. Think you can do that?"

Jones took a deep breath and shrugged. His face was flat white, and despite the cool night air of late February, Estelle could see the sheen of sweat on his forehead in the glare of the lights.

When Sam Ortiz was satisfied with all five sets of hands spaced to his satisfaction, he turned to nod at Estelle. "We want that head to stay real still, sheriff. Don't know what's going on inside, you know, or what that neck of his looks like. But he's studded enough that if I strap on a cervical collar, I'm just as apt to drive barbs right into all the wrong places." He shot a quick look at the other EMT and Noel Jones. "Now everybody just kind of work your hands in until you've got support."

He nodded, and almost immediately shook his head, making a sharp sucking noise against his teeth. "Easier said than done." Eurelio jerked once and then was quiet. "All right, he's passed out, so let's get it over with," Ortiz said. "On three." And on three, they lifted Eurelio Saenz out of the sand and transferred him to the waiting gurney.

"No straps," Ortiz said when his partner started to stretch one of them out. He shook his head. "Kind of like handling a porcupine," he said, and actually managed a smile at Estelle. "How'd this happen, you know?"

"No idea," Estelle said, although she could clearly picture exactly what had happened. "We'll meet you at the hospital." She turned to the trucker. His face was puckered up in a grimace, and he was digging at the palm of his hand in the glare of the ambulance headlights. "You all right, sir?"

"I got a spine in my hand," he said. "Jesus." He straightened up, sucking on his hand. "Got it, I think."

"Do you want one of the EMTs to take a look at it?"

"No, no," he said quickly. "That's not necessary. I got it."

Estelle extended her hand. Jones's grip was perfunctory. "Thank you, sir. We appreciate your help," she said.

"Need me for anything more?"

"No, sir. Let me jot down a couple things, and then you're free to go."

"I've got it, sheriff," Deputy Taber said. Her notebook was already in hand.

Estelle waited by her car, fingers drumming on the roof, until the ambulance had left and the big rig had pulled away, a cloud of dense, sweet exhaust hanging on the air. In a moment, the stout figure of Jackie Taber joined her.

"I've never seen anything like that," Jackie said.

"*Azote del espinos,*" Estelle said.

"A what of thorns?"

"*Azote.* A whip of thorns," Estelle replied. "My Uncle Reuben once told me about something similar happening light-years ago, when he was a teenager. He remembered hearing about some guy being surprised in the act by a jealous husband. Instead of shooting

238

him, the husband chased the man down, caught him, and then while some of his *compadres* held the guy, the husband went and cut off a cholla cactus plant at the ground." She made chopping motions with her hand. "He took his time, trimming off the spines at the base with a couple neat swipes of the machete so he'd have a clean handle, then whacked the cactus off at the ground." She held the imaginary cactus plant in her hand. "A cholla has all those neat limbs and prongs on it. Makes an efficient whip."

"Oh, you're kidding."

"No, I'm not. I wish I was. You talk to any of the old-timers, and they've probably heard the story."

"So somebody beat Eurelio with a cactus? That's what you think happened?"

Estelle nodded. "And then my guess is that they shot him for good measure." She stood with her hands on her hips, looking south. "I don't think he was pitched out of a vehicle from this highway. Most of his body was on the other side of the right-of-way fence. It looked like he'd been trying to crawl through somehow. Maybe under it. He got caught up in the wire. That's when the trucker happened by and found him."

She returned through the welter of boot tracks to the point where Eurelio had been found, and then played her flashlight on the sandy gravel. The scuffed, blood-flecked trail through the stunted desert growth was clearly visible. "What do you want to bet," Estelle said, and stepped carefully across the fence line.

"From the border, you think?"

"Sure. The border fence is about a hundred yards away at this point. That little hillock there makes it impossible to see it from the highway where we're parked. If there's a border fence there at all, it's just going to be a few strands of barbed wire."

Jackie snapped on her flashlight, and the two made their way carefully through the spotty vegetation. Only once did they lose the trail where Eurelio had been forced to work his way around a dense clump of greasewood. "I can't imagine this," Jackie said.

"That's the whole point," Estelle said grimly. A splotch of blood drew them back to the trail. "The misery of being flogged is only the beginning if you survive. Then you have to have all the spines removed. And each one has that nasty little barb on the end. And the spines are big enough, large enough in diameter, that they're lethal—not just little nuisances like those you might get off a Christmas cactus or something. And about ninety-five percent of the time, the wound becomes infected."

"Why didn't they just kill him and get it over with?"

"Well, they probably did, in the end," Estelle said. "Maybe the gunshot—if that's what it was—was a touch of mercy shining through. Put him out of his misery."

"That didn't work, then."

"No, it didn't. At least not yet."

They followed the trail as it wended its way south. Eventually, as they skirted the rise, they saw the narrow dirt path that was the border road. It paralleled a ramshackle fence, the steel posts bent and rusted. At one point, a single strand of wire drooped between two posts, the others snarled and rusted on the ground.

Estelle stepped to the nearest post, standing right at its base. She carefully played the flashlight on the ground, trying to imagine how the myriad of scuffs and digs in the desert had been made, splotched in several places with fresh blood. "There's no doubt he came through the fence right here, then."

"No doubt at all." Jackie played her light south. "But where from here, that's the question." She stepped over the wire and stood several paces firmly in Mexico, then turned and looked at Estelle. "What do you think?"

"I don't think that I want to let them go. I think I *really* want to arrest somebody."

"I hear that," Jackie Taber murmured.

Estelle took a deep breath. She knew that her friendship with Capt. Tomás Naranjo was built on a foundation that included Naranjo's respect for her family's *padrino,* Bill Gastner, thirty years undersheriff and then briefly sheriff of Posadas County. Estelle had met Naranjo a dozen times over the years in job-related encounters. She knew that the Mexican officer's good-natured, flirtatious hints earlier in the day had been just that. He had no authority to simply throw open the Mexican border to American law enforcement officers . . . and probably wouldn't, even if the authority were his to do so. Estelle knew that for her and her deputy to chase off into the Mexican desert, armed and official, was to invite a long vacation in a Mexican prison.

"You want to go on?" Jackie asked.

Estelle turned a full circle, head up as if sensing the air. The desert was quiet. "I need you to stay with Eurelio, Jackie. If they're able to save him, we might get a word or two out of him. And while you're waiting, be sure to call Paulita. She needs to be there with him."

"All right," Jackie said, but Estelle could hear the hesitation. "What do you plan to do?"

"For one thing, you're in uniform, and I'm not." Estelle reached around behind her back underneath her jacket and pulled the Beretta out of her waistband. She handed it to the deputy. "Here." She nodded toward the highway behind them. "If you'd lock that in my car, I'd appreciate it. I don't feature seeing the inside of a white-washed cell."

"This isn't very smart, Estelle," Jackie said. "Besides, the Mexican cops don't know we're here. We can just do a little scouting without any trouble at all."

"I know that," Estelle replied. "But someone needs to be with Eurelio right now. And I don't want to leave this." She waved a hand toward Mexico. "Just cover for me. I'm going to walk a ways and see what I can find. I'll take the little Olympus with the flash." She pulled the handheld radio from her belt and held it up. "I've got this. Stay tuned, as they say."

"You want me to get a hold of Naranjo?"

"Yes. Tell him exactly where I am, and what we need."

"What we need is some daylight," Jackie said.

"That's a couple of hours that I don't want to waste. It doesn't make any sense to me that whoever beat Eurelio did it somewhere else, and then drove him here to dump him. I can't see that happening. I *can* imagine them driving out into the desert, forcing him out of the car, and then taking their time to . . ." She hesitated. ". . . to do what they did. Then I can imagine them snapping off a quick shot to finish him off. Then they leave. And then he crawls toward the sound of the highway."

"Not that there's been much to hear," Jackie said.

"True. But even one car every ten or fifteen minutes would give him something to aim for. I mean, the poor kid probably couldn't see a thing." She took a deep breath, gazing south. "See if you can reach Naranjo for me. I'll be right back. I'll check with you at the hospital."

"You've got your phone?"

"Yes, I do. And it's switched off." She grinned. "I'll call you . . . don't call me." She didn't take time to explain to the deputy why she didn't want to make the call to Naranjo herself. It was the same stretch of desert, after all . . . the arbitrary line in the gravel that marked the end of one country and the beginning of another meant nothing to the rocks and plants and critters that lived here—or to the signals from her cellular phone. As she moved steadily south—even though only by a few feet—she wanted to concentrate on every sound, every waft of air, every smell that the Mexican desert had to offer. The last thing she wanted, when she needed absolute silence, was the sudden, jarring warble of the telephone.

33

❖❖❖

ESTELLE Reyes-Guzman was able to follow the traces of Eurelio Saenz's tortured crawl for what she estimated was well over two hundred yards before the relatively level desert gave way to a rumple in its complexion. An arroyo swept in from the northwest, cut when a small rivulet started off the flank of the hill just southwest of where the undersheriff's car was parked.

Standing on the arroyo's edge, Estelle swung the light to play on the tracks. The arroyo bottom a dozen feet below was cut by another small channel from the most recent rains—a month, two months, maybe six months before. A few deep pockmarks where cattle had stepped caught the light.

When Eurelio had crossed the arroyo, he had been staggering, but he'd been on his feet. He hadn't crawled across like a wounded lizard. The arroyo bottom was at least fifty feet wide, maybe sixty. The harsh beam of the flashlight made it difficult to judge. The shoeprints meandered like those of a drunken man.

He had reached the northeast side and then had been faced with an arroyo bank of eroded gravel that was twice as tall as he was—an impossible barrier for a man who could hardly walk, and probably could not see.

Estelle stepped as near the edge as she dared and turned the light downward. The tracks turned to parallel the arroyo side, running up a smooth wash of quartz sand. Estelle could picture the young man, one arm out against the rough bank for balance, trying to maneuver his way in the dark, desperate almost to madness from the pain.

Cattle were adept at finding their way down into and up out of arroyos. Once they discovered an easy route, that became their thoroughfare, hooves cutting the trail deep and hard. Eurelio Saenz had stumbled along the arroyo for almost fifty feet before he came upon the cattle trail that would save his life. The trail cut diagonally up the bank, up and out to the desert beyond.

Before descending into the arroyo, Estelle stood and listened. She hadn't heard Jackie Taber's county unit accelerate away, but the sound could easily be lost in the rolling hills. She looked up at the vast heavens. A full moon would have been helpful, rather than the little silver remnant that was already fading just above the eastern horizon.

Picking her way slowly, Estelle descended into the arroyo. Mingled with the tracks were copious blood spatters. She followed the tracks across, but even from the midpoint of the arroyo, still twenty or thirty feet from the other side, she saw that there was no matching cattle trail on the other side. Still, the footprints staggered from a spot directly ahead. She reached the southwest side of the arroyo and stopped. The edge above her head was crumbled, some of the edge freshly knocked loose.

On the arroyo floor was a series of imprints, a hodgepodge of impressions. No one had scrabbled down the arroyo side. The loose edge and churned gravel below indicated that at least one person had plunged into the arroyo from above. For several minutes, Estelle stood quietly, working the flashlight over every inch.

Had Eurelio Saenz cringed at the edge of the arroyo above, beaten and barely conscious, caught in the glare of flashlights, until a bullet had bowled him over the side? Had he been unceremoniously kicked over as he lay unconscious and bleeding?

Whatever the circumstances, the thugs had chosen a prime spot— out of sight of the highway, the border fence, any curious, prying eyes. A spring rain would shift and mold the contours of the arroyo bottom, hiding the few bones that coyotes, ravens, and vultures left behind.

Eurelio Saenz had fooled them. His attackers had been convinced that the young man was dead, Estelle was sure. They had taken the time to bury Rafael Smith, but Lolo Duarte had made them angry, and they'd left his corpse for the vultures. Apparently, Eurelio Saenz had made them angry, too.

With no way to leap up and out of the arroyo at that point, Estelle swung her light southeast, following the watercourse. The arroyo ran straight for fifty yards before sweeping around a corner. Estelle walked in that direction, staying on the ground beaten by cattle hooves. Just around the corner, she found a slump in the arroyo bank, and the trail led up on a long diagonal. She climbed out quickly, then turned to walk back along the rim.

She approached the spot above Eurelio's plunge with care. The vegetation was scant, dotted across the rugged desert, clustered here and there where there was shade or a natural water catchment.

It was the tire tracks that caught the flashlight beam first as she swept it back and forth. A rough cut in the desert, dodging the runty clusters of acacia and cholla, was marked by the occasional passage of vehicles—a rancher, shepherd, hunter, or rock hound, maybe a dozen in a banner year. Still, that was enough to make a permanent scar in the desert. The two-track had to meander eventually toward the main road from Tres Santos to Asunción.

Estelle stood and listened, wishing she was high over the desert in Jim Bergin's plane. She would be able to understand at a glance the spiderweb of trails and paths. Perhaps the path in front of her was the only thoroughfare in this area. If so, it must wind within shouting distance of the border fence behind the village of Maria, perhaps only a few thousand yards from where Estelle stood.

She stepped as if in slow motion, playing the light under every bush or clump of bunch grass. Twenty feet from the arroyo edge, she found the *azote del espinos*. Except for the pale gleam of the handle, it might easily have been a cactus somehow uprooted by an energetic Mexican steer, eager to tussle something with its sharp horns, not minding a few spines in the process. Estelle felt her pulse pounding in her ears. The cholla was the better part of four feet long, with three heavy branches forking off the main stem, each with its own clusters of branches. The limbs were broken and twisted, the spines bent and torn—or missing.

Reaching carefully, Estelle picked up the *azote* by the base, where several swipes of a machete or large knife had cleaned off the threatening thorns. Even with much of it broken away, the remains of the cholla bush weighed five or six pounds, a stout, vicious weapon.

She bent and laid the cactus fragment on the ground. After the last stroke, the thugs would have tossed the *azote* to one side, but it was heavy and awkward—it wouldn't go far. And sure enough, less than five paces farther on, she found the trampled ground where Eurelio had fought his attackers and lost.

Estelle stood rooted. How had they held him? An incapacitating, unexpected blow first? Or had they shot him, and then seen that he was still alive. The torn desert extended in a radius of several feet, as if the man wielding the whip had followed his target as Eurelio tried to scramble first one way and then another, frantic to avoid the lashing spikes of the cactus. Had they tied his hands behind his back? A rope around the neck like a dog?

A sharp pain in her left hand brought her back. She had been clenching her fist so hard that a fingernail had cut the palm.

She tucked the flashlight under her arm and shook both hands to ease the tension. The eastern sky was showing signs of life, the inky black overhead still star-studded but fading toward the horizon. Estelle closed her eyes and took several long, deep breaths.

"Okay," she said aloud. She skirted off to the left toward the two-track, counting the paces from the *azote* as she went. At twenty-two steps, she found the car tracks, a graceful crescent carved in the sand as the tires sprayed gravel and churned their mark. Because the vehicle had been cranked into a hard turn, the imprints of all four tires were distinct. One set was heavily treaded, the others showing scarcely more than a smooth, slightly dished imprint.

The scuff marks of several pairs of boots were clear . . . not enough to cast or photograph for detail, but distinct enough to mark passage until the next howling desert wind or late winter storm shifting things around again, smoothing the traces.

Estelle stood quietly, looking off to the north, flashlight turned off. Had the smooth rise of the hill not been in the way, she might have been able to see the sodium vapor light in front of Wally Madrid's gas station in Maria. Over the other shoulder, several miles toward the east, the highway would be visible. Once the job was done, had the thugs opened the back of the station wagon and enjoyed a little tailgate party, oblivious to Eurelio's agonizing escape?

She stood on her tip toes, trying to calculate the distance that Eurelio Saenz had crawled. Counting the long minutes when he floundered in the arroyo before stumbling upon the cattle trail, his tortured crawl could have taken hours.

If they had remained in the area, Eurelio Saenz's attackers would have seen the bob and weave of headlights from Noel Jones's big rig, the Christmas tree of its running lights clear and sharp before the rolling terrain hid it from view. They wouldn't have seen him hit the brakes, but had they held their breath and listened hard, they would have heard the big truck sigh to a stop. And, had they been patient enough, they most certainly would have heard the wail of the ambulance siren as it screamed down toward them from the north.

There was no reason for them to wait. They would have bailed out of the car, Eurelio Saenz terrified that his ride home wasn't turning out the way he'd hoped. They'd beaten him, flogged him, and then shot him . . . in unknown order. With the satisfaction of a job well done, they would have heard the sickening thud of his body as it hit the sandy gravel of the arroyo bottom. And then they would have left, driving off to whatever place they called home to celebrate another accomplishment.

Estelle turned the light back on, moved a step, and swept the desert. The light bounced off an aluminum can so bleached by the sun and weather that it was impossible to tell what the original product had been. A bit of rope, no more than three feet long, was half buried in the sand under a cholla that hadn't won the contest for selection as the *azote*. She pulled it loose, saw that it had been desert detritus for years, and left it in place.

The next instant, she sucked in her breath and her pulse jumped. The single shell casing was so bright in the gleam of the flashlight that it appeared illuminated by its own light source. Estelle looked at it in place for a long time before kneeling down.

"There you are," she breathed. She slipped the ballpoint pen from her pocket and hooked the point into the casing. It was large enough to slide easily over the pen, and she held it to the light to read the head-stamp. "You've become a favorite, haven't you," she said aloud, and brought the casing to her nose. The aroma of recently burned gunpowder was pungent.

She carefully pulled the lip of her left breast pocket open and slid the casing inside, then patted the pocket closed. For another long minute, she stood and listened to the air. Then she pulled the radio from her belt. She turned the volume knob off, then advanced it two clicks.

"Three oh one, three ten."

The reply was immediate. "Three ten, go ahead."

"Are you in town yet?"

"Negative. I'm still parked here behind your car."

Estelle felt a flash of irritation. "Who's with Eurelio?"

"The sheriff said he'd take care of it. He told me to stay down here. He's on his way."

"Any word from Naranjo?"

"Not yet."

"Okay. I've found the spot. I'd guess that it's a good three hundred yards from the border fence. Maybe more. There's a place here where an old dirt road skirts an arroyo. It looks like they stopped here. I found a fresh shell casing."

"Forty-four?"

"Yes. I'm going to flag the spot somehow and take some photos. I don't know what they'll show."

"Can you see our vehicles from where you are?"

"That's negative. There's a small knoll in the way."

"You be careful."

Estelle smiled. "There's not much out here, Jackie. A big open desert with a few tracks. That's it. I'm going to take some photos, then I'll head back. I found the whip, by the way. I'm bringing it, too."

"Ten-four."

Estelle turned off the radio so there was no risk of a sudden burst of squelch rattling the quiet of the night, and slid the unit back into its belt holster. After marking the spot where she'd found the shell casing with a half sheet of paper from her notebook weighted with a fist-sized rock, she turned to back away from the tracks, camera in hand. She froze. The sound drifted to her, muffled and guttural. Off in the distance, a single glint of amber light flashed. She snapped off her flashlight and dropped to a crouch even though a thousand yards still separated her from the vehicle that was making its way along the dirt trail.

34

ESTELLE waited. The vehicle appeared to have a single parking light illuminating its way. In a few minutes she could hear the crunch of tires, and the occasional ping of a stone spitting against the undercarriage. She eased the radio off her belt and turned it on.

"Three oh one, three ten."

"Go ahead."

"There's a vehicle headed this way, an older model of some sort." The car surged as the driver gassed it over a small rise. The engine was rough, hardly the silky whisper of Naranjo's government truck. "I'm going to make my way back your way."

"And quickly," Jackie Taber said.

"You bet," Estelle said. "I don't think I'm going to risk any photos just now." She holstered the radio. The growing light in the east was doing a fine job of illuminating Texas, but the desert under her boots was a mass of indistinct shapes and hazards. She cupped her hand over the flashlight, trying to direct just a tiny stab of light in the direction of the *azote*. With a sigh of relief, she was able to retrace her steps, and the battered cactus plant felt heavy in her grasp when she picked it up, like a huge, heavy, awkward broom.

Holding it out away from her legs, she walked as quickly as she dared along the arroyo edge until she estimated that she was close to the cattle trail. Without using the light, she was unable to avoid the indistinct shapes as they rose in her path, snagging either her clothes

250

or the heavy cactus. Turning her back to the direction of the method-ically approaching car, she turned on the flashlight, holding it close to the ground and shielded with her body. The arroyo edge yawned smooth and sheer in front of her. In the distance, she heard voices. The cattle trail remained hidden. She stopped, flashlight in her left hand. If she had gone too far, the trail down into the arroyo would be to her left. If not far enough, to her right. She crouched again and turned, watching the car.

The driver was using the illumination of a single parking light to wend his way through the scrub. His eyes would be on that little patch of yellow, unable to see far ahead into the darkness. On top of that, the growing light in the east would backlight anything he might see.

They were close enough now that if she stood up and turned on the light to survey the arroyo in front of her, Estelle knew that the occupants of the approaching car would see her. If she took her chances and dropped over the edge, a ten foot fall awaited her—jolt-ing under the best of conditions, crippling if her luck ran out. She remained crouched, watching.

In a moment the car turned east as it chugged around some obsta-cle in the desert, and Estelle took the opportunity. Releasing her grip on the *azote,* she cupped her hand over the flashlight and turned it on, once more holding it close to her body. Sweeping the light from left to right, she saw that she was still twenty feet from the break in the edge where the cattle trail broke the crown of the arroyo.

She snapped off the light, felt for the cactus and flinched as her hand grazed one of the thorns. She found the freshly cut handle, hefted the cholla to break it from the grip of a small acacia, and crouched low, scuttling along the edge of the arroyo, its core now a dark shadow off to her left.

Something stung her knee as she turned, sliding down onto the trail. A rattle of stones fell away, and she froze, breathing hard. The car was less than a hundred yards away, exhaust note deep and labored. A third of the way down the cattle trail and sheltered by the bank of the arroyo, Estelle turned on the flashlight, directing the beam up the arroyo. Around the corner, the spot where the cows ambled up and out of the cut was a good fifty yards away. She could reach the far side, and scramble up and out of the arroyo. If they saw her, she'd be on the open desert, racing toward the fence—a nice running target for a hunter.

If she stayed, they might not find her. And there was the chance that the approaching car carried someone altogether innocent—a late night check for wayward cattle, or goats, or whatever . . . even though there wasn't a single fresh patty or dropping to be seen.

Estelle knew exactly what had happened. They'd dumped Eurelio, and sauntered back to enjoy the rest of their booze under a stunted tree somewhere—maybe in a deserted shepherd's shack. And then they'd heard, piercing on the night air from miles away, the wail of the Posadas ambulance siren. The coincidence of that had awakened even their booze-fuzzed minds. With the night quiet again, they were returning, cautiously, to make sure that Eurelio hadn't somehow been resurrected when their backs were turned.

"Ay," Estelle whispered, and launched herself up the arroyo. She snapped on the flashlight and sprinted as fast as she could, lurching and weaving on the uneven ground. As she rounded the corner and headed upstream, a blast of light swept overhead. The driver had turned on his headlights as he swung around the final corner. They would be looking for their own footprints, moving cautiously. Estelle tightened her grip on the *azote,* kept the flashlight low, and locked her eyes on the cattle trail where it ramped up the side of the arroyo.

As she hit the incline of the trail, she heard a vehicle door open. The voices were low and urgent. She snapped off the flashlight and slowed her pace. The arroyo would shield her from view for a few seconds, and she made her way with careful steps, trying to avoid dislodging rocks. She reached the top and looked over her shoulder.

Behind her, the car was parked with its headlights on, but facing northwest, so the lights illuminated empty desert. A flashlight bobbed and weaved as at least one man made his way toward the arroyo. At one point, they stopped, the flashlight turning. Estelle could see two figures silhouetted against the headlights. Moving slowly, she shrank back away from the arroyo, keeping low.

By the time the two men had reached their side of the arroyo, she had managed to put nearly twenty yards between herself and the bank. She heard the rapid fire Spanish and paused, listening.

"Right here," one of the men said.

"Are you sure?"

"Certainly. I'm not stupid."

What followed was a string of volatile curses as they played the light across the arroyo bottom, seeing the tracks where Eurelio had dragged himself. Estelle held her breath, keeping her face turned away. The light stabbed this way and that.

"It's impossible," one of the men said. "You saw how he was hit."

"Let's find out, Benny," the other man said. "Let me get another light and the rifle."

Estelle took a deep breath, turned her head, and waited until the flashlight across the arroyo was headed back toward the car. She clenched the step of the *azote* in one hand, the flashlight in the other. Without the light, a sprint across the desert would be a hopeless demolition derby.

"Okay," she whispered, and driving as hard as she could, sprinted toward the border fence, keeping the light low. She had managed a good fifty yards when she miscalculated and crashed into a stout clump of greasewood. The cactus tore backward and slammed into her leg even as she pitched hard to the ground, her left shoulder grinding into the dirt. A shout echoed across the arroyo behind her, but she ignored it. She knew that the two men couldn't cross the arroyo and catch her—she was confident that she could outrun two drunks under any circumstances. But bullets were hard to beat.

She dashed no more than another two dozen steps before the first loud crack of a rifle exploded behind her. A bullet snapped by yards to her right. Another round sang over her head, and she took one last look down the beam of the flashlight and then snapped it off, running on memory. Three more reports and a symphony of shouts pursued her.

And then, breath heaving in painful gulps, she saw a dark figure ahead of her.

"I'm okay," she shouted. "Go on back."

She and Deputy Taber rounded the small hill and with a heartfelt groan of relief, Estelle saw the tangle of old barbed wire that marked the border. She stopped, dropped the *azote,* and bent at the waist, hands on her knees.

She felt Jackie Taber's hand on her shoulder. "You're all right?"

"Fine," she wheezed. "Out of shape." She straightened up. "They came back to make sure about Eurelio. They must have been where they could hear the ambulance siren, and got spooked." She sucked in a breath.

"And they saw you and tried for a moving target," Jackie said. Estelle heard the shake in her voice.

"Nah," she said. "Not to worry. I knew they couldn't hit me. Not at night, not with a scope."

"That's why you ran so fast . . . nothing to worry about."

Estelle managed a nervous laugh. "Yeah, well . . ." She held up the *azote* and turned on the flashlight so Jackie could see it. "I don't think they know that I have this," she said in triumph. She pulled at her pocket. "And a shell casing. And a name. They're dead meat."

"What's the name?"

"One of them called the other 'Benny.'" She heaved another deep breath and cringed at the stabbing pain in her leg. "*Por Dios,* but I want to arrest somebody right now."

35

♦♦♦

"IN here?" Sheriff Robert Torrez's voice was muffled by the examining room door, followed by a rap of his knuckle. The door swung open before Estelle had a chance to say "come in," and she pulled the flimsy hospital gown into a semblance of modesty.

The physician's assistant, Jolene Oliver, looked up and turned on her stool to glare at Torrez. "Do you mind?" Jolene carried her two hundred and thirty pounds on a five-foot-two frame, fourteen inches shorter than the sheriff. In contrast, she possessed hands so dainty they might have belonged to an eight-year-old. Her electric blue eyes peered at the world through gold-rimmed granny glasses whose lower rims nestled in deep troughs under her eyes. She pursed her heavy lips with disapproval and pulled an edge of Estelle's gown down to cover the area of thigh on which she had been working.

"You decent?" Torrez asked. He blocked the doorway with his body, holding the door against himself with his right hand. "You've got company." His eyes drifted to the stainless steel pan and the welter of stained gauze pads on the tray beside Oliver, the cotton swabs, the topical anesthetic, the antibiotic—and then to the long forceps in Oliver's hand.

"We could just sell tickets," Jolene Oliver snapped. "Now close the door, preferably with your bones on the other side."

Torrez grinned and pulled the door still closer to his own body as he leaned against the jamb. "Captain Naranjo is out in the hall," he said.

"Look," Jolene said with the withering patience of someone talking to a thick-headed twelve-year-old. "We've dug out thirty-six of these little bastards." She nodded at the stainless steel pan and its collection of cactus thorns. "And we've got at least another dozen to go, some of 'em hiding in pretty interesting places. So give us a break. Go find yourself a cup of coffee or something."

Estelle reached out and touched Jolene on the shoulder. To the sheriff she said, "What's the word on Eurelio?"

"Still in surgery. The gunshot wound was a raker. Broke two ribs, blew some bone chips where they're not supposed to be, and then took a chunk out of his triceps. No major vessels cut, though. He's lucky. I'm sure it *looked* like they'd killed him. The damage from the cactus is the hard part."

"I can sympathize a little bit," Estelle said.

"A *little* bit," Jolene sniffed. "Sweetheart, you're a mess."

Estelle managed part of a laugh until Jolene approached another thorn with the forceps, and then she sucked air through her teeth in anticipation. "I really need to see Naranjo, though, Bobby."

"Well," and he turned his head, leaned backward, and looked down the hall. "He'll wait. He's too much of a gentleman to come in now."

"See?" Jolene said. She pointed an accusatory forceps at Torrez. "Out."

"Yes, ma'am. We'll be in the coffee shop, Estelle." A frown darkened his broad face. "And I'm sure you've done dumber things than this border-jumping stunt. I can't remember exactly when, though." He started to close the door but thought better of it. "By the way," he said, "some interesting developments with the Popes. Jackie said you told her that you really wanted to arrest somebody? You might get your chance. I've got a meeting with the district attorney this afternoon." He saw the curiosity lift Estelle's eyebrows and grinned. "I'll tell you all about it when you're thornless," he said, and closed the door.

It was nearly an hour before Estelle Reyes-Guzman was thornless. She slipped into a set of clean clothes that Jackie Taber had delivered, consigning the ripped, pierced, and thorn-studded blouse and slacks to the hospital incinerator.

Tomás Naranjo saw her as she entered the coffee shop and immediately rose from his seat, his dark, lean face bearing a broad smile touched with sympathy. He stepped to one side and pulled out a chair for Estelle. "And what a night you've had," he said.

"Not as bad as Eurelio Saenz," Estelle replied.

"Of that I'm sure," Naranjo said. "Perhaps something to eat, then? Coffee?"

Estelle shook her head. "No, thanks. I don't have much appetite." She glanced at the thing that Torrez had been eating, a small, damp, and gooey creation that the menu optimistically called a breakfast burrito.

"Ah, perhaps later." Naranjo placed both hands around his Styrofoam coffee cup. "Tell me what you were able to discover."

"For one thing, I saw and heard the car. It's an older Ford station wagon, just like Paulita Saenz said. Only one parking light works, on the left side. It's the kind with the parking lights right on the end of the fenders, outside of the headlights." She pulled a napkin out of the dispenser and rapidly drew a front view of the car. "Like that," she said. "Its fenders look like cheeks, sticking out past the headlights. The headlights are stacked, not side by side."

"'Seventy-six Ford Crown Vic," Torrez said.

"With a bad muffler and bald front tires," Estelle added. "One of the two men called the other 'Benny.' Paulita said that she thought the two men *might* have been Benny and Isidro Madrid. I have the piece of cholla cactus that they . . . or someone . . . used as a whip on Eurelio."

"I saw that," Naranjo said softly.

"I'm sure there's enough blood on it that a DNA match won't be hard," Estelle said. "It'll either be Eurelio's or mine. And I found an expended shell casing, recently fired, of the same caliber as the one found earlier in Eurelio's truck. I'm sure it carries some prints."

"I saw that," Naranjo repeated, nodding.

"It won't be hard to do a match," the sheriff said. "We already looked at the primer indentions under the stereoscope. I'd be willing to bet they're the same. We'll see what the state lab says. We lifted a couple partials as well."

"But we do not have the rifle," Naranjo said.

"No, we don't."

"Deputy Taber tells me that she heard at least four shots."

Estelle nodded. "That's correct. I was running across the open, and they shot at me several times. Four sounds about right."

"That was a considerable risk," Naranjo said.

"I guess so. Not as much of a risk as it would have been if I'd let them catch me."

"You had no weapon?"

"No. Well, that's not true. I had the *azote*. That would have been good for a swing or two."

Naranjo grimaced. "So tell me . . . do you think that this young Mr. Saenz will be able to identify his attackers? Are we sure they're the Madrid brothers?"

"Yes."

"He's still in surgery," Torrez said. "A real mess."

"And whether he will talk to us or not is another question," Estelle said. "He was pretty stubborn before."

"But the *azote* is a great motivator, don't you think?" Naranjo said.

"Certainly."

Naranjo idly turned his coffee cup, marking the rim with his fingernail as he did so. "Let me tell you what I have been able to establish since I saw you last. The Madrid brothers live in a small apartment in Asunción, but were nowhere to be found. Although there are many neighbors, I hesitated to talk with them just yet. Once you express an interest, you see . . . you understand how it goes. But the Madrids know that Eurelio Saenz is in your hands now. They know they have made a mistake. He can identify them. So . . ." He spread his hands. "They're going to be most careful. I would not expect that they will remain at their home, waiting for us to knock on the door."

"If they were smart, they'd be in Texas already," Torrez said. "Get rid of the car, cut their losses, and split."

"If," Estelle muttered. "But there's one other thing."

"And that is?"

"They don't know that Mexican authorities suspect them of anything. You spoke of the murder of Juan Carlos Osuna. If the Madrids were involved in that, and faked their way through the interview with your officers, then they think that they're home free."

Naranjo nodded. "Unfortunately, the officers discovered nothing of suspicion."

Estelle nodded. "My point is that *if* it is the Madrid brothers who are involved with the homicides both north and south of the border, they have no way of knowing that we've made the connection . . . that we're working together."

"In fact," Naranjo said gently, "your little incident last night might help in that regard. That was not the sort of thing that a joint task force would undertake."

"They couldn't know for sure who I was."

"No, I'm sure they don't." He pushed the Styrofoam cup away. "It appears that our first order of business is to find the Madrid brothers, no? Have a little chat with them."

"More than a little chat," Torrez said.

Naranjo flashed a humorless smile. "A manner of speaking. We'll begin to tighten the net around their apartment in Asunción, and see where that leads us."

"I want to go along," Estelle said quickly.

Torrez's face remained expressionless, but Naranjo tilted his head with interest. "I don't need to tell you that in Mexico, you're a welcome visitor . . . but you carry with you no official capacity."

Estelle sighed. "No, Captain, you don't need to tell me that."

"But perhaps there might be some advantages in our cooperative venture," Naranjo said, and shrugged. "Perhaps so." He glanced at his wristwatch. "You're eager, then?"

Estelle nodded. "Yep." She picked at the corner of one of the small bandages on her right forearm, a fierce frown darkening her face. She turned to Torrez. "I meant what I said, Bobby. They're not going to get away with any of this."

36
◆◆◆

THE plan was simple enough. Sheriff Robert Torrez and Undersheriff Estelle Guzman would drive one of the county units as far as the border crossing in Regál, leaving it and their weapons behind as they accompanied Capt. Tomás Naranjo into Mexico. Torrez was skeptical about going anywhere unarmed, but both he and Estelle knew it was an understatement when Naranjo reminded them that his Mexican troopers had "weapons enough for everyone."

Estelle was grateful to Naranjo for extending the invitation—it certainly was not required of him. In fact, if the Madrid brothers could be implicated first in the death of Juan Carlos Osuna in Asunción and then in the attempted murder of Eurelio Saenz on the Mexican side of the border, the arm of Mexican justice would bury them so deep that extradition to face charges in the deaths of the two woodcutters in Posadas County was probably neither a possibility nor a necessity.

As they drove south on Grande Boulevard, Estelle noticed that the normally reticent Robert Torrez was even more quiet than usual. Perhaps he also had been mentally enumerating all the things that could go wrong when two American peace officers strayed south of the border. Whether by invitation or not, the arrangement was an informal one, depending entirely on the strength of Tomás Naranjo's word.

"I'd like to go through Maria," Estelle said as they drove through the interstate underpass.

"Regál is almost an hour faster to Asunción," Torrez said. He glanced over at Estelle, then into the rearview mirror at Naranjo's Toyota.

"I know. But we can cross at Palomas just as easily, and then catch Route Two back toward Janos." Torrez had already started to slow for the intersection with State 56, the highway west toward Regál. "I just have a feeling," Estelle said.

"All right." Torrez said. He passed the intersection and drove south on State 61. Naranjo followed, a discreet hundred yards behind. "So what's the feeling?"

"*Mamá y Papá* is the feeling," Estelle said. "We haven't talked to them. Francis and I stopped in Lucy's place for a few minutes whenever it was, but other than that, nothing. I'd be interested to hear what they have to say. Things have tumbled so fast, I haven't had the chance."

"I think they'd be the first ones to say that their boys are on their own," Torrez said. "It's Benny and Isidro who chose to live in Mexico. Their folks didn't force them that way."

Estelle sighed. "But they're up here all the time. That's what's bizarre." After a minute, she held up two fingers a quarter inch apart. "We were this close, Bobby."

"To what?"

"If those two had followed me across the arroyo, and then just a few yards farther into this country, we'd have had them. Dead to rights."

"The dead part is probably true," Torrez said. "And hopefully it would have been them."

"We were so close."

"And now . . ." Torrez said, and stopped in mid-thought.

"And now what?"

He accelerated the unmarked Expedition up to eighty to pass a pickup pulling a livestock trailer. "And now you're hoping that Isidro and Benny might slip back across the border to find out from Mama and Papa just what's going on. Try to find out what we know?"

"I would if I were them. Then maybe take off for some place that's a little cooler."

"For instance?"

"Guaymas, Guadalajara, Mexico City . . . somewhere out of the state, that's all."

"Or even Denver or Coeur d'Alene," Torrez said. "Or Central America someplace. Hell, with some money, they can go anywhere."

"We know they have a little," Estelle said. "The money from Osuna, the money from the woodcutters. At least that much."

"Nickel, dime," Torrez said. "We're not exactly talking about masters of the big haul here. I'm surprised that they haven't put the touch on the old man or the old lady yet." He turned and glanced at Estelle, the figurative lightbulb coming on over his head. "That's what you're thinking, isn't it."

She nodded. "And their aunt," she added.

"Paulita?"

"Why not? The *taberna* probably earns a pretty good bundle. Easy pickings. And after last night, they're not just going to sit around and wait for something to happen. They don't know if someone just dragged Eurelio's body away, or if he's still alive."

"Except for the ambulance siren on our side of the border. And they know that Mexican authorities aren't involved. Nobody chased them. They saw a figure running in the darkness—that's all."

"That's right. If Eurelio is alive, the Madrids have to assume that this time, he'll talk. But he's on our side of the border, and that makes for a nice, convenient complication that works in favor of the Madrids. I think that they beat Eurelio to scare him silent. Maybe he sold them that rifle in good faith, as a favor to a relative. Maybe they coerced it out of him. They figured a good beating would convince Eurelio to keep his mouth shut. And then one of them changed his mind and shot Eurelio, almost as an afterthought . . . one of them is trigger-happy."

"Not smart, but trigger-happy," Torrez said. He thumped his index fingers on the steering wheel in a fast drum roll. "A great combination." As they passed the dirt road that followed the power lines northward, he slowed the car. "Paulita is at the hospital with the boy?"

"Yes. And Jackie's with her."

"Okay. That's one out of the way then. I told Tony Abeyta to stay there until he heard otherwise." They rounded the sweeping curve that led into Maria, the red tile roof of the *taberna* visible on the right, and several abandoned, slumping buildings on the left. Torrez slowed the vehicle to an amble.

From the other direction, a large RV sporting white Texas license plates appeared, a small SUV hitched to its back bumper. The rig blinked its directional signal and turned into Wally Madrid's gas station. The RV was certainly taller than the small adobe building, and probably more square feet on the inside.

Torrez turned left in front of the gas station, drove far enough up the lane that he passed Lucy Madrid's restaurant and another abandoned building. Just ahead was a cluster of five homes, situated helter-skelter with lot lines that would have made a surveyor groan. Dominating the north end of the village, at the end of J Street, was la Iglesia de Santa Lucia, a low, flat-roofed structure plastered a rich rosy pink.

The dusty margins of the lane opened a bit so that Torrez didn't need to drive all the way to the church's parking lot to turn around. He swung the truck in a U-turn, idling back the way they'd come. Torrez pulled to a stop where a curb would be if Maria had sidewalks, just beyond view of the little café's front window. As they stopped, they saw Tomás Naranjo drive by on the state highway.

"I'll check the station," she said. Torrez sat with his chin resting in his left hand, gazing at the front door of Lucy Madrid's restaurant. Estelle climbed down out of the unmarked Expedition and strolled past the café, her hands in her trouser pockets. She continued up the lane to the service station. She rounded the corner in time to see the driver of the RV peering through the front door, his hand up to shade the glass.

"Don't guess they're open," he said when he saw Estelle. A smile split his round face. "You from these parts, *señorita?*" His voice carried the twang of west Texas. His eyes ran appreciatively up and down Estelle's trim figure.

"Yes, sir," Estelle said. "But they don't sell diesel here, anyway."

"They're missin' a good bet," he said. Estelle smiled pleasantly. The Texan was right, of course. But it was just one of many good bets that Wally Madrid had passed on over the years. "Probably should have filled up in Columbus, then," the man said. "What's the closest westbound, you happen to know?"

"Posadas is sixteen miles," Estelle said. "There'll be a big station on your left, just after you go under the interstate. They'll fix you up." She glanced toward the RV and saw a white-haired, plump woman peering out the door. The man appeared to be in no hurry to break off his conversation, perhaps happy to have found a native who spoke English in complete sentences. "You folks have a good day," Estelle said even as his mouth opened to say something else.

He nodded. "You too, young lady."

Estelle walked past him, glancing inside the front window as she did so. Wally Madrid's cluttered desk was visible in the far corner. If each piece of litter that constituted the landfill of his desk represented a successful business deal, Wally Madrid would have been a millionaire. The single overhead light was off.

She glanced down the street and saw that Naranjo had turned around and stopped at the curb fifty yards away. He lifted a finger off the steering wheel in salute, but stayed in the vehicle. Unlike Estelle and Torrez, Naranjo was in uniform.

The station, one room with a bathroom off the side, had been built onto the original adobe house nearly half a century before. Estelle walked around the side of the station, pausing at the door of the restroom. The door was ajar, and she pushed it open with her toe. The door cleared the commode with an inch to spare, revealing a dark, dank interior where the white porcelain of the sink and toilet had long ago stained to match the adobe walls. The fragrance was deep and pungent, and Estelle couldn't imagine stepping into the tiny room and actually closing the door on the flow of fresh air from outside.

She continued toward what appeared to be the front door of Wally Madrid's home. Two cinderblocks served as a front step, both loose in the dirt and waiting to tip should an unwary foot be planted wrong. She knocked on the door and waited, then knocked again. The blue porcelain doorknob included no provision for a lock. She turned it and pushed. The door opened effortlessly. The air inside was cool, and she could see an old sofa with an afghan on the back, a television with the round-cornered screen of the 'sixties black-and-whites, and a coffee table piled high with magazines.

"Mr. Madrid?" she called. The house was silent. From where she was standing, she could see the rump of the owner's red International Carry-All parked beside the house. She called his name again, a bit louder. With no response, she stepped inside and quickly walked through the house, taking no more than thirty seconds to tour all five rooms.

By the time she walked back outside, glanced inside the Carry-All and then rounded the front of the station, the huge Texas RV had trundled back out onto the highway, a plume of diesel hanging behind. She glanced back at Naranjo and shook her head, then walked back the way she had come, ignoring the restaurant.

"What did you find?" Torrez asked when she returned to the Expedition.

"Nothing. The station's closed and locked, his house is wide open. The coffeemaker's on in the kitchen. His truck is parked outside. Engine's cold."

"So. Maybe he's in his wife's café, having breakfast."

"He hasn't talked to Lucy in a dozen years. I don't think so."

"Want to go ask?"

"I certainly do."

Torrez opened the door, then hesitated. "Where's Naranjo?"

"Parked just down the street."

"You didn't see anyone else?"

"Not a soul, other than the Texan tourists."

"I was hoping that we'd see a big yellow Ford station wagon parked in the shade somewhere," Torrez said.

"They're not going to be that stupid, Bobby."

He shrugged. "And why not? Why change what works?" He stepped out of the vehicle, and then he and Estelle walked to the front door of Lucy Madrid's café like two curious tourists. Lucy's was open for business, the fluorescent bulbs in the single ceiling unit providing just enough light for customers to be able to find the saucer with their cup.

The first person Estelle saw was Wally Madrid, sitting at the same table she and Francis had used earlier in the week.

WALLY Madrid sat by himself, turned sideways so that he could see the door. His dark, long face struck Estelle as singularly melancholy, as if he were sitting there waiting for the end of the world. The sports section of the *Albuquerque Journal* rested on the checkered plastic tablecloth. Other than that, the table was bare. No food, no coffee, no utensils.

Wally was not alone in the café. Across the room, another much younger man sat at the far end of the short counter. Smoke from a cigarette in his right hand curled upward, untouched by anything so sophisticated as the downwash from a ceiling fan. The man turned and stared at Estelle when she entered. The light was behind her, and Estelle's eyes flicked a quick inventory of the room and its occupants. She didn't recognize the man at the counter, but his expression wasn't the idle curiosity of a man whose quiet coffee and doughnut break had been interrupted.

From behind, Bob Torrez put a hand on Estelle's shoulder and said, "Go ahead and find a table. I need to use the restroom." He made no effort to whisper, and what he said would have been clearly heard by Wally Madrid and the man at the counter. Torrez sounded like any other good tourist, too long on the road, rest stops dictated by the bladder. His grip on Estelle's shoulder was firm and directed her off to the right.

As watchful as he was, it nevertheless took the young man at the counter another couple of heartbeats before he recognized the possible danger, before he realized that the giant figure walking quickly across the small café toward him wasn't just a tourist who had brought his wife in for a midmorning snack.

Robert Torrez ducked to one side so that his head didn't brush the fluorescent lighting fixture in the center of the room. Benny hesitated for another instant, saw that Torrez's impassive gaze was locked on *him* rather than the small sign on the open door behind him that announced CABALLEROS.

From across the room, Estelle saw the man's left shoulder hunch upward. By the time a large revolver appeared in his left hand, sweeping upward to avoid the edge of the counter, Estelle's own Beretta had cleared her belt and jacket. But Robert Torrez was on the offensive.

As the revolver cleared the edge of the counter, Torrez barged into the man, knocking him off the stool into the lip of the counter. The sheriff's hand clamped across both the revolver and the hand that held it. With a vicious slam, Torrez smashed the hand down, the weight of the heavy weapon crushing the man's thumb against the Formica. The revolver discharged with a loud, sharp report and a cloud of blue smoke. The long-unused milkshake mixer on the back counter rocked sideways as the slug punched through its stainless steel housing, blew out the back, and embedded in the wall.

Torrez smacked the gun down again and the man howled, trying to bat him away with his right hand. The revolver skittered down the counter and pinwheeled to a halt, pointing toward the street.

With a deft twist, Torrez forced the young man's face down on the counter, at the same time pulling both of his arms behind his back. With a loud clack, he slapped handcuffs on both wrists with such force that the man's face crumpled in pain.

Shifting her own automatic to her left hand, Estelle crossed the room and picked up the revolver. Wally Madrid hadn't moved a muscle during the assault on his son. Both hands remained motionless on top of the table. His eyes grew wide as he watched Estelle thumb the revolver's cylinder open. The remaining cartridges clattered to the floor.

"*Como está,* Benny?" Torrez said. "Remember me?" He didn't

wait for an answer, but pulled Benny Madrid to his feet and pushed him against the counter. He kicked his feet apart and slipped two nylon ties out of his back pocket. With swift, deft motions, Torrez snapped a restraint around each of Benny Madrid's ankles, the ties looped through each other so that the man was effectively hobbled.

"Have a seat," Torrez said, his voice quiet and conversational. He caught Benny by the elbow and steered him toward the table in the back corner of the café, under the 1957 Firestone calendar that featured such striking photos of the Southwest that Lucy Madrid never had been able to throw it out. Benny managed the awkward, hopping journey, and fell into the chair. He glowered up at Torrez, who regarded him impassively for a moment. The sheriff rubbed the palm of his right hand, glanced down at the flash burn from the revolver, and then turned to Wally Madrid.

"You all right?" the sheriff asked.

Wally nodded and his eyes flicked nervously toward Estelle, whose Beretta hadn't wavered. The muzzle pointed at the light fixture, a short move from any target in the room. "Give me about ten seconds," Torrez said to Estelle, and he nodded toward the back storage room, the kitchen, and the bathrooms. He turned to Benny. "Where's your worthless brother?" Benny didn't reply. "Dumb as always," Torrez muttered. He pointed a beefy finger at Benny's nose. "If you move, she's going to put one right there," he said, and then rapped Benny hard between the eyes with his right index knuckle. *"Comprende, bato?"*

As Torrez rounded the end of the counter headed toward the small kitchen, he drew his own automatic, thumbing the hammer back as he did so.

"Nobody's back there," Wally Madrid called. His voice cracked as if it had been years since he'd used it. "They went to town."

"Okay," Torrez replied, and quickly checked the back rooms. He returned, weapon holstered, and walked across to Wally's table. The sheriff stepped close and reached out a hand, the fingers touching Wally lightly above the ear. "Did one of them hit you?"

"It's nothing," Wally said. As he turned his head, Estelle could see the dried blood near the corner of his left eye.

"Can you stand up for me?"

Wally nodded, but didn't move.

"I need you to stand up, Mr. Madrid," Torrez said gently, and the older man's hands fluttered with embarrassment.

"I'm sorry," he said. "I didn't understand." He leaned his weight on the table and pushed himself to his feet, the top of his head below Torrez's shoulders.

"Just stand still a minute, sir," Torrez said. He quickly ran his hands down the old man's sides and legs. "No hurts anywhere else?" the sheriff asked as he straightened up. He turned and nodded at Estelle.

"No, no," Wally said, and collapsed back in the chair. "I guess I wasn't moving fast enough for him, you know. That's all. He got impatient." A hand drifted up to touch his cheek. Estelle felt a pang of sympathy for the man. *Impatient* was nowhere near the top of her list of the Madrid brothers' failings.

"This one?" Torrez nodded at Benny Madrid.

"No. Not him."

"Where's Isidro, then? And where's your wife? Where's Lucy?"

Wally nodded. "They went into town."

"To Posadas, you mean?"

"Yes."

"When was that?"

Wally twisted so that he could see the small clock with the Holbein Dairies logo on the face. His eyes squinted. "It must have been about ten minutes to nine," he said.

Torrez glanced at his watch. "Twenty-five minutes ago," he said. "It's twenty minutes in, twenty back." He looked at Estelle and brushed one hand by the other. "We just missed them on the highway." Turning back to Wally Madrid, he asked, "What was Isidro after?"

"They went to the bank."

Torrez frowned, his left hand drifting toward the handheld radio under his jacket. Estelle had crossed to the table, and she sat down in the chair facing Wally.

"Isidro forced his mother to go to Posadas with him?" she asked.

Wally nodded. "I don't have much," he said, "but I gave them what I had. Lucy, though . . . she's got accounts. Over the years, she's got accounts. That's what they wanted."

"So they robbed you, took what money you had at the service station, and now Isidro is taking his mother to the bank?" Estelle asked. "Isidro isn't afraid that she'll turn him in?"

Wally pulled his shoulders up in a slow-motion shrug. "I guess she won't."

No, I guess she won't, Estelle thought.

Wally started to turn around to look at his other son, but didn't complete the motion. "There's been trouble, I guess you know that." Somehow, he managed to make it sound as much his own fault as anyone's.

"Yep, we know that," Torrez said.

"Was Benny supposed to wait here until Isidro returned with the money?" Estelle prompted.

"That was the plan," Wally said.

"You think Isidro will be back?"

"I don't know." Wally folded his hands as if to say, "what will be, will be."

"What were they driving?"

"They took Lucy's car. It's that black-and-silver Chrysler."

"Who's driving?"

"I think Lucy was."

Torrez looked across the room at Benny, who was studying the paint on the wall. "Your brother going to run out on you?" the sheriff asked. Benny ignored him. "Hell, I'd run out on him myself," Torrez said. "The worthless sack of shit." Estelle reached up and nudged the sheriff in the arm with the cell phone.

"They should still be at the bank," she said, handing the instrument to Torrez, then rising and slipped past him. On the back shelf behind the small, open cash register, she found a crumpled phone book. She quickly leafed through until she found the number of Posadas National Bank. "If you ask for Dottie Sandoval, she's got a good view of the entire bank from where she sits in her office."

Torrez nodded and dialed. Estelle could hear the cheerful voice of the bank receptionist as she answered on the third ring.

"Dottie Sandoval, please. This is Sheriff Torrez."

"I'm sorry, Sheriff. Dottie is with a customer right now. Can I take a message?"

"Who's the customer?"

"I beg your pardon?"

"Who . . . is . . . the . . . customer?"

"Well," and the receptionist hesitated. "I think it's . . . well, I guess I don't know who it is. It's an older man."

"Let me talk with Dottie, please. It's an emergency."

Once deviated from her cheerful, prepared phone message, the girl's polite good humor was quick to fade. "Well, wait just a second."

Torrez waited, gaze locked on Benny Madrid. The phone clicked and a pleasant voice came on the line. "This is Dottie."

"Dottie, Bob Torrez. Sorry to interrupt, but I need a favor that can't wait."

"Well, you just name it," Dottie said, her voice a rich contralto.

"Without being too obvious, can you tell me if Lucy Madrid is in your bank at the moment?"

There was a brief silence. "Sure. She's here. Do you need to talk with her?"

"No, no. I sure don't. Where is she?"

"She's here in the bank."

"No, I mean *where* in the bank?"

"She's with Mary Tuttle, the head cashier. Is there some kind of problem, Bobby?"

"Is she alone?"

"No. There's a young man with her. I think it's her son. It's been a long time since I've seen her boys, but I think that's who it is."

"How long ago did they come in, do you happen to know?"

"Oh gosh . . . I wasn't paying attention. I just don't know. It couldn't have been too long now. We just opened . . . about eleven minutes ago."

"Okay, thanks. Look, Dottie, I hate to do this to you, but it's really important that we know the instant that they leave, all right?"

"Well, sure. Give me a number."

"Let's just leave this line open. I'll hold."

"Well, all right. Do I get to know what's going on? Is there trouble we should know about?"

"How about not right now," Torrez said. He turned and glanced at Estelle, who was frowning. Had Isidro been planning to simply rob the bank, there would have been no need to take his mother along—and he'd have been in and out of the bank in seconds. If his plan was to recover as much cash as he could without raising an alarm, he'd hatched himself a pretty good scheme . . . as long as the smell of all that cash just over the tellers' counter didn't trigger a change in plans.

"Just let us know when they head out the door. I appreciate it. I'm putting Estelle Guzman on the line." He handed the cell phone to Estelle and said quietly, "I'll get somebody rolling from that end."

As Torrez picked up the café's telephone and set it on the counter, Estelle turned so that she could watch Benny Madrid. The young man sat quietly, following the sheriff's every move. His feet shifted as he tested the ankle ties, and she could see his shoulders hunch and then relax as he strained against the stainless steel cuffs behind his back.

"Where's the rifle, Benny?" Torrez asked conversationally as he dialed the phone. Estelle locked her hand over the phone mouthpiece so Dottie wouldn't hear, but Benny said nothing. "Isidro has it with him?" He lifted the receiver to his ear and waited. "Hey there," he said when his wife Gayle answered at dispatch. "Who've we got on the road just now?"

"Dennis is on duty this morning," Gayle Torrez said. "He's standing right here with Tommy Pasquale, who *isn't* on duty and should be home in bed. And Jack Adams is just heading out the door."

"Holler at Jack for me." She did so without covering the phone, and Torrez winced.

Gayle returned on the line. "You want to talk to him?"

Torrez could hear voices in the background, including New Mexico State Policeman Jack Adams's west Texas drawl. "No. But we're going to need him, so keep him close for a minute. Let me talk to Tom."

"Here he be," Gayle said.

"Yes, sir?" Tom Pasquale said.

"Your head on straight this morning?" Torrez asked.

"Sir?"

Torrez glanced over at Estelle, who shook her head. Life at Posadas State Bank was continuing apace. "Okay, this is the deal," the sheriff said, and quickly filled the deputy in. "Now listen to me," he said, and turned his back to Benny Madrid, walking the length of the phone cord toward the front window. His voice sank to little more than a murmur. "I don't want any kind of confrontation at the bank, Thomas. I don't want Isidro Madrid or his mother to see you, or to suspect that you're anywhere nearby. I want that son of a bitch out of Posadas, away from people. I want him to walk out of that bank with his mother with all the money they want, and I want them to drive out of town. Is that clear?"

"Yes, sir."

"We've got an open phone line to the inside of the bank right now. Dottie Sandoval is watching for us. If you park over underneath the portico of Salazar's Funeral Home, you'll have a clear view of the front of the bank. Park in the shadows. I don't want him to see you."

"Got it."

"When they leave town, I want you to follow *way* back. You understand me?"

"Yes, sir."

"He can't catch sight of you. If he does, Mama's a dead goose."

"Yes, sir."

"When they reach Maria, I want you to drive right on through. He's going to turn off, but don't follow him. He's going to be watching his back, and if he sees you, I don't want him to panic. No fanfare, no slowing down. You drive right on through. Stop just beyond the village where that big arroyo is. All you're going to do is keep us posted about what they're doing when they leave the bank. My guess is that they're going to head back out of town to the south, down Sixty-one. I'd be surprised if it's anything else, but we gotta know. That's all. Use the phone. I don't know if that bastard has a scanner with him or not."

"Yes, sir. I'm on my way."

"Move it, now. And let me talk to Dennis."

When he finally hung up, Torrez stood at the window for a long moment, and Estelle could tell by the expression on his face that he was replaying the game plan in his mind. Jack Adams of the State Police was already headed out of Posadas southbound on State 61, his black trooper car a blur of speed. He'd be far ahead of the Madrids, even if mother and son walked out of the bank that instant.

Deputy Dennis Collins had walked the few yards from the Public Safety Building to the small computer shop that faced the back door of Posadas State Bank, where employees or people wanting to talk to installment loan officers were apt to come and go. In the event of trouble, he could be across the street and into the bank in seconds. Tom Pasquale's county unit was poised a hundred yards from the bank's front door, waiting. And Lucy Madrid was taking her time remembering where her money was.

Torrez turned and walked over to Wally Madrid. "Where did they leave their car, Wally?"

"I don't know." He shook his head in wonder. "I never saw it. They walked into my station, and I never saw it. I never saw them coming."

Torrez shook his head and looked at Benny Madrid. "Where's your car?"

Madrid grunted something and looked at the wall, his lip curled.

With a shrug, Torrez held out his hand for the phone that Estelle held.

"No movement yet," she said.

"That's okay," he said. "We're in no rush. We need Naranjo's unit out of sight. You might as well invite him in to join the fun. I'll keep Dottie company."

"Is there someone else you can call in to keep watch at the back of the bank besides Dennis?"

Torrez shook his head. "If I had half an hour, sure. But they're not even going to go out the back door. Not to worry."

"You hope."

There was just the hint of hesitation. "With all my heart that's what I hope, Estelle."

38

ESTELLE closed her eyes and imagined herself in the backseat of Lucy Madrid's Chrysler as it headed south on New Mexico 61. Isidro would be sitting hunched forward with his face nearly against the dashboard, his pockets bursting with more cash than he'd managed to assemble during the previous twenty-six years of his life, his eyes searching for the first errant wisp of dust or glint of chrome that smelled of trap.

What did a mother and son talk about at a time like that? Was Lucy Madrid counting down the miles until she'd be rid of her two troublesome boys? When she'd turned over her life's savings to them, had she also given her best advice about which way to run? As she drove away from Posadas, did Lucy glance across the car at Isidro, see him sitting there with his fingers itching on the trigger of his rifle, and wonder what she had contributed to the creation of this monster?

Estelle shook her head to snap the webs. She opened her eyes and looked across the silent patio to the highway, and beyond that to the dirt lane that led past the café. Benny Madrid was safely trussed up inside the small restroom, no doubt struggling against the steel cuffs, the nylon ankle ties, and the duct tape that kept him quiet and trussed to the water pipes so he couldn't kick the door. Benny didn't think of himself as safe, Estelle was sure of that. She glanced down at the Beretta in her hand. She popped out the clip, studied the stacked pack of thirteen shiny rounds. "Ay," she said quietly, and took a deep breath, driving the clip back into the weapon.

From somewhere inside the house, she heard a hollow thump. Tomás Naranjo was finding himself a good vantage point in the shadows behind the small window. Estelle felt the warmth of morning sun touch her head, and she moved another step back to pull her shadow into hiding. At the same time, she heard the howl of tires on pavement from the east, and then the muttering rattle of a jake brake slowing the tractor trailer.

She lifted the radio off the tiles. "Bobby?"

"Go ahead."

"Traffic from the east. I thought Adams was going to block the highway?"

As she spoke, the huge truck rolled past, a polished stainless steel tanker with FRESH MILK in foot-high letters near the top access hatch.

"I told him to let the guy through. He's nonstop, and it'll look good for Isidro to see some normal traffic coming his way. If it's too quiet, he might get edgy."

"Where are they now?"

"Pasquale says that they're about six miles out. She's driving right at fifty-five. Pasquale's hanging a mile back. I told him to fade back a little more to give them some time. They'll be here in about six minutes."

"Okay. I'm in the patio. Naranjo is in the house. He's got a back window view."

"Ten-four," Torrez said. He sounded as excited as someone browsing through a library book sale.

Estelle placed the radio in a niche in the stack of tiles in front of her, transferred the Beretta to her left hand and flexed the fingers of her right, surprised at how tightly she'd been gripping the weapon. She looked at the welt left by one of the cactus spines in the back of her hand and grimaced. She could picture Eurelio Saenz lying under the flood of lights at Posadas General Hospital, the attending physicians wondering where to start.

She shifted her weight, transferring the Beretta back to her right hand. As she did so, the distant sound of an approaching vehicle reached her at the same time as Torrez's voice said quietly over the radio, "They're coming in."

Sheriff Robert Torrez wasn't often wrong. He had bet that Lucy Madrid would drive up J Street to the café. Isidro and Benny would leave the café together . . . after who knew what kind of farewell they had planned.

Lucy didn't do that. Estelle heard the vehicle slow, then heard the crunch of tires as the car pulled off the highway just west of the Taberna Azul, out of Estelle's line of sight.

"They've stopped west of the saloon," she whispered into the radio. "I don't know what they're doing."

She waited, head turned so that her peripheral vision would pick up motion approaching the rear patio gate, now ajar an inch or two, at the same time as she watched the highway and the front patio entrance. In a moment she heard the gravel crunch again, and the Chrysler appeared out front, turning up the lane toward the café. Lucy Madrid was driving, and she was alone.

Moving in slow motion, Estelle reached forward and turned the radio's volume knob to zero so that a random burst of squelch wouldn't tip off her position. She transferred both hands to the Beretta. Isidro Madrid was treading light, and she saw him before she heard him, his figure a shadow through the thin cracks between the boards of the patio gate. He walked quickly to the station wagon and reached for the door.

"Que chingado," Estelle heard him mutter in irritation that his brother had been so stupid as to lock the car. The rattle of keys followed, and then silence. Estelle shifted position just enough that she could see through the slit of the door. Isidro was standing motionless beside the car, keys in hand. After a moment, he jabbed the key into the lock and wrenched the door open. He held the short rifle in his left hand, and she could see a semiautomatic pistol in his belt. He slid into the car. Estelle heard the metallic clack of electric door locks.

Isidro leaned back as he passed the rifle across to the passenger side. His hands reappeared on the wheel, and Estelle shifted again. The rifle was no doubt resting on the passenger seat, its butt perhaps on the floor mat. His other weapon was still in his waistband. She could see his left hand on the steering wheel, and his head ducked as he shoved the key in the ignition. She waited, forcing herself to be patient. Even though both of his hands were occupied and she might be able to take him by surprise, Isidro was protected by the bulk of the station wagon and the ten yards that separated them.

The starter engaged, cranking the enormous old V-8. Isidro let it crank for three or four seconds, switched off, and tried again. Estelle saw the shadow of a frown cross his forehead. As if not believing his sudden turn of luck, he cranked the car over and over again until the battery started to fail.

After a final effort he slapped the steering wheel with a quiet oath. Twisting around, he looked out through the back windows, then relaxed in the seat. For a moment he was looking directly at Estelle, and she held her breath. Isidro would see the gap in the gate, but he wouldn't be able to see through the shadows beyond.

On the highway, a car roared past. Estelle didn't risk turning her head to look, but knew it would be Deputy Tom Pasquale. Isidro's head swung to follow the sound. Pasquale stuck to the original plan and drove rapidly through the village, the sound of his car tires fading quickly to the east.

It took another full minute for Isidro Madrid to make up his mind. Estelle heard him say something to himself as he wrenched open the door and got out of the car. He was a slightly built man, an inch or so shorter than Estelle. The large automatic was in his right hand. He stood motionless beside the car, pistol held high, its muzzle almost touching his cheek. Estelle could see that his eyes were closed as he listened. She held her breath, hoping that Tomás Naranjo had a clear view and that he wouldn't choose this moment to shift position.

Apparently satisfied, Isidro Madrid edged to his right, around the back of the station wagon. As he moved, he never took his eyes off the building. Once around the tailgate, he moved quickly to the front passenger door. The hinge groaned as he opened it, and Isidro gritted his teeth. Then he ducked down and came out with a short duffle bag and the rifle. Looping the straps of the bag around his left shoulder, he turned away from the car, not bothering to close the door.

"You're going to do it," Estelle breathed. Sure enough, Isidro

Madrid set off at a fast jog, due south toward the border fence. She toed open the gate just enough to slip through and sprinted the few yards to the cover of the station wagon. At the same time she heard a thump inside the building. Already twenty yards away, Isidro heard it too, and started to sprint, dodging through the short scrub and cactus.

"¡Alto ahí! Policía!" Estelle shouted. Isidro surely had sensed something wrong from the moment he had discovered the car locked—but still the barked command took him by surprise. Instinctively, he turned and in doing so tripped and fell hard. The duffle bag acted as a cushion, and he scrambled to his knees, the pistol seeking a target. Estelle crouched behind the fender of the car, Beretta extended across the wide yellow hood. Isidro was less than thirty yards away—an easy shot.

"No te muevas, Isidro," she said. Isidro didn't move, but not because of her command. He stared hard, searching for a target. He saw Estelle behind the car just as she shouted, "There's nowhere you can go, Isidro." She switched to English. "Drop the weapons."

An expression of incredulity spread across his face as he contemplated his chances with this slight, soft-voiced woman who now crouched behind his abandoned car. He could see the black automatic, could see that she held it steady and sure. The light played on the heavy, fresh scar that marred the corner of his left eye.

"And who are you?" he asked in lightly accented English.

"Drop the weapons, Isidro," Estelle repeated.

She saw his eyes flick to right and at the same time heard the faint shuffle of feet behind her. Tomas Naranjo had sidled to a position just inside the garden gate. The black muzzle of the shotgun protruded.

Estelle turned her head just enough that she could talk to Naranjo without taking her eyes off Isidro. "I want him alive, Tomás," she said quietly.

Isidro mouthed a curse and dove off to his left toward a stout clump of saltbush, leaving the duffle bag behind. Estelle snapped off two quick rounds, keeping her aim low, before the right windshield pillar interfered. Dust kicked behind Isidro's feet but the second round connected. It looked as if someone had jerked a rug out from under the fleeing man. He tumbled, his form nothing but a shadow behind the scrubby bush.

Fifty yards separated him from a gentle rise in the prairie. Behind her, Estelle heard the howl of a car racing into the village, its sound muffled by the buildings. In a moment, Tom Pasquale's Bronco appeared, shoveling dust and gravel with its front bumper as it careened around the east end of Paulita Saenz's home and dove across a sharp dip.

Isidro Madrid didn't wait to negotiate. He appeared from behind the saltbush, the automatic in his hand roaring. A slug whanged off the top of the station wagon, another chewed into the adobe to the left of Naranjo, and a third kicked sand in front of Pasquale's Bronco as it slid sideways to a stop.

So loud that it made her ears ring, Naranjo's shotgun bellowed, and Estelle saw the pattern of buckshot blow gravel to the left of Madrid's flying feet. He dodged sideways, legs pumping like a hotly pursued wide receiver. As he ran, he pumped rounds indiscriminately behind him.

Estelle took a deep breath and clenched the Beretta with both hands. She pulled the trigger at the same time that Naranjo blasted another round from the shotgun. Isidro Madrid was in midturn, trying to avoid a cluster of acacia. Instead he crashed into the stout shrub. Estelle saw the rifle fly from his grip.

Pasquale, gun drawn, sprinted toward Madrid. The man pushed himself to his feet, the automatic digging into the gravel and sand as he did so. Holding his automatic with both hands, Pasquale advanced on Madrid.

"Drop it," the deputy barked. Madrid turned and looked south. The cut border fence was less than fifty yards away. His left pant leg above the knee was blood-soaked, and his right foot refused to bear his weight. He turned back to Pasquale, and then watched as Estelle advanced toward him.

"Todo se ha acabado. Isidro," she said. "It's finished."

So sudden was his movement that both Pasquale and Estelle came within an ounce of squeezing the trigger. Isidro Madrid dropped the automatic, but at the same time collapsed backward to land on his rump, legs awkwardly folded under him. He supported himself on his right elbow and closed his eyes, swaying in pain. He opened them only when Estelle's shadow fell across his face.

She looked down at him, and found herself considering that a good swift kick would roll him into a small cholla cactus less than a foot behind him.

"No, you don't want to do that," Pasquale said. He stepped around Estelle and in a moment had handcuffed Isidro Madrid's hands behind his back. He pulled the handheld radio off his belt and keyed the mike.

"We're secure down here," he said. "Requesting an ambulance for Mr. Madrid."

"Ten-four," Torrez's voice said.

"I don't want to do what?" Estelle said to Pasquale. She watched impassively as the deputy quickly frisked Madrid, then sliced the blood-soaked trouser leg away from the man's thigh. One of the shot-gun pellets had raked a furrow four inches long, a nasty quarter-inch deep track that bled profusely.

"My foot," Isidro said through gritted teeth.

"Hurts, huh," Pasquale said. He secured Madrid's ankles with nylon ties, then looked at the neat bullet hole through the fancy leather around the heel of Madrid's right foot. On the other side, the hole was considerably larger. "You're not bleedin' to death, so we'll let the EMTs deal with that."

He straightened up and grinned at Estelle. "I could see it in your face, Mrs. Guzman." He reached out and touched the cholla gently with the toe of his boot. "Not that he doesn't deserve it." He pulled a small card out of his pocket. "Isidro, I'm going to read you your rights." Madrid mouthed an obscenity and Pasquale shrugged. "Well, all right, then. You don't need to hear it. We can drag your car-cass about fifty yards south, and Captain Naranjo can read you your rights in Mexico. How about that?"

Naranjo limped his way over, the shotgun cradled under his arm. He regarded Isidro with distaste. "I would consider that a favor for which I would be long in your debt, officer."

"You can't do that," Isidro Madrid said.

"We can't?" Pasquale said, and then shrugged. "Well, then, shut up and listen." As he read the Miranda statement, first in English and then in Spanish, Estelle walked over to where Isidro Madrid had dropped the rifle.

She lifted it carefully by the wooden stock. The scope was loose, perhaps jarred in the fall. The gun's caliber, .44 Remington Magnum, was stamped on the barrel. She turned the gun over and looked at the hammer. Sure enough, it was tucked under the body of the scope, difficult to reach. The small part that would have made it easier to use was tucked in an evidence bag in Posadas.

39
◆◆◆

"Do you have a minute?"

Estelle looked up to see Sheriff Robert Torrez standing in the door of her office. With the clock ticking at double speed before Benny Madrid's arraignment that afternoon in District Judge Lester Hobart's court, a sea of paperwork still needed to be processed and a dozen phone calls returned—including one to a federal prosecutor in Las Cruces who'd taken an interest in the border-crossing exploits of the Madrid brothers. Whether he was going to queue up with Mexican authorities to wait his turn was still open to question.

"No, but that's okay," Estelle replied. She saw the dark circles under Bob Torrez's eyes, but knew that his fatigue was nowhere near as consuming as his disappointment at missing the final chase. Isidro Madrid had simply run the wrong way, and the sheriff had been left to protect Lucy and Wally Madrid from their duct-taped, cuffed, and hobbled son in the bathroom. "Your office?"

Torrez nodded. "You need a break anyway," he said.

She patted him on the arm as she slipped past him. "*I* need a break, Bobby? You look like you qualify for the walking dead yourself."

"Tomorrow at this time, we'll all be wondering what to do with ourselves to stay busy," he said. "What's the word on Isidro, by the way? Did Francis know yet?"

The moment that the Posadas EMTs had sliced off Isidro Madrid's fancy running shoe and released the sea of blood and gore, it was obvious that it would take more than a Band-Aid before Isidro would be able to limp into his court arraignment.

"He's working with Brownell, the orthopedic surgeon from Deming," Estelle said. "The general consensus is that Isidro's heel bone is never going to be as good as new. 'Dusted it' is the way Francis described it."

"Good shot, then. You should have aimed a bit higher, though. Saved us all a lot of work."

"The thought crossed my mind." She followed him to the cubbyhole down the hall that he called his office. She was surprised to see Tom Pasquale sitting like a schoolboy waiting for the principal. Torrez motioned Estelle to the remaining chair and closed the door. The small office was stuffy, smelling of old leather and aftershave.

"Did you have a chance to read this yet?" Torrez picked up a folder from his desk and handed it to Estelle.

"Yes, I did." She leafed through Eurelio Saenz's deposition, four pages of single-spaced typing. Deputy Jackie Taber had been thorough, guiding the young man through the narrative, from the moment he had made the foolish decision to sell the .44 magnum carbine to his second cousins. Maybe the long, sorry tale had helped to keep his mind off the fire of the cactus thorns and the battering of his ribs. "The *azote* loosened his tongue, at least."

"Maybe that's what we should try on Isidro," Torrez said.

"Believe me, that thought crossed my mind, too."

Torrez laughed. "That's what Tom tells me."

"He's right."

Torrez hooked his hands behind his head and leaned back. "Benny's a good singer, though," the sheriff said with satisfaction. "He's telling us what we need to know. I think he hopes the DA is going to cut him a deal if he sings loud enough."

"He's dreaming."

"True. But . . ." He stopped and held up his hands. "The little bastard can always hope. He says that he stayed in the *taberna* when Isidro took Rafael and Lolo out to test drive the old pickup truck. Isidro and Benny had convinced Eurelio to sell the truck to the boys, do you believe that? Benny says he never went along for the test ride. He says that both he and Eurelio stayed in the bar, and that when

Isidro came back, he told him that Rafael and Lolo didn't want the truck after all, and that they'd hooked a ride home with someone else." Torrez puffed out his cheeks. "And Benny believed him when Isidro said he slipped jumping out of the back of the truck and cracked his head on the bed rack. Next he's probably going to tell us that he slept through the whole thing with Eurelio out there on the desert."

"It would be tough to sleep through something like that," Estelle said.

"For sure. Anyway, what I wanted to talk to you about . . . remember I mentioned some time or other that Tom had some interesting information about the Popes?"

Estelle's eyebrows lifted with curiosity. She had no recollection of that particular conversation in the great flood of events during the past few hours. The fire at Eleanor Pope's seemed a year in the past.

Torrez took that as agreement and said, "You remember in the hospital I said that I had some interesting news for you that was going to make you want to arrest somebody?"

Estelle nodded. "Yes."

"Collins is working on the insurance deal involving the Popes." He turned to Pasquale. "Tell Estelle what you told me, *Tomás*."

Pasquale cleared his throat and shifted uncomfortably on his chair. He hadn't spoken a word since Estelle and the sheriff had walked into the office—something of an accomplishment for him, Estelle reflected. In fact, he had studiously avoided opening his mouth, trying to blend in with the institutional green of the painted heater duct behind him. "Well, my motorcycle, you know?" he said, beginning in midthought.

"Your motorcycle?"

He cleared his throat again and leaned forward, forearms on the padded winds of the chair. "Yeah. You know, that big bike I bought from Tom Mears. When I first got it, I had a bank loan on it for a few months, and in order to do that, the bank required collision insurance." He held his hands out, palms up. "That was costing me an arm and a leg. So"—he looked embarrassed—"I borrowed a thousand bucks from Linda so I could pay off the loan. That way, I could drop the collision. Anyway, that's what I did."

He straightened in his seat and took a deep breath. "Then I happened to run into George Enriquez, and he said that he could cut me a pretty good liability policy for the bike that would save me some money. That he had an insurance company in his pool that gave bikers who qualified pretty good rates."

"Bikers who qualified," Estelle echoed.

"That means you have to own a bike," Torrez quipped, and Pasquale looked even more uncomfortable.

"And so that's what you did? You went with him? You dropped your collision with . . ."

"Arizona Mutual. Yeah, I dropped the whole thing with them and went with this company that Enriquez suggested."

"That was NMI?"

"No. Some other company in his pool, he said. I guess I didn't pay much attention. Anyways, Collins was lookin' through what he could find of the Popes' financial papers and couldn't find anything on insurance. The Popes had their cars insured with Enriquez. He found the insurance cards in the glove box of Eleanor's car. When they went through her checkbook, they found a check for a payment dated about three months ago. But they apparently didn't have home owner's insurance."

"What's this have to do with your motorcycle, Thomas?" Estelle asked.

"Well, see—" He hesitated. "Linda talked with Mrs. Pope not too long ago, down at the insurance office. She remembers Mrs. Pope commenting about how everything is going up, *including* her home owner's. But it turns out that Mrs. Pope didn't have home owner's with his agency," Pasquale said, as if that cleared things up.

Estelle frowned. "So what are you telling me?"

Pasquale shifted again. "Well, I don't have any paperwork that shows I have insurance with Enriquez, either. I mean, I got a proof of insurance *card* for the bike. Enriquez's secretary typed that out right there in the office when I took out the policy. Enriquez gave me a statement sheet that showed my payments, and said I'd be getting the regular policy from the company in a couple of weeks."

"And did you?"

The deputy shook his head. "Never got one. Nope."

"Did you check with Enriquez about where your policy might be?"

"No." Pasquale examined the nail of his left index finger. "It wasn't something that I was too concerned about."

"So where is all this leading?" Estelle said. She glanced up at the clock above the file cabinet. What she wanted more than anything else was a nap about 36 hours long.

"Well, I got to thinking," Pasquale said, and Estelle saw Robert Torrez's boot shift as the sheriff toyed with interjecting something. He let Pasquale continue. "What would be the point of burning down your own home if you didn't stand to collect some insurance? Denton Pope was sure up to something, but what did he stand to gain if there wasn't insurance? I mean, what was the point?"

"Murder comes to mind," Estelle said.

"Maybe he was tired of life with mother," Torrez added. "If he was trying for a tricky homicide, he succeeded. Or suicide, in this instance."

Estelle sat silently, looking at Pasquale. But it was clear that the gush of words had subsided. "Why don't you just call up Enriquez and say, 'Hey look, George, I need a copy of my motorcycle insurance policy. I'll be over this afternoon to pick it up.' Wouldn't that be the simplest thing to do?"

"I was going to do that," Pasquale said hastily. "I just got to thinking, is all. Like about the check."

Estelle sighed and glanced at Torrez. "The check?"

"Well, when I got the policy, I asked for comprehensive coverage as well as liability, and Enriquez said it was expensive, but he'd see what he could do. He called me in a day or so and said that he'd been able to add it to my policy—"

"Which you don't have."

"Right. And I was glad I went ahead and bought it, 'cause remember that wind storm we had in early January? That wasn't more than a week after I took out the policy. The wind took a limb off the elm tree in our front yard and that blew into my bike and bent the gas tank. I called Enriquez to see if my comprehensive covered it, and he had a check out to me that afternoon. A hundred and seventy bucks."

"And that's bad?"

"Well, no. I thought it was pretty cool. But when I'm thinking

287

about it here recently, I remembered that it was a personal check. Not from the insurance company. Not from Enriquez's company. It was one of his own personal checks. I didn't think much of it at the time. I was just glad to get the money, you know."

"George Enriquez paid you with a personal check? On an insurance claim?"

"Yes, ma'am."

"I don't suppose that you kept a copy of that check?"

Pasquale made a face. "Ah, no. I didn't. I cashed it, and that was that."

"Rates go up?"

"Pardon?"

"Did your insurance rates go up after that?" Estelle couldn't repress a smile.

Pasquale hesitated. "Well, I guess they did, a little. Enriquez sent me a new schedule. But don't they always?"

Estelle rubbed her face wearily. "Ay."

"What are you thinking?" Torrez asked.

She sat for a long moment with her eyes closed, head bowed. "Thomas, when you make your monthly insurance payments, how do you do it? Where do you send the check?"

"To Enriquez's office."

Estelle looked at him without lifting her head. "Where's the *bill* come from?"

Pasquale looked puzzled. "The bill?"

"The bill, Thomas. *La cuenta.* Someone has to bill you."

"Well, that's another thing, see. He told me that with the kind of no-frills policy that he wrote me, the paperwork would be faster if I just paid his office. So I do."

"Once every six months, or what?" Estelle knew what the young deputy was going to say before he opened his mouth.

"Well, no. It's due by the fifteenth, each month."

"Do you make out the check to him, or the insurance company?"

"I just write it to him. George Enriquez, CLU."

"So you never receive mailings from National. No bills, no policy, no nothing."

He shook his head. "Kind of makes you wonder, doesn't it?"

Both Torrez and Estelle laughed. "Yes, *Tomás,* it makes me wonder," Estelle said. "It makes me wonder why you don't call National's regional office, wherever that is, and ask if you have a policy with them." She smiled from the nose down. "That's sort of an investigatory thing to do."

She saw the flush creep up from Pasquale's collar and felt a pang of sympathy for him. "And just imagine," she added kindly. "You're busy, you're smart, you even work with the law all the time . . . and you step into something like this. Imagine Denton Pope and his run of luck. His grand plan was all for nothing, if he was after insurance. If George Enriquez was holding a fake policy, collecting every month from Eleanor, all he had to do was deny that she had a policy after the fire." She held out an empty hand.

"So what do you think?" Torrez asked again.

"I think," Estelle said, pushing herself out of her chair, "that Tom needs to make a discreet call to his insurance company's regional office and find out the simple answer to his question. If there's no policy on record, he could ask casually if there's such a thing as a discretionary policy that the agent writes himself. And if the answer to that is no, and we all know that it will be, then we go from there. And you're right, Bobby, the district attorney is going to be very interested. We would need to contact the state Attorney General's office for some guidance in this."

"There's not just going to be these two cases," Torrez said.

"No. Indeed not. What works once isn't tried just once. Folks like to keep a good thing going," Estelle said. "We need to move carefully. If the Popes thought they had insurance, but really didn't . . . and Thomas thought he had insurance and really doesn't . . ." She shrugged. "There's no reason to believe that they're the only two complaints. If George Enriquez has himself a little insurance scam going on the side, it'll be interesting to find out how many people got suckered in." She glanced at Pasquale. "Sorry, Tom."

"So what should I do?"

Estelle smiled at him. "Well, you've got about this much paperwork to do for the Madrids." She held her hand four feet off the floor. "We've got around-the-clock security at the hospital now, in two different rooms, to make sure that Isidro doesn't hobble down the hall

289

and jerk out Eurelio's tubes. I'm sure you'll take your turn at duty. If you can find time in all that to give your insurance company a call, then that's the first step. If they say you have nothing on file, then maybe you could saunter on down to George Enriquez's office and casually ask for a copy of your policy. I'd be interested to hear what he has to say."

"I can do that."

"Good," she said, heading for the door. "And tread softly. The last thing you want to do is tip him off. Enriquez's been around for a long time, and he's not about to run out of town tonight."

Gayle Sedillos met Estelle in the hallway. "Francis just called. I didn't want to interrupt you guys." She handed Estelle a small deck of While You Were Out notes, and then stepped past into her husband's office and handed him his own assortment of messages.

"He wonders if you have time to meet him for lunch," Gayle said. Out of reflex, Estelle's eyes drifted to the hall clock. "I told him I'd give you the message. And there's about ten other people who want to talk to you, too."

"Lunch sounds good," Estelle said, and handed the messages back to Gayle without reading them. "And then a long nap, and then the afternoon with Francisco and Carlos, and a long chat with my mother . . . would you stick those in my mailbox?" She grinned at the impassive expression that had settled over Robert Torrez's face. "Just kidding, Bobby." She turned to Tom Pasquale.

"And I'm serious about calling your insurance company, *Tomás*. It'd be really interesting if a little insurance fraud was tied in with that fire."

"Because I really do want to arrest somebody," Torrez said, with a fair imitation of Estelle's soft alto voice.

"Yes, I do," she said. "If Francis calls again in the next thirty seconds, tell him I'm on my way over to the hospital to pick him up."